A Tidy Ending

JOANNA CANNON

b

THE BOROUGH PRESS

The Borough Press
An imprint of HarperCollins*Publishers* Ltd
1 London Bridge Street
London SE1 9GF

www.harpercollins.co.uk

HarperCollins*Publishers*
1st Floor, Watermarque Building, Ringsend Road
Dublin 4, Ireland

First published by HarperCollins*Publishers* 2022
1

A catalogue record for this book is available from the British Library

HB ISBN: 978-0-00-825502-2
TPB ISBN: 978-0-00-825503-9

Set in Perpetua Std by Palimpsest Book Production Ltd,
Falkirk, Stirlingshire

Printed and Bound in the UK using
100% Renewable Electricity at CPI Group (UK) Ltd

MIX
Paper from
responsible sources
FSC **FSC® C007454**

This book is produced from independently certified FSC™ paper
to ensure responsible forest management.

For more information visit: www.harpercollins.co.uk/green

A Tidy Ending

Joanna Cannon's first two novels, *The Trouble with Goats and Sheep* and *Three Things about Elsie*, were both *Sunday Times* bestsellers and Richard and Judy picks. She worked as a hospital doctor before specialising in psychiatry, and lives in the Peak District with her family and her dog.

Also by Joanna Cannon

The Trouble with Goats and Sheep
Three Things About Elsie

Non-fiction
Breaking & Mending: A junior doctor's stories
of compassion & burnout

For Seth, who was always there

NOW

When people are asked to describe me, they'll probably say I keep myself to myself.

It's a silly way of putting it, really, because it makes it sound as if you've got something to hide, and I don't think there's anything about me that's interesting enough to be hidden. Not like some. You know what people are like, though, and newspapers always make something out of nothing, even keeping yourself to yourself. It's what you get for not following the crowd, I suppose. For not joining in. Even if people are pressed a bit harder, they will still find it difficult to dredge up a little anecdote, to pull some distant memory from the back of their minds to single me out. The reporters will want a picture, but they'll struggle to find one. 'No,' people will say, '*Linda isn't in any of those — she was never very big on parties*' or '*No, I don't think Linda was there that day'*. Then someone will have a brainwave and dig out an old school photograph from the loft, one that's faded and curled where time has eaten into us all, and they'll climb down from the stepladder and cough and brush the dust from their clothes, and they'll say, *'There she is, look, I've found her — she's the one at the back,'* and they'll have to point to make it clear: *'No, no, that one — the one you can't see very well.'*

That would be me. Linda. The one looking down when everyone else is staring straight ahead. The girl you can't quite remember. The one who kept herself to herself.

Except people forget that keeping yourself to yourself isn't always a decision you make on your own.

I wonder how Terry would describe me. He'd probably say, 'She's Welsh' or 'She's five foot nine' because Terry doesn't really deal in anything other than facts. He'd have our wedding photograph to show people, of course, although I'd really rather no one else saw that. Even when I dust, I don't look at it. I've never liked pictures of myself and I dislike that one more than any of them. It lives on the mantelpiece, with a carriage clock and a pair of candlesticks that will never find themselves being introduced to any candles. There it waits, trapped in a silver frame, watching me live my life and pointing out all my mistakes. When I do catch sight of myself, stood next to Terry with flowers stuck in my hair, I always think I look surprised. As though I stumbled into the day by accident and didn't realise I was expected to be the bride. I only put it out because Mother would have something to say if it wasn't on show.

I'm not really sure how Mother would describe me. All I know is you'd have to find yourself a seat, because she'd definitely take her time over it.

Newspapers will always sniff around, asking their questions, wanting answers and photographs and rummaging around in everyone else's business. It's started, even now. All those people who walked at the edges of my life over the years have begun to reappear. All those passers-by and all those silent voices have suddenly found something they want to say. Everyone is trying very hard to work out who they think I am, which is odd because they were never very interested in who I was before any of this happened. I suppose they want to make sense of it all, and they'll struggle because no one has all the pieces of the story, except for me. It won't stop them, though. *'Poor Linda,'* they'll say, *'she always was soft in the head'* or *'Poor Linda, I often thought she was a little bit strange'*, because we like to cast the heroes and the villains quite early on in a story, and then everyone knows where they are.

Mother's already had reporters yelling through her letterbox.

'Give us a quote about your Linda, Mrs Sykes,' they shout. *'We'll make it worth your while.'*

She doesn't, of course, because as much as Mother enjoys drama, she has always thought of it as more of a spectator sport. The journalists have kept at it, though. Very persistent, they are, standing outside the house all hours of the day and night, ringing the doorbell, climbing garden walls and knocking on windows. I told her to put some music on really loud and sing along with it so she can't hear them. That's what I've always done when I want something to go away, ever since I was a child. I don't know how I would have got through some days without my songs to drown out the world. Terry says I'm forever misunderstanding the lyrics, but he doesn't realise that there are always two ways to interpret everything in life. All you need to do is pick the version that suits you better. In the end, Mother stuffed the letterbox up with a pair of old socks. Now all they get when they shout at her is a mouth full of Marks & Spencer.

There are no letterboxes to shout through here, of course. No garden wall to stand on and no doorbell to ring. All the tiny details, all the quiet, unnoticed edges of the world have been taken away, and it's only when they're gone you realise how much you depended on them to make sense of everything else. There are newspapers lying around, but every time I pick one up it has holes in the pages where articles have been removed. Things that might distress people or make them feel uncomfortable. Although one person's distress is another person's couldn't-care-less, so I don't know how they decide which bits to take out.

'It would be nice,' I said to a woman sitting next to me in the day room, 'if life was like that. If you could just cut around the pieces you didn't care for.'

She didn't reply. Sometimes, they don't. Sometimes, it's

as though you haven't spoken at all, as if your world and their world are running quite happily side by side, but there isn't any way of moving between one and the other.

At least it means there's no sign of it here. No one knows who I am, because any mention of what happened has been deleted. It's all been cut away, leaving nice clean margins. I have been disappeared. The only problem is, you try to carry on reading, away from the gap where a story has once been, but — of course — the other side of the page is missing too, so that doesn't make any sense either.

You can't take a pair of scissors to one thing and leave the rest undamaged.

It's impossible.

1

'There was another one at the weekend,' I said.

That's how I remember the whole thing starting. Six weeks ago. Terry stood at the kitchen sink, not listening. You can always tell. Even from the back of someone's head.

Nineteen, she was. Frail little thing, blonde hair, smiling. Picture all over the front pages. I usually do a crossword on my lunch break, because I like to occupy my mind, but I popped into WHSmith instead and bought the paper that looked like it had the most coverage. Terry's never taken much notice of the news, but I thought this might catch his attention. It was only a few miles away, and people are always so much more interested if they think something might trespass into their own lives.

He was trying to scrub a day's work out of his hands, even though I've told him not to do it in the kitchen, even though he gets his muck all over the draining board. We'd only been moved into the house a couple of weeks, so it happened to be a different kitchen, a different draining board, but his tendencies hadn't changed one bit. I'd decided the move would be a fresh start. A chance for a different life, to leave all the old things behind us. Except nothing in it was new. We'd only moved to a different house on the same estate, one I'd had my eye on for quite some time, but everything was just as frayed and worn out as it had always been. We had the same discussions, the same unspoken rituals, lived through the same small machinery of our days, and the only fresh thing about it was that it was all played out to unfamiliar wallpaper.

'I'll have to get a clean cloth and go over that again later,' I said, but my voice disappeared into running water.

I unfolded the newspaper I'd bought and put it next to him when he was eating his tea, but he pushed it back across the kitchen table and said, 'Not now, Linda,' because he didn't seem to want someone else's misery interfering with his egg and chips.

'Nineteen,' I said. 'Her family are in such a state. Well, they would be, wouldn't they? I don't know what the world's coming to.' Because sometimes, I needed to be both parts of the conversation.

I watched the rise and fall of his throat as the food disappeared.

In the brief pause between a fall and a rise, he said, 'I heard it on the radio at work. It's not our problem to worry about, Linda.'

'Of course it is. There might be a serial killer out there.' I pointed at the paper. 'The paper says so.'

'The paper says a lot of things.'

'There are connections,' I said, pressing my finger into the headline on the front page, 'with this one and the woman they found off the M6 just before Christmas. Do you remember? Blonde, very slim. Lily someone or other.'

Because, no matter how distressing the story, no matter how disturbed we are by it, once the headlines become quiet again, our concern for the people they shout about quietens down too, until there comes a day when we can no longer remember their names.

Terry rested the cutlery at the edge of the plate and leaned back in his seat. 'What kind of connections?' he said.

'Well, they didn't say exactly. The police never do. They always keep their cards close to their chest, I know that better than most.'

He picked up his knife and fork again.

'I don't know why you have this obsession with the police and what they get up to,' he said. 'One minute you won't give them the time of day, the next you're falling over yourself to help them.'

'Because they *need* help, Terry.' I picked up the newspaper and stared at the front page. 'Just because I wouldn't trust a policeman as far as I could throw him doesn't mean I've abandoned my civic duty. Sorting out right from wrong is everyone's responsibility.'

He glanced at me and then back at his dinner. 'There's probably no connection between them at all. Just a coincidence.'

'But it says in black and white that there is. It wouldn't be mentioned, would it, if it wasn't true, and that makes it everybody's problem, Terry. Even yours.'

Sometimes I watched him eat, just to remind myself how miserable I was. Egg and chips. Steak and chips. Punctured, plastic lasagne in a microwaved square. Buttered bread pushed around the ruins of a meal and into his mouth.

He always said, 'Nice chips, Lind,' or 'Good bit of steak this, our Linda.'

Years of monotony had crept into the skin around his fingernails. His hands used to look clean. Hopeful. Somewhere along the line, he stopped being able to scrub away the remains of a factory floor, and they began to join us each evening at the kitchen table. He'd edge his empty plate forward an inch – only ever an inch, like an achievement – and he'd stretch the day out of his bones and scrape his chair back across the tiles, and then he'd leave me alone with the smell of a thousand other empty plates to come, and a clock that never stopped ticking, and he'd go off to digest it all in front of the snooker.

After he'd left, I always sat by myself in the kitchen, just for a minute. I needed to visit the silence. To be sure of it. When your ears are filled with the conversation of strangers and the scream of a television set, and the beat of distant traffic, when your head spills over with the unbroken whine of other people's lives, if you happen to stumble upon one of these pockets of nothing, you should sit in it for a while. It's the only way to make sense of it all, because it helps you to unpick the rest of the day. Mother always said I lived in a world of my own, but what she didn't realise was that was the very thing I could never manage to find for myself.

That night, once I'd filled up my ears with the silence, I gave the worktops a good going-over and filled the kettle. I put another load of washing in the machine. Backwards and forwards, measuring my life along the tiles. We think we're on a journey, but really we're just carving out the same little paths. Up and down a kitchen, an office, a factory floor, a supermarket aisle. Kidding ourselves we're moving forward, when all we're really doing is retracing the same life. Over and over again.

Afterwards, I stood in the carpet-quiet of the hall, trying to fit myself into an evening that waited behind a living-room door. There was still some unpacking left to do from the move and I looked over at it, stacked against the far wall. Most of our lives still lingered in cardboard boxes. We'd taken out all the things we actually used, and the rest just shifted around from room to room. DVDs we never watched, books we never read, things Terry hadn't touched in twelve months but still insisted he might need at some point, and clothes of mine that made me wonder if I used to be a whole other person. All these different versions of who we were and we didn't feel ready to let any of them go. I told Terry we should put them all in the back bedroom until we had a chance to sort through, but he'd already filled that room up with his junk and heaven knows what else, just like he did in the last house, and so the boxes drifted around, getting under our feet. I stared at them as I listened to Terry giving his opinion to a television set; I listened to the washing machine spinning out the soundtrack of our lives; and over the top of it all I listened to the noise of my own breathing. It filled the whole of the inside of my head, and I must have stood there for a good ten minutes before I managed to take a step into the rest of my night. To sit with Terry as he slurped tea out of his ugly football mug and talked back to the television.

The murder was the first story on the evening news, before the politicians and the footballers, and all the Americans arguing with each other. They used the same photograph as the newspapers, but they showed other pictures as well. Pictures from her childhood. Pony rides and ice creams. Party nights. University days. Evenings out with other girls – other, more fortunate girls. A family photo from last Christmas, everyone at a dinner table, raising their glasses and saying *cheers!* to the camera. Her entire existence unfolded on a television screen and nineteen years was over in a matter of seconds.

Terry tapped his fingers on the remote control.

'Where do they find all these photographs?' I said.

'They've taken them off the internet. People's whole lives are spread out on there. Anyone can steal a piece of it if they want to.'

I pulled a face. I'd never really bothered with the internet. I didn't see the point of it when I had my crosswords and my music.

The newsreader was just repeating everything I'd read in the paper, and so I stared at the picture that stayed on the screen. The girl was in a garden, her arms around this big dog. A Labrador, perhaps, or a Golden Retriever. I can never tell the difference. She was smitten with the dog, you could tell from her face.

'I worry about people's pets,' I said. 'No one thinks about the pets, do they?'

Terry didn't reply.

'I bet the poor thing wonders where she is,' I said.

I stared into the girl's eyes and tried to find something there, a clue that she knew what was about to happen to her. If your life was going to end so easily, if it would slide from your hands without a moment's notice and nineteen years was all you were going to be allowed on this earth, you would think, wouldn't you, that God would give a bit of a heads-up? Leave you some kind of Post-it note to make sure you made the most of the little time you had.

I was still staring when the scene changed to a press conference. A group of people sitting on plastic chairs in front of a big advertising board, like they have on the red carpet, except this one said 'West Midlands Police' all over it. There was an officer in uniform and a detective inspector, and next to them were the girl's parents. They were the same people they showed in the Christmas picture, although you never would have known if they hadn't put it on the bottom of the screen, because grief had stolen them both and distorted their faces beyond recognition.

The police did all the talking. They said everything in that special police language they always use, the kind that makes it sound like they know something you don't, going through the girl's last known movements and asking for people to come forward, to report anything suspicious. Although they didn't elaborate on what 'suspicious' might mean, and what's suspicious to one person is completely above board to somebody else. I've found that out to my own detriment. The parents didn't say anything. They kept their heads down, staring at a collection of microphones on the table and sipping water, but every now and then, one of them looked up with empty eyes, and immediately there was a feeding frenzy of lens shutters. Newspapers trying to capture their distress to put on tomorrow's front pages, a perfect snapshot of despair to sell a paper, because nothing dilutes your own unhappiness like feeding on the unhappiness of others.

It was only when they panned out that I noticed. Behind the parents and the detectives, and the microphones, they'd put a giant photograph on the screen. It was the picture of the girl with the dog. The girl's blonde hair rested on her shoulders and she had one of those fringes that wasn't really a fringe, but stray pieces of hair that fell perfectly onto her forehead and framed her face without any persuasion from a hairbrush. My fringe has never done that. My fringe has always had a personality all of its own. I frowned at the picture. Surely Terry saw it as well? It was so obvious. I looked over at him, but he was still watching the screen with one of his expressions and picking at a back tooth. I felt a breath catch in my throat and I was just about to point it out to him, to see if he agreed, but right at that moment he said, 'They haven't got a bloody clue who's done it, have they?' and changed the channel. It was a sit-com. A middle-aged couple sitting on a settee, watching television, and for a second I thought it was us.

The moment passed. There was no point in saying anything, because Terry never believes a word I say. Hysterical. That's what he calls me whenever I get in a state about something. 'You're being hysterical again, Linda,' he says and that's always the end of it. Instead, I stared at the traces of egg yolk around his lips.

'Most murder victims are killed by someone close to them,' he said, without his eyes leaving the television screen.

The egg yolk was gathered deep in the lines at the corners of his mouth, where it would probably stay until morning.

'I know they are,' I said.

2

Obviously, I would never go to the police about what I saw at the press conference. I'm no fool.

In the past, each time I've been – and I haven't been that often, I don't care what they say – they've just fobbed me off with one of those volunteer officers and a paper cup filled with lukewarm tea.

'*The thing is, Linda,*' that's how they always start. As though I have to have the thing pointed out to me by someone else, because I'm too stupid to recognise it on my own. It was the same when I reported the suspicious man in Boots, and when I asked them to check on a strange car parked up on the high street. Every time I've spotted a man they've shown on *Crimewatch* they've never been the least bit interested, and on the last occasion, when I went about a weird noise coming from across the road late at night, they kept me standing on the doorstep. They didn't even let me into the station. They get it wrong so often. Jumping to conclusions and judging books by covers. They're over-stretched and under-funded. You hear it on the news all the time, and they need help matching the right person to the crime and sorting the guilty from the innocent, or people will just keep on getting hurt. I try to help as often as I can, but you can only do so much. Although it doesn't mean I trust any of them because I've seen first hand the damage they can do.

One of them came to the house a while ago. A community support officer in a high-visibility vest with a short-wave radio swinging from his pelvis. I saw him making his way down the garden path and Terry let him in the front door. I could hear them, talking in the kitchen in their low voices, so I popped upstairs to get changed because I don't think it ever hurts to make a good impression. By the time I got back, he was gone and Terry was in his usual chair.

'What did he want, then?' I said.

Terry didn't take his eyes off the telly. 'Nothing much. Just a chat.'

Half an hour later, he turned to me and asked if I'd ever thought of doing an evening class. Terry wouldn't know an evening class if it hit him in the face. It would've been that community support officer, interfering. I thought they were supposed to solve crimes, not send innocent people to learn woodwork.

* * *

After they found that girl's body, nothing felt the same.

I couldn't quite put my finger on it, but there was a difference in the air. A gap where something else used to be. There were no kiddies playing out, for a start. You'd normally catch sight of one or two, whizzing past the house on their bikes after school, or you'd hear them somewhere over the hedges and the garden fences. Little voices in their imaginary worlds. Playing dress-up. Being doctors and princesses and models and film stars. Because that's the best thing about being a child; you can just turn yourself into whoever you want to be. The little voices were gone now, hidden away indoors. Back doors were kept shut. Bolts slid across. Latches dropped. The pavements stayed quiet, and if you did spot someone, they were never alone. It was more than that, though; it felt as though the whole estate was peering back at you, waiting to see what would happen next.

The following day I did what I always did and I watched Terry eat his breakfast before he went to work. I like to sit at the kitchen table and do a crossword with my first cup of tea, because crosswords keep your mind sharp. They make you think about how everything else fits together, because you can't answer one clue without considering all the others. The radio was on as well, because it made conversation for us and stopped anyone else from having to bother, but the disc jockeys seemed to have forgotten about weather reports and local travel news, and all the other subjects they usually fill the kitchen with, because the only thing they wanted to talk about was the murder.

Everyone had so much they needed to discuss, although most of it struggled to find its way over the top of Terry and his cornflakes. He's such a loud swallower. I've asked him on numerous occasions if he could do it more quietly, but he takes not one jot of notice.

They'd found her on some waste ground, down by the canal. She was taking a shortcut back from the supermarket and she still had her shopping with her, tins of cheap soup and a tube of toothpaste. Some of those reduced flowers with a little yellow sticker on the front. Mother always says that you can tell a lot from someone's shopping bag. It's a wonder someone found her so quickly, because it's so quiet down by the canal. You'd never know you were right near a main road, but that's the apron of trees, I suppose, shielding you from the noise of the traffic. It's one of the few places left where nature still has the upper hand and it's peaceful even in winter. I used to go down there all the time to get away from Mother because water always seems to swallow up all the other sounds, even the ones inside your own head. She was definitely killed in the place where they found her, everyone on the radio – and even the police – were very sure of that, except no one seemed to know exactly why the murder might have happened. They speculated. Talked about boyfriends and ex-boyfriends. Discussed things she may or may not have done, friends she may or may not have had. *'She was such a good girl,'* people said, *'until she got in with the wrong crowd,'* because you will always be judged by the landscape in which you stand, and being

murdered doesn't stop everyone running over your life
with their own particular set of rules and regulations about
how we should and shouldn't all behave. In fact, they probably do it even more, because you can't answer them back
when you're lying stone cold dead in a mortuary drawer.
It turned out the girl was in a lot of debt. *'I didn't even
know she had a credit card,'* said her mother. Which makes
you wonder how well you can ever really know the people
you stare at across a kitchen table each morning.

The body was deposited in dense foliage, the police said.

*The body was discovered by a passer-by who was walking their
dog.*

Of course, they didn't call her by her name any more.
She had become *the body*. They use a whole other language
after you've died. Even though you look the same, even
though the very last breath has only just escaped from your
lungs, it's as if in that moment you give up being you and
whatever remains becomes something that needs to be
deposited and discovered, and transported like a piece of
furniture. It was the same with my dad. *The deceased.* All
the way through the inquest they called him that. I sat in
the public gallery, looking down at the top of Mother's
head and at the tops of all the other heads. People who had
come to gawp and gossip and fill their stomachs. I wanted
to stand up and tell them all he was my dad, and they
should start calling him by his name, but of course, I didn't.
I stayed quiet, because if Mother knew I'd skipped school
to be there, she would have tanned my backside.

'They'll never find any clues.' Terry had moved on to toast, which was only marginally less boisterous than cereal.

'How do you mean?' I said.

He waved his butter knife towards the kitchen window, where February rain beat hard against the glass, dissolving the world outside until the view became just a smear of something you once recognised.

'It'll wash all the evidence away. Gone.'

'How do you know?'

'You see it on the telly all the time on these real-life crime shows. They never find anything in weather like this. If you're going to kill someone, it's the best time of year to do it.'

I stared at the rain. I'd never thought about murders being seasonal, like daffodils and trips to the seaside. How strange that something as simple as the weather could stop a murderer being caught. How clever we all pretend to be.

'You never know,' I said. 'They could still find something.'

I turned back, but he was in the hall, faffing around with his jacket and arguing with the zip. I wish he wouldn't hang it up with all the other coats, because it makes the whole house smell of the day before. I've pointed it out a million times. Then he started kicking at the bit of loose carpet near the front door, causing a big hoo-ha. I keep telling him that carpet needs seeing to. It's a trip hazard. There's the crack in the glass in the front door as well. It starts in the top left-hand corner and does this strange zigzag on the way down, exactly the same shape as you see on a heart monitor. When we moved in, I never noticed these things, but it's started to feel as though the house is splitting and breaking around our ears. I pointed it all out to Terry, but I might as well have told a brick wall. *'You were the one who chose this house,'* I always said to him. *'You were the one who found it, you were the one who went and asked if it was for sale'*, as though every crack and splinter was his fault. Of course, none of that was true. I'd chosen this house for us long before Terry even realised it existed, but sometimes, all you have to do is put something in a person's eye-line, and eventually they'll think it was their idea all along.

Terry came back into the kitchen, still trying to fasten himself up.

'You'll be home late?' I said.

He didn't look up. 'No, I'll be back for tea. There's no overtime.'

The rain hammered louder on the glass.

'There's always extra work this time of year,' I said. 'What's going on?'

I knew, of course, because he'd told me, in one of his notes that he was fond of leaving around. *NO OVERTIME FOR NOW* he'd written in big letters and filled up the whole sheet, and then *IT'LL HAPPEN AGAIN* on another one. Such a waste of paper.

I remembered it distinctly because it made me anxious. Not because I was worried about not having the extra money, but because I was worried about having the extra Terry.

He didn't answer. He just kissed me on the cheek, like he always did.

It felt like a handshake.

I watched him back out of the drive in that filthy van and he was gone. I was surprised he could see through the windscreen, what with all the muck and condensation. You can be fined for it, and get points on your licence, and he knows all this because I've told him enough times. Anyone else and I would've made a note of the registration plate.

I carried on with my morning after he'd left. I work part-time, which is just as well because it takes me the rest of the week to keep on top of the house. It's the small rituals, the empty habits you build over the years, brick by brick, that end up being your life, and I was halfway through a second bleach of the sink when I heard the post hit the doormat. I knew I'd have to wash my hands again afterwards because cross-contamination is an ever-present danger, but I couldn't help but go and have a look. You always hope it will be something worthwhile, something interesting to interrupt your day, but it was just the usual rubbish. Leaflets about car insurance and sit-on lawnmowers. A collection of takeaway menus. There was a brochure, which was a bit different, although everyone seems to have a brochure these days. Even our window cleaner has one. There's a picture of him on the front, holding up his squeegee and smiling, which is quite odd because I've never once seen him smile in real life. This brochure was much bigger, though, and wrapped in cellophane, and it was sandwiched between the gas bill and a flyer about the Conservative Party, and all the other nonsense that gets pushed through a letterbox.

I didn't even notice it wasn't for me at the time. You don't look at the name on something like that, and I was just about to put it in the pedal bin with the local Tory councillor, when I realised how heavy it was. I decided something that weighty must be worth a second look and it might make a change when I ran out of my magazines. Terry says it's a waste of money buying them, but I enjoy my magazines. Staring at pictures of all the people you might have been helps to pass the time. I took the brochure out of its wrapper and popped it in the gap next to the microwave, but it was only when I put the cellophane in the bin that I noticed the label. They'd got the right address, but the name on it wasn't mine. It wasn't Linda Hammett. Or Mrs L. Hammett. Or even Mrs T. Hammett, which is a pet peeve of mine, even though I'd never let on to Terry.

It wasn't addressed to any of those people.

I could see it, as plain as day, nestled amongst the potato peelings and yesterday's teabags.

It was addressed to someone called Rebecca Finch.

3

I am not in the habit of opening other people's mail.

I'm not that sort of person. I have a very firm moral code when it comes to rules and regulations, and the line where right crosses into wrong, where truth wanders into untruth, is very important. It's like those diagrams, though. The ones with different coloured circles. There's always a grey bit in the middle where all the circles overlap, where right and wrong bump into each other, where truth and untruth can't decide which one they want to be. Mother calls them white lies, as if changing the colour of something makes it more acceptable, but I do tend to agree with her. There are occasions when you have to look at the bigger picture. Sometimes, you think you've been deceived by someone, but that deceit is more to do with how you interpreted their words to begin with, rather than how they were delivered to you.

This was purely accidental though, and as the cellophane wrapper on the brochure had already been removed, I decided it wouldn't do any harm to have a look through. Some things are just meant to be and so I went into the front room to enjoy myself properly.

It was a clothing catalogue. Filled with people I used to think I could become. Elegant people. People who perched on the edges of bar stools and on the arms of settees. I very rarely did any perching because whenever I tried, it never seemed to end particularly well. *'Too weighty to be elegant'*, Mother always says. The faces of the catalogue people were all smoothed out and relaxed. Some of them were clearly in the middle of saying hilarious things to each other, whilst others stared wistfully into the distance. A population of slim, happy people, who sat on beaches and in restaurants, who leaned against car doors and stretched their legs out on settees and pointed their toes.

But it was an absence of things that made me stare, more than a presence. All the pieces of my life that were missing from the pictures. No Terry gazing deep into a television screen, no tower of dirty pots in the sink waiting to be seen to, no bus seat peppered with chewing gum and other people's lives. No Mother in the corner of the room, digesting her own opinions. Within each picture was a small story, and a glimpse of days lived differently to mine. The more I looked, the more clearly I could see how my life should have been, and I wondered if I stared for long enough, might I be able to find it for myself, because it was in there, waiting for me. I was sure of it.

Mother always said a vivid imagination would be the death of me, but I've often found it comes in quite handy, because I could imagine myself into the photographs of other people's lives straight away. It's amazing how easily your mind can unfasten itself from your own life and head straight into another one, even if there are times when your body might struggle a bit to keep up. I could see myself quite clearly, drinking tea from a mug that didn't have a chip in it. I could see myself having a smoothed-out face and making other people laugh with a hilarious, throwaway comment as I perched on the arm of a settee. It was easy as long as it stayed inside me. Everything was always perfect in my head. It was when all the things in my head tried to leave by themselves and happen in the real world that it all went a bit pear-shaped.

I reached the last page. There were two women sitting at a picnic bench. One woman had her arm on the other woman's shoulder and they were both laughing. They were clearly friends. They probably went shopping on a Saturday morning and had coffee together, and they never had a stranger ask, *'Is this seat taken?'* in the British Home Stores café and then drag the other chair away and leave them with just an empty space. They probably rang each other all the time. Had telephone conversations every evening and laughed about how ridiculous their husbands were. They remembered each other's birthdays and even went on holiday together sometimes, and they filled all the gaps in each other's lives so there was no room left there for any misery.

Perhaps this was the life Rebecca Finch lived in this house before we moved in. A life with no gaps. No empty space where a chair used to be, because the seat opposite Rebecca Finch was always taken. I decided I'd quite like to look through the catalogue again, so I stretched my legs out on the settee and pointed my toes.

I spent a lot of time looking, which threw me late with all my jobs and I was only halfway through my second daily crossword when I heard Terry's keys in the back door. I usually like to finish before he gets home, or he peers over my shoulder and interferes. He has no idea how crosswords work. If Terry thinks he knows one of the answers, he wants to fill it in straight away, in pen, and commit himself forever before he's really thought about it properly. He doesn't appreciate that you need to look at all the other clues as well, that you need to be sure everything matches up. Plan ahead. Take your time. It's Terry all over, marching straight in without a second thought for anything else. The problem is, Terry's handwriting is almost identical to mine, so you can't tell where I end and he begins. On this occasion, though, he didn't even notice the crossword, he just stood in the doorway with his mouth hanging open.

'Why aren't you at work?' he said.

'I swapped my day off.' I glanced at the clock. It was only a quarter past three. 'Why aren't you?' I said back. 'I thought you said you'd be home for tea?'

He turned to close the door. He took his time, because he was still fumbling with his keys when he answered me. Something about swapping to a shorter shift.

'I didn't hear the van pull in,' I said.

A bit of trouble with it, he told me. Left it at work. Didn't want to risk driving home, so he got the bus. I wasn't the least bit surprised. On the very few occasions I'd driven it – and I tried to do this sparingly, believe me – my heart was in my mouth every time I changed gear. That van was an accident waiting to happen.

Terry looked at the cold oven and the deserted hob.

'Well, I haven't got anything ready yet – you should have let me know,' I said.

He leaned across the kitchen table in front of me and took a Jaffa Cake. I wouldn't have minded, but I only had nine left.

'Note,' he said.

'Pardon?'

'Four letters.'

'What?'

'Six across. *Short letter college sent back.*' He picked up my pen. 'It's note.'

He filled it in. Just like that. I was furious. So furious, I didn't realise until he'd walked into the front room and shut the door behind him that his hands were as clean as a whistle. Which was strange, because he hadn't set foot near the kitchen sink.

* * *

The next day, I had an eye open for the postman after breakfast, wondering if he'd bring me something else. I kept getting up from my crossword and watching for him through the window, and he didn't disappoint. He marched down the path with something plugged into his ear, chatting away to fresh air like people do, and a great pile of things in his arms. Everything was for us. Except they weren't for us at all, they were for Rebecca Finch. Two big catalogues this time, one all about home furnishings and the other filled with different kinds of make-up. I'd never bothered much with make-up, but looking at the befores and afters on the front made me wonder if it was worth having a rethink, because it appeared as though you could turn yourself into a whole new person if you put your mind to it. I shouldn't have opened them, but it didn't feel quite as bad if you'd already done it before, which is a bit like being a serial killer, I suppose.

I'd got through my chores more quickly than usual. Perhaps I was trying to distract myself from thinking about the murder, or perhaps it was the rain beating time against the roof and hurrying me along. Either way, I decided to ignore my crossword for once and have a flick through the catalogues with a Jaffa Cake instead. Terry had long since disappeared to get the bus, so I spread everything out on the kitchen table. Perhaps Rebecca Finch had done the same when she lived here, made a collage of clothes and lipsticks and cushions. A comfort blanket stretched across a tablecloth.

Rebecca Finch's brochures weren't like any of the others I'd seen. Not like the ones that came tucked inside the TV guide, filled with handy gadgets you never knew you couldn't manage without. Not like Mother's wide-fitting shoes or Terry's fishing equipment. They were thicker, for a start, and the whole experience of reading them had a gloss about it. The first one was filled with pictures of beautiful rooms in beautiful houses. Furniture you wouldn't dare sit on. Ovens that looked as though they'd never cooked a meal and fridges so enormous, you could fit your whole life in there. I glanced around the kitchen as I turned the pages, and I wondered if the house looked as exhausted when Rebecca Finch lived here as it did now, because if it ever had any sparkle about it to begin with, it seemed to have worn off.

I stared at the middle pages of the brochure for a long time. There was a teal-coloured settee all on its own, with giant orange cushions and a coffee table in front of it. On the coffee table was a bowl that was big enough to hold the whole of Yorkshire. Further on there were shiny sideboards and occasional tables for every occasion. Lamps with no shades. Beds with no mattresses. There was even a whole section devoted to settees, and each one had been given a rating for how comfortable it was. *Medium*, it said. For all of them. Perhaps when something reaches a certain level of attractiveness, it has to let go of its ability to comfort you in order to make enough room for being so beautiful.

It wasn't just the furniture that drew me into the pictures, though; it was the absence of people. Every other homeware catalogue I'd seen had people in it. People lounging around on armchairs. People chopping carrots in a well-lit kitchen. People smiling at each other across a heavily discounted dining table. *This could be you,* the catalogues whisper, *living your well-lit, smiling life and chopping vegetables.* This catalogue had no one in it. Not a soul. I know, because I went through the whole thing from cover to cover three times. No one's feet on the footstools. No one's arms on the armchairs. It reminded me of a furniture store I once wandered into with Mother by mistake. We were at the retail park, investigating fridge-freezers, and Mother said, 'Let's just pop in here for ten minutes.' Two hours later we were still stuck there, mainly because we couldn't find our way out.

'*Follow the arrows on the floor, Linda,*' Mother kept saying. '*They exist for a reason.*'

Our arrowed journey took us past endless rooms, cross-sections of imaginary lives, but all the rooms were empty, just like in the brochure. The imaginary families had gone, leaving a discarded paperback on a table, a tea towel on a draining board, a casually placed throw at the end of a bed. As if the people who lived in those rooms had just disappeared into thin air.

Mother and I stood in front of one of the living rooms. It was all taupes and creams. The kind of colours you could melt into without any effort. Giant armchairs. Cosy rugs. No dust. No clutter. No Terry.

'I could live in a house like that,' I said, but Mother had moved herself on to potted plants.

Perhaps it was just easier to pretend yourself into an empty landscape. Perhaps, if there were no people to be seen, you could imagine you were the only one who was really meant to be there after all.

It wasn't just the postman who was after Rebecca Finch, either. There had been quite a few visitors over the past couple of weeks who were interested in her. Several men in smart clothes with clipboards. A very chatty girl and her dog who knocked on the door the day after we moved in. It's amazing how much you can learn about someone if you ask the right questions, and we had quite the conversation about Rebecca. The girl was on the doorstep for so long, I got the dog a bowl of water. I used Terry's cereal bowl. It said in one of my magazines that there are more germs in a human mouth than a dog's, and besides, he was out so he'd be none the wiser. Someone else turned up with a large brown envelope for Rebecca which they were determined to foist onto me, even though I told them they'd got the wrong house. I wouldn't take it from him, of course, because you never know where these things might have been, and I noticed that very little care and attention had been devoted to the underneath of his fingernails.

Everyone wanted Rebecca Finch. She was extremely popular, and sometimes, I felt like saying they'd got the right house after all, just to see what it felt like to be her for a while. She tip-toed around the edges of my mind and it was easy to let her live there, because the house connected us both, after all. We sat in the same rooms and brushed our teeth at the same sink. We looked through the same windows, and put the same key in the same back door, and unless she'd preferred one of the smaller bedrooms we even slept in the same space, staring up at the same ceiling. I'd find myself wondering what Rebecca would do or say or think about something and I'd read through her catalogues and wondered it to myself so many times, it wasn't very long before I knew exactly how Rebecca would behave. After Terry had left for work, I could almost hear her echoing around the house, her soft voice and the music of her laughter, Rebecca being graceful and petite and popular, and everything I thought I would never be able to be. But perhaps my life was finally taking a turn, perhaps moving into this house would be a new chapter after all, because you can't spend time in a place and not leave part of yourself behind for someone else to discover. For someone else to absorb. It's impossible.

4

'No one's safe.' Mother drew the curtains closed, as though four yards of beige velour would keep us both out of harm's way.

It was two days after they'd found the girl's body. I knew Mother would be in one of her states, but I always visit on a Thursday afternoon and I've learned that if there's one thing that stops you falling from the scaffolding of life, it's holding on to your routines, and so I made the short train journey and arrived in time to witness the beginnings of a case of mild hysteria.

'They reckon it isn't the first,' she said. 'They think there's a pattern. That girl off the motorway at Christmas, whatever her name was.'

I hung my coat over the back of a chair. 'It was further away from you than it was from us. I don't know what you're mithering about.'

She pulled the material into its place with a final sharp tug, and all the curtain rings danced along the rail. 'It may surprise you to know, Linda, that murderers are able to utilise public transport these days. They might even possess their own car, in which case they can drive all around the country at will, putting an end to whomever they please.'

When she released her grip on the curtains, her hands were shaking.

'It just brings it all back,' she said. 'Keeping the curtains closed.'

She took a deep breath and filled up her lungs, and by the time she'd released all the air out again she was back to the person she liked people to think she was, because nothing distressed Mother more than parading around a small weakness for all the world to see. Including me.

'We should have never left Wales,' she said. 'Unpleasant things like this never happen in Wales.'

I raised an eyebrow at her, because Mother was always very selective about which pieces of the past she chose to accompany her into the present.

'You were the one who insisted we left,' I said. 'You said you couldn't stand being there any longer!'

'You chose here, though, didn't you, Linda? I asked where we should move to because I wanted to make you happy again, and you picked this place. Although heaven knows why.'

'I read about it in a magazine,' I said. 'I thought it looked nice.'

'And now we find ourselves slap bang in the middle of a Stephen King film.'

'We've managed nearly thirty years without stumbling across any murderers. We haven't done too badly.'

'I've got my eye on a few people,' she said, and gave a small sniff.

'You think the serial killer lives here?' My mouth stayed open after I'd finished speaking. I couldn't help myself.

'You need at least three murders before you can call yourself a serial killer,' she said, because Mother watched far too many documentaries. 'Unless you know something I don't? Because if you do, I'm all ears.'

I shook my head.

'Next door but one, for a start. Always thought he was a bit shifty. Then there's Nigel from the butchers, because they very often turn out to be butchers, you know. Or people from the meat industry. It's the first ones they check.'

I was going to join in, but Mother was on one of her rolls.

'Or that young lad who collects the trolleys at Asda.'

I stared at her.

'Dirty fingernails, Linda. It speaks volumes.'

We stood in the half-darkness. She was right. It did bring it all back. It's strange how the smallest remembrance takes you on a journey of miles, of years sometimes. It's not the big memories, not my dad sitting at the bottom of the stairs with his head in his hands, and the shouting and the endless ringing of a telephone, it's the small memories that catch you when you least expect it. The curtains drawn in the middle of the day, the sound of a piano lesson behind a closed door, a vase filled with daffodils. The tiniest fragment can take you from where you are now, to where you used to be, as if you'd never even left.

'Of course.' Mother made an inch gap in the curtains and squinted through. 'The smart money's on number thirty-one. Mr Kemp.'

'Single Simon?' I said.

'He wasn't always single. There used to be a wife, although you probably won't remember her. Got dementia. Only forty-three. Ended up in a funny farm.'

She whispered the last sentence, because Mother seems to have this strange idea that if you say something within earshot of the universe, the universe might mistakenly think you are putting in a request for yourself.

'I really don't think—'

'I used to see him driving her around before she was taken away. Visiting places from when they were courting. The church where they got married. The school where she used to teach. Hoping it would jog her memory. As though she might have left a piece of who she was behind and there was a chance she'd be able to find herself again.'

'And did she?' I said.

Mother shook her head. 'He's never been the same since she went. All those miles he drove. For no good reason. He still does it sometimes, even though she's gone.'

'Do the police think it's Simon?' I said. 'Is he a suspect?'

'The police haven't got a clue. You could tell that from the press conference.'

I hesitated. 'Did you watch the press conference?'

'Did I watch the press conference?' she said and then she repeated the question a few times, with bigger and bigger gaps in between the words. 'Of course I watched the press conference. I watched it six times on catch-up. I even made some notes in my spiral-bound.'

She nodded over to a jotter, which was wedged between the remote control and this week's television guide.

'Not for anyone else's eyes, though,' she said. 'Just a few of my own thoughts.'

'Did you notice anything odd about it? The press conference?'

'Odd? What do you mean, odd?'

'Anything amiss? You know, unnatural?'

'It's a murder inquiry, Linda. Everything about it is unnatural.' Her eyes narrowed. 'To what, exactly, are you referring?'

'Nothing. No one.'

'Of course.' She returned her gaze to beyond the gap in the curtains. 'You know what they're saying, don't you? Freda heard it on a radio phone-in.'

'No. What are they saying?'

'They're saying the victims aren't random. They're saying it's nothing to do with opportunity.'

'What do you mean?'

Mother gave a small sigh.

'You're forty-three now. Do I still have to explain everything to you?'

I nodded and frowned, which made her sigh again.

'I mean the killer doesn't pick people by chance, Linda,' she said. 'It's all thought out. He chooses them for a reason.'

NOW

Every afternoon someone appears in the day room to do activities.

Activities you only usually do on Christmas Day when you try to feel like a family. When your mother paints her face with shiny determination, but your father refuses to leave his bed and eventually your mother's shine fades and everyone disappears back into themselves again. Board games and dominoes, a pack of playing cards, those kinds of things. You lead a life now where activities need to be unpacked from a box and laid out on a big table, because your activities have become things that need to be put in front of you in clear sight, and you have to be jollied along and repeatedly called by your first name to make sure you realise you should be doing them.

Sometimes, they bring a guitar or a dog. The dog is called

Kez and she wears a fluorescent harness, and everybody makes a big fuss. There's a strange sense of achievement when a dog likes you, even in here, because it makes you feel like the dog can see something in you that the human race has always managed to miss.

'Kez thinks a lot of you, Linda,' the woman always says. 'She likes you, she does.'

Dogs always like me, even though I'm not a dog person. Perhaps that's the reason. I'm not a people person either – a phrase Mother uses all the time – but that doesn't seem to work in quite the same way.

Whilst all this is going on, you might glance around and fool yourself into thinking this is an ordinary living room. Perhaps the residents' lounge in a seafront hotel or the waiting room in a dentist's, but so many clues give it away. For a start, there are no finishing touches, no casually draped throws or interesting scatter cushions, not like the rooms I stared at in Rebecca's brochures. There aren't any ornaments, and even if there were, they wouldn't have anywhere to live, because there are no shelves. No pictures on the walls, no mirrors, and if you want to know the time you have to ask someone, because there aren't any clocks in this room either. There aren't any clocks anywhere, as far as I can tell, apart from in the office behind the glass. There's no need for them in here because time has stopped serving any purpose. Days are punctuated by meals on plastic trays and the push of a drugs trolley. Meetings behind closed doors and silent handovers watched through chequerboard glass mark the hours and the minutes that were once thought to be so important. Time is now something which is manoeuvred around for you by other people, people who need watches and clocks to get through their lives, and everyone else is just swept along by the undercurrent. It's strange, because you can never quite measure how much you needed something, until someone takes it all away from you.

After an hour or so, when people have picked up the playing cards and stared at them, and felt the weight of the dominoes in their hands, and argued about which colour counter they want to be in the board games, the dog and the guitar both leave and all the activities are placed back into their cardboard box. Everything becomes still and quiet again, and conversation is buried in the bones of silence. People drift back to chairs and settees and corners, and seek out the bookmark of where they had left their life before the outside world came in and disturbed them all.

I am of the firm belief that you are either the kind of family that plays board games, or you are the kind of family that doesn't. We definitely fell into the second group, no matter how much effort Mother put into a round of Scrabble or setting up the Monopoly board every Christmas Day afternoon.

'It's what people do when they've watched the Queen,' she'd say, despite the fact that none of us gave the Queen a second thought for the rest of the year, unless there happened to be a wedding or a jubilee and we all got a surprise day off. It was Mother's way of hurrying us all through the festive period. Little rituals. Unfamiliar behaviour. Things she saw other families do in films and in advertisements, and so she decided we should be doing them as well. Perhaps she thought if we spent Christmas copying what she believed other people were up to, it would trick us into being a normal family for the rest of the year as well. Sadly for Mother, she never discovered whether it worked or not, because no one ever cooperated with her. I'd probably have given it a try, because I had nothing else to do, but my dad just stared at the dining room table, said, 'Give it a rest, eh, Eunice?' and went back to bed.

I spent most of the day in my bedroom as well. I even took my dinner up there on a tray, just like I did every other day of the year, because Mother always watched every mouthful I ate and it made swallowing feel almost impossible.

'Look at those chubby little arms,' she'd say, and pinch at my flesh whenever I wore a short-sleeved T-shirt. 'Look at those dimples!'

It should have made me want to eat less and less, but it actually did the opposite. I would smuggle biscuits up there and crisps and chocolate, because when the voices around you seem to echo the voice in your own head, when other people shovel fuel on your sense of self-loathing, eventually the only thing you can think to do is prove all of them right.

The girls who came for their piano lessons didn't sneak chocolate and crisps into their bedrooms. I could tell just by watching them as I sat on the stairs. They squeezed easily through the front door and past Mother and into the front room where my dad was waiting for them. They were the kind of girls that still held on to a tan from the previous summer. Skinny arms and legs and button noses, with hair just the right shade of blonde. Hair that fell to their shoulders and behaved itself. The kinds of girls who could sweep that hair into a ponytail without even once glancing in the mirror and they would still look perfect. Mother didn't pinch the tops of their arms as they walked past her. She didn't point out their dimples. She just ignored them and made her way back to the kitchen. Although sometimes, she would look up at me as I sat on the stairs. I'd wipe my mouth clean of crumbs and try to hide my biscuit or my crisps up the sleeve of my jumper, but she'd still shake her head and tut.

'Ever-open door,' she'd mumble to herself. 'That's our Linda. Ever-open door.'

Yet she seemed determined to keep shovelling food through that door. Mashed potatoes swimming with gravy. Stew and dumplings. Meat and potato pies and gammon and chips and pancakes for afterwards. Thick sausages, spitting out their fat in a frying pan. Bacon and eggs and black pudding every Sunday morning, because that's what other people did. Just like the board games on Christmas Day. Perhaps that's why it's so nice being here. Every day is Christmas Day and no one takes a blind bit of notice of what you eat.

They asked me my name when I first walked through the door.

It was only a matter of procedure, because the staff don't live a life where articles are cut away from newspapers and they all knew exactly who I was. You could tell from their faces. When I said my name, they wrote it down, because everyone seems to spend most of their time writing things down. Each conversation, each encounter. Even the smallest vibration of change has to be documented. It doesn't stop there, either. Without fail, on the hour, someone walks around and makes a note of what everybody is doing. Watching television. Sleeping. Smoking. They have a special form they fill in. I know, because I've seen it. It's called a head count. The only thing is, whatever your body is doing, your head is probably up to something completely different. There were plenty of times when my body was washing up or sitting in front of the television with Terry, but my head managed to be somewhere else entirely. Fraudulently strolling along a beach, or walking through a bluebell wood. It didn't really matter — I just needed my head to be somewhere other than where my body was. Perhaps we're all wandering around without really being there, but it doesn't stop the staff in here making a note of it. *If it isn't written down, it didn't happen.* I heard one of them say that to a student. It's an interesting way to look at life, but if that's the case then most of my own life didn't happen at all. Although there are definitely parts of it that happened just a little too much.

I watch them walking around, doing their head count and turning everyone into words, and I've seen the kinds of things they write, because once one of them left the sheet of paper on the arm of the chair when all these alarms started ringing.

Sitting in the garden, staring into space — refuses to engage
and
Sitting on the bed, laughing at nothing in particular
and
Looking at the television, but doesn't appear to be watching anything

I've done all of those things at home. Every single one of them. The only difference is, no one ever noticed.

5

I always listen to my music on the journey back from visiting Mother.

I still have the Walkman I got for my fifteenth birthday, and I bought myself some earphones from the pound shop. I make sure I stuff them in the minute I'm halfway down her garden path. If you fill your head with songs, it takes up all the space in there and stops anything else from getting in. The louder the better, really, because the louder it is, the further away everything becomes, until the rest of the world completely disappears altogether, and it's just you and the lyrics to a song and nothing else. Plus, if I don't listen to my music, Mother's voice follows me all the way home. It walks with me along cracked pavements, broken apart by other people's journeys. It accompanies me past plastic swings in an empty park, and we pause together before a smear of traffic, waiting for the lights to change. Even on the train, as it rattles its way through the country-side, without my music Mother's voice is there the whole time, pulling all my thoughts apart and interfering, and I had to make it go away that day, because my thinking needed to be all about Rebecca Finch. Of course, I'd already searched the house in case she'd left something behind. People do all the time. They leave pieces of themselves in buses and taxis, and hotel rooms at the end of a holiday. When we moved into our last house, we found a set of curlers in the cupboard under the stairs and it took Terry ages to clear the loft. Rebecca Finch had left nothing, though. No clue to say who she really was or where she might have gone next.

Mother says I always get fixated on things. I suppose she has a point, but when your life is very small it can fill up quite quickly, even with just one thought. Rebecca Finch began filling my mind from the day the first brochure arrived, and I'd grown the idea of her all week. She was something to think about as I sat through another evening with Terry, staring at the colours changing on a television screen, and laughing at a joke I didn't understand. She was a distraction as I wiped the pots or arranged washing on the clothes horse. When I lay in bed, trying to find my sleep, the idea of Rebecca Finch's life kept me company and ate away the silence.

I thought she and I might get along quite well; we had so much common ground that we could be best friends in no time. I started to wonder what her life might look like now. I knew quite a bit already and so I coloured in the rest of her existence with my imagination. Before we bought this house, I'd walked past it a thousand times, but I'd never managed to catch sight of anyone living here. Even so, it was easy to guess what Rebecca looked like. Her name gave it away for a start, because every name has a personality and you hear your name so often, you can't help but grow into it after a while. She was petite, of course. Not like me – no one has ever described me as petite, even when I was a child. They usually plump for sturdy or well built, and big-boned has always been popular with Mother. Rebecca was quite a bit younger than I am, that was clear. Perhaps even young enough to be my daughter at a pinch, but that wouldn't stop us getting along. Friendship goes beyond things like that and anyway, I'm extremely young at heart. No one would ever guess I'm forty-three. Rebecca didn't have children, but she had a job, and quite an important one, because no one sends brochures like that to someone who doesn't matter.

I embroidered Rebecca's life as I sat on the train, on the way back from Mother's. I took my earphones out, and for once, I could enjoy myself without the threat of any inter-ruptions, because the ticket collector put in an early appearance and my carriage was almost empty. Just two women across the aisle, deep in conversation. They must have been friends because they didn't have to explain them-selves to each other, not even in small ways, and they laughed a lot. They were talking about what their children got up to and I joined in a bit with the laughing, because I thought it would make them feel comfortable about sharing the carriage.

It was a bit more difficult to hear after that, but then I real-ised they were talking about a television programme from the night before. 'I watched that too!' I said and I did some more laughing to put them at ease. A couple of minutes later they got up and disappeared through the automatic doors, which was a shame because we were getting on so well, and we might even have exchanged numbers and definitely gone for a coffee at some point. They must have been getting off at the next stop, although when I scoured the platform to wave goodbye, I couldn't see hide or hair of them.

I had the carriage to myself then, and so I went back to looking through the window and thinking about Rebecca Finch. The journey slices into the landscape, cutting through towns and villages, stopping every five minutes at tiny concrete platforms with hanging baskets, and all the wood painted white. I didn't know the names of half the places we passed through, but I could spend the whole time just leaning my head against the glass and staring at all the back gardens. They're interesting, back gardens, because they tell you who a person really is. Not like the front of a house. The front is brushed tidy, with all the personality trimmed back, and it's always covered in a coat of what people would like you to see. The back garden tells you the real story. Last week pegged out along a washing line. Rusted basketball hoops and silent trampolines. Puddles of rainwater on top of rabbit hutches and the battlefield of a lawn no one cares about any more. It's even more interesting during the winter, in the darkness of a late afternoon. The lights go on, but the curtains aren't drawn as quickly at the back of a house, are they? All those little squares of other people's lives to look into. Women at draining boards and families staring into television sets, kids lost in computer screens. You can see everything from a train. Mother would have something to say about it if she knew how much I stared, but it can't do any harm. No one even knows you're watching them.

Perhaps Rebecca Finch lived in one of those houses now. Without realising it, I might have looked right into her kitchen on the way home. Perhaps a wedding-cake terrace on the edge of town, with a pretend balcony and swirls of white plaster, or maybe she'd just swapped one estate for another, and her wheelie bin was pushed out onto an Oak Crescent these days, or a Rowan Tree Close. She could have moved into one of those executive apartments they've built right near the railway station. The ones with an onsite health club and basement parking, and a big sign outside that says 'Executive Apartments', just in case any executives didn't realise that they were supposed to be living there. She could be any one of those people for all I knew.

Of course, the only way to find out for definite which one it was would be to find her. I've had bigger challenges in my life and it couldn't be that difficult, surely? Because if I managed to do that, we could become best friends. Perhaps she could come with me to see Mother and we could sit together on the train and not have to explain ourselves to each other and laugh a lot.

I just knew we'd get on like a house on fire.

6

Everyone on the estate had become a world expert in police investigations and they were all so busy playing Inspector Morse, it seemed like the perfect opportunity to start looking for Rebecca Finch. Besides, time was running out. She could easily move again or disappear completely, and I had so many plans for us. I thought we'd start off with something local, perhaps a coffee at the garden centre or a wander around the shops. She'd have to meet Terry of course, which was a fly in the ointment. I thought I'd keep that up my sleeve for later on in the friendship. because you can get around any setback if you work at it hard enough. The most important thing was to show Rebecca my best side, because I think that's where I must have gone wrong in the past when I tried to make friends. Mother says you have to make an effort if you want people to like you and I don't think my efforts were big enough. I just needed to know more about Rebecca, know what she was interested in, so I could be interested in it as well and then she'd see how our friendship was meant to be. Destined, almost.

It was quite clear from the outset that if I was to get any further, I'd have to resort to the internet, and that meant resorting to the back bedroom and Terry's endless clutter, because Terry wasn't so much an expert in the magic art of tidying, he was an expert in the magic art of making a bloody mess.

I wore my Marigolds, obviously. There's a big window in there and I thought it might help me see what I was doing, but the curtains were pulled to and I had to walk around Terry's mess just to draw them back. Boxes of nonsense. Jam jars full of nails and screws, bits of unfamiliar tools, piles of fishing magazines I knew he'd never read. It wasn't somewhere I'd usually venture, even in the old house, and I glanced around despite the fact that the sight of it made me nauseous. Like staring at a car accident on the opposite side of the motorway and thanking God that wasn't you. Most of the surfaces were impossible to see, let alone give them a good going-over, and the only free space in the entire room was a desk, right against the far wall in the corner. You could tell it was somewhere Terry went regularly because there was a clear path to it through the mess, and yesterday's coffee cup sitting next to the computer. I remember when he bought it at a car boot sale, one of those old-fashioned machines with a monitor that was more plastic than screen. It had a keyboard, but some of the keys had wandered off and there were just little spaces where they'd used to live, and the keys that had managed to hang on had marks over the letters where past fingertips had rested. There was a printer as well, all filled up and ready with paper. It was one of those giant box-shaped machines that take ages to churn out one page, and when it appears, after a lot of noise, it's full of smudges and wonky lines.

I walked over to the desk, along the path of carpet. The first thing I did was make sure my Marigolds were on tight, because keyboards are one of the worst culprits for germs and you can never be too careful.

I pressed the power switch.

It sprang to life.

It connected to the internet straight away. I knew because there was a little box at the top and it told me, and besides, Terry is always first in the queue when it comes to his own enjoyment, so he would have set this all up as soon as we moved in. I typed Rebecca's name into the blank space at the top of the page. Nothing happened. I pressed a few more keys, although it was difficult with some of them missing and I had to guess at what they might be. Still nothing happened. I took Rebecca's name away and typed in the names of the murdered girls instead. All of them, one by one, very carefully – because I knew the internet was particular in the way that you spoke to it. I'd seen it enough times on the television.

I'd just typed in the most recent girl's name when I thought I heard the postman. It was a struggle manoeuvring my way around all of Terry's nonsense to the top of the stairs, and in the end it turned out to be a false alarm because it was some pizza shop leaflet or other, but by the time I got back, the picture on the computer screen had started to change to a newspaper report. The pictures were missing and some of the writing seemed to have got stuck, but at least it meant the machine actually worked. It was just slow and lazy. A bit like Terry. The computer was fine, which was all that mattered, because if my plan for Rebecca Finch was going to work out, I knew I'd need the internet's help.

I turned it off again and gave the room a good coat of looking at before I closed the door. I didn't want Terry knowing I'd been in there, because it would only lead to his endless questions. It took the biggest effort not to pick up yesterday's coffee cup and give it a good wash, but I left it just where it was, because he'd never imagine in a million years that I'd have that much discipline.

Sometimes you have to look at the bigger picture.

7

The next day, the rain had eased off and I decided to walk to work.

Terry told me I shouldn't be walking anywhere on my own in the current climate, as though people being murdered was just a spell of unpleasant weather, and so I told him I'd get the little bus that wound its way through the estate. I couldn't face it in the end. I don't mind trains, but buses are a breeding ground for bacteria, filled to the top with gossip and other people's germs. I always carry hand wipes with me, but no matter how many I get through, I never feel as though I've managed to completely wipe everyone else away. Besides, the fresh air always clears my head and helps me to think. If I'm struggling with a particularly tricky crossword clue, you can guarantee I'll have worked it all out by the time I get to where I'm going.

Terry would never know, anyway. He'd set off for work by the time I got downstairs and put on my coat, and the only thing he'd left was a mess on the kitchen worktop and one of his ridiculous notes. This time, it was about the dripping tap and it took three separate pages.

I'VE TRIED TO CALL THE PLUMBER BUT THERE'S NO ANSWER

WOULD YOU RING HIM TODAY BECAUSE IT'S GETTING WORSE

and

IT'S DRIVING ME MAD IT'S GOT TO STOP

Because when it comes to melodrama, Terry is an expert. Not quite as much of an expert as Mother, obviously. If they gave out awards for melodramatics, Mother would definitely be up there on the tallest podium.

I also like to walk to work because it's reassuring to remind yourself of the familiar. Some people don't pay any attention to detail, but it's always been my strongest suit. Eventually I joined up with the route I used to take from our old house, and I know that walk like the back of my own hand. The spire of St Oswald's church as it appears between the rooftops, the peeled paintwork on a garden gate, the row of newly planted cherry trees that guard the windows of the old people's home across the bypass, the crooked steps leading up to the dentist's. Other people walk past these things without caring, but I always see them. I always have. Mother says I take far too much notice of the world, that I hold on to things when everyone else has let them go, but it's just the way God made me and you never know when that kind of information will come in useful. I can hold on to a detail for ages, years sometimes, just waiting for the right moment for it to shine.

The sky was watery and pale, and as I made my way down the road the pavements were polished clean from the downpour. The only thing the weather seemed to have left behind was a silence. There are many different kinds of silence. This wasn't my kitchen silence, which wraps itself around my mind and stops me from thinking too much. It wasn't a Sunday silence, when the world has a really good stretch, when church bells ring out into the quiet. *Nothing really changes, nothing really changes.* It wasn't a hard silence, either. Not the silence at the coroner's inquest, when they read aloud the things my dad was supposed to have done. When all the people turned to my mother and forced her to accept their hard silence, until the weight of it bowed her head and curved her shoulders, and she stayed that way forevermore. This was another kind of silence. More of a pause. The kind of silence that made you certain something else was making its way towards you. Steadily. Unquestionably. Because if everything felt different in the house after they'd found the girl's body, it felt even more different when you walked the streets.

The quietness was everywhere. In the paint-box sky and the shiny wet pavements and all the things in between. It found the houses and the driveways, and it wound around the trees and stopped them from swaying in the breeze.

My footsteps sounded endless, a crash of leather on concrete, and even though I tried to walk more quietly to blend in with the rest of the world, my feet couldn't help but be heard. I'm a size nine, you see, and size nine feet weren't designed to walk softly. I echoed all over the estate.

The sound of my feet made people stare. Three men standing on the corner of the next avenue even turned around. They were obviously talking about the murder, because you could see how it filled the gaps in their faces where empty space usually lived. They must have been standing there for a while because one of them had a little black dog, and the dog had given up and was lying on the grass verge, licking at its paws. They stopped speaking when I walked past. They stopped looking at me when I got closer. Instead, they looked at their boots and at each other and at the dog. A few steps later and one of them said something, I wasn't sure what it was, but the other two laughed – the kind of laugh that you fetch up like phlegm from somewhere deep in your throat – although I wasn't really that bothered. I was used to conversations disappearing whenever I went near them.

Further down, a woman was putting out her dustbin. It had the number of her house painted on the side in white paint. Mother does this as well, but she put a little green sticker on hers. I've never quite understood how anyone can be possessive of a dustbin. I've said as much, but Mother always gives me a strange look and says you can get attached to anything in life, given time, even rubbish. The woman frowned as I got closer. I frowned back because I thought it was rude, but then I realised she was looking at a man across the road. A stranger, walking along the pavement with his hands in his pockets. Because people can get possessive of their towns and their streets, as well as their dustbins.

At the bottom of the road, Malcolm was standing by a post box looking furtive. Everyone was familiar with Malcolm. I'd known him since I married Terry and we bought a house on the estate, but the move meant that Malcolm and I were now living on the same street. On the day we arrived, he squeezed through the front door along with the removal men and we've never really managed to shake him off since. Every street has a Malcolm. Except our Malcolm is more Malcolm than most.

'Nasty business,' he said, when I got close enough.

I nodded and tried to walk around the edges of a conversation.

'Have you heard anything?' he said, when I thought I'd got away with it, because Malcolm was the kind of person who collected other people's thoughts and then spent the rest of the day moving them around the inside of his own mind until he'd turned them into something he felt happy with.

I stopped and shook my head.

'I heard she was strangled.' He put his hand to his throat, in case I couldn't work out what strangled meant. 'With her own scarf,' he whispered.

'Oh,' I said.

'Mrs Cooper mentioned it in the post office queue. Also,'

Malcolm leaned in, 'she said Single Simon was seen driving the streets late that night in his Ford Fiesta.'

'Single Simon?'

Malcolm nodded. 'Not for the first time either.'

I could feel doors to a subject being opened.

'And for no good reason,' he said.

Malcolm's eyes didn't look the kind of eyes that had room in them for another person's opinion and so I turned away.

'No good reason!' he shouted.

After three steps I had a change of heart.

'Malcolm?' I looked back.

'Hmm?' His hand was still clasped to his throat.

'Malcolm, I don't suppose,' I said, 'you know about the woman who used to live in our house? Where she went after she left here?'

Malcolm looked up the road, as though Rebecca Finch might be standing there, waiting to be described.

'Renter,' he said. 'I don't bother getting to know the renters, because they never stay long.'

'Anything at all?' I said.

Malcolm decided to give my question his full attention, and he let go of his throat. 'She was one of those fancy types, you know?'

I didn't.

'Always dressed up,' he said. 'As though she forever had something important to do. Although she can't have had, can she? No one leads a life like that all the time.'

I couldn't remember ever living a life like that, even for five minutes.

'She had a gentleman friend.' Malcolm said 'gentleman friend' in the same way Mother did, making it sound vaguely suspicious. 'Picked her up in his fancy car. Brought her back all hours of the day and night, revving his engine and making a big fuss.'

'You don't know where she moved to?'

'No idea. She never spoke to any of us. One day she was here, the next she was gone. Why?' Malcolm's hand went to his throat again. 'Do you think she's connected to the murderer?'

I said, 'No,' a few times and threw in a 'Nothing like that,' and eventually he let me go. He clearly hadn't noticed anything at the press conference either.

I was halfway down the street, and a safe stopping distance from Malcolm's ears, before I answered him properly.

'I think there's a chance that she might be,' I said under my breath.

8

Before I'd even reached the charity shop, I'd worked out exactly what I was going to do about Rebecca Finch. I'd need to pay a few more visits to Terry's computer, obviously. Even though it was slow and half the writing didn't show up, it was still going to be very useful. There was more to be done, but it was like a crossword really, you just needed a bit of time to sort out all the other clues, move them around a bit until everything made sense.

I've worked at the charity shop part-time for the last fifteen years, and that's not counting the seventy-four weeks and three days I was there as a volunteer. I started helping out mainly as a way of getting away from Mother. Eventually they offered me a permanent position, and Mother still can't get her head around the fact that they pay me now.

'*When are you going to get a proper job, Linda?*' she says. '*One that brings in real money?*'

or

'*I don't know what your grandmother would have said. Or your Uncle George.*'

Because Mother likes to summon up the dead to support all her arguments.

I always tell her I like working in the charity shop. I tell her it gets me out of the house and gives me something to think about. The truth is, it was only ever meant to be a stopgap. That's the trouble with stopgaps, though. They always end up being not very easy to stop.

When I was eleven, I decided I wanted to become a hairdresser. I quite fancied turning people into whoever they wanted to be, because hair can do that. It can transform you into someone else. It's amazing what a pair of scissors can achieve. Like magic. Or perhaps it's the person holding the scissors who has the real magic, the real power to change you, because people can do that, too. Dad was all for it, even though it would have meant moving out after I left school and living miles away. But then all the trouble happened, and nothing ever became of it. Mother said it was just as well. 'You've got the wrong name for a stylist,' she said. 'Creative people have names like Kiki and Nina. Not Linda. No one ever trusted their hair to someone called Linda.'

And so no one ever did.

Now she takes every opportunity to tell me about all the other things I could be doing instead of working in a charity shop, although she manages to turn a blind eye when I give her first dibs on a brand-new Marks & Spencer cardigan.

When I first started, they put me in the back room by myself, sorting through the clothes and steaming them. It's amazing the things we get donated. When you look through the bags people leave, it feels as though they've taken their whole lives and dumped them in our doorway overnight. Sometimes, they don't empty their pockets or the little compartments in their handbags, as though they were in such a rush to reinvent themselves, they didn't even want to hold on to the smallest reminder of who they used to be. I've found all sorts. Train tickets, chewing gum, letters, money. Of course the change goes in the charity tin, but the rest gets thrown away because there's no way of knowing where it came from, or who it was that left it there, so we don't have any choice. There's a lot of rubbish, of course. Used tissues. Sweet wrappers. Heaven knows what else. *'You'll have to wear gloves, Linda,'* Mrs Gadsby said when I first started, and she wasn't joking either.

When Mrs Gadsby left with her hip, I thought they might make me manager because I was allowed on the tills by then. I even had some input into pricing. I was eyeing up a suit on the occasion-wear rail, because you have to dress the part for a job like that, but they brought in Tamsin instead. Not that I minded because I've never really got on well with responsibility. Mother said, *'You'd only have got yourself in a state, Linda,'* and she was probably right. I did hint at my disappointment when the area manager paid a visit, but she said my strengths were on the shop floor. *'We need you at the coalface, Linda,'* she said. *'A big strong girl like you. An army is nothing without its foot-soldiers.'* They made me fourth keyholder instead, after Tamsin, Tamsin's mother and Nigel the butcher next door. So if all of them happen to lose their key at the same time, I'll be the one to save the day. Except my key still hasn't come through yet. *'It'll be here soon, Linda!'* the area manager always says. *'It'll be here soon!'*

I couldn't resent Tamsin, even if I tried. She's a few years younger than me, but I don't see any reason why that should stop people being friends. Several times I asked her if she'd like to go to the pictures one night, or maybe a coffee after we close up, but she's such a busy person and there was always something else she had to do. I gave her a present in the end, a scarf she'd admired in a magazine. I thought it might start the friendship off nicely. *'Surprise!'* I said, when I handed it to her. She was knocked for six, I could tell by her face. *'I can't accept that, Linda,'* she said, and she made a big fuss, because that's what people feel they have to do. I insisted, though. I made her take it, and she gave me the exact same smile as she gives to all of the customers. I think she was just a bit overwhelmed. In fact, I know she was, because she hardly spoke for weeks afterwards. Went out for her lunch every day, scurried off as soon as it was closing time. Some people find it difficult to accept friendship, which is a shame, really. Although I suppose it could be worse. As Mother likes to remind me, I've always got

Terry, which is probably more than I deserve when all's said and done. *'Beggars can't be choosers, Linda,'* that's what she says.

I just can't help but wonder, sometimes, what my life would have been like if he wasn't in it.

It didn't take long to get to work that morning, although I probably walked a little faster because I was doing so much thinking about Rebecca. Apart from Malcolm, I didn't see anyone else I knew. Towns are like that now. Every face belongs to a stranger and no one looks you in the eye any more, although sometimes that can be used to your advantage. The estate was so big now, it had got out of hand. There were cul-de-sacs and avenues I never knew even existed. Velux blinds and ornamental fishponds I'd never clapped eyes on, people I didn't recognise. There were two workmen looking into a hole they'd made in the road and some young lad pushing leaflets through letterboxes, but most people had demisted their windscreens, or boarded buses and trains, and disappeared into their day.

I crossed the car park and walked down the alley and on to the little square with the statue and the park benches. There was usually a busker outside the Co-op, but even he wasn't there, and across from the supermarket there was always a small stall that sold flowers. I usually avoided looking at it, this time of year, but I glanced across to check and it was closed up and covered in tarpaulin. The high street was as busy as usual, although the people on it seemed to have more of a purpose about them. A sense of needing to do what they had to do without lingering for too long. Although they'd have you believe there's safety in numbers, I've always thought it was a strange thing to say, because you can never quite be sure of who's wandering around in those numbers with you.

As soon as I walked into the shop, I could see Tamsin standing next to the till because she has the kind of hairstyle that always seems to catch your eye.

'I'm early for once,' I said. 'I would have been even earlier, but Malcolm held me up with all his gossiping. This murder's the only thing people seem to want to talk about these days.'

I didn't spot the two policemen until I'd folded the raincoat over my arm.

'Oh,' I said. It's always a surprise seeing a uniformed policeman close up, because they're much bigger than you think they are, like cows I suppose, and if I haven't prepared myself they make me say things I don't mean, or mean things I don't say. I learned my lesson a long time ago, so I try to say as little as possible now. Mother says it's the best approach when it comes to an unexpected encounter with anyone wearing a uniform.

They didn't pay me much attention, but even so I didn't hurry putting my coat away in the back room. I could hear Tamsin say thank you and the sound of them making their way out of the shop, past the little carousel of sunglasses and the display I'd made of shoulder bags by the entrance.

Their radios started to crackle as they left and when I peered around the door I could see them crossing the road, heading towards the estate agent's and talking into their shoulders.

'You can come out now, Linda,' Tamsin said. 'It's nothing to worry about.'

'I wasn't worried,' I said. 'I was just hanging my coat up and anyway what did they want?'

'They're going round all the shops. It was just routine.'

'They always say that,' I told her. 'They say something's routine, but before you know it they've put you in the back of their panda car in front of the whole street and taken you in for questioning.'

Tamsin started to laugh, but then she stopped laughing and frowned, first with her eyebrows and then the whole of her face.

'You see it on the telly all the time,' I said, 'in police dramas,' and my words made her frown disappear.

'Well, this isn't a police drama, Linda, this is real life, and they just popped in to give us advice on staying safe and keeping our eyes open.'

'My eyes are always open, don't you worry about that.'

'Open a little bit more than usual then,' she said. 'Especially considering the kind of place we work in. People bring all sorts in here.'

She started relaying everything the police had said. Any kind of donations we should look out for. What to do if we thought something was suspicious. How to contact them in an emergency. I stopped listening after a bit because anything to do with the police always makes me anxious, and my gaze wandered around the shop instead. Most things can look peculiar if you stare at them for long enough, but there's something especially curious about other people's clothes. Rows and rows of discarded lives, suspended on hangers and waiting for their new beginning. Even when you've steamed them and pulled away the loose threads and taken all the tissues and the sweet wrappers out of the pockets, you can't quite empty away who the clothes used to belong to. Some things more than others, of course. Jackets and coats don't hold much of someone else, but hats and scarves and shoes seem to easily become the person who wears them. Or perhaps it's the other way around. If you can dress for the job you want to get, perhaps you can dress for the person you want to become as well. Perhaps all you need to do is find the right outfit and the right hairstyle, and you can turn yourself into whoever you want.

'This is important, Linda – are you listening?' Tamsin said.

I repeated the last few words to come out of her mouth – which is a trick I learned a long time ago with Terry – and it seemed to be enough to convince her.

'I still don't trust them,' I said. 'Perhaps we should ask them to come back and go over it again?'

'Linda, they're fine. They both had a very positive aura.'

Tamsin believed in the kind of things Terry likes to describe on a good day as utter codswallop. Crystals and healing. Fairies. Homeopathic medicine. Guardian angels. And she's very big on aloe vera. *'Don't go annoying Tamsin,'*

Terry always says, *'she'll sweep you up with her broomstick,'* and he laughs at his own joke far longer than you'd think anyone could ever manage. Mother is more open-minded, because she watches a lot of documentaries, but I haven't quite made a final decision on the matter.

'What's an aura?' I said. I already knew, but mainly because it meant she'd stop talking about the police.

'Everyone has an aura, Linda,' she said. 'It's like an energy field around you. It tells you about someone's personality, their past. Even their future. Different colours mean different things.'

'And you can see them?'

'Oh yes, yes,' she said. 'Those policemen were both predominantly blue – intuitive, calm, truthful. Blue is an excellent aura.'

I leaned back against the wall, in a little gap between a poster about saving water and a display of exotic candles. I smiled at her.

She smiled back uncertainly.

'Well?' I said.

'Well what, Linda?'

'What about mine? What colour am I?'

'There isn't one,' she said.

'I thought you said we all have them.'

'We do, but I can't always see them.'

'Can you see my mother's?' I said.

'Definitely not.'

She said this so quickly, she must have been very certain.

I was sure the police officers would come back, but they didn't, and the rest of the day passed in its ordinary way. Tamsin even admired Rebecca Finch's brochure.

'What's this, Linda?' She picked it up because quite by accident I'd left it right in the middle of the chair where she always sits.

'Oh, we're revamping the house,' I said, because Tamsin and Terry hardly ever crossed paths. 'Just getting a few ideas!'

She spent ages looking at it. I've taken things to work before on numerous occasions and she's not given them a second glance, but she couldn't get enough of this.

She stopped at the middle of the brochure and admired the teal settee. 'They're quite pricey, Linda, aren't they?'

'We could go to the showroom together?' I said. 'Have a look around and make a day of it?' but she just ignored me and turned the page, so I wandered over to the *New Arrivals!* rail and started flicking through. I tried to imagine which clothes Rebecca might pick out for herself. All dressed up and fancy, Malcolm had said, but the hangers just seemed to be weighted down with greys and beiges, and polyester.

When I glanced up, Tamsin was watching me.

'Are you looking for something in particular, Linda?' she said. 'You seem to be concentrating very hard.'

'Oh no not really I'm just searching for an outfit to wear for when I meet my friend her name is Rebecca and we get on like a house on fire.' The words flew from my mouth in a big storm before I could do anything to stop them.

'I see.' Tamsin put down the brochure and tilted her head very slightly. 'I've not heard you mention this Rebecca before, is she a new friend?'

'We've known each other ages,' I said. 'Ages and ages.'

'Right, I see.'

'We've got so much in common. We're like twins, really.'

'Right.'

'I mean we're the same person,' I said. 'Practically.'

I carried on looking through the bobbled sweatshirts and the elasticated waistbands of other people's lives, I even did a little bit of whistling to cover my tracks, but when I looked back over the top of the rail, Tamsin was still standing there. Watching me.

As the day went on, we had quite a few donations. Some had been left on the doorstep, some were brought in. Others were sent from different branches – ones that had too much stock, or couldn't manage to sell something. Tamsin carried the bags into the stockroom for me to sort through, then she disappeared back into the shop and chatted for half an hour to whoever had brought them in. Mainly about the murder, even though Tamsin usually gave a wide berth to controversial subjects. I was starting to wonder what we'd all talked about before it happened.

I usually hated being stuck in the stockroom all day by myself, but it kept me away from conversation and theories and hearsay, because you can only take so much before your ears feel too full. Plus, it meant I could open a new packet of Jaffa Cakes and put my music on very quietly without

Tamsin giving me one of her looks. I could still hear them talking, though, and as I sorted through the bags, I tried to match the voice to the clothes. Some were obvious. A gruff-sounding man who brought in a bag full of tired shirts and a grey overcoat. A woman with a sing-song in her voice who donated several frilly blouses and an Alice band. A middle-aged woman who seemed to have given up on her youth overnight and packed it all into two black bin liners.

It's amazing what people give away sometimes. It makes you wonder what their reasons are. Tamsin says I have an eye for things. I can spot a designer handbag from five hundred paces, even though Tamsin says we shouldn't exploit people, so she always picks my label off and puts on a lower price. I didn't see anything exciting in that day's donations, though. At least, not until I got to the final bag. It was one of the collections redirected from another branch and it was a mish-mash of things, really. Shoes, children's clothes, a couple of board games, but right at the bottom was a man's leather jacket. It was an unusual colour, not your typical black, more of a burgundy. Heavy, too. I was just lifting it out when Tamsin walked in.

'That'll fetch a bit,' she said.

I held it up to show her. 'Terry's got a jacket just like this,' I said. 'Although it can't be his, he'd never part with it.'

'I expect it just looks the same,' she said. 'They're all very similar, aren't they?'

The little bell went and Tamsin returned to the shop. I turned the jacket back around and studied the front. It was there, right at the bottom, under the pocket. You could only see it if you knew where to look. A black line where Mother had swiped Terry with her marker pen the last time we all went to bingo.

NOW

The staff seem quite pleasant. Some more than others, of course, but that's what you get in a place like this.

It takes a special kind of person to work here. I said that to one of them. Vahri, she's called. What an interesting name. If you study her closely, you can see it written on a badge, peeking from behind her cardigan. I'd put it on display, a nice name like that, if it was me. She's tall and slim, with beautiful Irish blue eyes and the loveliest nature. You can spot it a mile off.

'Vahri,' I said one day, 'do you enjoy your work?'

She was straightening all the chairs in the day room.

'I do,' she said. 'Very much. I like helping people.'

She even stopped straightening them to answer me, which I thought was very telling.

'Vahri,' I said again, because I quite liked saying her name out loud. It felt oddly satisfying. 'How long have you worked here?'

She hesitated, halfway through moving a chair. 'Since I left college,' she said.

Whenever anyone mentioned time, I measured it against my own life and put them side by side. When Vahri was leaving college, I'd probably just got married to Terry.

'That's forever,' I said. 'An eternity.'

She smiled at me, as if she knew. As if she'd stood next to me for every one of those years and seen all the tiny pieces of misery walk with me through my life. Some people are like that. They understand, even if you've never really explained it to them properly.

'Do you live locally, Vahri?' I said, but I don't think she heard me because she just smiled and carried on tidying up.

From where I sat you could hear the simmer of conversation through the walls from the room next door. Occasional laughter, the door to the garden opening and closing. Friends and family bringing the reassurance of ordinary lives. That's what visiting time was. The restoration of hope. It might look like an opportunity to give someone magazines and chocolate and cigarettes, to relay news from home, to ask how things were going, but really it was about replacing something which had been mislaid. It was about trying to fill the space where hope once lived.

Vahri looked over at me. 'I'm sorry,' she said. 'You know, some people just don't like visiting.'

'Vahri! I'm fine! Honestly!' I tried to brush it off but sometimes my voice comes out louder than I mean it to.

She took a step back and said, 'That's good, that's really good, Linda.'

'People are strange.' I widened my smile, just to make sure my face matched my words and she knew I was all right about it all. 'They get themselves into such a state about a place like this, don't they, thinking it's something to be ashamed of?'

She nodded.

'When really it's quite delightful. I'm surprised people aren't queuing up to spend time here.' I waved my arms about to demonstrate how delightful the place was. 'Everyone who works here is so lovely.'

I stopped waving my arms.

'Especially you, Vahri. I think you're the loveliest of them all.'

I made sure my smile stayed where it was, because some people say things they don't mean just for the sake of it and I didn't want her to think I wasn't genuine. I'm fairly sure I succeeded. I was going to ask to make sure, but right at that moment, she remembered something she'd forgotten to do and off she rushed. It must have been important, because she left a couple of chairs still skew-whiff. I went over and tidied them myself. I wouldn't want her to get into trouble and besides, it's essential to keep up your standards, no matter what might happen to you in life. Mother said this when the police took my dad in for questioning and I've stuck to the principle ever since. She sat us all down at the kitchen table with a pot of tea when they brought him back. It was two o'clock in the morning and I was only eleven and I'd never stayed up that late before. The strip light above my head was fizzing and clicking because the bulb needed to be changed, and the noise was so loud it seemed to dance around my mother's voice and join in. Everything was loud at that time in the morning. All the colours seemed brighter as well, and the room smelled of yesterday's food. Like when you've had the flu and you venture downstairs for the first time and the world seems too overwhelming, and so you go back again.

'We have to hold our heads high,' Mother said, and she straightened her shoulders and jutted her chin out, perhaps to show us how it could be achieved. 'No one's done anything wrong and we need to carry on just as we are, or they'll assume we're guilty.'

She clearly meant my dad, even though she looked straight at me as she spoke. Probably because I was the only one taking any notice. My dad had his hands over his ears and his head bent forwards, as though he wanted to vanish into the tablecloth and disappear forever.

I tried very hard. The following Monday I got ready for school and put the thought right at the back of my mind. It was only when I stood in the hall and stared at the daffodil painting that the thought travelled to the front of my head again and made itself a nuisance. Mother caught me staring into the sickly bright yellow of the flowers and she said, 'Go on, Linda – you've got nothing to be ashamed of,' and so I pulled myself up and stuck my chin out, just like she'd told me to.

Everyone knew. You could tell. It was obvious from the crackly silence when I got on the bus. Thankfully, there was a free seat right at the front, but I didn't sink into it like I usually would. Instead, I sat down very slowly and kept my head up. I even tried a small smile, just to be sure people knew my dad was innocent, but I'm not certain anyone noticed. Mother would have been very proud, because I kept my head up even when those girls got on a few stops later. They stared at me as they walked past and I stared back at their full faces of make-up because as the term went on, school dress code seemed to be getting sloppier and sloppier. I still kept the smile on my face though, because I wanted them to know I had no hard feelings.

One of them was still standing in the aisle, looking back at me. I thought of her as the ringleader, because she was the one who started it all. The others just followed suit. She wasn't smiling. She was just watching me. Sharp black eyeliner and pale pink lips. She carried on watching, even when the other girls pulled her into the seat beside them and whispered in her ear. I'd love to have known what they whispered. I'm usually very good at hearing other people's conversations, but this was too quiet. Too quick. Because I couldn't hear, I couldn't reply, so I made my smile even bigger to make up for it. I even laughed a little bit. Just to put them at their ease. It was a misunderstanding, that's all. My dad said so.

9

I challenged Terry about that jacket. I just wanted to see what he'd say for himself.

It was Friday night, and we were getting ready to go to the pub. We often did on a Friday night, whether we wanted to or not. I most definitely did not because I'd much rather have stayed in and looked through that morning's mail instead, but in the end I managed to talk myself into it. I found a lipstick at the back of the bathroom cupboard and I thought it might be the kind of shade Rebecca would wear, so I put a coat of it on before I came down. Terry was positioned at the bottom of the stairs and he looked up and said, 'What have you done to your face?', so I wiped it all off on a tissue.

'Why don't you wear your leather jacket?' I brushed past him and stuffed the tissue in my coat pocket. 'It'd go nicely with those tan slacks.'

I waited.

He stood in front of the hall mirror, fiddling with the zip on his coat. All fingers and thumbs like he usually is.

'I can't be bothered to change now,' he said. 'It means going back upstairs.'

'Oh, go on. It's smart, that leather jacket. The coat you've got on looks like it needs a good hour on forty degrees.'

The fiddling stopped, but his eyes didn't leave the reflection in the mirror.

'I don't know where it is. I must have put it down. Left it behind somewhere.' He said all this very fast, because people have the strange idea that if words leave your mouth in a hurry it means that they don't carry any weight with them, when truth be told, they carry so very much more.

I told him he shouldn't be so careless, that money didn't grow on trees, all the things he says to me when the fancy takes him.

'I think someone must have nicked it,' he said. 'I don't remember the last time I wore it. Perhaps I left it somewhere. You know what they're like around here, anyone could have taken it.'

I thought of all the people we knew, or thought we knew. All the front gardens we stared at, without ever seeing what lay at the back. As much as I hated agreeing with Terry, he was right. You never really know anyone.

'It'll turn up,' he said. 'Sooner or later.'

I didn't reply. Instead, I lifted the house keys from the hall table and walked ahead into the night, past the cracked glass and the loose carpet, and all the other fault lines in our lives, into the shock of cold air that stole all the warmth away and made me wish, for once, I'd admitted I didn't want to go. But that's the problem with routines, they creep up on you when your back is turned and before you know it, your life is littered with every kind of nonsense you'd rather not be doing, and so those unsaid words joined all the other unsaid words in the back of my mind, where they gathered, waiting for their chance to be spoken.

The Red Lion was packed. It was always busy on a Friday, but the need to share out their opinions on the murders had pulled people from television sets and out of armchairs, and it seemed to be even more crowded than usual. We'd walked there because it was quicker than arguing about who was going to drive, and after pavements filled with nothing but the sound of our own breathing, pushing open the doors felt like hitting a wall made out of lights and lager and shouting.

'Busy,' Terry said, because even though he'd barely said a word on the walk down, he now felt the need to declare the bloody obvious to anyone within earshot. He usually told me to find a seat, but there wasn't much chance of that, so I waited next to a coat stand whilst he tried to push his way towards the bar.

I could see faces I recognised, heard familiar voices drift over the hammer of conversation. The Red Lion was right in the middle of the estate and people seemed to be drawn towards it no matter where they lived, persuaded by the slot machines and the cheap beer, and the chance to get away from an evening staring at their own front rooms. But even in a pub, there are still boundaries. Restrictions. It might look accidental, arranged by chance, but people only ever sit with their own tribe, glued together by geography and genetics.

To anyone passing through, the estate might seem as if it had just unfolded by chance, across fields and time, but within its sprawl of crescents and avenues lay a map of the town's history, raised from one small terrace originally built to house factory workers. A factory that had long since fallen quiet. They still called it Tin Town, even though the cans of condensed milk and rice pudding weren't made there any more and the factory chimney stood cold and silent, never again to heave the black smoke of a day's work across the rooftops. After that small beginning the factory had grown, and with it grew Tin Town, sending rows of houses across the meadows. The terraces turned into semis, yards turned into gardens. The alleyways disappeared to make room for off-road parking and ornamental fishponds. Kids stopped playing in the middle of the street. Soon, the semis weren't enough. They started building detached houses gathered into little cul-de-sacs, which were so close together, you could stand in your front room and entertain yourself with someone else's television across the road. People didn't seem to mind, and the new properties filled with families. Commuters. Outsiders. Locals became strangers. No one cared any more about the land or the lives lived on it. The latest houses they built, right at the top of the estate, had Georgian pillars and little iron gates. All the things inside them were ready fitted. The bedrooms, the kitchen. Everything measured and made. All you had to do was slot yourself in there alongside the furniture. I forced Terry to look at them when we were choosing where to move to. I even persuaded him to walk around the show house. I'd no intention of living anywhere like that, because I already had my mind set on this place, but I didn't think it would do any harm. He drifted from room to room like a draught, with his hands in his pockets, staring at ceilings. He didn't even open a cupboard door.

'What do we want with four bedrooms when there are only two of us?'

It was all he said the whole time we were in there. That was that. We didn't even leave with a brochure. The house we eventually bought was only a bit further down the estate from where we were already living. I'd had my eye on it for a long time. I always made sure I walked past it on my way to work, and sometimes I'd stop by the gate on the pretext of searching for something in my handbag or adjusting my coat, but really it was to steal glances into its dark windows or stare for a while at the silent front door. I never saw Rebecca Finch, no matter how many times I walked past, but some houses are like that, they have the look of being hollow even when someone is waiting inside them. I let Terry think it was his idea, of course. Casually pointed out how much bigger the garden was than ours when we walked past on the way to the pub. Commented on the width of the drive. 'A drive like that would be better for parking your van,' I said, and I carried on walking and left it at that. It doesn't take long, especially with a man. It's like supermarkets, putting the biscuits in the tea and coffee aisle and letting you think throwing a family pack of Hobnobs in with your jar of instant was your own idea all along. It was exactly the same with Terry. I read about it in a magazine. You don't have to hand it to them on a plate, though. Like the biscuits, it needs to be placed very carefully, just within sight. It didn't take long. One Friday night, on the way to the Red Lion, he stopped and put his hands on his hips, and he stared at the house and he said, 'It looks empty – I wonder if it's for sale.' The next day, he knocked at the door. He must have spoken to Rebecca, but I didn't ask. No need to push it by then. Because I've found in life that if you wait quietly for long enough, eventually your turn will come.

The rooms in the new house were a few inches longer, the flowerbeds a tiny bit wider, and Terry had more room to park his filthy van, but we still lived the same life. We just stared at it all from a different angle. We walked to the Red Lion, the same as we always had, we just took a slightly shorter route to get there, and I still found myself looking into a crowded bar for the umpteenth time and trying to figure out where I was meant to sit.

The old estate, the Tin Towners, were always at the back.

They were observers, mainly, witnesses to the lives that spilled and passed in front of them, choosing their words quietly, carefully. When they did speak, they were listened to, earning their seat and the right to be heard by the bones of their forefathers, which grew in the soil of the church-yard. The rest of us sat in little groups, carved out by our roads and avenues. I could see Malcolm, squashed into a seat in the far corner, so I tried to make my way over, between the backs of strangers, past other people's lives and elbows and conversation. Newcomers who hadn't yet found a refuge. I would have been one of them if I hadn't married Terry. My face didn't fit. My accent didn't fit.

'*Are you from London?*' people say sometimes, even now. Because it's the only other place they can think of when I tone down my accent.

I just agree with them. Mother and I put as many miles as we could between us and what had happened, so a few more imaginary ones wouldn't hurt, because the last thing we needed was people putting two and two together.

'Evening, Linda.' Malcolm greeted me with a raised pint glass and the hint of froth on his top lip. 'Busy, isn't it?'

I nodded and smiled, and said the right words to fit his ears, because the thing about the Red Lion was that everyone had the same conversations every week, passing them backwards and forwards between them like the lyrics to a song. You could disappear for twelve months and walk back in, and you wouldn't have missed anything because everyone would still be singing the same tune. Except now there was the murder, of course, and they all had something fresh to talk about. It was strange how someone else's death had given everyone in there a new lease of life.

I found a few inches of seat on the end of a bench that ran the length of the big bay window. It meant being closer to Malcolm than God had ever intended, but it was either that or stand, and I'm not very good at standing in a pub. I never know what to do with my arms and legs, and I always get through my drink so much faster when I'm on my feet.

I looked around the table. There were people I recognised from our road. The old woman who lived on her own in the row opposite Malcolm. She always had a tomato juice, just the one, and more often than not there was still half of it left at closing time. Malcolm's neighbour sat at the far end of the group. He was next to his wife. Blonde. Small. Wearing a bit too much make-up, although Terry would have you believe there's no such thing when it comes to other women. I smiled at her. Whenever I walked past their house it always seemed like they were in the middle of an argument. I'd seen them through the windows and sometimes I'd pretend to be looking for something in my bag and I'd stop and listen. Raised voices. They threw their arms about a lot when they were quarrelling, like people do when they can't get their point across just with words, so they start involving their limbs as well. They hadn't been married very long, I don't think, because they were at the stage when you still have things you care enough to argue about.

'Hello,' I said.

She said hello, but it was one of those half-hearted ones that barely leaves your mouth before it goes back inside again.

'You must know Steve and Ingrid, Linda?' Malcolm said. Malcolm was the kind of person who enjoyed being in charge of introductions, because it meant he knew more people than you did. 'They're only just down the road from you.'

I shook my head.

'Linda hasn't been moved in very long,' Malcolm said, because he felt the need to explain me. 'Came up from further down the estate with her husband, didn't you, Linda?'

'We've only been here a year ourselves,' said Steve. 'Moved from Manchester to be near Ingrid's mother. You never see the same person twice on this estate.'

On first impressions, Steve didn't appear to be the sharpest knife in the cutlery drawer, but he was right on that score. The estate was so big now, it smothered the landscape, stealing the light with its endless rooftops and satellite dishes. It had grown even in the time we'd been there, and if you kept your head down, if you didn't draw any attention to yourself, no one would even notice you were there.

Malcolm raised a half-empty glass in the direction of Steve, who just wiped lager from his mouth with the back of his hand.

'Oh, he can never do enough for my mother, can't Steve.' Ingrid suddenly found her voice and sent all of it in the direction of her husband, who just grinned back at her.

I studied her make-up. She'd drawn those sharp little wings at the edges of her eyes. The ones that make you look like a cat. The ones you see in magazines. I'd always wanted to paint my eyes like that, to make them tilt towards the sky in a state of constant curiosity, and I imagined Rebecca Finch drew them on herself all the time.

'He's there morning, noon and night,' she said.

Her sweater was quite nice, too. One of those fluffy ones that seem to have a mind of its own. I bought a pink one home from work once, but Terry said it made me look like a house side, so I took it back again. Ingrid didn't look a house side. She looked tiny.

'He's at the beck and call of my mother, aren't you, babe?'

'Terry's just the same,' I said.

They all looked at me.

'He is?' said Malcolm.

'Oh, he is. Always offering to help Mother. Never complains. Goes out of his way for her all the time.' I spotted Terry and a tray of drinks weaving their way across the bar towards us. 'Don't you, babe?'

Terry put his tray on the table and a fraction of his pint slipped over the edge of the glass and was lost. 'Are you talking to me?' he said.

Everyone laughed. I'm never sure if I'm supposed to join in, but it got quite loud so I felt forced into it. I couldn't understand why Terry didn't just say 'yes'. He did it all the time at home. Slotted yes and no into the conversation without caring what he was yes-ing and no-ing to.

Terry and Steve and Malcolm, but mainly Malcolm, started having a conversation about the latest police statement, and I couldn't stomach any more police, so I turned away and found myself looking straight at Ingrid and her catty eyes and pink pouty lips. She asked me about the new house.

'How are you settling in, Linda?' she said, with a little head tilt. The kind of head tilt that people do to make it look as though they're making a big effort to listen by putting their ears at a special angle.

Fine, I told her. Fine.

'Of course, you'll have to put your stamp on it.'

The little black wings at the edges of her eyes looked quite tricky to do.

'You know,' she said. 'Make it your own. Apparently, it's been rented out for so long, and no one's really done anything with it.'

I didn't reply, because I was still thinking about her eye make-up. Perhaps she could teach me how to do them because I'm a quick learner. I only have to be shown something once.

'Home decor?' she said. 'New furniture?'

I hesitated. 'Oh yes, new furniture. We're ordering some.'

'Great,' she said. 'What have you gone for?'

Her jumper was so fluffy, little clouds of wool stood out from the sleeves, as though they were trying to escape. She wore a scarf, too. One of those scarves that stay on even when you're indoors because they might masquerade as a scarf, but really they're just there to decorate your neck.

'Teal,' I said. 'A big teal settee. With orange cushions.' I glanced over at Terry, but he didn't hear.

'Nice!'

'And a coffee table,' I said. 'With a giant black bowl. It's huge. You could put the whole of Yorkshire in there, if you wanted to.'

'Nice!' she said again, only she stretched the word out even further.

She took a sip of her drink. 'Any holidays planned, Linda?'

'Several,' I said. 'I like your scarf.'

We were in the Red Lion until long after last orders. Terry always buys himself two pints as soon as the first bell goes and then I have to sit there and watch while he drinks them. I didn't mind so much this time, though, because I had Ingrid to talk to.

'Ingrid and I have so much in common,' I said to Terry on the walk home.

'Really?' he said. 'She's a lot younger than you – you conveniently forget your age sometimes, Linda.'

'I'm only forty-three,' I said, but he was too busy laughing to answer and the words just disappeared.

There's usually no point elaborating, because if you click with a person, it never sounds the same when you try to put it into words for someone else's benefit, but I tried to explain to Terry just the same. It turned out Ingrid was a hairdresser, and I always wanted to be a hairdresser. We were both big fans of *Coronation Street*, although Ingrid didn't know many of the characters I talked about, even when I explained them at great length, because she didn't always have the chance to watch it. She'd never really taken much interest in crosswords, but she had brown eyes like me, though, and both our fathers were called David. When I said the last bit, Terry stopped walking and looked at me.

'You didn't tell her about your dad?'

'Of course not,' I said.

'Only people wouldn't understand, Linda. They'd probably get the wrong idea.'

'I know,' I said. 'People always have. That's why I never say anything.'

Mother and I left Wales because of people getting the wrong idea. People we didn't know, people who turned around to stare at us in the street, or in shops. People in those shops who refused to serve us. People who threw bricks at the windows and pushed dog muck through the letterbox. Then there were the people we did know. People who edged around the subject, trying to find a way in. People who eventually gave up edging, and trying to be quiet and careful, and who became the people that just said, *'Linda, do you mind if I ask you something?'* The thing is, you're never allowed to say, *'Well yes, actually, I do mind and I'd really rather you didn't,'* because it's one of those pretend questions people fasten onto something unacceptable, just to make themselves feel better about opening a door to a room they shouldn't be in.

I always said I didn't know anything. I had no idea. It

wasn't anything to do with me. That's what Mother told me to say, but I would have said it anyway, because the problem with answering their question any other way was it gave them the green light to ask anything they wanted.

'You'll have to speak to my dad,' I used to say, knowing full well they'd never dare. Then, of course, he wasn't around any more and they couldn't ask him anything, even if they'd wanted to. None of us could. Six months later Mother started talking about moving away. She wasn't the only one. Other families disappeared too after everything that happened with Dad. The family of the first girl went first, the one I blamed more than any of them because she started all the lies, then the others followed suit, because people are like sheep. Even families who had nothing to do with it all decided to move on. I thought Mother might change her mind, but she didn't.

'Where would you like to move to, Linda?' she said one day. 'You can pick anywhere you want. It's your choice. It's up to you.'

I said a few different places to begin with. Places I knew she hated, just to test the water.

'What about Blackpool?' I said one day, knowing full well she'd throw a fit.

'I've always fancied living in Scotland,' I told her the next time it was mentioned, because I knew she hated the cold.

'What about London?' My mother didn't trust London or anyone in it.

It was only then, after I'd explored all the places I knew

she would reject immediately, that I mentioned moving here. Because if you plant something in a bed of nettles, it's always going to look appealing.

'Oh,' she said. 'That sounds interesting. What's made you pick there?'

I told her I'd read about it in a magazine. I told her the views were pretty and the air was clean, and there was hardly any crime.

'That sounds perfect!' she said.

I didn't tell her about the conversations I overheard on buses. There was never any need.

'Because I can't stand another minute under this roof,' she said.

Except it wasn't the roof that was causing us any trouble, and whenever you try to run away from your problems, your problems join you for the ride, and no matter how far you travel, you can always rely on them to keep you company. They were there even as I followed Terry through the estate that night, along empty pavements. I'd told him most of it over the years. Not all of it, mind, because it's always best to have some corners of your life that no one else ever knows about. My dad taught me that.

'Smells like rain,' Terry said, over his shoulder.

I stared up at the sky, black and starless, a spill of ink resting on our heads. 'It doesn't look like it,' I said.

'Malcolm reckons it's going to chuck it down. He heard we're in for a real storm.'

It turned out to be the most accurate thing Malcolm said all night, because when we woke the next morning it rained for six solid days.

Perhaps if it hadn't, they wouldn't have found the next body.

NOW

They bring the drugs round here on a trolley. It reminds me of the cinema, in the days before shiny counters and baseball caps, when a woman appeared in an apron during the interval, with a tray strapped to her shoulders and little tubs of ice creams.

I've never taken anything stronger than an aspirin, but they give out all sorts from that trolley. Things to make you more happy, things to make you less happy. Except it's someone else deciding exactly how happy you need to be, which is a flaw in the system no one else seems to acknowledge. The drugs trolley is very popular, at least with some. They're queuing up ready for their turn long before it's time, waiting for a tiny plastic cup containing just the right amount of happiness. Others aren't so keen. They have to be hunted down and taken to the clinic room and someone checks their mouth afterwards, to make sure what they're given isn't being spat out later when no one's looking. Secreting, they call it. *'The patient has been secreting their meds again,'* you hear them say, because it's always 'meds', and never 'medication'. Perhaps shortening a word makes the whole thing sound more bearable.

It breaks up the hours, the drugs trolley. Twice a day, sometimes more, its wheels squeak their way across the lino and everyone knows a little time has passed since the last time they thought about it.

They don't just use drugs to sweep out the corners of your mind either. They use conversations as well. People disappear into a side room for hours on end so someone can pull out all the words no one has ever heard before. It's called Talking Therapy. I know, because it says so on a poster taped to the noticeboard. I often wonder if it helps. Perhaps when you stay silent about too many things, all those words you keep to yourself eventually clog up your mind like a big traffic jam and it stops working properly. If you let them all out, it frees everything up a bit. Talking on its own is no good, though. I can talk to Terry until the cows come home and I never feel any better for it, because he never listens. It's the listening that matters. They should call it Listening Therapy. Except no one ever teaches you how to listen, they only ever teach you how to talk. Which is a recipe for disaster, because it means everyone is walking around saying things, but no one ever really hears them.

There are other ways, too, and other things they use to

unclog your head. There's a room down the corridor where it all happens, but of course I've never seen inside. Just a glance, occasionally, as I walk past. A glimpse as its double doors swing open or someone adjusts the blinds on its tiny windows. It's strange that a treatment should cause more upset and commotion than the illness it's supposed to help, and you wouldn't think three little letters would cause such controversy, but they do, because sometimes society makes you pay a price for becoming well again. Even if it's almost certainly society that made you ill in the first place. That's the thing with people, though. They spend all that energy breaking you, bending and snapping until there are only tiny little fragments of you left, but then a little while later they return to the scene of their crime to enjoy the applause when they manage to put you all back together again.

10

The first we knew of it, they'd closed off the lane down by the river.

'Perhaps it's flooded?' Tamsin said, the umpteenth time one of the customers mentioned it. 'Or maybe there's been a car accident?'

I knew straight away, of course. I didn't say anything, because people always think you're strange, but I got this weird feeling in my chest, as though my ribs were a size too small. The feeling stayed with me all day. If anything, it got worse every time the little bell went, because with each customer, I thought there might be some more news, but of course there wasn't. It was just the same thing but said in a large variety of different ways.

'You're very quiet, Linda. Are you okay?' Tamsin said as we were closing up.

'I'm fine,' I said. When someone asks if you're okay, this is the answer they're looking for, because I have learned along the way that most conversation people have is based on a script, and there are certain lines you're expected to say. If you make a mistake and wander off the script and absentmindedly tell them how you're really feeling, they're always very shocked and never quite know what to do with your words, so you're really better off just keeping quiet.

Terry was on an early. He'd already left when I'd got up that morning and there were pages of his notes on the kitchen table. I couldn't speak to him during the day, he said, because they weren't allowed mobile telephones on the factory floor any more due to health and safety. It was too noisy anyway, he said. It suited me because it meant I could use his mobile telephone whenever I wanted to. It just sat there on the coffee table, waiting to be picked up and I very often rang people on it instead of my own, which meant I didn't use up all my credits. Anyway, this particular series of notes was about lightbulbs.

WE ARE OUT OF BULBS

and

I'LL GET TWO ON THE WAY HOME

they said, and I screwed them up and put them in the bin, because they were no good to me. Terry wasn't very keen on anything practical. All fingers and thumbs, he was, and with a house that seemed to be falling apart at the seams, it wasn't an ideal combination.

Because of the early shift, he was already at home when

I got in that evening. He was sat in front of the telly, watching the news. One of those twenty-four-hour channels that repeat the same stories all day long and have a ticker running along the bottom of the screen. I could hear it before I was halfway through the back door.

'Something's cracking off down by the river,' he shouted, before I was even out of my coat.

I didn't answer.

'Doesn't look good,' he shouted again.

I wanted to listen, because not knowing is sometimes worse than knowing, but not knowing meant I was still allowed to imagine the road was flooded or there was a car accident, like Tamsin said. That's the strange thing about hope, it usually causes more problems than it solves and there are times when your life is so much simpler without it. In the end, I stood in the hall, watching through the doorway.

'I thought you were interested in all this stuff?' he said, over his shoulder.

'It just winds me up, Terry. It's all people can talk about.'

'Come inside and close that door, you're letting all the cold air in,' he said, and so I did what he told me to and sat on the edge of the settee. I wasn't stopping. You could tell straight away the people on the telly knew no more than anybody else, and there was cleaning to be getting on with.

On the screen, there was a reporter holding a microphone and stood in his overcoat not two miles from where we were sitting. His collar was turned against the wind and you could see the rain reflected in his hair with all the camera lights.

Cordoned off since mid-morning today, said the reporter.

'Poor sod,' Terry said. 'I bet they'll make him stand there all night, just in case something happens.'

No official statement

In the background was blue and white police tape, wrapped around little poles, and it snapped and cracked along with the wind. You could see the very beginning of the river, the tall reeds that marked the edges of the water, and there were the first few notes of spring, dotted yellow and white in the grass.

Local reports state that a body has been discovered by a passer-by.

But beyond that, nothing. Just the black of the evening, deep and quiet.

Speculation is rife that this could be the third victim of what the media has now labelled the Hexford Strangler.

'Look – you can see the church spire!' Terry pointed. 'There, behind his head!'

'You can stand on the landing and treat yourself to a far better view of it,' I said, but it fell on deaf ears. For some reason, Terry found it much more interesting to watch it all on a television screen.

The reporter put one finger in his ear, trying to listen to what the newsreader in the warm, comfortable studio was saying.

Yes, Dermott – everyone here is terrified, he shouted into the microphone. *It's a small community, but a community in turmoil.*

I glanced over at Terry. There didn't look as though there was any turmoil about him. He appeared more relaxed than usual, if anything. The remote control was out of reach, for once, and he sat back in his chair, arms behind his head, drinking it all in.

'I'll go and put the kettle on,' I said.

The police gave a statement on the ten o'clock news. I was going to call it a day, but I hung about for a bit, just to see if they said anything new.

A police officer stood on some steps in front of a crowd of journalists.

'Nowhere I recognise,' Terry said.

I was going to say did it matter, but it would have meant talking over the top of the detective on the steps. Except he couldn't have been a detective, because he was in uniform. Perhaps all the detectives were busy, detecting things, and he was the only one left.

The policeman said it was the body of a woman. He said they didn't know who she was, but she'd been there for some time.

'How can nobody have missed her?' I said, but Terry shushed me and pointed at the screen.

Police were alerted at approximately 10.05 this morning following the discovery of a woman's body in the River Tame adjacent to Conygree Lane. The discovery was made by a member of the public, although it is believed the body had been there for some time. The woman's death is currently being treated as unexplained.

'Unexplained.' Terry stretched all the syllables out. 'It's either unexplained or no suspicious circumstances. There's never any middle ground.'

It was my turn to shush him.

The officer looked down at his notes. 'An investigation is underway and inquiries are in their early stages. No formal identification has yet been made. We would appeal to anyone who uses the area of Conygree Lane, and who may have any information which could help. If you were on foot or cycling in the area and noticed something which you thought was out of the ordinary, or if you have any information at all, no matter how insignificant you think it may be, then please make contact with the police. There will be no further statements at the present time.'

I looked at Terry. 'Isn't that near where you go fishing?' I said.

He didn't answer.

Mother was in such a committed relationship with her television set, she left me on the doorstep until it was time for a commercial break.

'It's like OJ Simpson all over again,' she said when I finally got into the house. 'I daren't leave it for a second in case I miss something substantial.'

It was a good job she wasn't watching it on BBC, or I never would have got through the door.

'We don't even know if it's anything to do with the other girls.' I decided to put the kettle on for myself, because she showed no sign of stirring. 'They've never said one way or the other.'

'Of course it is. It stands to reason. You were right all along, Linda. It *is* a serial killer.'

'What?'

'This is number three. Or it might be number two. Or even number one. That body could have been there for months.'

The man who found the body was interviewed on the lunchtime news. He was one of those water bailiffs, the ones who patrol the riverbanks and stop people fishing where they shouldn't. The heavy rainfall had caused part of the river to flood, and he had gone down to take a look. Mother sat poised with her jotter and a biro, in case he said anything she needed to mull over later.

'I thought it was a mannequin at first. You know, a shop dummy,' he said.

Mother turned to me. 'What would a shop dummy be doing in a river?'

'What would a body be doing in a river?' I said, and she turned back to the television.

The interviewer pushed the microphone a little further towards the man. 'How does it feel,' he said, 'to find someone deceased under those circumstances?'

The man looked at the interviewer and then stared into the camera. 'I just thought it was a shop dummy.'

'Yes, but how does it *feel?*' The microphone was pushed even nearer.

The man just gazed at it and said nothing.

'How does he think it feels?' I said. 'How would anyone feel, finding someone dead like that when you don't expect it?'

I stared at the side of Mother's head, at the tiny grey curls which still held on to the shape of the rollers she'd slept in the night before.

'It's something you never forget,' I said.

She realised what I meant, but the grey curls didn't move an inch.

The police stopped all the cars on the top road for a whole week. They put cones out and pulled people into a lay-by and asked them all sorts of questions about the girl, and what they might or might not have seen.

'I suppose they're trying to jog people's memories,' Tamsin said.

We were arranging Easter cards on a little carousel near the door. It was only the end of February, but Tamsin said if people saw the display, it might make them think Easter was a lot closer than it actually was, because very often people only need a gentle push in the right direction and they'll begin to believe in all sorts.

'I know,' I said. 'Mother's been round so many times with Freda from across the road, the police have started waving them straight through. They even take Freda's dog with them and make a little trip out of it.'

'Terry must have been past there on his way to work – did he say what kind of questions they were asking?'

I held up one of the cards. It was a little yellow chick bursting out of a rainbow egg. *'Surprise!'* it said across the top, although what you could find surprising about the crucifixion of Christ was anybody's guess.

'He says he's been cutting across country and going into work the back way,' I said. 'To avoid the hold-ups.'

'That must be a four-mile detour.'

'He said it saves a lot of bother. The queues, you know?'

I looked at Tamsin, but she'd turned away and was lifting more cards out of a box.

She didn't ask any more questions.

11

I was with Mother the day I decided what to do.

She had that effect on me sometimes. Forced me into a decision. Started a ball rolling that no one could stop. We'd arranged to meet in my lunch break. Mother's loyalties lay firmly with The Swiss Cottage, where she'd eaten the same lunch at the same table for the past fifteen years. 'They plate it up for you, Linda,' she said. 'I don't trust any establishment where they expect you to be responsible for collecting your own cutlery.' I suggested we might go somewhere else for a bit of a change – somewhere a bit more upmarket, a place where a person like Rebecca Finch might eat, but Mother was having none of it. She'd already made a beeline for the arcade, quickening her pace along the high street, weaving her way between lines of school children and women wielding pushchairs, and a queue of people trying their best to get into a bank. She didn't even say 'Maybe next time,' or 'My mind's set on a hotpot,' she just gave me a tut instead. Mother's tuts were always impressive. They managed to hold a thousand words, without the need to ever waste any energy on fashioning them into a sentence, and by the time we reached the arcade I was quite out of breath.

The Swiss Cottage was right by the main entrance, and the smell of car park kept making its way through the doors and mixing with the gravy. There was very little Swiss about it, to be honest. Our waitress was called Courtney. She was dressed in an embroidered pinafore, but it was worn over the top of a Grateful Dead T-shirt and not enough sleep. The Swiss Cottage was decorated with tired wallpaper and melamine, and in front of us on the table there were endless sachets of tomato ketchup, stuffed into a miniature replica of the Matterhorn. My mother turned the Matterhorn upside down once. 'Made in China,' she read out loud. 'Who would have thought it?'

'Are you watching your weight?' Mother didn't look at me as she spoke, she just dug her fork a little bit further into a pavlova.

'I just fancied a coffee,' I said.

'Because it might be worth keeping your north eye on it, Linda. Women thicken up as time goes on.'

My mother, who had spent the whole of her adult life losing and gaining the same three pounds.

'Like custard?' I said.

She didn't laugh. 'Did you buy those clothes at work?' she said.

Perhaps I shook my head a little too quickly, because I saw one of the slim smiles she likes to give out to people from time to time, and I pulled the cardigan further around my shoulders.

'I don't understand how you can call it a job. Helping in a charity shop.'

'I get paid.'

I wasn't listening. I didn't have to listen. I knew all the lines off by heart. Instead, I watched Courtney in her Alpine fraudulence, making a bad job of pushing a damp cloth across tabletops and staring through a window at the river of people who passed by on the other side of the glass.

Mother slid the last piece of pavlova into her mouth and replaced the fork on her plate without even a sound. Neat, my mother is. Everything about her. Her clothes, her footsteps. Even her criticism has a certain tidiness about it.

I pulled a paper napkin out of the dispenser and tried to spare Courtney the job of cleaning up spilled coffee.

'I don't think Dad would have minded what I do.'

The napkin began to disintegrate.

'Your father thought butter wouldn't melt in your mouth. That was half the problem.'

'Or Uncle George,' I said.

'Linda, you're making it worse.'

I abandoned the napkin and tried to avoid Courtney's gaze.

Mother glanced across at the doors. 'I need to browse Marks & Spencer,' she said. 'Something for Freda's seventieth. She's having a joint do because it's the dog's birthday as well. I had an invitation from them both through the post.'

I thought of my collection of Rebecca Finch's brochures, nestled against the microwave, and the life that lay within them, waiting to be understood.

'Your face has gone funny. What are you thinking about?'

I stared at the ceiling, with its clouds of Artex, and tried to work out the point. It would be a devil for cleaning, I thought. All those hidden places. All those bits you couldn't see. I kept looking at it until I felt the conversation had drifted away from us, then checked my watch.

'Did you want to have a walk around the shops?' I said. 'Because if I'm calling at yours on the way home, we'd better get a move on.'

We left our table and edged around gatherings of spindle-back chairs towards the doors, past a silent cuckoo clock and a 'Cheeses of Switzerland' map.

As I followed my mother into the crowds, she said, 'I don't know how you can call it work, Linda.'

I don't think she even knows she's doing it half the time, this silent conversation that runs alongside all of her other words. By the time we walked through her back door, she was talking about someone else's daughter.

'Married a man in IT,' she was saying. 'Whatever that means.'

I nodded without really knowing why. I was looking around at her house instead, reminding myself not to drop any crumbs or leave any dirty marks on the carpets, because I knew she'd trace them back to me. I wondered how I ever used to live here, because there was a stillness in every room. Most places have a feeling of movement in them, as though the scene you stumble into is just a snapshot of someone's life. My mother's house was motionless. Rigid. It felt resentful of either of us even being there.

'I knew it wouldn't last,' she said, taking her coat off.

She hadn't changed anything in thirty years. The furniture was dark and uncomfortable, dressed up in antimacassars and unhelpful cushions in different shades of brown, and the curtains were made of the kind of material you find on church altars and never looked as though they were ever keen on being fully drawn back.

'I'd never say anything to Freda, but it was obvious he wouldn't stay with her longer than five minutes.'

It was the neatness, though, more than anything.

'Wandering eyes.' She switched the kettle on. 'You could see it a mile off.'

It felt like a dare. It made you want to move an ornament or very slightly change the angle of a picture frame. The house was like Mother. Settled and methodical. Everything in it had found its position in life and would never feel the need to ever move again. My mother lacquered herself into place every morning with half a can of hairspray, and it felt as though the house did exactly the same thing.

'See what a mile off?' I said.

'That he wouldn't stay with her,' Mother repeated, very slowly, as she took the tea cosy out of its drawer. 'I hope you take more notice of your husband than you do of me.'

'Perhaps they drifted apart,' I said. 'People do.'

'Nothing to do with drifting anywhere, Linda. She went up a dress size and her husband was through that front door faster than a streak of lightning. Would you like a slice of cake with your tea?'

I had to have a break halfway through. I said I needed the toilet, even though I didn't, just to have a few minutes away from her. I didn't even go to the bathroom, I just stood at the telephone table in the hall, taking a few deep breaths. The telephone rested on a lace doily that had 'Cromer 1982' embroidered on the bottom of it although I didn't remember ever going there. Next to the phone was Mother's telephone book and a notepad and pen. I flicked through the pad as I stood there. All the pages were blank.

When I went back into the front room, she'd made another pot of tea.

'Stay a bit longer, Linda,' she said. 'Make an evening of it. Reminisce. It'll be just like the good old days!'

I agreed with her, even though I could never quite remember what the good old days were and why she always thought old days were better than new ones. There must have been a point, although I couldn't quite decide when it was, that she stopped talking about the future and only commented on the past, as if she needed to visit there as often as she could, to feed and water her memories until they grew into something she was happy with.

'Did we ever go to Cromer in the good old days?' I said.

She frowned, and I nodded back towards the hall.

'On the telephone table?'

'Oh no,' she said. 'I wanted to, but your father put a stop to it. Reckoned it was too far to drive. Too much hassle. We stayed at home instead, so I embroidered the little tablecloth to pass the time.' She smiled. 'Next best thing!'

Perhaps Mother had spent so much time looking over her shoulder at the past, she'd managed to embroider the whole thing into something she wanted it to be, rather than the thing that it actually was.

Mother spent the afternoon explaining other people's business. Details she had collected in supermarket queues and on the top decks of buses, stolen from strangers or excavated with the stealth and dexterity of a deep-sea diver from other people's conversations. I tried not to involve myself. I didn't know who most of her victims were, but if I admitted that, she would whip a photo album from the shelf and point at strangers for the next three hours. My mother is a surrogate for other people's lives, stacking the empty shelves of her mind with nonsense. If my concentration went, even for a minute, it was difficult to work out if she was talking about a real person or a character in one of her programmes.

'Ran off with her brother-in-law,' she was saying. 'Brighton, I believe. Or somewhere equally ridiculous.'

'Really?' I stared past the church altar curtains into a garden that had slept since Mother had embraced her arthritis. It idled in shades of brown and grey. Moss had hijacked the paving slabs, reaching out beyond the gaps between the stones towards the edges of the patio. Raindrops clung to the washing line, waiting to fall. Leaves spilled onto the concrete, and darkness had soaked into the stone and the soil. Something was there, though, if you looked hard enough. Pinpricks of snowdrops, fighting to be noticed beneath the darkness of a hedgerow. A scattering of crocus, peeping from behind the rockery. Small mentions of hope, edging their way forward, in a garden that was dressed in the colours of winter and had yet to find its spring.

'What happened after they got to Brighton, then?' I said, because all Mother needed was the occasional pull on the reins.

'Well, I don't know, do I? Freda rang me in the advert break and I missed the whole of the second half.'

I glanced back at her. 'Pardon?'

'Thank heavens for catch-up. I hinted I was in the middle of something, but she didn't take a blind bit of notice. Never does.'

'Why did you even answer the phone?'

As soon as the words left my mouth, I wish I hadn't asked. In my mother's house, the telephone was seen as so important, it had its own table.

'Linda.' She clasped her hands on her lap, which was how Mother usually sat; it always made it seem as though she was on the verge of delivering a sermon. 'When a telephone rings, you answer it. When an invitation arrives, you say yes. You of all people should know that we need to grab at any little opportunity life bothers to throw at us.'

'Meaning?'

'Meaning, dear, that people like us are never going to be the names at the top of anyone's list, are we?'

I never knew whether 'we' included her or not, or whether she just added herself in there out of politeness.

'So, if you lead an unimaginative life and something comes along to break up the monotony, you embrace it.' She paused. 'When life's telephone rings, Linda, you must answer the call.'

I studied her face. There were lines there I hadn't noticed before. They were made deeper by the light from the window, spreading across her cheeks like a map. People say we look alike, although I can never usually see it. I saw it then, though, as we watched each other across the width of a dining-room table. I glanced down at my hands. They were clasped together in my lap. I unclasped them and looked up again.

'Have you ever opened someone else's mail?' I said, before my head had a chance to put a stop to my mouth.

She made her eyes very narrow. 'You do know that's a criminal offence. Whose mail were you thinking of opening?'

I hesitated. Mother isn't someone I would generally

confide in, because I know, even years later, my confession will come back to visit me. She stores everything, does my mother, in the neat little drawers of her mind. She can cross-reference it all, if the need arises. Every comment. Every opinion. Ticked off and recorded, and safely delivered into a future argument.

'No one's,' I said. 'Nobody's. It was on the telly. A drama on the telly.'

I knew I hadn't made a very good job, because her eyes were still narrow and she'd shifted forward a good few inches.

'Well, I hope they were arrested,' she said.

'Who?'

She sat forward a little more. 'The person on the telly,' she whispered.

12

They set up a Portakabin. Malcolm said they would, because he seemed to know more about these things than most people. It appeared early one morning, a week later, on the patch of waste ground between our road and the next. By eight thirty, there was a queue forming.

'Nice and convenient,' I said to Mother, on one of her perfectly timed visits. 'If you crane your neck just right, you can almost see it from the landing window.'

'I'm not sure I'd want to,' she said. 'I wouldn't like a daily reminder that there's a killer on the loose, thank you very much.'

'This isn't about murderers, Mother. This is about staying safe. It says so on a poster stuck to the outside. You can go in there any time you want, and they'll advise you on how to keep out of harm's way.'

'They shut at five o'clock,' she said. 'Most harm wanders around all by itself in the woods after dark. We both know that.'

We stared at each other through the hiss of the kettle.

'I thought we were going to put that on one side,' I said. 'I thought we weren't going to mention it.'

'That Portakabin has got very little to do with neighbourhood watching and everything to do with making the police look as though they're doing their job.' She inched the conversation along, on an endless piece of string. 'You'll stay away from it if you've got any sense. Don't draw attention to yourself. Anyway, I thought you hated the police.'

'I do,' I said. 'I'm just interested in who they think it might be. That's all.'

'You can bet your bottom dollar, whoever the police think it is, it'll be someone else entirely. Won't it?'

She held the question in her eyes and I couldn't look away.

'Won't it?' she said again.

I reached over and switched the kettle off. 'It will,' I said.

Malcolm had placed himself in a supervisory role, obviously. I persuaded Mother to have a wander over during a commercial break and we found him making sure people in the queue were a suitable distance apart and no one was cluttering up the pavement.

'Leave adequate width for a buggy,' he was saying. 'Remember women and children first.'

The door to the Portakabin was closed, and a thick chain and padlock had been slid through its handle.

'Gone to lunch,' Malcolm said. 'I suppose the police force have to feed themselves, even in a time of national crisis.'

I stared down the line of people. People from this part of the estate. People I recognised from the Red Lion. There must have been at least twenty, and they had ignored Malcolm's instructions and were gathered into small knots of conversation. Some of the voices were angry and loud, and flickers of confrontation sparked along the pavement. I leaned back and frowned all the way to the end of the queue.

'Everyone seems to be taking the opportunity to speak to the police,' said Malcolm. 'Understandably so, given this morning's events.'

'What events?' Mother said. 'We've been fully engaged with *Judge Judy*. What's happened?'

'The letters.' Malcolm's voice went down at least an octave. 'It's all nonsense, of course, but they've caused such a hoo-ha.'

Mother leaned forward. 'What letters?'

'Even I've had one. Anonymous, of course.' Malcolm tapped the pocket of his overcoat.

'Someone sent you an anonymous letter?' I said.

'Not just me,' Malcolm said. 'This lot have all had one.'

'Our Terry hasn't,' I said and I heard Mother mumble, *How would you know?* under her breath.

Then she said, 'What did the letters say?' at normal volume, and I could hear excitement spread around the back of her throat.

'Well, they're not telling, are they?' Malcolm bobbed his knees very slightly and peered up the road. 'But it's touched a few nerves, it's obvious.'

I followed his gaze. It was difficult to tell the indignation from the fear, the anger from the worry, because sometimes, your head says one thing but your face decides to tell everyone a completely different story.

'The only problem is,' Malcolm said, 'the letters are . . . quite threatening.'

I looked at Mother but she was staring very hard at the pavement. 'Threatening how, Malcolm?' I said.

'They say that if we don't come clean about our secrets, we'll be "next". That can only mean one thing, can't it? The letters must have come from the killer.'

'They could have come from anyone,' I said. 'Someone playing a prank. Kids with too much time on their hands.'

'Oh no, no, no.' Malcolm shook his head very vigorously. 'Far too professional for that. Printed envelopes. Reasonable quality A4 paper. At least 80 gsm. This is someone who means business.'

'What's the rush?' Mother was at least five paces in front and I had to speak to the back of her head. 'Don't you want to hang around and see what happens when the police have finished their lunch?'

I looked back over my shoulder, but no one was taking

any notice of us. They were all too busy ignoring Malcolm and arguing amongst themselves.

'There's no point, Linda,' she called back. 'I've got nothing to say to any of them.'

I abandoned trying to keep up with her and watched her march further ahead. 'You've usually got plenty to say. There are often not enough hours in the day to give a voice to all the thoughts inside your head,' I shouted.

Her footsteps slowed and she turned to face me. I wasn't sure when it had happened, but at some point when my back was turned, my mother had become old. Time had sloped her shoulders and hollowed out her face. It had crumpled her eyes and her mouth, and stretched out the veins on her hands. She had become slight and shrunken, or perhaps her frame hadn't altered at all, but everything within it had just become quieter and more insignificant. When we were in Wales, she had been loud and strong and invincible. Now, it seemed as though the slightest breeze might carry her away forever.

She walked back towards me.

'What are you so afraid of?' I said.

'I'm afraid it's all going to start up again,' she whispered, when she was close enough to be heard. 'This is exactly how it was over your dad. People getting angry. Out of control. We got letters. Don't you remember? History is going to repeat itself, I just know.'

'Why on earth should it?'

'Look at them, Linda.'

We were quite a distance from the Portakabin now, but arguments were beginning to spit and flare along the line, and the voices were carried towards us.

'Nothing will start up again,' I said. Although the words didn't sound as convincing as they did in my own head.

'You don't remember what it was like because you were too young,' Mother said. 'It was me who bore the brunt of it. It was me who had to go out and face people while your father sat at home with his head in his hands.'

'You had nothing to be ashamed of,' I told her. 'Those girls were lying. All of them. The police twisted my words. It was that first girl who started it. She was deranged.'

'Of course.' She reached out and squeezed my arm. 'Of course she was.'

'I shouldn't have walked in on them. Dad said never to disturb him in the middle of a lesson. If I'd done as he said, the police wouldn't have had anything to twist.'

'It wasn't your fault,' she said.

'Then you should have held your head up high.'

'It's not as simple as that, Linda. People see what they want to see. They reach out into the world and choose the pieces of it that suit them best. Your father . . .' She petered out for a moment. 'Your father wasn't very well liked.'

'We liked him. That's all that matters, and we should stick together.'

'We should. Which is why we should stay safe and away from Portakabins and gossip.' She still held on to my arm, but I began to wonder if it was for her benefit, rather than mine. 'Although I'm beginning to wonder if anywhere is safe now.'

Back at the Portakabin, a policewoman had appeared and was unfastening the padlock and sliding the chain from the handle. People were pushing in the queue, trying to move forward and elbowing each other out of the way.

'Why would you think that?' I said.

'Because whoever wrote those letters must know us all really well. So well they just blend right into the landscape and we pass them by without a second thought. Do you know why?' she said.

I shook my head.

'Because the best place to hide a book is in a library.' Mother let go of my arm and pointed. 'They're probably standing in that queue right now,' she said.

13

I knew there was something amiss as soon as I picked up the telephone.

Mother never usually introduces herself, she just launches into whatever she has to say and assumes you'll work it out for yourself at some point. She always stops as abruptly as she starts, as well. One minute she's there, one minute she's gone. Like a telephonic whirlwind.

This time she said, *'It's your mother you need to come over now'* all in one breath, and then put the phone down very quietly.

I stared at the handset for a minute, wondering if she might reappear, and then I put it back in its cradle and lifted my anorak down from the coat peg. I wasn't at work that day, which was just as well because when Mother issued a request, it was better to just go along with it. Any dilly-dallying and you'd only end up paying for it later.

'Mother's,' I announced to Terry, who was on a late and sitting with his football mug in front of some quiz show.

He looked up. 'You were only there yesterday.'

'It'll be something or nothing,' I said. 'One of the neighbours has probably looked at her the wrong way or Tesco haven't got the right brand of margarine on their shelves.'

Terry shrugged and went back to the third-round accumulator. No offer of a lift, although in all honesty I preferred the train. Every time I sat in that van I had to put a towel down and it made everything I was wearing smell of damp.

'I might go down the pub after work,' he said, as I pulled the front door to. 'I'll leave you a note.'

I didn't bother answering.

It's only a short train ride to Mother's, but I took my earphones with me and plugged myself into Andy Williams because you can never have enough music and it stops me from having to endure pieces of other people's business. Snippets of dull conversation floating around amongst the seats, kids playing up, people explaining the monotony of their lives for everyone else to hear. It means folk don't start talking to you either. It used to be rare that people struck up a conversation on public transport, but the murder seemed to make everyone sociable and so much more cheerful, and perfect strangers began speaking to each other like old friends and asking what the latest update was. A bit like when it snows.

There are times, though, when I reach down and put my music on pause. If I think there might be an interesting conversation to listen to, or someone I don't know gets on the train. As long as you keep your earphones in, they assume you can't hear them and they speak much more freely. Because people look at you and see what they want to see. I've heard all sorts, I have, sitting on public transport.

Once I get off the train it's only a short walk through the town to the bottom of her street. She usually keeps me on the doorstep, but I could see her behind the curtains as soon as I turned the corner, and by the time I reached her gate she was by the front door with her arms folded.

'You took your time,' she said, and I took my earphones out and followed her inside. She double-locked the door behind us and I walked behind her down the narrow hallway which was made more narrow by ornaments and furniture and unnecessary chairs from the past, an obstacle course of my childhood. We entered the kitchen at the back of the house and she pointed to the table.

'What?' I said.

She pointed a little more dramatically. 'Look, Linda. Look at that!'

There was an envelope on the tablecloth, face up, with Mother's name and address on the front in block capitals.

'That's nice colour stationery,' I said. 'Although I'm not sure if you'd call it lilac or blue.'

'Never mind the bloody colour,' she said. It was quite unlike Mother to curse and it made me wince ever so slightly. 'Read what's inside!'

I took a sheet of paper in the same shade of blue out of

the already-opened envelope. It was a very brief letter, written in capital letters again. It was strange how something so short could have had the dramatic effect that it did, but sometimes the shorter the message the more troubling it can be.

I KNOW THE TRUTH. I KNOW ABOUT YOUR HUSBAND.

STOP PRETENDING IT DIDN'T HAPPEN OR YOU'LL BE NEXT.

'Well?' she said. 'There's no signature. No return address on the back of the envelope. What do you make of that?'

I looked at her. She didn't seem upset or frightened, just angry. Very angry. The kind of anger that drains your colour away and thins your lips to almost nothing. Mother never did like being told what to do, even by an anonymous letter.

'How would they know about Dad?' I said. 'Because no one knows the whole story, do they?'

'Clearly they do. Or they think they do. Have you been opening that big mouth of yours again, Linda?'

I shook my head.

'Because I didn't move us all this way to have everything start up all over again.'

'No,' I said. 'You didn't.'

'And the only other person who was witness to it all is you – and that isn't your handwriting. You're much scruffier. Even in capitals.'

'What do they mean by "the truth"?' I watched her eyes as I spoke, because as good as people are at lying, their eyes can never quite manage to be as deceitful as the rest of their face.

She shrugged. 'One man's truth is another man's false-hood. People think they know the facts and they know nothing of the sort. It's the "you'll be next" that bothers me the most.'

'It's only the kind of thing people write in chain letters and add on to things to make them sound sinister. Why are you worried? I wouldn't let that bother you.'

'Well it's obvious, isn't it? The letter's from the serial killer. Just like Malcolm said.'

'It is?'

'Who else would it be? And you know what that means, don't you?'

I waited.

'It means I'm going to have to come and live at your house until they catch him.'

'That could be months,' I said. 'There are some serial killers they never manage to find.'

'I know,' she said, and she smiled. 'So you'd better help me get that big suitcase down from the loft.'

Terry talked her out of it in the end. I gave him a quick call and he pulled up outside in his van not ten minutes later, even though he was supposed to be at work, which under the circumstances was very considerate.

'Cometh the moment, cometh the Terry.' Mother laughed through her nose.

'It'll be kids playing games, Eunice,' he said as he wiped his boots on the doormat. 'No need to panic.'

He said if she was that worried, she should go to the police, but I knew she wouldn't.

'I don't want to rake all that up again, Terry,' she said. 'Water under the bridge.'

Although I wasn't sure how you could rake water, I kept my mouth shut. Any encouragement might have swayed the conversation back to moving in again, and that would mean Terry clearing out the spare bedroom. I'd made several visits to that computer in my Marigolds since the first time, and I didn't want Mother barging in and upsetting all my plans for Rebecca Finch.

'I'll sleep on the floor!' Mother said when I explained the state of the spare room, and she even said, 'I don't mind a bit of mess,' at one point, which under any other circumstances would have made me laugh out loud.

Terry checked all her locks and mended a bolt on the back gate and it seemed to pacify her. She followed him around the house as he did it.

'You're a good boy, you are, Terry,' she said in between windows and doors. 'A real hero.'

It wasn't often Terry got called a hero, and he lapped it up. 'Only doing what any son-in-law would do,' he said, but the whole time his chest was all puffed out as if someone had offered to pin a medal on it. 'We want to keep you safe, Eunice.'

'I'll be forever in your debt,' she said, 'protecting me like this. I'll make sure everyone hears about it.'

Terry and his chest pottered about a bit more, behaving

like people do when they think they've accomplished something worth writing home about. Pretending they're being selfless when there are very few people in the world who do anything unless it's for their own advantage.

While he loaded his tools into the van, I glanced over at Mother and she smiled back at me from the sink.

'Cromer 1982,' I said.

'Pardon?'

'It's a nice shade of lilac, that notepaper. Quite distinctive.'

'I have no idea what you're talking about, Linda,' she said, and turned to the window.

'You couldn't bear it, could you? Being snubbed. Even by a serial killer. You wrote that note to yourself. Don't tell me you didn't, because I happen to know for a fact that you did.'

'I'm sure I don't know what you mean.'

Which was Mother's equivalent of a full stop.

14

I'm the kind of person who usually sticks to the rules, because if everyone did whatever they pleased, it would be chaos, but there are times when you need to break a few small regulations for the greater good. Push the boundaries a little. Think about the destination, rather than the journey – especially when it's something so necessary. Although the strange thing is, as nervous as the letter made me feel, it only sat on the kitchen table for a few hours before Terry spotted it and put me out of my misery.

The rota had given me an extra day off. I'd already been into town and picked up a few bits. I'd normally spend a few hours wandering around the shops, just to see if I bumped into anyone I knew to pass the time, but that day I thought I'd get home instead, spend a bit of time doing research on Terry's computer and then start on the vacuuming. Cleaning gives your mind something to hold on to and stops it from shuffling all the other things around in there. Mother taught me that when my dad died. I put my music on first, for a bit of company, and then I began in the kitchen and worked my way around. I always do the upstairs last. Terry was on a long shift, so it was a chance to give everything a good going-over without him getting under my feet. I can cover the whole house in a day if I get my skates on. When I finally finished, I treated myself to a coffee and a flick through Rebecca Finch's life whilst I waited for Terry to get home. When I caught sight of him halfway down the garden path, I tucked the brochures back down the side of the microwave and tried to look as though I was making a start on his tea.

I was reaching for a tin of baked beans at the back of one of the cupboards when he walked in, and I didn't have to look, because I knew exactly what he was doing. The sounds were the same every night. Van keys hitting the hall table. A coat thrown on a peg. Taps running. An extra breath of effort as he kicked off his boots. He was an orchestra that only knew how to play one bloody tune. This time, though, he seemed to be standing around the kitchen more thoughtfully.

'Who's this meant for, then?' he said.

When I turned, he'd picked the envelope up off the kitchen table, and he was squinting at it.

'Someone must have pushed it through the letterbox this morning,' I said. 'Hand-delivered. I found it lying on the hall carpet.'

He turned over the envelope and placed it back in the middle of the kitchen table.

'Do you know who's it for?' I said. 'Because I don't.'

'Someone called Rebecca Finch, by the looks of it. Although the typing's all smudged. You want to write *not known at this address* and pop it back in the box.'

'They probably are though, aren't they,' I said.

'Are what?'

'Known at this address.' I tipped the beans out and watched them creep towards the edges of the saucepan. 'It must be the woman you spoke to when you asked if the house was for sale.'

'But that was months ago.'

'Anyway, it was hand-delivered, so it's nothing to do with the postman. What's the point in putting it in a letterbox?' I lit the gas and stared at all the yellow tiles on the kitchen wall.

Terry prodded at the envelope and pushed even more dirt into its whiteness with his forefinger. '*Not known at this address*,' he said. 'Let them deal with it.'

The letter stayed on the table and it sat between us while Terry had his tea.

That evening, as I sat in my little pocket of silence, the letter sat alongside me. I had my Marigolds on, of course, because you can never be too careful, and I picked up the envelope and stared at the place where Terry's finger had left its dirty mark. I wondered if Rebecca Finch was sitting in a kitchen somewhere, with a sink full of dirty pots and the sound of snooker commentary drifting through a dividing wall, and I decided that she most probably wasn't.

I put the letter in a little plastic bag, so it didn't get spoiled, and it lived at the edges of my mind. I thought about it each time I walked past the drawer where it was living. The thick, white paper and the typed address. It reminded me of the rest of Rebecca Finch's life. Just . . . *different*. Different from photocopied days. Different from yellowed tiles on a kitchen wall. Different from a sink filled with someone else's dirty plates. Different from the junk mail and the electricity bills, and a brown-envelope life.

Something not known at this address.

And I still hadn't made up my mind about who should be the one to open it.

In the end, I chose Mother. Because if anyone was bound to take action, it was Eunice.

15

'Linda, you have to do something!'

The letter still sat between us on the tablecloth. Mother hadn't taken her eyes off it since it had been opened. It was strange how flexible Mother's moral code became once curiosity got the upper hand.

'What can be done?'

'This woman has to be warned. She needs to know the killer's watching her – she should be protecting herself.'

'He can't be, though, can he? Or he'd know she'd moved.'

'Well, he's going to easily figure that one out and he'll find her.'

I tilted my head and stared at the letter. The dark scratch and smudge of capital letters. The neat fold of the paper. I reached forward.

'Don't touch it!' Mother shouted. 'At least put your gloves back on, this could be vital evidence!'

DON'T WORRY, YOU'RE NEXT

the letter said, typed in the same smudged capitals.

'I don't know who she is, though. I haven't even got a clue where she lives now,' I said.

'Then you need to take steps to find her. Before he does. It can't be that difficult. People find other people all the time, even people who aren't particularly in the mood to be found. This should be a piece of cake.'

'I'm not sure I want to get involved,' I said.

'Linda!' She got up from her seat and put her hands on my shoulders. 'This is your chance to do something worthwhile. You could save this woman's life – she'd be forever in your debt. This is your chance to finally prove yourself!'

'Do you think so?' I said.

She leaned forward and whispered in my ear. 'Go out there and shine, Linda.'

The laptop sat on a side table in the back room. Two years ago, my mother had been talked into buying it by a very enthusiastic salesperson in John Lewis and it still had the plastic cover on the screen and a swing ticket hanging from its backside. She'd only paused briefly in Home Electricals for a coughing fit.

'I didn't like saying no,' she reported back at the time. 'He was such a nice young man.'

She had no idea how to use it and neither had I, but I knew it would be a lot more useful than Terry's, and so I sat in front of a blank screen and stared at it.

'You've got to switch it on, Linda.' Mother appeared with a mug of tea, which she placed on a coaster by my right elbow. Mother was the kind of person who had far more coasters than people she knew.

She got on her knees and searched under the table for a socket and after a couple of minutes, the screen came to life and a picture of the Grand Canyon appeared.

'Arizona is none of my doing,' she said and left.

I looked at the Grand Canyon. I'd always presumed that using the internet was a skill I would never be able to manage. It joined a lot of other things throughout my life that, in my mind, I'd never get the top side of. Netball. Make-up. Dancing. I don't know why my mind felt that way, because it just seemed to choose these things at random and decide I'd be bad at them. Perhaps I'd accidentally tried them once and I wasn't very good and so I gave up, or perhaps I'd never bothered trying them at all, just to be on the safe side. Whenever anyone mentioned any of them, I'd say, *It's no good asking me, I'm hopeless at anything like that*' and eventually people started saying it for me – '*Oh, it's no good asking Linda, Linda's hopeless at anything like that*' and my mind would nod and smile, and agree with everyone. The trouble is, if you tell yourself something for long enough, if you apologise for yourself before you've even started, if you fasten a few words onto every opinion telling people to ignore anything you might happen to say, before you realise, it becomes knitted into the very soul of who you are and it's a devil of a job to try and unpick it all.

The Grand Canyon looked back at me in silence. Perhaps I could prove myself wrong after all.

In the end, it wasn't nearly as difficult as I thought it would be, because it was much easier to operate than Terry's monstrosity, and every time I wanted to do something, a box popped up and explained how it could be achieved. The only tricky thing was finding the internet, because it was one of the few things in life that Mother didn't possess. When I tried, a little list came up of all her neighbours. I chose Freda, because it was the first name I recognised, but next to Freda's name was a tiny padlock and the need for a password.

I hesitated.

'What's Freda's dog called?' I shouted.

Mother stuck her head around the door.

'Heathcliff,' she said.

'But it's a poodle.'

'I know,' she said.

I typed it into the little padlocked box and I was in. I didn't realise the internet was so obliging.

After a few false starts, I managed to bring up a search page and I typed Rebecca's name into the little space at the top. Quite unlike Terry's computer, the screen changed immediately and there were Rebecca Finches of all shapes and sizes. Thousands of them. I gazed at the screen and wondered how I could ever know which one belonged to me. Some, I could rule out immediately, because they were too old or from the wrong country. Some just didn't fit, because when I clicked the little arrow on their faces, they had husbands and children and jobs in industry and business, and I was fairly sure my Rebecca Finch didn't come equipped with any of those. Even discounting all the obvious ones, though, I was still faced with hundreds of people to work my way through and I wasn't even sure how I'd realise who she was when I did finally find her.

Most of the time, when I clicked on someone, I was taken to a page filled with photographs of anything I might want to look at. Terry was right, people's entire lives were spread out all over the internet and it was like flicking through someone's family album when their back was turned. They didn't seem to care that complete strangers could explore the inside of their houses and their back gardens, and stare at their children and be informed about what everyone ate for their tea last night. They were quite happy for us to tag along with them on holiday and admire their new car, and sit with them in a restaurant and choose from the menu. They couldn't wait to tell us all about the arguments they had with their mother and how the school asked impossible things of their children, and we were encouraged to go with them on days out and keep an eye on their house renovations, and when all that was over, they insisted we sat with them at their kitchen tables and listened to them talk about how inadequate their husbands were.

That's how I found her. The kitchen. I was looking through yet another album, this time being treated to a series of photographs showing a cup of coffee with a heart shape on the top, when I spotted my yellow tiles. There was no mistaking them. If that wasn't enough, in the background, you could see an electrical socket where the coffee maker was plugged in, and there was a tiny swipe of paint right in the corner of it. I'd asked Terry to scrape that paint off a thousand times because it was an eyesore, obviously to no avail, and beyond the coffee maker and the swipe of paint, you could see the edge of a wall cabinet. The one I keep my teabags in. It was a photograph of my kitchen.

I carried on clicking, past endless cups of coffee and yellow tiles, until I found a photograph of a man smiling into the camera. He was very good-looking and I stared at him for quite a while. He reminded me of the men in Terry's fishing catalogues, the rugged ones posing on river-banks in waxed jackets, the ones you are never likely to stumble across on a riverbank even if you walked Britain's waterways for the rest of your life. He had jet-black hair and a polo-necked jumper, and the kind of lopsided smile women always seem to fall for and bitterly regret later on. It was quite peculiar to see him stood next to my draining board and it threw me so much, I had to pause just to take it all in.

A few photographs later I found her. Rebecca Finch. She was standing next to the back door. The same back door Terry slams every night when he comes in from work. She had curly auburn hair, right down to her shoulders, and sharp green eyes that laughed along with her face. There were freckles dotted across her cheeks and she had that relaxed look people get when they've been on holiday and their tan hasn't quite worn away yet. Her T-shirt had a little hole on the shoulder. If I wore a T-shirt like that, I would look as though I needed to go and get changed. Rebecca Finch didn't. She looked perfect.

She was everything I knew she would be.

All I had to do now was find out what happened to her after she left my kitchen.

'You've been in here hours.'

Mother was standing in the doorway. I could hear her latest soap opera drifting from the television in the front room. Everyone in it was arguing, because clearly there wasn't enough arguing in the world already and people felt it necessary to watch made-up arguing as well, in their spare time, just to top themselves up.

I shut the laptop lid.

'I'm still looking,' I said. 'I can't find her anywhere – I was just going to give up.'

'Oh.' Mother frowned at the closed lid. 'Nothing at all?'

'Not a thing,' I said. 'I'd tell you if I did.'

Mother has always been very good at spotting untruths and scooping them out of their shells, like whelks. Even when I disguised a lie in a wide avenue of truth, she could still manage to find it, because all she had to do was stare at me for long enough and out it would pop and wave at her.

'Do you mind if I take the laptop home with me?' I

fumbled around under the table to unplug it. 'I'll bring it back when I'm done.'

'Do whatever you want,' she said. 'Linda?'

'What?' I said, from halfway under the table.

'It's not really that important, you know. Finding this girl. Don't get into one of your states about it.'

I didn't answer.

As soon as Terry started snoring, I went downstairs and plugged the laptop in. I slid out of bed as quietly as I could but there was no real need. Once Terry is asleep I could cartwheel several times across the bedroom carpet and he wouldn't notice.

I found Rebecca's page straight away. She was where I had left her, standing against the back door with the heart-shaped coffee in her hand. I zoomed in on the picture and travelled across it. Her eyes were a khaki green. There was a tiny hole by her left nostril, where there must have been an earring at some point, or whatever it should be called, and she was laughing into the camera and lacing her fingers around the coffee cup, just like the people in the catalogue. The man in the polo-neck must have taken the photograph, because a few frames later he was standing in exactly the same place and smiling into the camera in exactly the same way, except his fingers weren't laced around the coffee cup, he was holding it by the rim like people do in films when they're in a hurry, but no one actually does in real life. There must have been thirty photographs in that album. I didn't understand how someone could take so much interest in a cup of coffee and a back door, but having wandered around the internet for several hours, I had begun to realise that people could find anything fascinating if they looked at it for long enough.

I clicked on another album, and then another. There was something odd about them, but I couldn't put my finger on it. One was all about the back garden. Rebecca and the man sitting in deckchairs with glasses of wine. Never together. First one and then the other. Cheers to the camera. Wide smiles. The next was the man standing by a car in the drive. He was leaning against the driver's door, looking extremely proud of himself for just being there with a puffed-out polo-necked chest and folded arms. Malcolm was right. It was fancy. I knew nothing about cars, but I could tell from the shine on the paintwork and the shape of the bonnet that it was the kind of vehicle that didn't leave your clothes smelling of damp. When I zoomed in, I could see Rebecca's reflection in the car window. In one hand, she was holding her mobile telephone to take the picture, while the other hand seemed to be giving directions to the man, holding her palm out like a stop sign. All the pictures were like that, as though some of them had been taken only seconds apart and it seemed as though all the photographs were from the same day, because neither of them ever seemed to change their clothes. That was it. The odd thing. I couldn't believe I hadn't noticed it sooner. On all the other pages I'd visited when I was looking for

Rebecca, people had documented year after year of their lives. Hairstyles altered. Houses changed. Friends came and went. Children started school, grew in and out of different uniforms, left school and disappeared to university. Christmas trees were decorated and abandoned. Lines grew on everyone's faces. Rebecca and the polo-necked man stayed the same. As if their entire lives had taken place in just the space of five minutes.

I found a little button that said 'About' and I clicked on it. There was nothing except a date of birth that made her twenty-six and a list of all the television programmes she liked watching. No clues as to where she might be now. Nothing written on her page to give anything away. I went back and clicked across all the pictures and stared at my kitchen through someone else's eyes. I was just about to give up and go back to bed and Terry's snoring, when I noticed a name pop up when I moved the arrow over a picture of the handsome man. 'Jolyon King' it said, in a little box, so I clicked on it and it turned out that his page was much more interesting than Rebecca's.

Jolyon King lived in a flat with leather settees and no curtains. One of those apartments that was so high it didn't warrant as much as a blind or a set of decent nets, although I'd still feel exposed if it was me, even a hundred feet up in the air, because you just never just know. Everything in his front room was heavy and expensive – you could tell, even through the lens of a camera. Thick rugs were spread across stained floorboards. Weighty ornaments crouched on wide shelves. There were books, too, but they were placed at right angles on a coffee table, and they didn't look like books anyone would ever want to pick up and read. Jolyon was in some of the pictures. He was in groups with other people, laughing and drinking and talking, the kind of photographs people take of you when you don't know they're doing it. Not like the pictures in Mother's albums, where everyone has at least ten minutes to prepare themselves and sort out what they're going to do with their face.

Jolyon went on holiday a lot. You could tell he was abroad because the light was different and the sky looked bigger. Jolyon on a beach at midnight, surrounded by campfire and the glow of distant ships. Jolyon at the top of mountains and posing in front of skyscraper trees. Jolyon pointing at a wide range of landmarks – the Great Wall of China, the Eiffel Tower, the Statue of Liberty, places I'd only ever seen in books – just in case anyone viewing the photograph was so busy looking at him, they hadn't spotted it was there. When Jolyon wasn't on holiday, he was eating in fancy restaurants with thick white tablecloths and lolling around on other people's identical leather settees and drinking wine.

Rebecca wasn't in any of the photographs. I know because I looked at every single one.

I sat back in the chair and pinched at the bridge of my nose. Even though my eyes were shut, I couldn't stop the pictures and lights and colours travelling past the inside of my eyelids. I wondered how people stared at these screens for any length of time, because it felt as though I'd overfed my mind with other people's lives and my head had developed indigestion and didn't know what to do with it all. When I opened my eyes, the kitchen clock stared down at me from the wall. It was a quarter past four. Terry would be awake in a few hours and apart from finding out the polo-necked man's name, I didn't feel any the wiser. I tried the 'About' section, but it just said he was forty-two and self-employed, although Mother has always viewed anyone calling themselves self-employed with deep suspicion.

I decided it was a waste of time. Perhaps the internet wasn't the answer to finding Rebecca Finch after all. Perhaps this was never meant to be. I searched on the computer screen for how to turn it all off and that's when I noticed the picture. It was Jolyon in a bar somewhere, one made entirely of chrome and glass, lifting a glass of wine to his mouth and doing his lopsided grin over the rim of the glass. It wasn't so much the photograph itself, though, it was the comments people had made underneath it. One in particular. Someone had written, *'Not seen you in ages, Jolyon — we must catch up!'* and all these little smiley faces afterwards. Jolyon had replied. He'd put *'Yes, mate — I'm in Harley's most lunchtimes. Come and find me!'*

I'd never been to the Great Wall of China or the Eiffel Tower or the Statue of Liberty. I'd never been to Harley's, either. But I knew exactly where it was.

Harley's was in the middle of the town, resting on a bridge that separated the old from the new, the silent from the unsilent. It separated the brass letterboxed solicitors and the quietly polished banks from the hairdressers and the nail bars, and the shops that only seemed interested in selling one thing. Like milkshakes or jelly beans. I walked past Harley's every day on the way from the bus stop into work. It was one of those places that was deliberately raised up from pavement level, so everyone inside could look down at the tops of people's heads, and all you could see as you walked past was a tangle of bar stools and other people's feet. Laced brogues in just the right shade of tan. Well-heeled court shoes. Pointed, patent, a brand logo punched into the leather somewhere, just in case you weren't smart enough to realise how much they'd cost and you needed a little bit of extra help in order to be impressed. Mother thinks a person's footwear says everything you need to know about them, and the shoes in Harley's said we are feet that belong to people who go for lunch, rather than feet that have a lunch break.

I'd never been inside. Not unless you count Mother and me poking our heads around the door when it first opened, because she said she needed a closer inspection of the upholstery. I'd studied the menu though, written on a blackboard nailed to the wall in a small porch. Everything had a line of symbols after it, meat-free, dairy-free, gluten-free, a list of all the things it didn't contain. Some of the dishes had so many symbols, the list of what you weren't eating ended up being longer than the list of what you were. I'd tried to persuade Mother to go in properly a few times, just to see what it was like, but it would take more than a fancy chalkboard to drag Mother away from Courtney and her Matterhorn.

I never meant to eat my lunch there. I was going to get a meal deal like I always do, but on the way to the Co-op, I poked my head round the door of Harley's, just to see what I might be up against and if anyone in there looked like the man in the photographs.

Strange name, Jolyon, although people seem to call their children whatever they want these days. The woman up the road named her child after a root vegetable. I didn't know anyone called Jolyon, nor am I ever likely to because I'm settled into my own landscape. Every day, the same people standing at the same bus queue, the same people serving you in the supermarket, the same faces, the same journeys, backwards and forwards, you see them out of the corner of your eye, but they're just a wallpaper to your own life. Unimportant. Incidental. You might know their names, but you don't think to find out who any of them really are. It's no wonder people lie dead in a council flat for six weeks before anyone notices.

'*That'll be me,*' Mother always says. '*Eaten by German shepherds.*'

'*You don't own a German shepherd,*' I say, but my mother just glosses over it, because when it comes to creating a dramatic scene, she has never been very big on the small details.

I'd only loitered in the doorway for a couple of minutes when a girl appeared, dressed all in black with a tiny butterfly tattooed on the inside of her left wrist. It turned out she was a waitress, and before I could make an exit, she sat me down at a table with a bowl of olives and half a stick of French bread. I have never liked olives. I've always seen them more as a small punishment.

'For one?' she said.

I made a noise at the back of my throat, which the girl must have taken to be a yes, because she put a menu on the table in front of me and poised herself. It wasn't the kind of menu I was used to – although I don't read many menus, it has to be said. When Terry and I do go out, which isn't very often, we tend to plump for a carvery, and what we're eating is either perfectly obvious or written on little laminated cards, so everyone knows where they are. This menu was typed on a sheet of paper. Not properly typed, either, but done on an old-fashioned typewriter. One that needed its ribbon changed, by the look of it, because some of the letters were so faded, it was difficult to be sure of what you might be eating.

I read through the menu and looked up at the girl, who was still holding a pencil with its point waiting on a blank pad. She seemed to take this as a cue, because she launched into a description of every dish, like a small piece of theatre. I would've interrupted, put a stop to it because it was all so unnecessary, but she didn't leave any gaps between the words and there was nowhere for my opinion to squeeze itself in.

I ordered a sandwich in the end and played it safe. It wasn't called a sandwich, it was called something completely different, but that's what it amounted to, no matter how many other bits and pieces swam around on a plate with it, and if Terry knew how much I'd paid, he would have had a coronary right there and then. I looked around for Jolyon whilst I waited for my completely different sandwich, but I couldn't spot him anywhere. I couldn't spot anyone I recognised. This wasn't a place for Malcolm, or Tamsin, or even Steve and Ingrid. It was filled with strangers. Smooth, untroubled existences. Impossible faces. People dressed in clothes I would have saved for a wedding, eating their completely different sandwiches and living their completely different lives.

It only took three visits to Harley's before I finally found him. I became almost a regular, and the all-in-black waitress stopped reading the menu out to me and poising her pencil, and just brought me my sandwich without any argument. It cost me a fortune. On the last visit, when she put the plate in front of me, I thought I'd grab my chance.

'I don't suppose,' I said, 'Jolyon is in today?'

I assume she looked surprised because she wasn't used to customers making conversation with her, rather than because the question caused some confusion. To know one person called Jolyon is quite an achievement. Two would be something close to a miracle.

She nodded over to an area by the bar. 'He's over there,' she said. 'In his usual seat.'

I hadn't noticed him, tucked away like that. Holding court within a small alcove. A handful of tables and chairs. A group of men, suited in money and being clever and noisy, like groups of men in suits often are. I walked past on my way out, just to get a better look. Rebecca wasn't with them, but it was Jolyon all right. I recognised him straight away and when I was level with the table, I took a breath of his aftershave. It was exactly the aftershave I expected him to wear.

Wooden benches can be quite comfortable if you know how to position yourself correctly, and it's a good job I do, because I sat on one for two hours and fifteen minutes before Jolyon finally walked out of Harley's. Some people have no concept of time. He'd left all the others behind and he turned up the collar of his coat and walked up the pavement by himself. Handy for me, because it meant I was less likely to be seen, but then again, there is no law against walking, quite briskly, along a street right behind someone else. Even if that person isn't aware that you're there. Mother always says what you don't know can't hurt you, which is absolute nonsense of course, but on this occasion it happened to be true. He crissed and crossed through the traffic and I crissed and crossed with him. Jolyon is the kind of person who doesn't bother even pressing the button for the little green man, whereas I wait for the little green man even if there are no cars coming, but he forced me to take my chances just to keep up and in the end it felt quite exhilarating. Eventually, he stopped outside a very tall, grey building, paused to take a key from his pocket, and disappeared inside. I walked up to the tall, grey building and stared at the little row of buzzers. I saw his name straight away. KING. Right at the top.

NOW

A new person arrived yesterday.

You can tell, even before you've set eyes on them, because the whole feeling of the place changes. People very easily arrange themselves into little groups, but when a newcomer walks in, they start questioning if they want to be part of that group after all because there might be something better on offer.

You see it everywhere, not just in here. The girls who accused my dad were in a little gang. Before it all happened, I'd see them at school, clustered at the bottom of a staircase or sitting on the desks at break time, swinging their legs. They were the kinds of girls that life was favourable to, because everything came easily to them. Homework, boys, good looks, friendship. They had it all. It was as if God had been feeling generous on the day they were born and He said, *'Here – take it! Have the lot!'* and with people like that, you find the more they have, the more life seems to want to shovel on top. The problem was, it left people like me scrambling around for all the leftovers.

They were a little bit older than me, but I didn't see why that had to stop us being friends. I made a big effort, because Mother says you have to show the best of yourself if you want someone to be friends with you. I always made sure I sat next to them on the bus and waited at the edges of the playground, so I could listen to their conversation and join in. If I knew what they were interested in, I could be interested in it too, and then they'd realise how much we had in common, and I'm very good at hearing things, even when people speak quietly. I even tried wearing some make-up, because that was all they ever talked about, but Mother stopped me as I was leaving for school and said it would probably be better if I practised a bit more before I went out in public.

They came to the house for their piano lessons, one by one on weekends and in the evenings, because they were the kind of girls who had piano lessons and rode horses and did ballet with satin slippers. I never did any of those things. *'What's the point, Linda?'* Mother would say. *'You're too tall and clumsy'* or *'You're tone deaf'* or *'You need grace to be a ballerina'*, so I just watched everyone else from the sidelines. I'd make sure I was around, though, when they came to the house. I'd arrange it so I was in the hall or standing near the front door. I'd sit opposite the daffodil painting until they arrived, but they'd just walk past me without saying a word and disappear into the front room and shut the door. I could still hear them as I sat with the daffodils. The same tunes played over and over again, until they were perfect. Arpeggios and scales travelling up and down a keyboard. I would sit on the stairs and listen, and sometimes I thought I could hear music but it turned out to be laughter, because even their happiness sounded graceful and musical. Plus, you can't always tell what something really is until you're really close up to it. I've learned that much for nothing.

Sometimes, though, it was quiet. No crotchets, no quavers. No travelling arpeggios. I'd stare at the door and into the silence. I asked him once, my dad, what the silence meant.

'Theory!' he said. 'Life isn't all fun and games, Linda. It's like everything else — you have to understand something before you can truly be the boss of it. There's no point expecting all the good things in life to land on your door-step if you haven't put the hard work in first.'

It was during one of these silences that I decided to walk in and I saw what I saw, and everything was different after that. They fell like dominoes, those girls. One after the other. Repeating the same lies.

I tried to be friends even harder afterwards. I thought if we were all friends, I could explain that my dad would never do anything like that and they'd realise their mistake and tell everyone they were sorry for the misunderstanding, and everything would be all right again. In the end, the headmaster called me into his office. He said he understood I must be going through a difficult time and they were going to arrange some counselling, but it might be best if I kept my distance from those girls until then. Stayed away. Kept myself to myself. So I did. You can still watch people, though, even from a distance. And besides, I still hadn't decided yet if I hated them or if I wanted to be one of them.

16

I had to have my lunch in Harley's twice more before I saw him again.

It wasn't too much of a hardship, because sitting in the alcove was quite the experience. From there, you could see everything going on in the bar, but no one could really see you, and it's a shame life in general doesn't contain more alcoves if I'm honest. A few times, people made their way inside, eyeing up the table Jolyon usually occupied, but I managed to put them off by patting the seat next to me and saying hello, because people are very predictable and always seem to do the opposite of whatever you might suggest to them.

The third time, I was just about to give up and go back to work early, when he walked through the door. You couldn't miss him because he made such a palaver, saying hello to everyone and waving at people across the room. There was such a hoo-ha, I didn't notice straight away. He wasn't on his own. A few steps behind him was Rebecca.

People never look like they do in their photographs. People in real life are usually wider and shorter, their eyes sit closer together and their noses are often much larger. I've found that when you meet someone, they never quite match up to their picture. You can recognise them, but it's more as though they're a distant relative.

Rebecca Finch looked exactly like she did in her picture. Right down to the tiny hole in her nostril and her deep khaki eyes. The only thing that was completely different was her hair. In the pictures on the internet, she had auburn curls right down to her shoulders, but as she stood with Jolyon in the entrance to the alcove, it was ice white blonde, and it felt to her shoulders in a sharp bob. They both stared at me.

I didn't smile or pat the seat or do any of those things, instead I looked away and carried on eating my food very quietly. I had ordered quiet food deliberately, because some food is prone to noise, and no matter how hard you try it just brings it out in you.

'Is this table taken?' Jolyon said, and I allowed myself to look up and say, 'No I don't believe so,' and I went back to my quiet food.

I'm not very good at many things, but I'm exceptionally good at being unnoticed, especially when I pretend to read a paperback I've borrowed from work, so it wasn't long before the pair of them started talking as if I wasn't even there. They talked about nonsense mainly. Different people they knew, something they'd watched on TV the night before, things that don't hold any interest for me. At one point, they began discussing some kind of business venture – it must have been a business venture because they started whispering about money – and then they had a little squabble about what they were eating, but it was a meaningless squabble. The kind of squabble people have when they really want to argue about something bigger and more important, but neither of them have the courage to do it. I'm very good at hearing things and it never takes me long to fill in the gaps, but with these two it was even easier. All the post I'd read. All the people who'd come knocking at the front door. The girl with the dog was the most useful, but each of the visitors had had something useful to offer. People always do, if you take the time to listen. The whole time, I was dying to get a better look at Rebecca. It was all I could do not to turn my head and give her a really good staring-at, but I knew I had to bide my time. Think of the bigger picture.

They left before I paid my bill and didn't give me a backward glance.

Just how I wanted it.

A few days later there was some progress because Jolyon gave me a little nod when he sat down. Halfway through, I asked if I could borrow their salt because mine had run out. Of course, it hadn't. I'd just emptied it all into a napkin before they arrived, but it gave me a chance to have a good look at Rebecca. She had quite a bit of make-up on her face – a lot more than she did in the photographs I'd seen – and she was wearing a crisp white shirt. The kind of shirt you only usually see in catalogues, because, within five minutes of wearing them in real life, they've collected creases and dirt around the collar, and little stains down the front from whatever you've just been eating. Rebecca's didn't look like that at all. Rebecca's looked perfect. I smiled at her when she passed me the salt. She didn't exactly smile back, but her face changed shape a little bit, which was a start. I listened in again, of course, to their whispering and their squabbling and their discussions, because even the most ordinary infor-mation can prove useful, if you hold on to it for long enough.

They quietened down a bit when their food arrived and I took the opportunity to lean forward.

'I don't suppose,' I said, 'you'd watch my bags for me whilst I nip to the ladies', would you?'

I had quite a few bags. Nice ones, they were. From fancy stores. Someone had used them to bring in their charity shop donations and I'd folded them up and stuffed them into my handbag before Tamsin knew they even existed. People treat you differently if you're using nice bags, even if they're actually filled with the usual rubbish and nonsense you carry around with you.

I could see Rebecca arching a brow at my posh carrier bags.

'The toilets here are so pokey and small, aren't they?' I said. 'And I've no idea why they have silly blue mood lighting in there – you can't even see your face, let alone put your lipstick on.'

Rebecca laughed into her soup and I laughed back quite loudly. It made Jolyon join in as well, which was nice because all three of us shared a good joke.

As I squeezed past the chairs on my way to the loo, I could see my purse resting on top of the biggest carrier bag, but it didn't matter because all that was in there was three pounds fifty and yesterday's bus ticket. Everything else was safely pushed into my pocket.

'You're very trusting,' Jolyon said, when I got back from the toilet.

'Oh, I'm a firm believer in trust,' I said. 'I try to see the good in people, give to those in need, you know.'

They knew, because they both said yes a few times and nodded quite vigorously.

'Very Christian!' said Jolyon.

'Well, you should always treat your neighbour as you would want to be treated,' I said, 'because that's when good neighbours become good friends. Just like the song!' and I hummed it a little bit, to make sure I got my point across.

The third time, they both said hello when they sat next to me, and I saw Rebecca give Jolyon a little nod. Jolyon even made a comment about weather when he shook his umbrella out. One of those bubble-wrap comments that only exist to fill up a bit of space, but it made me decide that today was the day. It was now or never.

'Terrible, isn't it?' I said, and reached for my coat and scarf from the back of the chair. 'Not fit to be out and now I've got to go back into it!'

They did polite smiling. Rebecca was sitting the other side of Jolyon with her arms folded, but I could see the edges of her face. The kind of smooth, well-attended face people get when they spend a lot of time in front of a mirror, staring at it.

I waved at a waitress to bring over the bill, and she wandered over with her little card machine. She struggled to fit it onto the table, what with my umbrella and my coat and all the leftovers of an expensive sandwich, and she tried to move things around like a game of chess.

'Oh, I don't need that,' I said and I fished a twenty-pound note out of my purse. 'I always use cash. I never bother with cards.'

The waitress and Jolyon both stared at me.

'You don't have a card?' said the waitress. 'At all?'

'Only to get money out of the little hole in the wall,' I said.

'How quaint! Jolyon laughed and from the edges of my eyes, I could see Rebecca lean forward and stare.

'Well, I've never had any real need' – and I said 'Real Need' with capital letters like Mother does from time to time to make the words stand out from all the others.

Jolyon looked across at me and smiled. A proper smile this time.

'I don't think I've ever met anyone who doesn't own a credit card,' he said. 'It's quite a novelty in this day and age.'

'I don't believe in debt,' I said. 'Paying for things with imaginary money, getting yourself into all sorts of messes.' Then I took my change from the waitress and I left.

They were still staring at me as I walked out. You can tell sometimes. Even without turning around.

It doesn't take much to make friends with people, if you're willing to put the effort in, because the next time I went to Harley's, Rebecca and Jolyon were already sitting in the alcove and they both looked up when I walked in and said, 'Hi!' in very loud voices. I said 'Hi' back again and sat next to them, and we had another nice little conversation about the weather.

A few minutes later, Jolyon took his credit card out of his wallet and placed it on the table, which seemed a bit previous because they hadn't even ordered their food yet, and he pointed at it and said, 'I should follow your example, shouldn't I, and only use cash?' and everyone laughed quite a bit.

'Don't you struggle?' Rebecca spent her whole time leaning forward now, and her arms weren't folded, because she was using one to prop up her head. 'I mean with wages being paid in and everything?'

I considered her question very carefully. People don't think for long enough about the words they use and the right words can make all the difference, especially when you're trying to make a good impression.

I thought about Terry's wages. 'I have a private income each month,' I said. 'Although I do a bit of charity work, just to get myself out of the house, you know?'

They definitely knew, because they both nodded.

'So I've never really had the need for a credit card,' I said.

'I'm Jolyon!'

He pronounced it in a strange way, like he'd got a boiled sweet in his mouth, and he thrust a handshake towards me so violently, it made me jump backwards a little bit.

'And this is Rebecca!' he said.

I'd considered several different opening lines over the past few weeks. *Good Afternoon* seemed a bit formal, but *Hi* smacked too much of indifference now we were being formally introduced, so I decided to plump for something in between.

'It's very lovely to meet you,' I said, and went in for a handshake, but Rebecca's hands were both occupied playing with her hair so she just smiled at me instead.

'And you are . . . ?' Jolyon said.

'Linda. My name is Linda.'

'Liiiiinda!' Jolyon had discovered a way of saying my name that made it sound far more important than it actually was. 'Linda, Rebecca and I have been talking and we think the three of us have quite a lot in common.'

'We have?' said Rebecca, but Jolyon ignored her and carried on.

'We might even have a little business proposition for you, eventually, if you'd be interested?'

'Oh yes, Jolyon?' I felt a little flush travel all the way up to my forehead and back down again. 'I'd be very interested.'

'Excellent! Why don't we all go back to ours and carry on this chatting there?'

'What, now?' I said. 'Aren't you going to order any lunch?'

'No time like the present!'

Which wasn't strictly true, but I reached for my coat anyway and whilst I was putting it on I heard Rebecca whisper, 'Jolyon, are you drunk?' and he said, 'Not yet!' and it made me smile because it was just the kind of thing I'd say to Terry and it only went to show how much we had in common. We were practically best friends already.

I crissed and crossed the streets again, just as I had a couple of weeks earlier, except this time I was following Rebecca and Jolyon. I kept my distance a little bit, because they were having quite the heated discussion. Jolyon had his hands stuffed into his coat pockets and Rebecca was throwing her arms around continuously, and she was still doing it, even when we got to the tall, grey building.

'Oh, *this* is where you live!' I said, quite loudly. When we got inside, Jolyon ignored the lift and started taking the steps two at a time, with Rebecca marching behind him, and I lost them quite quickly. I had to stop to catch my breath for a bit on one of the landings, but eventually I heaved my way up to the fourth floor and stood on the mat outside their door. It was still slightly ajar, but it was one of those heavy doors that close all by themselves and I had to use my finger to hold it open.

'Hello?' I said.

'Linda!' Jolyon flung the door open and I jumped backwards. 'Come inside! Come inside!'

And I found myself standing in the flat I'd stared at on the internet.

Very much like Rebecca, the room looked exactly the same as it had in the photographs. The rugs were just as thick and the ornaments were just as heavy. The walls were a pale grey, matching the sky beyond the curtainless windows. The place was messier, though, as if it hadn't been expecting any visitors and was a little surprised. A pile of laundry spilled from a basket in the corner of the room and there was a film of dust covering the giant television screen. The leather settees looked as though they needed a good going-over with a cloth and all the books on the coffee table were at the wrong angle. I adjusted one as I sat down on a settee, and Jolyon smiled.

'Sorry the place is a bit of a tip, Linda. We didn't know you were coming and neither of us is very big on housework.'

Rebecca made a strange noise with her nostrils. She sat in the corner, curled like a cat into a large brown armchair.

'Oh, I love it,' I said. 'You could say it's one of my hobbies.'

Rebecca leaned forward in her chair. 'You enjoy housework?'

'I suppose it gives me a sense of purpose,' I said, startling myself, because there are times when you don't even realise a thought is sitting inside your head until your mouth discovers it and it's given somewhere to go.

'I don't suppose you'd like a cleaning job?' Rebecca said.

I laughed but she didn't laugh back, even though I thought it was quite a funny joke.

Rebecca's gaze travelled from my face right down to my shoes. 'I just thought, you know, with the clothes you're wearing you could maybe start straight away.'

Which was a real compliment, because she must have meant I looked like I was going to an interview or something, and I shuffled around in my seat and crossed my legs, to give myself the best chance of looking even more presentable. As I did, there was a strange crackling sound underneath my left thigh.

'Oh . . .' I said, and looked down.

'God, sorry Linda. All sorts of crap gets pushed down the sides of sofas, doesn't it?' Jolyon reached over and pulled out an envelope. 'Ha – it's like a magic trick!'

'Nothing magic about that letter.' Rebecca arched a brow and all the coppery eyeshadow she was wearing twinkled back at the room.

'Bex, don't start. I've told you, it's just a joke of some sort.'

'It doesn't seem like a very funny joke to me,' she said.

'How do you mean?' I said.

Rebecca said, 'Go on then, Jolyon – you tell her all about it, being as you think it's all so bloody funny.'

Jolyon gave a big sigh, took out a piece of paper from the envelope and put it in front of me. I didn't touch it because Mother always says you look with your eyes, not your hands. I didn't have to look very hard though, because I knew exactly what it said.

'Don't worry, you're next!' Rebecca shouted and made me jump. 'Bloody psychopath. On what planet, Jolyon, is that a *joke*?'

I had a whole speech prepared. I'd rehearsed it so many times at the kitchen table and in my head on the way to work. I'd gone through it when Terry was watching his television programmes and I'd repeated the words to myself lying in bed at night, to the sound of him snoring. It was a speech that would make Rebecca realise what a great friend I was. A speech that would make me shine.

In the end I didn't say very much at all, because I've discovered that the rehearsals which turn and turn in your mind and the performance that life actually provides for you, will forever be two completely different things, and when something you have longed for is eventually placed in front of you, sometimes the shock is so great, you don't realise it was even there until it disappears again and it's too late.

'Lots of people have had one of these,' I said. Very quietly.

'See!' Jolyon pointed at me. 'Even Linda thinks it's nothing serious!'

'Oh, I wouldn't go that far,' I said. 'They seem to think all these letters are linked to the murders. You know, the serial killer ones.' Because I didn't want them to get confused about which murders I meant.

'Oh, we're more than aware of those.' Rebecca took a long drag on her cigarette. 'We even knew the second girl.'

'Bex.' Jolyon's voice went very low all of a sudden. 'I don't think Linda needs to be burdened with all that.'

'I know exactly how you feel, Rebecca.' I wanted to reach out and pat her shoulder, but she was sitting too far away. 'Bloody psychopath.'

'Have you had one of these letters then, Linda?' Jolyon said.

'Well, no . . . but lots of people on my estate have. Except my husband. He hasn't had one.'

'How very strange.' Jolyon picked the letter up. 'If everyone else has.'

'He should thank his lucky stars!' Rebecca shouted and made us both jump again.

'She's been under a lot of stress,' Jolyon whispered. 'Just lately.'

I nodded at him and we both smiled.

'I would have been the first to know if Terry'd had one,' I said, 'because the post always comes just as I'm doing the second hoover of the hall carpet. It's amazing how much you can miss the first time around.'

Rebecca looked up from lighting another cigarette. 'Are you sure you don't want a job?' she said.

Jolyon went to make everyone a drink. I could hear him opening and closing cupboard doors and cursing to himself.

After a moment, Rebecca uncurled herself from the chair and followed him into the kitchen. I could hear them, whispering, because my ears are very tuned in to other people's conversations. Even the quiet ones.

Rebecca said, 'Why on earth did you invite her back here?' and 'What were you thinking?' which is such a shame, because she should know I'm not the kind of person who expects people to stand on ceremony, but she obviously wanted to make a good impression.

I didn't hear all of Jolyon's reply, because it disappeared into the slam of a cupboard door, but he did say 'useful' and 'new recruit' which made me a little emotional, because it's always nice when people try to make you feel welcome.

Then I heard Jolyon say, 'You could make friends' and I heard Rebecca say, 'Old enough to be my mother', but they must have started talking about someone else because I hadn't told them my age and you'd never guess just by looking at me, and then Rebecca flung herself back into the room like a small storm and sat down again with such violence, a cloud of dust escaped from a cushion and hurried towards the ceiling.

'Men are terrible at making drinks, aren't they?' I said. 'Terry hasn't got the first clue how to brew a decent cup of tea, but don't you worry about it – I'm not that fussy!'

Jolyon walked back in the room.

'There's no bloody milk.' He stood in the doorway with his hands on his hips.

Rebecca didn't reply.

'Would you like me to go and buy some?' I said. 'I've got my purse on me, it's no trouble!'

'Don't be silly, Linda – you're a guest.' He did a small tut at Rebecca and disappeared back into the kitchen.

I sat back on the leather settee and admired a few things around the room. The painting above the mantelpiece to begin with, although I wasn't sure what it was supposed to be because it was one of those paintings that could be anything you wanted it to be, depending on what mood you were in. Then I admired a cushion. Then I admired Rebecca's T-shirt. I could tell she was still bothered by the letter because she didn't say a word back to me, she just kept leaning forward in her chair and peering towards the kitchen. In the end, I decided to enjoy sitting there and drink in being a guest, because it wasn't something that happened to me very often.

'Sorry, Linda – it has to be black coffee.' Jolyon appeared holding three mugs and closed the door into the kitchen with his left foot. No sign of a biscuit, but I suppose some people are more spur of the moment about these things.

I took it from him and smiled, even though black coffee always plays havoc with my small bowel. I was just on the point of explaining, but Jolyon's mobile telephone rang and the moment was lost. Mother says sharing intimate details of your health problems is a way to bring people closer together so I thought I'd keep my digestive tract up my sleeve for another time.

Jolyon walked into the hall with his telephone conversation, but you could still hear him talking. He said, 'No can do, mate' and 'We need it pronto' and 'Don't you worry — as it happens, I've got one lined up here and ready to go'. He said quite a few other things as well, but I couldn't make them out properly because Rebecca started moving things around on the coffee table and then she experienced a rather violent coughing fit. I did ask if she wanted me to fetch her a glass of water, but I don't think she heard.

Jolyon walked back into the room just as she stopped coughing. He sat opposite me on the other leather settee and reached for his coffee, but he misjudged and it spilled onto the rug.

'Let me get a damp cloth,' I said. 'The faster you tackle it, the more chance you have of getting it out.'

'Don't worry about it, Linda.' Jolyon rubbed at the mark with the tip of his shoe and ground it further into the pile. 'It just adds to the ambience.'

'This whole place is filled with ambience,' Rebecca said. 'Floor to bloody ceiling.'

Jolyon glanced around at the rugs. 'I suppose they've seen better days. Maybe we need some new ones.'

'No need for that,' I said. 'I've got some magic spray at home that would get all these stains out in seconds.'

'Really?' Rebecca looked up from her ashtray and her eyeshadow twinkled again.

I smiled at her. You can bond over small things like that. I saw it with Ingrid and with Tamsin; all it takes is some common ground.

Jolyon was the kind of person whose mobile telephone

rang every five minutes, and he was in and out of that room like a yo-yo. I said I didn't mind if he answered his phone in the front room, but he seemed insistent on going into the hall and out of the way, and it meant Rebecca and I sat in silence a lot of the time. It was fine, though, because friends can do that. For ages sometimes.

Although the flat was on such a busy road, there was hardly any noise at all. I suppose it was because of how high we were. The traffic and the people and the rest of the world were so far away, the sound of them became unsure. Something you thought you could hear, but couldn't be certain of. To my ears, the cars were running water, a fast-moving stream. The people sounded like starlings, arguing and pecking and squabbling over food. Beats from a car radio were the drum of impatient fingers. Because the further away you are from a thing, the more likely you are to mistake it for something else.

'Well, this is nice, isn't it?' Jolyon said, as he walked back in for the umpteenth time and he smiled at us both.

'It is nice, isn't it and so what about this business proposition then?' I meant to separate the words, but they ended up all being in the same sentence.

Jolyon laughed. 'If you're going to do a little business with someone, it's always best to get to know each other first, isn't it?'

'Oh yes,' I said. 'I don't get the chance very often. To get to know people.'

'Don't you have much of a social life, Linda?' he said.

'Not really.' I frowned and tried to pick out the bits of my life that were sociable. 'I suppose that's why I don't bother with credit cards and things like that. I just don't go out much to use them.'

'You've got a bank account, though?' said Jolyon.

'Oh yes, I've got one of those! I just don't take money out very often. I only usually put it in.'

I saw Rebecca give Jolyon a little smile, and Jolyon said, 'See,' without any noise coming out and he smiled back at her.

'For goodness' sake pop out and get some milk,' she told him. 'Linda hasn't even touched that black coffee.'

We made quite the afternoon of it in the end. When Jolyon returned with the milk, he brought a box of doughnuts with him and the doughnuts had rainbow sprinkles all over the top.

'No, no, they're all for you,' they said, each time I tried to offer them around.

I was going to hold back and save a couple for them to eat later, but before I knew it I was licking my finger and dabbing at the last remaining sprinkles on the inside of the lid.

'They're very moreish, aren't they?' I said and Rebecca found this very funny, even though I never really meant to make a joke.

We talked about so many different things. They were so interested in my job and how long I'd been working there and whether it paid well. Rebecca asked so many questions because she'd always been interested in charity work. I thought that was a nice gesture because I couldn't ever imagine her fishing used tissues out of coat pockets and trying to make a window display out of nothing but thermal nightwear. She even wanted to see my ID badge.

We talked about how unreliable banks are and how useful store cards can be. I told Jolyon I'd probably get a store card of my own at some point, because they're so convenient and you get all kinds of rewards for having them. Things you never imagine you need until someone offers them to you and you realise just how much your life was lacking in that department. Rebecca said I was very wise and nodded a lot.

Jolyon had an even better smile in person. Much nicer than Terry's.

It was a shame I had to go home, but all good things must come to an end, as Jolyon said on several occasions. Rebecca had commented more than once on how fast time was going, but it was only when Jolyon stood up and said, 'Wow, it's almost five o'clock!' that I realised it wouldn't be long before Terry would be home. I hated disappointing them, because I could see how much they were enjoying the afternoon, but Terry always gets in one of his moods if his tea isn't on the table.

I explained it all to them, as I was halfway through the front door. It was quite complicated, because I had to make it clear what Terry was like about his meals being on time, but I think they understood.

'I really like your T-shirt,' I said to Rebecca again, just as I was leaving. It had little pink and silver hearts all over it, like confetti, and a giant pink heart just over where your actual heart is.

'Hang on,' she said and disappeared back into the flat.

When she returned, she was holding a packet wrapped in plastic.

'For you,' she said. 'It's exactly the same. Brand new. We got a job—'

'It's a spare,' Jolyon said, and he glared at her.

The plastic crackled as she handed it to me. Like electricity.

'Now we have matching T-shirts,' I said, 'everyone will know that we're friends.'

Rebecca did a small laugh, although it didn't seem to travel very far around her face. 'Yes,' she said. 'Yes, I suppose they will.'

'We'll be in touch!' Jolyon said. 'Do you know your way back to the bus station?'

'I do.' I smiled at them both. 'Thank you very much but I know exactly where I am.'

I held on to the T-shirt all the way home on the bus.

I didn't dare take it out of its wrapper, because dirt and germs would get all over it, but I stared at the little pink and silver hearts through the plastic. I decided I'd definitely save it for best because you wouldn't want to waste a T-shirt like this on any old occasion. Or I thought I could just wear it in the house to keep it nice. Underneath my dressing gown, perhaps. Or with my black leggings. Just like Rebecca. Even though I didn't own any black leggings, I could ask Rebecca where hers were from and then I could buy some quite easily.

I was in two minds whether to tell Terry about where I'd been. On the one hand it would do him good to know I had a life outside of the kitchen sink, but on the other hand I had found in the past that when you share a thing with someone it always ends up getting broken. In your head it exists perfectly, flawless and untouchable, but the moment you allow it to escape from your mouth, it shrinks and becomes damaged and weak. Just as I was leaving, Jolyon had invited me back. He brought up the business proposition again, the one he mentioned in Harley's. I wondered when he was going to say something, but I suppose you have to make sure you get along with somebody first. Check you're all singing from the same hymn sheet, that's what Mother calls it, and from that afternoon, it was clear the three of us got along like a house on fire. Jolyon said it was something that would benefit all of us, but if I told Terry, he'd lean back in his chair and laugh, and he'd repeat what I'd said in a cartoon voice. He'd keep doing it, again and again, and the thoughts I'd grown, all the ideas I'd fed and watered and taken care of, would become smaller and smaller, and quieter and quieter, and eventually they would all disappear. It was a talent Mother had too. The only person who ever fed and watered them with me was my dad.

I put the T-shirt right at the bottom of my bag and got off the bus at the end of the road. I was staring at my feet and trying to fathom out an excuse as to why I was so late, and so I didn't look up until I crossed over just outside Malcolm's. It was only then I realised. There was a police car parked right outside our house.

17

'Afternoon, Linda.'

I tried to walk past and pretend they weren't there, but they were having none of it. They were different police officers from the last two. Straight away I knew these ones were detective-somethings, because they wore their own clothes and looked more dishevelled. There was one in a uniform, but he stayed in the driver's seat of the car. It must be nice to have someone chauffeur you around everywhere all day and not have to worry about germs and public transport.

I didn't say good afternoon back to them. I just put the key in the front door and kicked down the bit of loose carpet as I stepped into the hall.

'Mind if we join you?' one of them said, although she announced it when she was halfway inside, so it wasn't as if I had much choice in the matter. They took off their coats and hung them up, and didn't even wipe their feet. I did make a point of looking down at their shoes, but immediately regretted it. You'd think there would be some code of conduct for police footwear, but apparently anything goes. Even loafers.

They both went straight into the front room and sat themselves down in the chairs either side of the fireplace as though it was their God-given right. The one sitting in Terry's chair leaned forward with his elbows on his knees and said he was Detective Inspector Nahdi and his colleague was Detective Constable Andrew and they just wanted a little chat. I deliberately asked their first names – Mo and Caroline – because it was Linda this and Linda that as though we'd been friends all our lives, and if first names were fair game for them, they were fair game for me as well. They didn't realise I was wise to their nonsense and I already knew the police speak in a back-to-front language. Whatever they say always means the exact opposite, so I was fully aware that a little chat would end up being a long conversation.

'Shall we have the kettle on, Linda?' DI Mo smiled at me. 'I could murder a brew.'

I closed the door to the kitchen and for a few minutes I sat at the table next to my own breathing. I hadn't even taken my coat off and my handbag still hung from my shoulder with the new T-shirt waiting deep inside it. I knew that if Detective Inspector Mo or Detective Constable

Caroline saw the new T-shirt, it would be spoiled forever-more, because thoughts very easily glue together in your mind and I knew that if they did see the T-shirt, whenever I looked at it in the future, I would always see a police car parked outside my house and filthy shoes treading all over the Axminster. I have no idea what makes thoughts do that. It's like they can't bear to be alone and they have to find company in each other, and sometimes it makes the most harmless things become almost unbearable.

I used to love daffodils, but after Dad died I couldn't bear the sight of them. They made me feel physically sick. More than that, they made me angry. I couldn't work out why, but then I remembered that after I'd found him, when I ran back into the house, the first thing I saw was that bloody painting in the hall. All yellow and happy and smiling. My eyes were still full of what I'd just seen, and the daffo-dils stopped me in my tracks because I couldn't understand how something so cheerful could exist in the same moment as something so horrific. It still turns my stomach if I see a bucket of them on a market stall. The counsellor they gave me said it was shock. They said your mind holds on to little details when you go through something like that to stop you from focusing on whatever it is that's upset you. They said my head was still full of caterpillar thoughts and I should try to turn them into butterflies. They said a lot of things.

'Are you all right in there, Linda?' DC Caroline called. 'Do you want a hand?'

I shouted back that I was fine. I had half a mind to walk through with three mugs of black coffee in my hand and shut the living-room door with my left foot, but instead I got a tray from the cupboard and a fresh doily, and arranged some fig rolls out on a side plate, because you have to maintain your standards, even with police officers. I was going to give them Terry's mug, but I thought better of it. Whilst I was getting it all ready, I could hear them moving around through the dividing wall. Heaven knows why, there was nothing to move around for.

When I went back in, DI Mo was standing by the fire-place with my wedding photograph in his hand.

'Nice picture,' he said, although we both knew full well it wasn't. 'You and Terry been married long?'

I put the tray down on the coffee table. 'Ten years this August,' I said. 'Help yourselves to milk and sugar.'

I looked around for somewhere to sit. That was the trouble when you had other people in the house, the seating arrangements became all too haphazard. I decided on the settee in the end, and I sat on the very edge of it so they'd know I wasn't intending on being there for long.

'Like we said, it's just a little chat, Linda.' DI Mo put me and Terry back on the shelf. 'Nothing to worry about.'

I wondered if I looked worried. Sometimes, my face does things I'm not aware of.

'Where is your Terry?'

The photograph was definitely off-centre and would need adjusting as soon as they'd gone.

I looked at my watch. It was just before five. 'He's at work, of course. Where else would he be?'

I saw them look at each other.

'And where does he work these days?' said DC Caroline.

They knew the answer to this full well. I looked at one and then the other, but their expressions gave nothing away because their faces are especially trained to always run in neutral gear and keep everything to themselves.

'At the tyre factory,' I said. 'Over in Tyldsley.'

They glanced at each other again.

'Why?' I said.

'That's a few miles' drive each day,' said DI Mo. 'What time does he usually get home?'

They were very good at that as well. Ignoring your questions and summoning up ones of their own instead.

'It depends on what shift he's doing. Whether he's on overtime. Why are you asking me all this?'

It was the same with my dad, even before he died.

Tell us what you saw, Linda

and

When you walked in the room, what do you remember seeing?

Because sometimes people keep asking you the same question over and over again, in all sorts of different ways, until you give them the answer they're searching for. To be honest, it gets to the point where it's worth saying what they want you to say, just to shut them up.

'Linda?' DI Mo said.

'Sorry, what was the question again?'

'What time will Terry be back tonight?' DC Caroline said very loud and slowly, as though I was hard of hearing or away with the fairies.

'Search me,' I said.

DC Caroline raised her eyebrows.

'I mean, I don't know,' I said. 'It varies so much. Sometimes, he says he'll be back late and he turns up at four in the afternoon. Sometimes I dish his dinner up and me and the plate both sit there waiting for him until gone eight.'

'That must be frustrating. Maybe a bit lonely?' said DI Mo in that special police voice they use when they take you by the hand and lead you along a path you never intended walking down in the first place.

'Not really,' I said. 'I quite like being in the house on my own.'

'Are you on your own a lot, Linda?'

'Not really,' I said, because I didn't know what the right answer was, so I reused the words I already had in my mouth, just to be on the safe side. 'Why are you so interested in Terry's shifts all of a sudden?'

'No reason.' DI Mo moved his weight about in Terry's armchair.

'Just making conversation.' DC Caroline did the same in mine.

'Are you making conversation with everyone else on the street?' I said.

DC Caroline did polite laughing.

'Of course,' she said. 'We're just trying to get a feel for

what's been happening on the estate for the past couple of weeks, you know?'

I didn't, but I kept it to myself.

'Do you mind if I use your toilet, Linda? It's a bit of a drive back to the station.'

DC Caroline got up from her chair, even though I hadn't answered.

'Upstairs, is it?'

I followed her up there, even though she said she could find it by herself, because the fewer rooms those dirty shoes walked around in, the better.

'This one, is it?' She went for the back bedroom.

'No, that's Terry's study,' I said, because I couldn't think of a better word for a room where someone stored all their unnecessary clutter. 'It's here.'

I opened the bathroom door and nodded my head towards the lavatory pan because it struck me that DC Caroline needed more instructions than most people.

'I can find my way out, Linda,' she said before she closed the door. 'I'll see you downstairs.'

I waited for a moment and she smiled and nodded, and I smiled and nodded back. I'd have to put some bleach down, of course, and change the hand towel.

When I got downstairs, DI Mo was standing in front of the window with his hands behind his back. The police car was still out there, with the uniformed officer at the wheel. Against the backdrop of suburban beige, it looked overdressed.

'You've not been here long, have you?' DI Mo's gaze didn't leave the street. 'Settling in all right?'

I told him I was. I almost mentioned Rebecca, but I managed to stop myself just in time. Mother always said my mouth had a habit of running away with me and I didn't want to spoil Rebecca by passing her on to a member of the police force unnecessarily.

'Wales, isn't it, where you're from originally?' DI Mo turned and looked straight at me.

I wasn't expecting Wales. He slid it into the conversation as if it carried the same weight as everything else, but I could see from his face that he knew full well it was far heavier than all the other words in the world put together. I couldn't answer him for a minute because it made everything else in my head shrink away.

'It's all right,' he said. 'I know with your background, you probably haven't had the best experience with the police up until now.'

I thought I could see sympathy in his eyes, but I've made that mistake before.

'But if there's anything bothering you, Linda, even if it's something small, you know we'd be only too glad to help.'

I searched around his face for a clue. Lots of things bothered me. I could probably have listed them every one of them, if we'd stood there for long enough, but I didn't think DI Mo was thinking about the potholes on the high street or the way next door had their television on too loud. The problem was I couldn't always tell the size of something until it had gone past. Small things could fill my head right up, yet something really big could come along and I wouldn't notice it had been there until someone pointed it out afterwards. Like the photograph from the press conference. I still hadn't made my mind up when I should mention it to them. I wondered if DI Mo would be better than I was at sizing things up.

'The thing is,' I said, but just as I was about to tell him what the thing was, there was an almighty crash from upstairs. It made the whole room shudder and all the light-bulbs rattled in the light fitting.

'What on earth is she up to in that toilet?' I said.

There was another, smaller crash.

'DC Andrew can be a little on the clumsy side of life.' DI Mo winced at the ceiling. 'Even though she very often takes her time over things.'

'I'd better go up there,' I said, but I only got as far as the hall when DC Caroline appeared at the top of the stairs.

'No need to panic!' she said. 'Had a bit of trouble with the door. Sticking. Change.'

'Change?' said DI Mo, who'd followed me through.

'In the weather,' said DC Caroline. 'It happens all the time.'

Of course, I marched straight up there to see what damage had been done. I'd noted there was a distinct lack of a flush and so I was expecting the worst, but everything was unchanged. The hand towel still sat in a perfect square. Even the toilet paper was folded into a point, just how I'd left it.

I leaned over the banister to say something, but they were putting on their coats in the hall.

'We'd better be off,' said DI Mo. 'Leave you in peace.'

'Yes,' I said. 'Yes, I expect you've got lots of other people you need to talk to.'

DC Caroline smiled at me and turned up her collar.

I watched from the front door as they walked down the drive, back to the waiting police car. Halfway along, DI Mo turned and looked back.

'You take care of yourself, Linda,' he said, and it's so strange because out of all the words they said to me that afternoon, even including the bit about Wales, those were the ones that bothered me the most.

18

I'd knocked on Ingrid's door five times since that night at the Red Lion. Her mobile hairdressing must have been doing really well, because she never seemed to be in, but we'd agreed to have a coffee and I didn't like to disappoint her. To be fair, it was me who did most of the agreeing, because Ingrid said she worked strange hours and it was best not to make a firm arrangement, but I'm a person of my word and I didn't want her to feel I'd let her down.

The last time I knocked, I swear I heard a noise, although it could have been a cat, I suppose. Malcolm was in his front garden and I asked him. 'Do they have a cat?' I said, but he just shook his head.

'I can't get a reply, Malcolm.'

He leaned on his dustbin. 'I thought they were in,' he said.

He was holding a pair of lawn shears, but the edges of his lawn looked like they'd long seen better days and I knew for a fact all the houses on that row just had yards at the back, which made me wonder what the shears happened to be doing in his hands in the first place.

'You shouldn't be out on your own, Linda.'

I nodded and turned to leave, hoping it would be enough, but I should have known better.

'Good evening at the Lion the other night,' he said before I could escape. 'Exchanging ideas. Theories. It's how criminals get caught, Linda. Any policeman will tell you that.'

I smiled and tried walking away again, but he wasn't having any of it.

'Interesting points of view,' he said, only he turned the end of the sentence up which made it so I had to stop. 'Of course, local knowledge will solve this, you mark my words.'

'Why? Do the police think it's someone from round here?' I said, because if he was going to hold me up, I wanted to make sure it was worth my while.

Malcolm gave a little watered-down smile. 'Well, it's obvious, isn't it?' he said, even though it hadn't been obvious to him until someone else had pointed it out around a pub table. 'Local knowledge. Where the bodies were left – that stretch of woodland off the motorway where they found the first girl – you can only get to it if you know the back roads.'

'I suppose so,' I said.

'And where the second girl was discovered, that bit of waste ground the other side of the industrial estate, it can't even be seen from the road. You'd never know it was there unless . . .' He paused very slightly. 'Unless you were local.'

'One of us, then?'

The watery smile disappeared. 'Oh, yes,' he said. 'Almost certainly one of us.'

I looked down at the shears. Malcolm's grip had tightened, because his knuckles were blanched ever so slightly and there was a very fine tremor, right at the tip of the blade.

'Do you think we should be worried, Malcolm?' I didn't take my eyes off the shears. 'Do you think it's going to happen again—?'

'Oh, yes, definitely it will happen again,' he answered before my voice had even found the question mark. 'They won't just stop at two or three, will they? Murderers never do. They get a taste for it, Linda. They keep going until someone catches them.'

'And do you think they will?'

He frowned.

'Catch them?' I added. 'Do you think the police stand any chance?'

His jaw tightened and he gazed over the rooftops. 'We have to put our faith in the emergency services, we've no other choice,' he said. 'The boys in blue, the bobby on the beat. They always triumph. In the end.'

'Jack the Ripper?'

Malcolm didn't look at me, but I saw his jaw tighten a little more.

'Lord Lucan?' I said.

Mother had been watching documentaries about unsolved mysteries, and I tried to remember the long list she'd reeled off.

'Shergar?' I added.

Malcolm sniffed. 'All the more reason for our eyes to be watchful.' He looked at me now, and the blade began to wave about with so much enthusiasm, I thought it wise to take a step back. 'To pull together, as a community. To be observant.'

'How do we know what to observe though, Malcolm, when we don't know what we're looking for?'

'Anything suspicious!' The blades seemed to acquire a mind of their own. 'Anything out of the ordinary! We need to learn how to be good neighbours again!'

My eyes followed the shears. 'Malcolm, I'd feel so much better if you'd put—'

There was the slam of a front door, which made me jump, although Malcolm didn't seem to flinch. It was Steve. I was surprised to see him, because he'd just emerged from exactly the same place where I'd been knocking for the last ten minutes.

'Cheers, Malc!' He reached over the hedge and took the shears from Malcolm. 'I'll pop them back when I'm done.'

'I thought you had a cat,' I said, but Steve didn't reply, just nodded at Malcolm and smiled. There are times you discover that to some people, you are so insignificant, so unimportant, you grow smaller and smaller and quieter and quieter, until you eventually end up becoming invisible.

'Not a problem. Any time.' Malcolm smiled and gave a little wave to the back of Steve's head.

Malcolm returned his hands to his trouser pockets and transferred his smile back to me. 'See?' he said. 'Being neighbourly.'

'Right . . .' I said.

'Any time!' Malcolm turned and shouted again, but the front door had long since slammed.

I stared at the door. 'Malcolm . . . what's he going to do with them?'

Malcolm turned back. 'Hmm?'

'The lawn shears. Why does he want to borrow them?'

We both looked over the hedge at the smooth black tarmac that covered the whole of Steve and Ingrid's front garden.

'He doesn't have any lawn,' I said.

Malcolm's mouth made a few different shapes, but no words managed to find their way out of it.

19

On the Friday after they found the third body, another two policemen came knocking at the door.

Down the hallway from the kitchen I could see the blackness of them, silhouetted against the glass. I knew who they were straight away, because nobody else makes a shape like that. I turned my music down and I took my time taking my Marigolds off and smoothing down my hair because with police officers, I've found it always pays to gather yourself first.

I tried to look relaxed when I opened the door, but I'm not sure it came across properly.

'What do you want?' I said, and I kicked the bit of loose carpet down.

I saw them glance at each other. They were different from the last two, both men for a start, and different from the ones who had come to the charity shop. It seemed the police force had an endless supply of people who wanted to interfere in your life. These two were both tall, but one was a bit shorter and God had blessed him with a slightly kinder face, so I sent all my conversation in his direction.

'I'm in the middle of hoovering,' I said. 'Just because people are being murdered, it doesn't mean life stops for everyone else, does it?'

The taller one looked beyond my left shoulder, into the darkness of the hallway, where the vacuum cleaner sat in silence, backing me up. Its flex spilled and spiralled all over the carpet. I'd actually been sat at the kitchen table, looking through Rebecca's post, so for once I was grateful for a mess.

They said they were just advising local residents on security. They said it was something they did from time to time and it was nothing to do with the murders. They didn't actually say 'murders', they said 'recent events', because sometimes the police like to treat you as if you were born yesterday.

I looked at the taller one and then I looked at the shorter one, and I said, 'You think he lives on this estate, don't you?'

They shifted their weight from side to side, and the taller one stared down the road for a bit.

'We can't comment on an open investigation, Linda,' the shorter one said.

Even though I didn't remember telling them my name.

The taller one finished looking down the road and said,

'We're just here to give some friendly advice on staying safe, updating your security – that kind of thing.'

'My husband's all the security I need, thank you, and I don't think he's in need of updating right at this present moment.'

Although I have to admit, the second part was more of an afterthought because updating Terry sounded quite appealing.

'Terry?' said the taller one.

'Yes,' I said. 'Terry.'

'Is he at home, your Terry?' the shorter one said.

The policemen shuffled about and peered over my shoulder a bit more. I could tell they were all for coming in but I thought I'd give them a taste of their own medicine and leave them on the doorstep.

'He's at work,' I told them. 'Where else would he be at this time of day?'

I couldn't quite fathom what they were saying with their eyes, but they looked at each other when I said that.

'A little extra vigilance never did anyone any harm,' said the shorter one, and he attempted a smile.

I could have had quite the discussion with them on that particular topic. I also toyed with the idea of bringing up the press conference, of showing them up because nobody else seemed to have spotted what I'd seen, but I looked into their faces – at the vacancy in their eyes, the kind of blankness police officers and doctors and firefighters get when they've witnessed all the misery life has to offer and they've run out of expressions to give back to it — and I knew I couldn't face hearing 'The thing is, Linda' even one more time, so instead, I told them I had to get ready for work. I told them I was in a rush.

The taller one tried to start a conversation about whether I walked to work or if Terry gave me a lift in his white van, but eventually I managed to see them off. I watched them leave from the window.

The taller one looked back over his shoulder.

I lied, of course. It was my day off. They wouldn't know that unless they decided to watch the house, so I stayed by the front-room window to be certain they'd gone. In the old days, I would've switched on the short-wave radio and had a good listen in to what they were up to, but everything's gone digital now and it doesn't work like that any more. I still have the little radio, even though the counsellor said I should get rid of it. *Let go,* they said, *move on.* I never wanted to see a counsellor in the first place, but the school insisted so I had to go along with it. What do counsellors know anyway? Sometimes, you hold on to your habits for so long, they become part of who you are, and if you let them go it turns out, even if you search and search forever, you will never be able to find the person you used to be.

I've always noticed an unplanned conversation with members of the police force can be quite a draining experience, so I decided to treat myself to five more minutes at the kitchen table. I'd usually sit and do a crossword to quieten my mind, but instead I thought I'd turn the music back up and look through Rebecca Finch's latest brochure. I had quite the collection now, nestled at the side of the microwave.

If you didn't read the writing on the front, you'd never have guessed what they were trying to sell you, because it was just picture after picture of people lounging around on settees and armchairs, being thoughtful. The models in Mother's catalogues smiled straight into the camera with their hands on their hips, but these people looked away from you, as if they were deliberately being stand-offish. Or perhaps they didn't even know you were there, feeding on the half-drunk coffees and discarded magazines, and silently looking in on their unexpected lives.

I was right in the middle of staring at a picture and imagining myself into it when I heard the noise. I wouldn't have noticed if the CD hadn't been between songs, but it was there. Definitely. A slow creak. It felt as though it was coming from upstairs and I tried to follow the sound as it moved across the ceiling. It stopped and then it started, but just as it did Elvis piped up again and it was lost in the lyrics to the song. I stared up at the light fitting. It was a different house, that was all, and different walls and different ceilings all creak and grumble in different ways. Every house has its own voice. I just hadn't got used to this one yet. I decided to ignore it and I flicked through the brochure until I reached the middle pages where there was a woman lying back on a large grey settee filled with large blue cushions. She had long, dark hair and a look of such contentment, you would be forgiven for assuming she had been placed there by the hand of God Himself. She drank coffee holding onto the whole mug, like children do, or people in films, and she was wrapped in a beautiful white dressing gown. It looked like a cloud. It had a giant collar and deep pockets, and a wide belt to pull tight around your waist. Even as I looked at the photograph, I knew exactly who this woman was. I knew how people would talk to her and the way she would be treated in shops. I knew no one would push in front of her in a queue, or ignore her when she said something and carry on as if no one had spoken. I knew she'd never sit in a canteen, eating her lunch on her own, and at school she'd walk home with a big gang of other children, and she wouldn't know what it felt like to always walk home on your own and have kids shout things at you and throw stones. I knew all of that just by looking at the picture, because she was wearing the kind of dressing gown that carried all sorts of other invisible things along with it.

My dressing gown carried invisible things along with it as well. It was the last thing I saw each night before I went to sleep and the first thing I saw each morning when I opened my eyes, because it was looped over a hook on the back of the bedroom door. Mother would insist on describing it as a housecoat, but I always think calling it a dressing gown makes it so much more sophisticated, although if you stared for long enough, you'd soon realise my dressing gown wasn't very sophisticated at all, because this is the thing when you see something every day. Your eyes get too used to it.

It was quite fancy when I bought it. Quilted. Powder blue. Little press-studs on the pockets and a ribbon around the neckline, although the ribbon soon disappeared deep into the washing machine, never to be seen again. I'm not sure when the dressing gown started to look tired, or when it stopped being fancy, because no one bothers to tell you these things. You just put it on, time after time, day after day, until you happen to catch sight of yourself in the mirror and realise your dressing gown looks just as exhausted as you do. I was all for throwing it out, but Mother said, 'Everything comes back in style, Linda, if you wait long enough,' and so I kept it. Even though some of the little zigzag stitches on the quilting had started to unravel and the press studs didn't work properly any more. The blue wasn't quite as blue as it had been, and the hem didn't hang very straight, but it felt comfortable. Familiar. But the kind of familiarity that sometimes carries with it an edge of the ever-so-slightly dangerous.

I didn't just wear my dressing gown in between dressing, either. I popped it over my clothes when I was doing the housework, because Terry wouldn't let me have the heating on all day and it kept me nice and cosy. I wore it when I was doing my crosswords, and when we watched telly of an evening. Because it wasn't just a dressing gown, it was a whole feeling all to itself.

As I walked back into the hall, the voice of Elvis fell into its closing notes, and I glanced up the silent stairs. No groaning. No grumbling. The house slept on and yet even in the emptiness, it didn't feel right. Perhaps I was distracted by the photographs in the brochure, or perhaps quiet can sometimes be even more unsettling than unquiet, and the sound of nothing ends up being the most distracting thing of all. Before I switched the hoover on again, I stared at the hallway and wondered what it had seen. Maybe Rebecca Finch wore her dressing gown all the time as well. A muted grey existence, spent lounging on a giant orange cushion with her fingers wrapped tight around a coffee mug. No wonder the house groaned and grumbled. Me and Terry must have been such a disappointment to it.

It was only when I put my hand up to the collar, as I bent down to plug in the hoover and felt where the ribbon had once sat, that I realised I'd also worn my housecoat to answer the door to the policemen. If I'd been wearing a beautiful white dressing gown with a giant collar and deep pockets, and a wide belt pulled tight around my waist, perhaps the policemen wouldn't have glanced at each other, or asked me if I was driven to work each day in Terry's white van.

Although when I thought about it, I didn't remember ever mentioning Terry's white van in the first place.

NOW

You can't tell who's staff here and who isn't.

It confused me at first, because everyone gets to wear their own clothes, but then I learned to look for the lanyard. At the end of it is a tiny piece of plastic that says you're allowed to leave every evening, to go back to wives and husbands and children, and a life far removed from plastic cutlery. When you look at people's faces at the end of a shift, though, it makes you wonder which life they'd rather be living. You can see them from here, through the window, trudging across the car park, all shoulders and elbows, their hands stuffed into coat pockets. I suppose your destination doesn't always end up being what you imagine it will be. You fill a house with all the things you think you need, you work all hours of the day and night to pay for everything, and yet one day you realise you're not in any rush to get back to it all.

Other than the staff, it's always the same faces, sitting in the same seats, watching the same television screen. There's a little garden, but apart from people going outside for a cigarette, nine times out of ten it's deserted. It makes it feel as though the landscape never alters and everyone has been sealed into some kind of vacuum and lost to the world forever. Visitors are scarce underfoot. You'd think people would make more of an effort to come in, but it's only been a few days so perhaps I'm being a bit harsh. It's almost certainly for the best. The whole thing takes a bit of getting your head around, and perhaps there are times in life when you just need to let the dust settle. I see Mother most afternoons, and of course, she's still making a big song and dance about it all because it's something different to decorate her life with. Terry sits with his arms folded, hardly saying a word, letting Mother carry on with it. He's probably waiting for her to get everything off her chest, which is never a speedy process with her.

'I didn't see this coming,' she keeps saying. 'Never thought you were the type.'

I don't comment. No point in it really, because once folk have made their minds up about what type people are, there's never any shifting them, no matter what you say. The staff here are the same. They'll have made up their minds about me as well, as soon as I walked through that door. From where I'm sitting, I can see them behind a glass partition, huddled into a little office, tippety-tapping away at their computers and filling a whole screen with who they think I am and why they think it all happened. Watching me keep myself to myself. Working out my type. Even I don't know what type I am, so there's not much hope for anyone else. But people see what they want to see and then they spend all their time gathering evidence to back themselves up, because there's nothing in life more delightful than proving yourself right.

What none of them realises is how easily you can cross from one path and onto another. It only takes a moment, a slight hesitation, and you can find yourself facing a completely different direction in life. It could happen to any one of them because it happened to me. I think it happens to all of us at some point, but we don't usually spot it because the ridiculous thing is we're so busy walking, we don't take any notice of exactly what it is we're walking towards and whether we really wanted to be walking in that direction in the first place. No one ever bothers to look up, not even Terry with his eternally folded arms, or Mother with all her flapping. I'd take the time to explain if I thought it would make any difference to anyone, but I know I'd just be wasting my energy. All the staff in the office behind the glass screen would feed words into their computers, words that didn't make sense, words that made me sound foolish. Words are like that. You can shape other people's words into anything you like, because when someone writes down what you say, what you say doesn't belong to you any more. It belongs to the person who writes it down, and all the other people who read it, and everyone can look at your words and see whatever it is they want to see. What you actually meant by your words disappears behind all their opinions, hidden somewhere in the paragraphs and the sentences and the full stops, and the story is lost. Especially if that story is something people would struggle to understand in the first place. I know, because it's happened to me before.

When the police in Wales asked me about my dad, there was so much I wanted to tell them. You're probably not supposed to have a favourite parent, but I much preferred Dad's company to Mother's. There was always a more interesting conversation in it, for a start, and whilst Mother always hunted down what might go wrong in a situation, my dad managed to figure out what could go right. He made me feel like I could belong somewhere. Eventually.

'Give it a try, Linda — why not!' he'd say, or 'You can do that, no problem!' whenever I presented him with an idea.

Whereas my mother spent most of her time hunting down potential catastrophes and always seemed vaguely disappointed if she didn't manage to locate one.

When I was very little, my dad and I spent all our time together, but the police didn't seem very interested in field walks and fishing trips, or weekends at the seaside. They just wanted to know what I saw the day I walked into one of Dad's piano lessons.

He only started giving lessons as a hobby. A bit of pin money, Mother called it. But the pin money grew and grew, and because no one else in the town offered them, it wasn't long before it became Dad's proper job.

'Why don't you go for a walk with your mother,' he'd say, when I waited for him on a Saturday morning, sitting in my coat and hat in the hall. Staring at a painting of daffodils that hung on the wall above the telephone table, wondering how it could manage to look so cheerful. *'Spend a bit of time with her instead?'* Mother was too busy pouring her day into a television screen, watching her soap operas, passing away her life by staring at other people's. I never even bothered asking. Instead, I'd take both the packed lunches I'd made, paste sandwiches and orange juice in cardboard cartons, and little silver triangles of Dairylea, and I'd go for a walk on my own. I took the route we always used to take. A slow climb out of the village, up onto the top road, where a little broken stile made a path into the first field. It was a huge meadow, looking down at all the houses. I called it my *Sound of Music* field and I would spin around like Julie Andrews and make Dad laugh, but if you didn't concentrate properly, you wouldn't realise which way you were supposed to go next. It was just a giant green meadow falling into the landscape, no obvious path, no way through. But there was always a way through, my dad taught me that.

'Look carefully, Linda,' he'd say. *'Stare at what's ahead of you, and if you stare for long enough, you'll find what you need to do.'*

He was right. Because if you concentrated really hard, if you screwed up your eyes really tight, you could see the faint outline of a path where the grass had been trodden down, where the meadow was a slightly different colour of green, and once it had been spotted, it made you wonder how you didn't ever see it in the first place. That was the thing with my dad, he made you realise things you knew all along.

I told the police the truth, because back then I thought truth and lies were two different things. I know better now. These days I can see that life is never that simple, but back then I hadn't walked as many miles on my own. I told them I'd got back from one of my walks and the front room was silent. No waves of arpeggios. No faltering hands on the piano keys. Not even the beat of a metronome. I thought he must be in there on his own and so I did what I was told never, ever to do, and I pushed open the door of the front room, and I walked in.

I told the police everything I saw. I told them it wasn't how it seemed at all, but they didn't seem very interested in that. When I tried to explain, they stopped writing. They just glanced at each other and stared at the floor until I'd finished speaking.

'It was a misunderstanding,' I said. 'It wasn't what it looked like.'

It never is. But it's a bit like when people tell me something funny and I don't get it, and they always shake their heads and look away, and say, *'Perhaps you had to be there, Linda.'* There are some moments in life when you have to be there, and it was the same with this moment – you had to be there. Or perhaps you had to be there long before any of it happened, because no moment exists solely on its own. Every moment in life hangs on a thread of other moments. Lines of moments stretching back throughout your life, as far as you can see, each one pulling very gently on the next. If you retrace your steps, if you walk through the past, take your time and have a proper look around, you soon realise nothing sits quietly on its own. Everything you do and say and think is tied and knotted forever to something that went before. It's why I'm sitting here. Because of all those small moments, and because of all the things they became tied and knotted to. What I saw at the press conference and all those brochures, and then Rebecca. Perhaps most of all Rebecca.

I do have to agree with Mother on one thing, though. You never see it coming.

20

I decided not to mention the police visits to Terry.

I could tell the police had started to rattle him, even if he tried his best to hide it. Anyway, I didn't see the point. They were only casual, after all, so there wasn't any need to bother him. Plus, Terry always gets this look on his face whenever I talk about the police. He rolls his eyes and makes a *pffftttth* noise like whales do when they come up for air, and I wasn't in the mood for his eye-rolling and his whale-blowing noises, and so I kept quiet. I couldn't have said for certain, but I'm sure the police knocked on every door in the street before they got to ours. It wasn't as though they'd singled us out.

The next morning, Terry was up with the lark, off on a fishing trip like every Saturday morning. Each weekend, he went fishing with his work friends, although who those friends were, I couldn't tell you, because he never brought them home. *'They'd only mess up your kitchen, Linda,'* he always said. *'Make a nuisance of themselves and get marks all over your clean surfaces.'*

I've never known anyone so enthusiastic about fish. Tearing round the house getting ready, whistling to himself, and there was no point attempting to have any kind of conversation with him because he was too busy living in a world of his own. I wouldn't have minded, but that loose carpet was getting looser by the minute and all the glass in the front door might go through if that crack wasn't fixed. Had I let those policemen come in, and one of them had tripped, we might even have litigation on our hands. You see the adverts all the time on the telly, because Mother writes the numbers down in case she ever goes head first on a wet floor.

I set to as soon as he was through the back door. Terry thought housework was a piece of cake, but that's because he never did any. For a start, he made more mess than he thought he did — he never rinsed out the sink properly when he'd had a shave, footprints all over the kitchen floor, and I was forever hoovering bits of him up. Hair, muck, grease. You could follow a trail of him around the house like breadcrumbs in a children's story. Heaven forbid if he decided to have a bath, because it always took me a good hour afterwards to get everything back to the way it should be. I always tried to put him off. *'Have a shower,'* I'd say. *'It's much quicker.'* He never took a blind bit of notice. Although he had recently begun to make more of an effort, in all fairness. He'd started going for a shower as soon as he got in. Even put his own clothes in the washing machine. It was like most things in life — it probably just takes a bit of time for people to come around to your way of thinking.

That morning I had a mountain in front of me. Sticky fingerprints all over the worktops, heaven knows how many crumbs down the side of his chair, and Terry had managed to get a strange mark on the side of the washing machine that on its own took me a good fifteen minutes to get rid of. I'd got through half a packet of anti-bacterial wipes and I hadn't even left the kitchen. It was past ten o'clock before I was ready to put the hoover away, and that's when I found it. Pushed to the back of the cloak cupboard in the hall. I was trying to put the vacuum back without touching any of the coat sleeves, because they harbour so many germs, coat sleeves, and it would have meant washing my hands again. I thought it was the end of the vacuum cleaner handle, or part of the flex, or even that little nozzle that attaches to the front. But it wasn't. It wasn't any of those things. I decided it was best to just ignore it. There are always two explanations for everything and it's silly to plump for one explanation without giving proper consideration to the other, and so I turned my music up instead and carried on singing, because if the music was loud enough, and if I chose the right song, it always stopped me moving all the thoughts around inside my head.

He'd probably forgotten it. Or borrowed someone else's. Or perhaps he'd bought another one and I just didn't realise.

I put it back behind the coat sleeves.

It was Terry's fishing rod.

When Terry got home, he hosed his boots off in the back yard and headed straight upstairs in his stockinged feet. He nodded to me as he walked through the kitchen.

'Make us a brew, Linda,' he said, as he brushed past. 'It's freezing out there.'

Even though I was already filling the kettle not two feet from his face. Because people always have their words ready before they've even studied the landscape.

When I lit the gas, the blue light gave its little hiss of comfort and I listened to Terry march up the stairs. You could follow his journey across the ceiling because he made all the light fittings shake, one by one. The airing cupboard opened and closed and the shower sprang to life, and the immersion heater sighed and heaved with the effort of it all. That was the thing about my husband. He used up an entire house just by being in it.

For all that noise, when he came downstairs he looked no different. Just a bit more red in the face.

He reached across the draining board for his mug of tea and sat at the table to drink it.

'Any good?' I said.

He looked down at the drink.

'The fishing, Terry. Was the fishing any good?'

He said it was. He gave a little weather report and ran through a list of different species of fish and rounded it all off with how much traffic there was on the bypass.

'I never see anything of these fish,' I said.

'That's because I throw them back in.' He took a sip. Even his tea-drinking managed to make a din. 'You know that.'

'Then I don't understand why you go,' I said. 'What's the point if no one ever sees what you catch?'

'Because I see it. You don't have to show something off to people to prove it happened.'

'Everyone generally does, though,' I said.

He pushed his empty mug across the tablecloth. 'We show them off to each other. Me and the lads.'

'Do I know these lads?' I said.

He sat back and folded his arms. 'You ask a lot of questions, Linda.'

'I've been saving them up,' I said.

He said they were people he worked with and he ran through four or five names. Names like Bob and Ben and Tony. Names I didn't recognise. Names that can slip quietly into a conversation, unnoticed. I shook my head with each one.

'You know Bob,' he said. 'He fits carpets in his spare time. The one with the good-looking wife.'

I blinked.

'Quite good-looking.'

'Oh,' I said.

'Not as good-looking as Tony's wife, obviously. Is there any more tea in that pot?'

As I poured the tea, I watched my reflection, etched into the glass of the kitchen window. I couldn't tell where I ended and all the scenery began. The tired blue of my dressing gown drifted into the lawn and the shed, and a washing line twisted with forgotten pegs, and all the wrinkles on my forehead crissed and crossed over the wooden fence, because there must have been a point in life when I'd frowned at something and my face had forgotten to stop.

'What makes her so good-looking, then? Tony's wife?' I said to the etching in the window.

'You know.' I could hear Terry shift around in his seat. 'Dresses up all the time. Wears a lot of lipstick. One of those glamorous types.'

I couldn't imagine Jolyon describing anyone like that. He had far more decorum.

'Oh,' I said. 'One of those.'

'Some women are, aren't they?' he said. 'They always look as though they're off to a party.'

Just the way Malcolm described Rebecca Finch. Except nobody lives a life like that all the time, do they?

I could imagine Terry and his friends, all sitting on the riverbank, staring into the water, comparing their wives in exactly the same way they compared their fish.

* * *

I don't very often get a Saturday off and I like to make the most of it, so I left Terry and his second mug of tea in front of a television screen and got the bus at the bottom of the road. I didn't think he'd even notice I was gone. I shouted as I pulled the front door to, but there was no reply, because he was staring at sport of some kind. It didn't really matter what sport it was, as long as it provided him with an opportunity to pick a side and get angry with it.

I caught the twenty past twelve. Every bus has a personality of its own, and a Saturday lunchtime bus is always full of teenagers and people with too much time on their hands. I had to push past a couple who couldn't stop kissing and a gang of sniggering youths just to get a seat to myself, and even then I had to share it because a woman got on three stops later with a large collection of carrier bags and a sense of entitlement. I was forced to breathe her germs in all the way into town.

When we pull into the station, I always wait for other people to leave first, just like I do at the pictures, and so I leaned my head against the glass and watched the bus pour everyone out. You could work out exactly where they were all going. Well-worn paths waited to take them to the shopping centre or to the parade, or to the little café across the street, where you could sit on a stool just a bit too high for your legs and watch all your time pass away through a big window, until another bus arrived to take you to somewhere else. There were no surprises. Nothing out of the ordinary. I wondered sometimes, when I got to the end of my life, whether I'd lie there trying to remember it all, only to realise there was nothing that happened which was very much worth remembering.

It was at that point I decided I'd stay on the bus.

I never stay on the bus. It goes all the way into the city, and the only time I visit the city is for the odd hospital appointment or if Terry needs a new multipack of boxer shorts. It's too much messing around. Too many people. Too much of a palaver. But I decided, as I stared out at all that familiar out-there, that a palaver was probably just what was needed. The driver glanced over his shoulder and gave me a look, but then we were off. Away from the high stools and the chewing-gum parade, and a day that would have always remained unremembered.

It's a straight road all the way to the city centre. A stop-start journey of traffic lights and pedestrian crossings. Little towns made out of housing estates and high streets had spread like ink stains from the city, each blending into the next, until you couldn't be sure where one place ended and another began. A string of shops moved past the bus window. Takeaways and dentists. Betting shops and pawn-brokers. Great Georgian houses refashioned into nursing homes, where wheelchairs and walking sticks looked down from a double-glazed life at an army of young women with pushchairs and toddlers. It was all there. The carpet of life spread wide across a pavement.

Forty-five minutes later and we were at the bus terminal. Terry wouldn't know I was missing, even less so if there was extra time. He'd just sit there drinking tea out of that horrible red mug and giving his opinion to an empty room. He wouldn't even notice. You can get a bus to anywhere from that terminal. The very tip of Scotland, and all those little islands that look like biscuit crumbs on a map, back to the watercolour hills of South Wales, even down to London and onto the Eurostar and then to heaven knows where else. It's a crossroads. A place where decisions are made. A place for changing your mind. When I stepped off the bus, the smell of diesel and wet concrete crept into my nostrils and I looked up at a board above my head. A list of shiny new towns, all in orange lights, and I could understand them, the people who walked into a crowd and never looked back. The people who changed their minds.

The best thing about city-centre buses is that the terminal is usually right next to the shopping centre. It waits for you, just over the road, pulling you across with a steel smile and whispers of warm air escaping through its doors. The whole of the outside of this one is mirrored, so if you're still unsure about visiting, you can study your reflection from a distance and appreciate just how much you need to go inside and make adjustments to yourself. I couldn't spot me at first. I stood by the pedestrian crossing staring into the mirrors, trying to find myself, and it was only when the lights changed and I walked a little bit closer, I realised I'd been looking straight into my own eyes for the past three minutes. It's strange how your face drifts along without you and becomes somebody else's the moment your back is turned.

I didn't intend to go shopping. I didn't need anything, but being as I was there, gazing at the shopping centre, I decided I might as well go in and have a look around. It would be like Terry and his fish. You didn't have to take anything home with you, you could just admire it for a little while and then throw it back in. The undercurrent of strangers pulled me through the doors and I washed up right outside a department store. It wasn't any old department store, either. It was the very shiniest kind. One whose name fell from your lips in a whisper, and who wrapped up your purchases in bright yellow bags with ribbons and tissue, and described shopping as an *experience* rather than just something you endured because you needed to replace something you'd run out of. I was having my experience before I knew anything about it, because a shopping centre isn't like a high street. It's all very open plan, like life really, and before you realise it, you've crossed over a thin silver line on the floor and off you've wandered, out of your own world and into theirs.

21

It's the smell that hits you first. Sweet and costly.

A thousand fragrances mixed into one, a smell that climbs into the back of your throat and then decides it would quite like to stay there for a bit. It made me cough at first and my eyes felt full of water, but after a couple of minutes I got used to the taste and it began to feel strangely soothing, like a lozenge. I started to walk around, the weird, wandery path you take in a shop when you don't really know what you want to look at, and so you end up back where you started and none the wiser. Around every corner, and as far as you could see, there were counters. Little islands of hope. Shiny displays of palettes and brushes, pots and crayons. Just like being at school, except instead of painting sheets of sugar paper, you'd moved on to painting your face. Women circled between these counters. Women in dark suits with sharp shoulders. Women with impossible faces, faces that had been painted into something else entirely. I'd seen them before, of course. I'd glanced in when I walked past with Terry, but I'd never looked at them close up and I probably stared a bit more than I should have done. Mother says I've always been a Staring Stanley, but when people fluff themselves up like that, they're almost inviting you to go ahead and have a good gawp.

I didn't linger. I kept moving, because I've found it pays you not to pause for too long in a shop like this one, unless you want someone to talk you into buying something. That's how Mother ended up with a laptop. A few of the women glanced at me and weighed me with their eyes. A couple of them smiled, but they weren't smiles that held on to anything, and for the most part, I was ignored. It was only when I stopped to look at a poster that someone spoke to me. The place was full of posters. Giant ones suspended from the ceiling, photographs of women mainly with their eyes closed. Women giddy at the thought of how soft their legs felt, or overwhelmed by the wonderful smell of their own armpits. Women who had nothing of me in them at all. The picture I stopped for was different. The face in it was tired. Pale. Lines unfolded from the edges of its eyes and pulled at the corners of its mouth, and for the first time I found something I recognised, but it was one of those electronic pictures, and as I was staring, it started to change. All the little pixels drifted into something else and before I realised it, I was looking at the same woman but all her wrinkles had disappeared and she was covered in make-up and throwing her head back and laughing. I wondered if people actually did throw their heads back in real life. Whenever I laugh, more often than not I have to keep it to myself because it's usually about Terry. I certainly can't ever remember finding something so hilarious I felt the need to throw my head back, but perhaps that's because the world hasn't really given me anything that amuses me enough to make me do it.

I was about to watch it change for the third time when I heard the voice behind me.

'Would madame like her make-up refreshed?' it said.

For some reason I found it more difficult to ignore a madame than a madam. It's surprising how much difference an 'e' can make to you. The thing is, I never wear any make-up, so I wasn't sure how you could refresh something that had never been fresh in the first place.

When I turned, I was head to head with one of the women in the dark suits. She was so close, I could see all the little grains of powder on her cheeks and the thick black lines that travelled the length of her eyelids. She stared right into my soul and then her eyes did a little journey around my face.

'Madame?' she said.

'I don't think so,' I whispered.

I must have backed away a little too quickly, because the next thing I knew, I'd reversed into a stand on the opposite side of the aisle, and all the little pots and packets were rattling and shaking with the effort of keeping upright.

'Oh dear!' A woman appeared from behind the stand. She was clearly in charge of the pots and packets, because they were all wearing matching outfits.

She looked across at the dark-suited woman. 'They can be a bit . . . assertive over there, can't they?'

I said, 'Yes they can,' and she smiled a smile that made you smile back, and a second later, I was sitting on a high stool and having my face wiped with something that smelled of aniseed. It wasn't altogether unpleasant.

'Linda,' she said, because at some point, I must have told her my name. 'You have such clear skin.'

'I do?'

'You do,' she said. 'What do you use?'

I thought about it for a second. 'Soap and water?' I said.

The aniseed cloth paused just above my right eyebrow.

'Nothing else?'

'No,' I said. 'Nothing else.'

When I looked up at her, it seemed as though a small orchestra of joy was playing behind her eyes.

'Linda,' she said. 'I have so many things to tell you about.'

She pulled a brown cape from out of nowhere and made such a display of wafting it around and draping it around my shoulders, it felt as though I had suddenly become part of a magic trick.

I didn't listen to what she was saying. A catalogue of names I'd only vaguely heard of and didn't really understand. It was a bit like the shipping forecast. Faraway places I would never visit. Unlikely words that fell into my mind by accident and left just as quickly as they'd arrived. But when the names were joined together and formed a line, it became strangely comforting. A reassurance, almost. Like a small prayer.

'And that, Linda, is why it's important to have nanotechnology in our eye cream!'

I agreed with her, because it seemed the polite thing to do, and she said, 'Now – make-up!' and she smiled again and I couldn't help but fall into it and so I offered up my face to her like a large plate.

She put my name into every sentence.

'This foundation is such a good match for you, Linda,' and

'Linda, do you have a favourite colour for your eyeshadow?'

I said, 'My friend Rebecca wears coppery eyeshadow, so I'd like coppery, please,'

and she smiled and fluffed one of her little brushes into the palette.

It made it feel as though we'd been friends for ages and ages, and she was just using my name a lot to make up for all the years she hadn't had the opportunity to say it. Every now and then, she'd step back and tilt her head, and stare like an artist stares at a canvas, as if I had turned into a bowl of fruit or a vase filled with chrysanthemums. I tried to make conversation, but I was always opening my mouth when it needed to be closed and closing my eyes when they needed to be open, and in the end I just threw the towel in and stayed quiet. I usually find not talking quite difficult, but there was something about the touch of a powdery brush on my cheeks and the smell of something unnecessary that made speaking easily avoidable. It's amazing how you can sit in a silence when someone is being kind.

'There!' she said, twenty minutes later.

'Are we done?' I kept my eyes shut until I got the go-ahead, just in case.

'Oh yes, we're done,' she said. 'This is some of my best work, Linda.'

When I opened my eyes again the world was too bright and shiny and blurred, but when it all came back into focus, she was standing in front of me with a big smile and a little hand-held mirror.

'Look!' she said.

And so I looked. The face in the mirror must have been my face, because when I scowled it scowled back at me, but besides that there were no other clues. My new face seemed so much more relaxed than the last one I'd had, even with all the scowling. There were still lines, of course, but they seemed more acceptable now. More as though they were a part of who I was, and hadn't been chiselled into my face as I slept, by a lifetime of wishing when I woke up that everything would be different.

'Do you like it, Linda?' she said.

For the first time, I noticed the little brass name badge on her lapel. *Natalie*, it said. Underneath, it said *Advisor*. I wondered how many other subjects she would be able to advise people on. Most things, I suspected, judging by her smile and how she'd made my face turn into something I actually enjoyed looking at.

'Oh yes,' I said. 'Very much.'

'We've used some of our bestsellers on you today – and they're all included in our special "Find the New You!" promotion.'

She pointed to a display in the middle of the stand. There was a photo of a woman who had found the New Her and was clearly delighted about it.

'Oh, the exclamation mark's fallen off again.' She crouched to reach under a display of lipsticks. 'The exclamation mark made all the difference in the marketing trials.'

Whilst Natalie recovered her punctuation, I stared over at the trolley, and the aftermath of a war that had just taken place on my face. There must have been twenty things on there, bottles and jars and pencils and tubes, all missing their lids, and that wasn't counting the brushes, which lived in a little belt around Natalie's waist.

Natalie stood up, clutching her exclamation mark, and she looked at me, and I tried to find a smile.

'I understand, Linda,' she leaned forward and whispered. 'Finding the New You can be a bit of a shock to the system, can't it?'

I nodded.

'I'll tell you what,' she said, but instead of telling me what, she vanished behind a little door. Whilst I waited for her, I perched on my high stool and watched everyone walk past me. I tried to imagine all the New Yous that crouched beneath the overcoats and the scarves, all the fresh starts and the reinventions, all the different editions of people yet to be discovered, each one biding their time until it was their moment to appear. Perhaps we could just keep on unpacking ourselves, like Russian dolls, until we found a version we thought we might get along with.

When Natalie came back, she was carrying a shiny yellow bag tied with ribbons and bows, and for a second I was worried I'd been talked into buying something without realising it.

'For you!' she said. 'Free samples!'

I reached out to take the bag. 'But!' she said, and took a step back, 'You must promise me something, Linda.'

I nodded, without taking my eyes from all the shiny yellow in her hands.

'You must promise me you'll come back and let me know how you got on with everything. You're very important to me, Linda, and I won't rest until I know what you think.'

I nodded, potentially a little bit more vigorously than was needed, and she handed the bag to me. I knew straight away that this was not your ordinary carrier bag. It was heavy. It had a gloss about it. It stood out a mile, because this was a carrier bag that clearly held something far more important than all the other carrier bags I was used to. The ones that slouched in an unhappy crowd at the end of a supermarket checkout. The ones I shoved inside another carrier bag on a shelf in the garage. Even the ones we kept under the counter at work for people whose bag for life always lived somewhere else.

Natalie smiled her smile and studied my face, and then she reached across and pushed my fringe back, away from my forehead, and my eyes started to fill. I wasn't sure if it was because of the coppery eyeshadow or because of the bright lights, but perhaps it was because I didn't remember anyone ever pushing my fringe back like that to give my face a better chance at life. Not even Mother.

I slid from my stool. I'd been sitting there so long, my legs felt unhappy about the thought of standing up and whilst they were getting used to the idea, Natalie said, 'Remember, Linda. I need to know how you get on.'

I thought I might buy a small notebook to record everything. One of those pretty ones with a floral cover and a bookmark made out of ribbon, because Natalie was obviously very big on detail, and I looked back to ask her whether I should go for plain paper or lined, but she'd turned away and was smiling her smile at some girl in a black leather jacket. It was understandable. Even when you clearly have a connection with someone, they still have to do their job and as much as Natalie would like to spend all afternoon talking to me, she'd probably get in trouble if it was all that she did. As I left the stand, I looked over at the woman in the black suit, who stood watching with an arched brow and her arms folded. She had a smile sitting right at the edges of her mouth, and I'd have one too, if I'd just watched someone else treat a customer properly without any intention of trying to sell them anything.

The escalators in the store zigged and zagged and slowly carried us all towards the sky. You could look down to where you had once walked, and stare at the tops of everyone's heads. As they drifted further away they became a kaleidoscope. Patterns of people, constantly changing, but no matter how much they moved and shuffled, and tried to rearrange themselves, they would forever remain just the same; small beads of existence. I was only after the toilet, but department stores never like to make it easy for you, so I thought I'd start from the top and work my way down.

The higher up you go in a shop, the more silent it becomes. The chaos of the beauty hall fell into a distant memory as we climbed, and when I reached the very top floor, it was strangely empty. The advisors were different, too. They weren't even called advisors up there. They were called 'associates'. There was no smiling Natalie, either. Not even any women with sharp shoulders. People floated around in navy blazers or cream trouser suits, and with the best will in the world, it was difficult to decide if they were customers or staff. You had to search for the little brass badge if you wanted to be certain. They watched me from a distance, with sharp eyes, as if customers only made a nuisance of themselves by cluttering up the place.

Everywhere I looked there were handbags. Handbags of such consequence, each one had a shelf all of its own, and a little spotlight to emphasise how important it was to take the time to enjoy it properly. When you studied them more closely, though, you soon discovered that the handbags were all chained into position. They even had padlocks. Perhaps the people in the navy blazers and the cream trouser suits were so fond of their handbags, and so unhappy to see any of them leave, they liked to make it as difficult as possible for you to actually buy one. I was peering around the back of a bright purple clutch when one of the associates gave me such side-eye, I decided to move on to shoes and belts where it might all be a little more relaxed.

Even there, it still wasn't what I was used to. Where I usually bought my shoes, the pairs were all arranged on racks in order of size and there was a little machine in the corner to measure you up. But here, there wasn't a rack anywhere to be seen. Instead, the shoes were displayed on small platforms. Straps ribboned across marble tabletops and six-inch heels balanced themselves on blocks of wood. There was a little plaque by each one as well, to tell you who'd created it, like it was a small sculpture. I would have examined some of them a bit more closely, just out of curiosity, but even though there were no signs telling you not to touch, there wasn't anything about the place that seemed to encourage picking things up. Perhaps you were supposed to know you wanted something just by staring at it for a while. There wasn't even a measuring machine up there. If there had been, I'd have stuck my foot in it, because I'm a size nine, and Mother always says you have a propensity to spread after forty.

In the end, I took the escalator back down a floor to see if I had more luck with finding any facilities there, and as it dropped me off in lingerie and nightwear I caught a glimpse of myself in a mirror on one of the displays. I looked the least like me I'd ever looked in my life. It wasn't just the lipstick and the eyeshadow. It wasn't just the way Natalie had arched my brow and dusted colour across my cheekbones. It was the way I stood. The way my shoulders had relaxed and my back had become straight. I also realised I hadn't bumped into anything, or knocked anything over, the whole time I'd been walking around. I always crashed into something, mainly because there's so much of me. I usually dropped my handbag, or spilled something down myself, or tripped up over my own feet. I hadn't done any of those things because – although there was still the same amount of me walking around – it felt as though it deserved to be there. More than anything, though, it was the way my head lifted up, but perhaps it's so much easier to look up when your face feels like it has something worth looking up for.

I could see a sign for the toilets right on the other side of the shop floor, next to a café, and I made my way over, brushing past lace and silk, garments that had long since left behind my own definition of underwear. It was then that I spotted them. A display of dressing gowns. Just like the ones in Rebecca Finch's brochure. There was no lace on them. No quilting. No powder blue ribbon around the neck. They were white and clean, and raised up on a little stage. A small altar. I stared. They weren't hanging on mannequins like in the shops I usually went to, they were hung over pieces of wire. Ghost people, inviting you to step into their clothes and live the rest of your life bathed in soft white light and one hundred per cent cotton.

Because I'd stopped, a shop assistant emerged at my left elbow. They have it down to a fine art. Any hesitation. Any slight deviation from your path, and up they pop, ready to whisper in your ear. This one had had a slick ponytail, which made her head look like polished mahogany, and the ponytail was so high it left her eyes in a constant state of surprise. She looked at the shiny yellow bag Natalie had given me, and the coppery eyes Natalie had also given me, and she smiled and said, 'Would madame like to try?'

It could have been the soft white light or the smell of comfort. Or it might have been because my head had found a reason to be lifted up, but I heard a voice saying yes please, and then I realised that the voice I had heard was mine.

The high ponytail showed me to a cubicle. I say cubicle, but it was at least twice the size of our back bedroom. It had a giant mirror with swirls of gold all around the edges and lighting that made it appear as though you had turned into someone else entirely. There was a small shelf with tissues and hand cream, because it was so comfortable I should imagine that once people had stepped inside, they might want to loiter around for a while and moisturise their hands. The dressing gown hung on its peg, waiting for me to try it on. Waiting to see what it felt like to be someone else.

'Madame?' said the woman, and relieved me of my anorak.

The dressing gown was taken from its peg and slid onto me, and I felt all sorts of things disappear. The reflection of blue quilting etched into the garden shed. Terry, twenty miles away, parked in front of a television. Mother whispering in my ear about none of us getting any younger. The body of a girl, left in a field, and all of its nineteen years flashing by in a second. Everything was hurried away by the weight of something uncalled-for resting on my shoulders and the relief of pockets so deep, I could have buried my hands in there and lost them both forevermore.

'Madame!' said the woman and her hands clasped together in solidarity.

I pulled the belt a little tighter, and gave myself a small hug.

'It's beautiful,' I said. 'It's the most beautiful thing I've ever seen.'

'It was *made* for madame,' said the woman. 'It was *meant* to be.'

I stared into the mirror.

Perhaps it was.

Perhaps some things were, after all.

'How much is it?' I whispered, because there are some things in life that can only be whispered.

She whispered back a number.

It was almost a week's wages.

The pockets felt deeper, and the cotton felt softer, and somewhere within the fabric of that dressing gown, I felt the pull of a thing I didn't even recognise.

'Does madame have a store card?' said the whisper.

I shook my head.

'If madame takes out a store card today, there will be ten per cent off!'

It was presented as a battle cry. A *fait accompli*. The hands clasped together again in joyful union.

It was strange because all of a sudden, ten per cent of a week's wages seemed much more money than an entire week's wages, and some things were worth holding on to. I don't mean holding on to the belt around my waist or holding on to the heaviness that rested on my shoulders, but holding on to the feeling that I was a person who was worth a week's wages. Because if you weren't worth a week of your own wages, were you really worth anything at all? Plus, when I stayed over at Rebecca's – which I was bound to at some point – I'd need something suitable for my overnight bag.

'Okay,' I said. 'I'll take it.'

And a sick excitement found its way deep into my stomach, and I found the discomfort strangely enjoyable.

The heavy, glossy bag I was given was much heavier and glossier than Natalie's. The dressing gown wasn't just put inside all by itself, it first had to be ribboned and bowed, and then buried within a deep coffin lined with tissue paper. I signed all sorts of forms that meant I was allowed to take it away. I ticked boxes and circled statements and agreed to all the terms and conditions, without really knowing what the term of my condition was.

'The card will be posted to your home address!' said the

woman, and she handed me my ten-per-cent-off life, all wrapped up in yellow, and smiled at me and walked away. I wandered around the little stands for a while, holding on to my new dressing gown, because I was worried that the minute I left, the feeling in my stomach would disappear and I'd never be able to find it again. I passed the high ponytail woman once more, by chance, right next to a row of silk pyjamas, but she looked straight through me as if we'd never met, and we had become strangers again.

My wanderings took me from nightwear into kitchen appliances, objects which didn't really look like useful appliances at all, more suggestions of what you think a kitchen should look like until you have one of your own. Primary-coloured and whistle-clean; devoid of any used teabags or scraped plates. Kitchen appliances melted into rugs and cushions, an expanse of embroidery and padding to soften the edges of your unhappy life. I wandered back and forth, holding on to the feeling, enjoying the yellow weight of my carrier bag, until I found myself standing in front of a row of coats. They were black and shiny, like dustbin liners, and they had giant collars and giant cuffs, and I wondered how they could ever be practical, because you'd have to devote all of your energy into fighting with your outerwear in order to get anything done.

'Madame!'

Another voice. This time it was a man's. He had the same slicked-back ponytail as the woman, and I wondered for a second whether the store had a secret basement where they manufactured shop assistants with shiny, mahogany heads and an ability to make you immediately lose the power of speech and agree to absolutely anything they wanted, because before I knew it he had buttoned me into one of the bin-liner coats and was telling me about all the things in life that were meant to be.

'Madame looks fab-u-lous!' he said and he gave that little fingertip kiss people do when they talk about food.

I searched for my reflection and he gestured to the far end of the shop floor, where a row of mirrors lay in wait, eager to introduce people to their meant-to-be selves. I had no intention of buying a coat – I had plenty of coats at home because the charity shop had an endless supply – but there was no harm in taking another peek at a parallel universe, if by chance you were offered an opportunity. I was making my way over there, squeezing through rows of unlikely outfits, when I heard someone say my name.

'Linda?'

It wasn't the usual way of saying my name, it was more of an exclamation of surprise. A shout of unlikeliness. I turned and Ingrid was standing three feet away with her little cat eyes, tilting her head to one side and allowing her mouth to hang open in a very unattractive fashion.

'Linda,' she said again.

She was with another woman, who had exactly the same hairstyle and exactly the same tilt of the head.

Ingrid looked at the yellow bag and my new and improved face.

'Linda,' she said for a third time. Perhaps if she said it

enough, she'd be able to reassure herself it really was me. 'What are you doing here?'

I looked around at the landscape. The unlikely outfits and the army of mahogany heads.

'A fishing trip?' I said.

Ingrid and her friend laughed in exactly the same way, as if they'd been practising it for many years together behind closed doors. I joined in because Mother always says I'm the kind of person who manages to be funny by mistake, and sometimes, it takes much less energy to go along with something than it does to fight it.

'Linda, you are funny,' Ingrid said. 'Stephanie and I were just on our way to soft furnishings.' She looked at the black bin liner. 'I like your coat.'

'Do you?' I studied her face, because there have been a lot of times before when people have said things and I've believed them and then I found out it was a trick all along, but this didn't seem to be one of them.

'Thank you.' I reached down and tucked the price tag into one of the sleeves.

'I didn't realise you were . . . so up to date, working where you do. I mean, no offence. But that's how it is, isn't it?'

'That's how it is,' said Stephanie.

'And your make-up looks fabulous.'

'It looks fabulous,' said Stephanie.

It must be nice having someone following you around all day, providing an echo. It must give you endless reassurance about everything you say.

'We need to do coffee,' said Ingrid, although she seemed to be addressing the coat more than me, to be honest. 'Have a proper catch-up!'

'That's great, because I'm free now as it happens!' I said, but they'd both turned away and were making their way down a corridor of trench coats. They looked over their shoulders, but I don't think they could have heard me because neither of them said anything back.

'I could meet you in the café in a bit,' I shouted, but they were too far away. The only person who did hear me was the man with the mahogany ponytail, who was making a path towards me, and who had quickened his pace quite considerably when I started shouting.

'Madame?' he said and gestured to the coat.

I didn't look at him. I watched Ingrid instead, walking away from me. Stopping to look at something on a rail. Laughing with her best friend Stephanie.

'I'll take it,' I said.

I stared at the yellow bags all the way home. I didn't take my eyes off them. They sat next to me on the bus. They took up a whole seat all by themselves, but I didn't move them, not even when a woman got on at Dewsbury and gave us all a stern look.

For once, Malcolm wasn't loitering around his front gate and I managed to walk up the road without anyone giving me a second glance. I shut the door as gently as I could and took my shoes off in the hall, but it all turned out to be completely unnecessary because Terry was still slouched in front of the television screen. I could see him through a crack in the door. His chin was on a certain path down to his chest and I knew for a fact he'd dozed off because the horse racing had come on and he doesn't hold with horse racing. Says it's cruel. It's a pity he doesn't feel the same way about the fish he catches, but it's strange how someone can have feelings towards one creature and not towards another.

When I got to the top of the stairs, I opened and closed the bedroom door as gently as possible and looked around the room. I'd never really needed a hiding place before, because my life has never had anything in it worth hiding, and Terry and I aren't big on Christmas presents. I needed to keep quiet about this, though, because there'd only be questions if he caught sight of everything I'd bought. In the end I put them behind my wedding dress and Terry's funeral suit, which hung together in a strange unison, right at the far end of the wardrobe. I kept everything in the yellow bags, because it all seemed to belong together somehow and anyway, they were too nice to throw out.

If someone died in the near future, I'd just have to look for another hiding place.

NOW

When I was little, I caught chickenpox.

It was all Mother's engineering. She sent me to play next door with a little boy who was covered in it, hoping I'd get covered in it too, and it worked. A couple of weeks later, they began to appear. Furious little spots all over my body, red and unhappy, demanding to be scratched. Mother was delighted. I was, too, once I realised it meant I'd have to stay off school.

For once, I had something to show for myself. My dad always believed everything I told him, but usually, when I felt so ill I needed to be kept at home, I would have to persuade Mother into believing me. A headache or a stomach ache needed to be elaborated upon and given its own witness statement. With chickenpox, all I had to do was lift my vest and show off my tummy, and she didn't put up even a small argument.

It's a little like that here, I suppose. No one has anything to show for themselves. No angry spots, no calamine lotion; everyone wears their own clothes and no one has to lie in bed all day, unless of course the mood takes them. Perhaps if they did, it would be a lot easier for everyone else involved because people are so much more afraid of the things they can't see. That's why visiting hours have become such a problem. Why I always end up sitting here on my own. People are afraid. Ashamed. There are plenty who don't want to visit and many more who don't want to be visited. Perhaps they think it's like chickenpox, and if we all sit in the same room for any length of time, two weeks later they'll be covered in it as well.

It would solve a lot of awkwardness if we all knew where we were. The other day, a man came into the day room. Quite rough clothes. Looked a little dishevelled.

'You're new!' I tried to sound friendly because it doesn't cost anything to be pleasant. Some people are quite anxious when they first get here and I know the staff rely on me to put people at their ease. 'I haven't seen you before!' I said.

He said yes, yes, he was new. Hadn't been here very long at all, apparently. His name was John. Married with two children. Just moved into one of those houses that overlook the bypass, because it's amazing what information people give you when they feel comfortable and you keep asking questions. We had a nice little chat about the weather and I was just about to ask him which doctor he was under, when he walked over to the broken radiator on the other side of the room, took some tools out of his bag and started fixing it. You could have knocked me down with a feather.

22

They provide a public service.

That's what Rebecca told me when I asked what she and Jolyon did for a living. Rebecca had rung me, just as she promised. I was at work when she called, and I was so shocked, I had to dive behind gentlemen's overcoats and catch my breath. People often don't, you see. Keep their promises, I mean. I have a growing list of people's promises in my head still waiting to be kept. Some of them have been there for years. But Rebecca had kept hers, and now we were sitting in Jolyon's front room again.

'A public service? Like libraries?' I said. 'Or fast-food outlets?'

'Absolutely like that!' Rebecca said. 'We supply whatever people need and we do it as cheaply as possible. There are far too many big companies charging far too much money for things – so we bypass them!'

'You don't really make any profit, then?' I said.

'Hardly any at all!' Rebecca smiled, and it was one of those smiles that stay on your face for ages and don't really want to leave.

'So you're like a charity?' I said.

'Exactly like a charity,' said the smile.

Rebecca hesitated for a moment and put her face closer to mine. 'Are you wearing eyeshadow, Linda?' she said. 'Sparkly eyeshadow?'

I'd spent ages messing around with the samples Natalie had given me and I'd been waiting for Rebecca to notice. 'I am!' I said. 'It's just like yours – do you like it?'

She must have loved it, because she was obviously lost for words, and sat back in her seat and stayed quiet for a minute.

'We're in the same line of business then, aren't we?' I said. 'When you think about it.'

'Oh, we *are*, Linda,' she said.

'We're like Robin Hood!' Jolyon kicked open the door with his foot and brought the tea in on a tray with a plate of Jaffa Cakes, because I'd told him they were my favourite and Jolyon was obviously the kind of person who listened to what you said. Not like Terry.

'Thank you for the Jaffa Cakes, Jolyon,' I said and I smiled at him and he smiled right back.

I was waiting for one of them to mention the business proposition, but neither of them did. They just kept looking at each other every time I spoke. I suppose I had to pass some kind of test first, like a job interview.

'Anyway, as I was saying.' Rebecca must have been in a good mood that day, because she was trying very hard not to laugh. 'We act as a . . . middle-man . . . between the consumer and big companies.'

'And banks.' Jolyon sat on the settee and put his feet on the coffee table. He was still wearing his shoes. It's something Terry liked to do as well, but no one's perfect and these habits are easily got rid of, given the right encouragement.

'Banks?' I said.

'Oh, yes.' Jolyon smiled again and I suddenly found it quite easy to forget about his feet. 'Banks are charging their customers extortionate amounts in fees and we've found . . .'

'Loopholes,' said Rebecca.

'Yes,' he said. 'Loopholes that mean we can recoup some of that and distribute it more fairly.'

'How wonderful,' I said. 'Anything else?'

'Sometimes we acquire large amounts of a product, which means we can deliver them to our customers at a much cheaper rate,' Rebecca said. 'And we do fun things as well.'

'Oh good, what kind of fun things?' I took another Jaffa Cake.

'We have blind auctions,' said Jolyon. 'Where people bid on a mystery box. We raise quite a bit of money through that.'

'For charity,' said Rebecca.

'For charity,' repeated Jolyon.

'How exciting,' I said. 'What's in the box?'

245

'That's the mystery, Linda!' said Jolyon, and he laughed quite a bit.

I finished all the Jaffa Cakes by myself. I felt quite bad about it, because when Rebecca and Jolyon went into the kitchen to clear away, I heard Rebecca say, 'Thanks for the Jaffa Cakes, Jolyon,' in a squeaky voice.

If I'd known she liked them too, I would have saved her one.

23

The first I heard of it was on the lunchtime news.

It was midweek, which meant I was over at Mother's. She always has the television on in the background, or sometimes in the foreground, depending on how interesting she finds your conversation. Talking to her often feels as though you're in a competition with someone far more exciting in the corner of the room and you're constantly having to up your game to stop her ears wandering off.

They were in the middle of a piece about farming and Mother and I were staring at a herd of cows somewhere in Shropshire, when the picture unexpectedly cut back to the newsreader. The newsreader clearly found it unexpected as well, because he pressed a finger to his earpiece and fumbled around with his words for a minute, and then he announced they had some breaking news on the Hexford Strangler.

'Breaking news!' my mother said, and she reached for her jotter and sat forward a good few inches.

I squinted at the screen. The picture had changed again to something I recognised, but my mind couldn't catch up with my eyes.

'Isn't that your avenue?' Mother said, because her mind always caught up much more quickly than mine.

It was.

I could see the tall hedge and the little brick wall near the post box, and the gap where Malcolm always put his wheelie bin, and behind it there was Malcolm loitering on his doorstep and staring.

'An ordinary avenue in suburbia . . .'

the reporter said and he appeared at the edge of the picture, clutching a giant fluffy microphone. It was the same man they'd put on the riverbank a couple of weeks earlier and he looked like he hadn't even been allowed home for a change of clothes and a hot meal.

'which last night became anything but ordinary for these two women . . .'

The cameraman panned across, away from Malcolm who was craning his neck and doing his level best to stay in shot.

Two women stood in front of a garden gate. They were both wearing jeans and T-shirts, not dressed for the weather at all, and the camera was so close you could see goose-bumps travelling across the tops of their arms. The wind lifted the sleeves of the T-shirts and pushed their hair across their faces, and they held on to each other as though they were both afraid of being blown away. They were as pale as paper. I didn't know one of them, but the other—

'I'm sure I've seen her before somewhere,' Mother piped up. 'Isn't she one of your neighbours?'

She was.

It was Ingrid.

She wasn't wearing any make-up, though. No catty eyes. No pink lipstick. Her face was lost and tear-stained, and she was wearing the same T-shirt as the last time I'd seen her. I knew straight away it was Ingrid as soon as she started speaking.

'We were running out of milk,' she said, 'and I just nipped out to the twenty-four-hour garage. It was late. My husband said he'd go, but he was full of cold and I told him not to be silly. I said I'd stick to the main road – it's only a few minutes away.'

The other woman squeezed Ingrid's shoulder and nodded and they both looked at each other.

'What happened next, Ingrid?' The reporter pushed the microphone towards her.

'I bought a few things and then I decided to take the shortcut back home.' Her voice began to waver and the squeeze on her shoulder tightened. 'I shouldn't have, but you don't think, do you? You don't think anything will happen to you.'

'And you were about halfway down the alleyway when the attack took place?' the reporter said.

Ingrid nodded. 'I didn't hear anything. No footsteps. All of a sudden there was an arm around my neck and someone

twisting my scarf. I couldn't breathe, let alone shout. I tried
to push him off, but he was too strong.'

The reporter pointed his microphone at the other
woman. 'And that's where you come in, Tiffany?'

Tiffany. What kind of a name was Tiffany?

The other woman nodded. 'It was about eleven thirty.
I'm a barmaid and I was walking home from work. I'd just
turned into the alleyway.'

'And what did you see?' said the reporter.

'It was dark, there's no lighting down there, but I could
make out two figures in the distance and I knew straight
away there was something wrong. You could tell.'

'So what did you do?'

'I shouted. As loud as I could. I can't even remember what
I shouted, I just knew I had to make a lot of noise, and it
worked. The man ran off towards the park. Then I hurried over
to Ingrid and helped her up. Her shopping was everywhere.'

'It was,' Ingrid said. 'The milk carton had come open.
The biscuits I'd bought as a treat were all smashed.'

'Do either of you remember anything about the attacker?'
said the reporter.

Both women shook their heads.

'Taller than me, and very strong,' said Ingrid, who was
probably all of eight stone wet through. 'But he was behind
me so I couldn't see his face.'

'There wasn't enough light,' said Tiffany. 'Especially when
someone's wearing dark clothes – maybe even a ski mask
– and he disappeared as soon as I shouted.'

'That was very brave,' said the reporter.

'It was instinct,' Tiffany said. 'Anyone would have done the same.'

'Anyone wouldn't.' Ingrid wiped her face with the back of her hand.

'And you two don't know each other?' said the reporter.

'No,' said Ingrid. 'But we do now because Tiffany saved my life. We'll be friends forever.'

Ingrid hugged Tiffany and Tiffany hugged Ingrid, new best friends, and the camera zoomed in a little bit closer.

'And it's back to you, Dermott,' said the reporter.

Mother turned down the volume. 'Well,' she said.

We sat in the silence for a moment.

'It's a pity Terry wasn't around; he would've chased that attacker and pinned him down until the police got there,' she said.

I picked at the material on the arm of the chair.

Mother turned the television off. 'What's the matter, Linda?'

I looked at her and looked back at the arm of the chair. 'I use that alleyway most days,' I said. 'I'm always walking down there. That could have been me.'

'Linda!' She reached over and put her hand on mine. 'You mustn't dwell on those kinds of thoughts. Thank heavens you weren't the one who was attacked.'

'I don't mean that.' I looked back up at her. 'I mean I could have been the one who saved her.'

* * *

'The place is still crawling with reporters and television crews. I've had to draw the curtains.'

I rang Terry a few hours later, thinking he might offer to pick me up. I didn't fancy getting the bus, listening to people talking about nothing but Ingrid and Tiffany. They might even realise I lived on the same avenue and start asking me what I thought and I wasn't sure what I might be tempted to say. Their names joined up together really well, *IngridandTiffany*. It sounded like they were meant to be friends all along.

'I'd stay over at your mother's if I were you,' Terry said. 'No point coming back to this chaos. Besides, you don't want some reporter sticking a camera in your face again after all these years.'

'We could get past them in the van, though, couldn't we?' I said. 'No one would take any notice of us.'

He said it wasn't worth it. He said he wasn't sure he could even get the van off the drive with all the commotion.

'You're better off staying put,' he said.

I went back into the front room where Mother had been listening to the whole conversation through the dividing wall with the television on mute.

'I'll go and air the bed in the guest room,' she said.

The mug of cocoa grew cold on the bedside table.

I didn't know why she'd made it for me, because I never drank it even when I lived at home, but even when Mother seemed to do things for other people, she was only ever really doing it for herself. I lay in the bed, under a shiny quilted eiderdown, and stared at half-familiar shadows. There was a vast oak wardrobe throwing darkness across the whole room and a dresser with a strange triple mirror that took what it saw and gave it back to you threefold in a way you always struggled to recognise. Furniture that had travelled with us from Wales, along with the guilt and the shame. Although Mother got rid of a lot of our things. One minute she was lying in a dark room, refusing to even look the world in the eye, the next she was putting everything she could carry on the front lawn with a sign telling people to help themselves. And they did. I watched them from my bedroom window. Word got around and the whole village seemed to turn up to choose a souvenir of our downfall. Even the families of the girls who'd accused my dad. Some of them I was glad to see go – the ugly pot dogs from the mantelpiece, the loud fruit bowl my mother kept on the dresser in the kitchen. Someone even wanted the nasty painting of daffodils that used to hang in the hall, although I couldn't for the life of me see why. It was the family of the first girl that spoke up, which seemed appropriate in a way, because the nastiest person in the village ended up with the nastiest item of all, and after that I studied all the people as they wandered around the garden, and tried to second-guess which piece of our life they would choose to take home with them.

Everything went in the end and we just brought the big furniture with us when we moved. Except Dad's piano, of course, which was the first thing to disappear. I came home from school one day and it had gone. Although sometimes I thought I could still hear it. Students in the back room practising their scales and arpeggios. Tiny, unsure notes climbing up the stairs. Even though Dad had gone and even though his piano had gone, it seemed like the crotchets and quavers still wandered in the air and refused to leave. I wouldn't go in the room to check, though. I wouldn't push the door open. Because I had done that once before and I had seen something I should not have seen, and I would never make that mistake again. He was just comforting her. I told that to the police. But they twist what you say, and before you know it, your words have turned into something else.

Mother made sure we left everything else behind us, but perhaps the mistakes we'd made and the bad memories they left still lived inside the brass-handled drawers of the dressing table and lay quiet on the deep shelves in the wardrobe. Perhaps they hung in the creases of tired curtains and crept along the seams of a shiny eiderdown, and perhaps we would never be free of them unless we completely unfastened ourselves from the past, and Mother would never do that. The past was her motherland.

We weren't in Wales any more. This was a different room and a different life, but lying there in the darkness, it felt as though I had crossed from one into the other. If I listened hard, I could hear the sound of the woods at the back of the house. The shout of men's voices moving through the trees. Mother calling up the stairs and telling me not to come down again. An iron full of steam on a damp funeral dress and the smell of rain on gravel. I could feel the itch of a prayer cushion on my knees. I could hear the vicar talking about an unpardonable sin and yet we all still bowed our heads and asked for my dad to be forgiven.

The past was so loud, I switched on the bedside light and tried to make it quiet again. The darkness of the oak dresser disappeared, and the only shadow was my own, waiting for me on the far wall. I moved my head and lifted my arms, just to check, and I watched them move with me. When I was little, my dad used to make shadows. He would lace his fingers together and rabbits would appear. The rabbits would turn into camels and the camels into elephants, then the elephants became butterflies and they flew away and disappeared behind the big oak wardrobe.

'What is it now? What is it now?' I'd shout, each time he moved his hands.

He would smile at me. 'Things are however you want to see them,' he'd say. 'They can be whatever you want them to be.'

My dad was the only piece of the past Mother didn't bring with us from Wales. She made sure his memory stayed there, and we packed our bags and left without him. He was cut away, leaving nice clean margins. Disappeared.

But you can't take a pair of scissors to one thing and leave the rest undamaged.

It's impossible.

24

They called a meeting for the following week. When I say 'they', I mean Malcolm.

He knocked on the door the following day in the middle of the evening news.

'You missed all the action yesterday, Linda,' he said, when he'd run through all the whys and wherefores of where everyone had to assemble the following week. 'Quite the commotion, it was.'

Terry shouted, 'Who is it, Lind?' from the front room, and so I pulled the door closed behind me and the sound of ITV disappeared back into the house. I stood on the front step in my old dressing gown, because I couldn't risk showing off the new one and Terry asking how it came to be in my possession. It still sat in its yellow bag at the back of the wardrobe. The cool evening air made me pull my old dressing gown a little tighter around my shoulders. Malcolm, padded into his parka, didn't seem to notice.

'I thought it best to stay at my mother's overnight, what with reporters swarming all over the street.'

'They were gone by mid-afternoon,' he said. 'Once Ingrid had given them an interview, they were satisfied and off they went.'

'Are you sure?' I said.

'Oh yes, quite sure. I monitor every movement on this street these days. I'd got extra teabags in, but everybody had gone before I'd boiled the kettle. Complete waste of time.'

'I must go over to Ingrid's,' I said. 'Check she's okay. She'll be wondering where I am.'

'Oh, I wouldn't disturb them.'

'Them?'

'Ingrid and Tiffany. She's in there with her now. Inseparable, they are, since it happened.' Malcolm smiled and looked over at Ingrid's house. 'Understandable, really. If the police aren't helping us, we need to look to each other for support.'

'We do?'

'We do.' He turned back. 'Which is why we need an urgent community meeting.'

'What will that achieve?' I said. 'If the police can't catch him, what chance have we got?'

Malcolm waved his hand at the deserted road, where abandoned pavements met driveways crowded with cars, where privet hedges and block paving marked out the edges of everyone's lives. The kind of road where people only bothered to mow their own grass verge.

'We need to be vigilant,' he said. 'There's a killer out there. He could be watching us right now, even at this very moment. Look at Ingrid.'

I stared beyond Malcolm and into the street. The only movement was the flicker of television screens behind silent glass.

'You think it's someone on this road?' I said.

Malcolm tutted. 'Well of course not. Not on *this* road. Cavendish Avenue is far too upmarket. You wouldn't get a killer living in a place like this.'

I waited.

'The other side of the estate, though,' he whispered, 'is a different story.'

'How do you mean?'

'Polesworth Close, Caledonian Way, Barlow View.' He stretched the names and his neck stretched along with them, pulling out their significance. 'They want to concentrate their efforts around there.'

'Do you think so?' I said.

'Have you seen the state of those places? Kiddies' bikes in the middle of the road. Dogs barking. Chippings everywhere – no one sweeps their chippings up, Linda. It's a disgrace.'

'So who's your money on, then?' I said.

'It's not the Grand National.'

I waited again.

'Well, if you're pressing me and if I must be pressed.'

Malcolm checked beyond his shoulder again. 'I think they could do worse than look at Harry Slater.'

'Hard Harry?"

Malcolm nodded. 'Nasty piece of work.'

'Weren't you at school with him?' I said.

'Or Frank Taylor.'

'Tricky Taylor? Weren't you at school with him as well?'

'That's beside the point, Linda.' The whites of Malcolm's eyes had gone very shiny and little strings of saliva gathered together in the corners of his mouth. 'Always up to no good, the pair of them, making other people's lives a misery. I've a good mind to go down to that Portakabin and tell the police all about it.'

You'll have to wait your turn, I thought, because there'll be people camped outside with thermos flasks and space blankets if this goes on much longer, like they do for Wimbledon tickets. I was going to mention it, but he was halfway down the drive before I had a chance.

'Tuesday, seven o'clock sharp,' he said.

I watched him march across the road, heading for number fourteen.

'And for the love of God, please don't bring your mother,' he shouted.

Mother took her knitting.

Malcolm queried her on the door, of course — 'You're not even from the estate, Mrs Sykes, you live four miles away' — but she had her coat off before he'd even finished

259

his sentence. She gave him her speech about murderers and public transport, and then she said she had a vested interest because of me, so he had to let her sit in the corner with a tonic water.

We had the meeting at the local hall, mainly because it's the only place that could fit us all in. It's called the Empire Ballroom, even though there isn't much of an empire left, and it has a lot less to do with ruling the waves now, and more to do with tae kwon do classes and Slimming World. Although that's still an empire of sorts, I suppose. Malcolm had set up a trestle table on the stage. He even had a small gavel, and he tested it out a few times as we were all finding our seats, which confused everybody and made it difficult to tell when he really meant it.

'I wonder where he got that from,' said Mother, in between a knit and a purl. 'They don't sell those in John Lewis.' But Malcolm is the sort of person who is always prepared for any occasion, even one requiring a gavel.

Terry went to get a pint of lager and never bothered to come back. He blended into a group of men at the bar, hunched denim jackets, tired jeans, work boots resting on the foot rail, like a line of soldiers. I watched them from where I sat and played spot the difference, and I thought how easy it would be to take the wrong one home, if you happened to not be concentrating properly.

Malcolm banged his gavel. It made not a blind bit of difference. The volume of voices got louder, if anything. People weren't talking about the killings, either, they were talking about the roadworks on the high street and the price of petrol, and whether they'd get home in time for *Silent Witness*. Tiny threads of normality. Because when something extraordinary happens, if you concentrate on the ordinary things instead, it stops you from having to look at it all too closely.

'Now then, now then!' Malcolm called out from the front. His shouting blended in with the gang of kids in the foyer, who were running in and out from the car park and knocking into a macramé display and an A-board advertising guitar lessons.

'Come along now.' Malcolm banged his gavel with a bit more conviction, and slowly the voices began to disappear, one by one, until we all stared back at him in silence. Malcolm did one of those coughs you invent to use up all the space, because now he had our attention, he didn't seem to know what to do with it.

In the end, he started it off with a minute's remembrance for the three girls, which everyone respected, thank goodness, because you always worry, don't you? Even the kids piped down. I looked around during that minute, because I never know what to do with my eyes. Most people were staring at their feet. Some were looking across to the windows and out into the car park. I wondered if anyone knew them personally, these girls. Probably not the first one, because she was a student. No family nearby, according to the police. The second and third ones, though, someone might. They weren't from this estate, but it's only when you walk from room to room that you realise what a small place we live in, how very few steps there are from one person to the next. I didn't see any tears, though. No one seemed emotional. When the minute was up, everyone just looked relieved and we smiled at each other in that strange, congratulatory way, because we had all managed to keep our mouths shut for a whole sixty bloody seconds.

'Now then,' Malcolm said again, and he looked down at his notes. 'The first thing I want to do is pass on the reassurance that the police are doing everything they can to apprehend this individual—'

'That's copper talk.' Mother's needles didn't stop clicking, even when she spoke. 'That's a direct quote.'

'—and we are all to remain calm and leave the investigation of this matter to them.'

'Where are they, then?' someone shouted from the back. 'Why aren't the police here?'

Malcolm looked across the room. One of the Empire's bulbs lit up his whole forehead and he squinted into his audience. 'I didn't invite them,' he said. 'I thought we could speak more freely if they weren't present.'

'Well, he got something right at least,' Mother said.

I would have tried to shut her up, but it was like halting the tide.

'The most important thing, the thing we need to consider, the thing we can have some control over, is how we can all stay safe.' Malcolm paused and we all paused back. 'We can learn a lot from last week's near miss and how we all need to be Good Samaritans.'

A few arms folded. A young woman in the front row hushed a small child on her knee and the old woman opposite us put down her bottle of stout and stared at the stage.

'How you propose we do that, Malcolm?' she said. 'When two young girls couldn't manage it?'

Malcolm coughed again and shuffled his notes.

'The first thing I'd suggest is that until this situation is resolved, women don't go out on their own.' He looked up again. 'Especially after dark.'

'Why just women?' one of the voices said. 'What about the elderly?'

'And the children,' my mother whispered, but no one heard her.

'The police believe young women are being targeted, even though there's no . . .' Malcolm petered out, like a small engine. 'No sign of . . .'

My mother tutted along with her needles. 'For heaven's sake, he's a grown man.'

'. . . there isn't . . . wasn't . . . the police don't believe there was a sexual motive to any of the crimes.' Malcolm found the steering wheel again. 'But it would be wise for us all to be vigilant. Whoever we are. We all need to watch out for each other.'

The room looked at itself, as though we were all seeing each other for the first time. There were families there, and generations unfolded along rows of chairs. Children played at the feet of their grandparents. Fathers and sons, mothers and daughters, shoulder to shoulder, living their mirrored lives. Everyone on a different leg of the same car journey. There were the newcomers, too. Outsiders, commuters, unfamiliar figures that stood at the edges, waiting to be included.

'It's also been suggested,' Malcolm continued, 'that we don't open our doors to strangers. Offer lifts to people we don't know. Accept lifts from someone we're unsure of. And so on.'

'And so on,' said the woman with the bottle of stout. 'None of those girls did that, though, did they?'

Malcolm stared into the spotlight, and a glaze of sweat covered his forehead.

'We're not sure what they did,' he said. 'The police think they were killed where they crossed paths with their murderer and their bodies left for someone to find. We just know that they were strangled.'

My hand went to my throat. It couldn't help itself.

'And?' said the woman.

'And the killer probably has local knowledge. From where the bodies were discovered, the police think he might know the area quite well.'

'So, Malcolm, what does that tell you?' The woman was old. Probably the oldest person in the room. The anatomy of her life was drawn in the lines across her face and the shapes of the bones that pressed into her skin.

Malcolm remained silent. He shifted his weight from side to side.

The woman sighed. 'What it tells you, Malcolm, is that these women almost certainly knew their killer. They might have got in a car with them without a moment's hesitation, or invited them round for tea. They trusted them.'

'Probably so,' Malcolm said into his notes.

'So not opening our door to strangers isn't going to help, is it? Because this killer could be our milkman, our postman, our friend. The person we sit next to at work. The conversation we have on a bus. We shouldn't be wary of the people we don't know, we should be wary of the people that we do.'

No one spoke, least of all Malcolm. Even Terry and his friends turned and leaned back against the bar and I saw Terry put down a pint of lager and fold his arms.

'Who is that woman?' I whispered to Mother, who had abandoned her ribbing stitch and was as still as I'd ever seen her.

'I don't know,' she said. 'But she's got a point, hasn't she?'

Everyone else seemed to agree as well, because even though Malcolm stammered on from the stage about neighbourhood watching and not starting any witch hunts and trying to carry on as normal, no one was paying any attention to him. They were paying attention to each other instead. I could tell. Finding the small, unremarkable details. Searching for the weightless, the inconsequential that might one day find itself heavy with a consequence. An unopened packet of cigarettes. The thick brown leather of working boots. A brush of mud at the bottom of a pair of jeans. The notes in a margin that might, one day, become a headline. We drank them all in.

'Are there any questions?'

People pushed back their chairs and gathered up their children. If there were any questions, they would be asked later, quietly, at kitchen tables and around television sets, finding their answers amongst themselves. Even Malcolm finally folded his notes and reached for his coat.

'I've got a question!' someone shouted.

Malcolm returned his parka to the back of a chair. 'Yes?' he said, squinting into the spotlight. 'Go on then.'

'My question' – the voice came from somewhere in the far corner of the room, near the wall – 'is who do *you* think it was, Malcolm?'

Malcolm's throat struggled under a tight collar. 'What I think is immaterial,' he said. 'My thoughts are no more important than anyone else's.'

'Come on, Malc. Tell us who did it!' someone shouted, and laughter travelled across the room, as brittle as an egg.

Malcolm stared down, as though an answer to the question might be written somewhere in his folded notes. 'We all have our own ideas,' he said very quietly, without raising his head. 'That's not the point.'

'That's exactly the point,' the same voice said. Louder now. More insistent.

The laughter disappeared into nothing, and we all craned our necks to see who was speaking. Even Terry and a few of his mates unfastened themselves from the bar and moved forward, their pints waiting in unhurried hands.

The nothing grew.

'Well?' said the voice.

It was Harry Slater. I spotted him. Stood against the wall in his shirt sleeves. Arms folded. Bookended by his sons, who looked exactly like Harry, except life hadn't quite finished souring their faces yet.

Malcolm coughed again. 'I'm not going to be drawn. I'd rather not say.'

'Strange that,' Harry said. 'Because our Daryl here reckons you've been knocking on doors and saying it rather a lot. That's what you heard, isn't it, Daryl?'

One of the bookends raised his head a couple of inches to distinguish himself from his counterpart, and he nodded.

The glaze on Malcolm's forehead travelled across his face, pushing his glasses beyond the bridge of his nose and forcing him to remove them and find solace in the floor.

'I'm sure I don't know what you mean. I don't believe in idle chit-chat. Gossiping gets you nowhere,' he said.

'Ah, but that's where you're wrong, Malcolm.' Harry leaned forward and his sons leaned with him, as though they were all connected by invisible string. 'Gossiping is what's going to solve this case. Local knowledge. Hearsay. Insider information. As long as you're careful of who you gossip about' – he tapped the edge of his nose – 'gossiping is going to get us everywhere.'

* * *

We walked home through the estate.

'Well that was a bloody waste of time.' Terry was ahead of us, hands in pockets, some kind of purpose in his step.

It was barely after eight, yet it might as well have been midnight. The day had been abandoned, and the roads were left quiet and still. Even the teenagers, who usually circled in packs through the streets, spilling time and opportunity, even they were nowhere to be seen.

'No one feels safe. It's obvious.' Mother walked beside me. 'I was right to get Terry to drive me home. I could find myself on a train with him. He could even be the driver.'

I half listened to Mother embroider another of her stories about murderers on public transport, but I was really thinking about the press conference and what I'd seen, and where it might fit into the crossword. I studied the rows of houses we passed as we walked. They all looked very similar if you weren't paying attention, the same patterns of glass and bricks, thrown together in the 1970s. Each house a mirror of its neighbour. A folded page. It was the tiny details that made them unalike, though. One window of bright curtains in a home otherwise made out of beige, a flowerbed filled with weeds but no flowers. An abandoned toy. An empty dog kennel. Each house held a small story.

'Threw his body out of the train window – they found it on an embankment,' my mother said.

And all those small stories were kept in place by the

lines drawn around them, by the fences and the hedges, the gates and the walls.

'Couldn't get away, poor chap – like a sitting duck.'

We passed a long wooden fence, the timber boards so close together, not even a breath of air could slip through.

'And that's why they put corridors on trains,' she was saying. 'Because of that German tailor.'

'Right,' I said.

Another brick wall. Brick walls were very popular. Perhaps people enjoyed the symmetry. The idea of their lives being held in place by neat lines of cement.

'I know you're not listening, Linda. No one ever listens to me, I have it on good authority.'

I turned to her. 'Was this a film?'

She stopped walking, briefly, in order to devote all her energy into tutting and shaking her head. 'No, it was real. I watched a documentary on catch-up.' We began walking again. 'A Victorian man, murdered on a train, but in those days there was no corridor, no escape, you see? No way out.'

'No,' I said. 'No way out.'

A hedge so tall and so dense, it looked like a wall of ink.

'So after that, they started putting corridors in railway carriages,' she said, 'so people could escape.'

'Or get in,' I said.

'What?'

'The same corridor that allows people to escape also allows people to get in, doesn't it?'

She frowned.

'You can't have one without the other,' I said.

'No, I don't suppose you can. You're so melodramatic, Linda. Heaven knows where you get it from.'

Terry put her in the van as soon as we got back. I suppose I should have offered her a cup of tea before she went, but the thing is with Mother, you can only stomach so much of her in one go, a bit like a strong Cheddar, and my stomach was telling me it was full.

'You've had a drink, Terry,' she said when she fastened her seatbelt. 'Don't go throwing me about.'

'Only the one, Eunice,' he said. 'Only the one.'

I knew he'd had two. I didn't say anything, because with Mother, there's never any need to throw coals on the fire. She does that quite nicely on her own. I could have taken her back myself, of course, but I've always been a bit frightened of driving in the dark. My dad used to say that you learned fear. He said that no one is born afraid of anything, and we just collect all our anxieties as we move through life. He always made me feel as though I was bigger than the thing I was afraid of. *What are you so worried about, Linda?* he used to say. *Why do you always expect the worst to happen?* Not knowing that the very worst thing would eventually happen all by itself, and as it turned out it was not a thing any of us could ever have expected. Aside from the dark, though, I can't be doing with Terry's van. Filthy, it is. I only drive it when I have no other choice. So instead of taking Mother back, I sat at the kitchen table with a mug of tea.

I could hear the van's engine long after they'd left. I could imagine them winding their way through the estate, crossing the lights at the top of the high street and climbing the hill out of town. Mother running through all her theories, Terry gripping the steering wheel, collar up, wishing the miles away. Mother never used to talk as much when Dad was alive. These days she never shuts up, as though she needs to make up for his silence. With me and Terry, it's different. The house is much easier without him in it. It's not as though he makes much noise, if you don't count the television, and he really doesn't take up a great deal of space. It's just so much simpler when he's not there.

I was in bed by the time he got back. I listened to the van pull in on the drive as I lay there. It was so quiet, I could hear the snatch of a handbrake and the sound of his boots eating into the gravel. Footsteps on the stairs. Bathroom light going on and the shower running. When he came back into our bedroom, the darkness changed shades and I followed the outline of him stumbling around, trying to not make a noise.

'That took a long time,' I said.

The outline paused. I could hear his breathing, snatched and hurried, just like the handbrake.

'Bit of traffic.'

I listened into the silence beyond the window and felt the bed sink and the outside creep in under the duvet.

'Right,' I said. 'Right.'

NOW

Everything here is assessed for risk.

I know all about this, because I went into the office behind the glass to ask about leave, and I saw one of their long yellow forms. The person I was asking had to turn away to answer the telephone and so I managed to have a good read. There was a box to tick for everything. Risk of hurting someone, risk of hurting yourself, risk of self-neglect, risk of wandering off. Each of these risks had its own question, and within those questions were more questions, and answering them helped the person filling out the form to decide if a risk was worth taking or not.

'There is no such thing as a risk-free situation' said a sticker on the top of the form, and I couldn't decide if that was designed to be a comfort or a worry. Mother would have approved because she manages to pinpoint danger in most scenarios. Whatever you might be thinking of trying, she's very good at coming up with the most unlikely and calamitous outcome she can, to put you off ever thinking of it again.

When you've finished filling out the yellow form and you've answered all the questions and the questions within the questions, it presents you with a score, just like the quizzes in my magazines, and with that score in mind you are supposed to decide whether to go ahead with your risk or not. Whether to roll the dice. Whether to stick or twist.

I wish I'd had one of those forms when I married Terry.

The first time I met Terry was in a pub. I wasn't even supposed to be there. I was supposed to be partnering up Mother at a whist drive. Some people might call that fate, and I probably would have said the same thing at the time, but now I'm not so sure. I don't think fate has very much to do with any of it. You make your own fate at the end of the day, but if you pretend you're not really in charge of anything you do, it makes your mistakes feel as though they were all somebody else's fault.

'What did you think when you first saw me?' he says sometimes.

I tell him my heart skipped a beat. I tell him I was captivated. I tell him I didn't have eyes for anyone else. Those cut-out words you see in magazines, the lyrics from a record. Phrases scooped straight out of love songs and handed around to keep people occupied. He takes it all in. He nods and goes back to whatever he was doing at the

273

time, reading the newspaper or watching some silly quiz show on the television. I'm not sure if you're supposed to be completely honest with your own husband, but I've never really found it to be a necessity.

The truth of the matter is, I thought he was a bit loud. He stood at the end of the bar with a group of other men, enjoying the sound of his own voice, because Terry's the kind of person who can paint a whole room with his own opinion. He's still like it now. Especially if you get him onto certain subjects.

'The thing is, Linda . . .' he'll say. Like the policemen.

I just drift off.

He bought me a drink that night. Made a fuss. Nobody had ever really made a fuss of me before. Mother said to get to my age without all that stuff and nonsense was quite an achievement, especially under the circumstances, but it was nice, you know, for someone to notice. So I ignored the loudness and the opinions, and the way he picked at his back teeth every five minutes, and I went along with it. You never know when the next bus will come along, so it's best to go with the one that's right in front of you.

Mother seemed pleased when we got engaged. Relieved almost.

'Babychams all round!' she said, and gave one of those laughs that have nothing inside of them.

Small wedding. Nothing fancy. Not like it is these days when people have to take six weeks off just to plan it all. We got married on a Wednesday. Mother said having a midweek wedding was 'in vogue', but I think the real reason was because it meant the reception was half price. Most people went back to work afterwards. It was fine at the time, because I didn't really have any expectations. It's strange, because you only discover you have expectations long after something has gone, years later when you're woken one morning, by the sound of snoring and the weight of your own disappointment. When you leave your sleep and open your eyes, and face each day like an enemy. When you look at the body lying next to you, and you realise that's it. You've dropped your anchor. Here is the view for the rest of your life. It's only then you realise you did have had some of those expectations after all.

I try not to dwell on it, but there are times I just can't help myself. When I glance over at Terry laughing at some stupid joke on the telly. When I flick through Rebecca Finch's brochures and see all the people I could have been. When I look out of the bedroom window at the estate, at the endless rooftops, pinned to the landscape as far as you can see. Row after row of houses. All those lives reflecting straight back at mine. They look like a theatre audience, waiting for a performance to start.

'What are you staring at, Linda?' he shouts. 'Draw the curtains and come back to bed.'

'Nothing,' I say. 'I'm staring at nothing.'

25

I never usually bothered switching on my mobile telephone. Terry never rings it, of course, as he's fond of leaving notes instead, and so it lay at the bottom of my bag, gathering fluff and sweet wrappers, and waiting for an emergency. Since Rebecca had started calling me, though, I kept it on all the time. Even at night.

Sometimes, I took it out and stared at it, just to make sure it was working properly, and I'd wander about the house, lifting it up to the ceiling to get the biggest number of bars and working out where the best place would be to speak to her when it finally did ring. But for all my wandering around with the phone, when Rebecca did eventually call, I always seemed to be at work.

This time, I'd just finished rehanging all the cardigans on the knits and woollies rail when my phone started singing and jumping around in my jacket pocket. I didn't know what it was at first, but I ducked behind a large puffa jacket on the end of the ladies' coats and anoraks stand and pressed the green button.

'Linda! You're there!'

You couldn't mistake Rebecca's voice. It was light and sweet, like someone singing a beautiful song.

'Hello!' I said.

Whereas my voice sounded difficult and awkward, and I knew I was probably speaking a lot louder than I needed to, because Tamsin's head popped around the other end of the rail to check on me and I was forced into a crouch.

'Linda, are you free tomorrow?'

'Yes!' I said, even before the last syllable found its way to my ears. I wasn't free at all, in fact; I was supposed to be at work. Everyone took sick days, though. Where Terry worked, they even gave you an allowance, and if you didn't use them up you could glue them all together at the end of the year and spend a week in bed.

'I'm having a dinner party.' Rebecca's voice tumbled down the phone line. 'And I'd love it if you could come over?'

'You do look a bit pale, Linda.'

Tamsin put the back of her hand against my forehead.

'Perhaps you're running a temperature,' she said. 'Or sickening for something.'

'I feel *dreadful*,' I said.

I leaned against the till and tried to think how someone

who felt dreadful would behave, because for that moment the idea of it seemed to have escaped me, so I put my own hand to my head and closed my eyes very shut.

Nothing happened and so I opened one of them again to see Tamsin glancing at her watch.

'Perhaps it would be best if you left a little early today,' she said.

My entire wardrobe lay scattered around the room.

Acres of skirts covered the bed. A column of tops had risen so high, a few of them had launched themselves onto the bedroom carpet where they now sat, waiting to be judged. Several pairs of trousers were arranged, inside out, in a crop circle around my feet and in the corner was a special pile of clothes which had made me so angry, they had been screwed into a ball.

I'd never been to a dinner party before. Mother once did a small finger buffet for a royal wedding, and when Mrs Gadsby retired we all stood around in the shop with a glass of dry sherry, but nothing like this. Nothing so important.

All of my clothes seemed unremarkable. I'd looked through my magazines for ideas, but the models in the pictures were shiny and uncomplicated, and everything I owned felt tight and took up far too much energy. Prints were too loud or too quiet. Checks were too checked and stripes were too stripy. Skirts were too long or too short. Trousers were too casual. Dresses were awkward to walk around in. Some outfits were passable, but they held on to

memories of the last time I'd worn them. A wedding reception when Terry had got drunk and vomited on one of the
bridesmaids. A restaurant meal when Mother had taken
umbrage with a waitress and we'd all left early. A birthday
party where I hadn't known a soul and had spent most of
the time in a toilet cubicle wishing I was at home in bed.
Rebecca's dinner party deserved better. It deserved something new. Something I could always look at and say, *'This
is what I wore to my first dinner party at Rebecca's'* and Rebecca
and I would laugh together about it, because there would
have been so many other dinner parties and so many other
memories made by then.

I looked at the clock at the side of the bed. Terry would
be home soon and I had to be at Rebecca's for three o'clock
the next day, which I thought was a strange hour for a
dinner party, but perhaps she wanted us to spend some
time together first. I wouldn't have a chance to go into
town and buy something, but the online shops did next day
delivery and I had my store card. And Mother's laptop.

The box they sent was enormous.

I'd selected next-day delivery before 9 a.m. and the
courier knocked on the door when Terry was barely out
of the drive. They must have passed each other on the road.
The delivery driver wore a brown uniform and he struggled
up to the front door with a box so big, I could only see
his hands and the top of his cap. He put it on the doorstep
and said, 'Delivery for Ms Hammett' and made the Ms

sound like an angry wasp. He tipped his cap when I'd signed for it, which I thought was a very pleasant gesture and one that wouldn't go amiss in a few more situations. After I'd washed my hands, because heaven knows how many fingers had touched that pen, I knelt down on the hall carpet and began opening it, because it was far too big and heavy to carry up the stairs.

I'd chosen a black trouser suit in the end, although it wasn't the kind of tailored trouser suit people wore to an office or a funeral. It was silky and flowing, and on the website, it looked as though someone had poured it onto the model like ink. The price made me feel slightly nauseous, but it was worth it because I knew Rebecca would approve. She might even ask if she could borrow it and of course I would say yes straight away.

I had to buy some shoes as well, obviously, because I didn't possess any that would go with a black inky trouser suit, and then I needed a new handbag. I owned quite a few handbags because the charity shop was always overrun with them, but the ones I had would look tired and unhappy against a smart outfit like this and I couldn't go to Rebecca's dinner party in anything but the best. It meant using more money on my store card, but Terry wouldn't find out about it, and accessories can make or break an outfit. I know this because I read it in a magazine.

I laid everything out on the bed. When you treat yourself to something new, there's always a little spark of excitement in your chest, but somewhere between the hall and the top of the stairs, the little spark disappeared. It was the same with everything new I bought. Once I'd taken it out of the packaging and admired it, and hung it up or put it in a drawer, it blended in with everything else and the spark of joy disappeared because it had become part of me. Until the next time.

I spent three hours getting ready. I had a bath and put my big white dressing gown on, and used all the little pots and packages Natalie had given me. I had to guess what some of them were for, because everything was written in French, but it seemed to work out in the end and the bedroom smelled quite heady when I'd finished. I put the trouser suit on, slid my feet into the shoes and picked up my handbag. When I looked in the mirror, I was the person I always imagined myself as, whenever I wandered off into a daydream. She was right there, staring back at me, in a beautiful black trouser suit and her hair pinned up to the side. Just like Rebecca.

I put a big coat on, because I would imagine Rebecca's dinner parties went on until very late and even if Jolyon offered to drive me home – which he almost certainly would, being such a good friend of Rebecca's – it could still get quite chilly, even in a car. I would have called at the Co-op for a bottle of spumante, because this is what people always seem to do, but Rebecca said not to bring anything with me, because she had everything she needed there, and so the only thing I took was a page I'd cut out of one of my magazines. It was called 'How to Be Interesting at Dinner Parties', and there was a little list of bullet points to get a conversation started. Asking people what they do for a living and if they've got any holidays planned, that kind of thing. I also wrote a few of my own at the bottom: *Coronation Street* is a sure-fire winner because everyone watches it; and asking people about their health concerns is something my mother does all the time and it always seems to break the ice.

Terry was never bothered where I was, but I still left a note and a cheese and pickle sandwich, and I walked to the bottom of the road and caught the ten past two. All the way into town, I practised the conversation starters on the magazine list. I thought I kept most of it in my head, but the odd word might have escaped because one or two people gave me funny looks. By the time I got to Rebecca's front door, I knew it almost off by heart, but it wouldn't matter if I pulled it out of my handbag and had a quick glance, so I wasn't too worried.

She took an age to answer the door, even though she'd just buzzed me in. When she finally opened it she stood there in jeans and a T-shirt and for a minute, I thought I'd got the wrong day, but then she said, 'Linda! You made it!'

I did a little bob with my knees and spread my arms to the sides, to show off the outfit, but she'd already disappeared back into the flat. I followed her into the hall. I couldn't smell any cooking. I couldn't smell anything that might fall under the description of a dinner party, to be honest, just the usual stale ashtrays and remains of Jolyon's coffees.

When we reached the sitting room, she turned to face me. She smiled, but nothing happened afterwards, so I said, 'I know you told me not to bring anything with me, but I couldn't resist getting you this!' I handed her the gift bag I was carrying. 'I bought you a present!'

'A present?' she said.

'I thought you might be a bit upset about the letter. It's to cheer you up!'

She stared at me. She was quite taken aback, I could tell.

Jolyon was travelling through the house with his mobile phone pressed to his ear and he said, 'Well, isn't that nice?' as he went past.

Rebecca took the present out of its blue and gold bag. It was a mug I'd chosen especially off the internet, because giving gifts for absolutely no reason whatsoever is something best friends do all the time. It was all the colours of the rainbow and it had a gold cherub for a handle. I'd even had it personalised. 'Rebecca', it said, in beautiful gold script around the rim. She stared at it and turned it over.

'Do you like it?' I said.

'Fantastic,' she said. 'Brilliant.' And she pushed it under the settee, right to the back where it would be safe.

There was a pause.

'I didn't bring anything else,' I said. 'You said you had everything you need', because I was worried she was waiting for me to hand over a wine bottle or a small box of Ferrero Rocher.

'Oh, I *have!*' she said. 'I've even got a can of that magic spray you told me about.'

She pointed to the coffee table, where a group of canisters and bottles formed a small line, alongside a pile of yellow dusters.

I stared at the table. While I was staring, Rebecca disappeared and when she returned, she was dragging a large vacuum cleaner behind her.

'The bag probably needs changing. Sorry,' she said.

I watched her plug it in by the window.

'I thought you could start in here and then maybe the kitchen next; the caterers will be here in a few hours. You can leave the bathroom until last, because I need to get ready and I always make a huge mess.'

'Right,' I said.

'The guests won't be here until seven at the earliest, so you've got plenty of time. Although you'll need it.'

She laughed and I heard myself laugh along with her, even though I didn't remember feeling one start up anywhere.

'Good job you're only wearing old clothes, this place is a bloody tip,' she said, wandering back into the hall. 'I blame Jolyon. He lives like a pig. I've never known anyone so untidy.'

Her voice floated away to somewhere else in the flat and I was left alone with the cans and the cloths, and the hoover.

'Best make a start then,' I said to them.

* * *

You can still take pride in your work, even if it isn't work you expected to be doing. There was something strangely rewarding in getting all the marks out of the rugs and polishing the shelves until they shone. There would be plenty of time afterwards to tidy myself up ready for the dinner party, if I got my skates on.

After an hour or so, Rebecca wandered through in a dressing gown with a towel around her head, and she said, 'Good job, Linda!' as she passed, which gave me a little boost, even though I wasn't sure which bit of the room she thought was a good job because she didn't seem to be looking anywhere in particular.

I moved on to the kitchen. There were so many dirty pots covered in the patterns of meals gone by, far too many for the dishwasher, and so I ended up washing a lot of them in the sink. I miss washing pots in a sink; there's something quite relaxing about it, the slip of warm water between your fingers and the smell of the soap. We didn't have a dishwasher in Wales, of course, so when everything happened with Dad, and Mother took to her bed, I spent a lot of time at the sink. It gives you a chance to swim around in your own thoughts and find a way out of them again. The counsellor said I shouldn't fight my thoughts. She said stopping yourself from thinking about something takes up too much energy, and it was much healthier to stop and acknowledge my thoughts and then let them go. I acknowledged a lot of thoughts at that kitchen sink, but not many of them managed to leave. I fed and watered them, and they grew over the years and flourished instead. Thoughts about all those girls and what they'd said about my dad. Thoughts about all the lies they told. Thoughts about what I'd seen and heard that day and how the police took apart what I'd said and rebuilt it into something else, until I wasn't even sure of it myself any more. 'Just tell us the truth, Linda,' they said. 'You've only got to tell us what you saw.' Except what you think you see and what you're actually looking at can be two different things and before you know it, one has crossed over into the other and you can't find your way back to the truth.

The hall needed a good going-over, but then again halls always do. Filthy shoes and coats. Mud all over the carpet. A mirror you could barely see your face in, it was so covered in dust. It was one of those ornate things with a swirling gilt frame. Endless crevices. I was trying to riddle some of the muck out of it when Rebecca's reflection appeared in the glass. It didn't look like Rebecca at all because the dirt stole away all her features, but it's amazing how much detail you fill in with your imagination.

'Not my taste at all,' she said, nodding to herself in the mirror. 'It was my gran's. I only kept it because it might be worth something. And that painting, it might fetch a bob or two.'

She nodded over to a picture on the far wall, next to the front door. I glanced at it and looked away again. I didn't mind flowers, but you could have too much of a good thing and this was far too gaudy and loud. Obscene, almost.

'Is that an heirloom as well?' I said.

'I suppose so. Not sure where Mum got it, but when she died, it ended up with me. God knows what I'm going to do with it.'

It was strange how the past was handed backwards and forwards, until it found a person who wanted it. Someone's once-loved treasure found itself abandoned on a trestle table at a car boot sale. Pictures of unnamed faces filled never-opened photo albums. The charity shop was over-flowing with other people's unwanted past. My dad used to say if someone dusted your photograph after you'd died, you'd done very well for yourself, and I often wondered if anyone would bother to dust mine. Certainly not Terry. I couldn't imagine him picking up a cloth and a can of Pledge.

When I'd finished in the hall I went to open one of the other doors, but it was locked.

Rebecca heard me trying the handle.

'Don't worry about in there!' she shouted. 'It's the office!' and so I wandered through into the bedroom Rebecca shared with Jolyon. It didn't look too bad at first, because a lot of things can hide in a shadow and it was only when I drew the curtains back I realised it was probably the messiest room of all. Great piles of clothes in every corner, a queue of coffee cups on the bedside tables, overflowing ashtrays and a bin that looked like it hadn't been emptied in weeks.

'It'll have to be done, I'm afraid,' Rebecca said over my shoulder. 'People will be putting their coats in here.'

I wanted to ask her how she managed to get to sleep in a room filled with so much chaos, but then I remembered how busy she must be, far too busy for housework, and she was only turning to a good friend for help.

'You leave it all to me,' I said. 'Of course I don't mind.'

I looked around the room, floor to ceiling, and when my gaze reached the top of the wardrobes, I saw them. A row of severed heads. At least, that's what they looked like at first glance, but they were wigs. So many different styles and colours, and each with its own blank polystyrene face. I even spotted the curly auburn one she'd been wearing in the pictures I'd found on the internet.

'Goodness,' I said. 'What are those?'

'Oh they're just my wigs everyone has wigs don't they?' she said, very quickly I thought, because the words seemed to tumble all over themselves on their way out.

'Do they?' I said.

'Of course. They let you mix it up a bit, you know. Change your image.'

I stared at the heads, and they all stared back at me from the top of the wardrobe. I was going to answer, but Rebecca had moved on and was waving her hand at the piles of clothes on the carpet, a mountain range made out of silks and cottons.

'While you're here, could you sort out all the laundry out into whites and colours for the machine?' she said. 'I'm hopeless at that sort of thing and I bet you're really good at it. Would you mind?'

'I don't mind at all,' I said. 'Perhaps I could take your wigs home with me at some point. Give them all a wash and blow-dry. I'm quite good with hair, you know.'

I turned to smile at her but she'd already wandered off, a hairdryer in one hand and a mug of coffee in the other. As she turned into the sitting room, coffee slipped over the edge of the mug and spilled onto the carpet I'd just scrubbed at for the last twenty minutes.

'You won't even notice they're gone,' I said.

It took until a quarter to seven to sort the bedroom out. The caterers arrived in the middle of it all and I had to let them in and get them settled in the kitchen, because Rebecca was busy with her hair and didn't want to leave her curling wand unattended.

'Do you mind, Lind?' she shouted.

When Terry called me Lind it rubbed me up the wrong way, but when Rebecca said it, it made me smile because it sounded as though we'd known each other far longer than we actually had.

I didn't know what they were cooking in that kitchen, but I hadn't eaten since breakfast because I was saving myself, and the smell of it made my stomach yawn. I looked down at the silky trouser suit. It hadn't fared very well during the cleaning, it had to be said. A couple of buttons had escaped from the jacket and the hem of the trousers had come loose. Poor workmanship, clearly. There were splashes of bleach on the cuffs from cleaning the bathroom and the whole thing was creased and damp, but the other guests weren't arriving for another half an hour, so it probably gave me just enough time to tidy myself up and put a fresh coat of lipstick on. Before we all had a glass of dry sherry and got to know each other. I'd just finished vacuuming under the bed, and I was winding the flex around the hoover when Rebecca walked back into the bedroom.

'Ta-da!' I said. 'All done!'

'Linda, you are *such* a star,' she said. 'Good job, you.'

I couldn't stop smiling. I was about to tell her if a job was worth doing, it was worth doing well, but she stopped me in my tracks because she fished a ten-pound note out of her back pocket and tried to hand it to me.

'You don't have to give me any money!' I said. 'Friends don't need paying, do they?'

'But you came all this way.'

'I was coming anyway, though,' I said. 'A few hours didn't make any difference.'

But she just frowned at me and looked at her watch and said, 'If you're sure then, Linda,' and she ushered me out into the hall.

'Oh, I've already done out here,' I said. 'If I could just tidy myself up, I'm all set!'

'You look fine!' she said, and opened the front door. 'Just fine!'

Which I thought was very kind of her, because I could see myself in the mirror I'd cleaned and I looked a bit of a disaster. Certainly not presentable enough for a dinner party.

She looked at her watch again. 'It's just, they'll all be here any minute. If you hurry, you can catch the ten to seven bus from the bottom of the road.'

'The what?'

'Or the twenty past, if you miss that one.'

We were by the lift now and Rebecca reached past me and pressed the down button.

'Thanks again, Linda, you're such a good egg. I really don't deserve you.'

Jolyon appeared behind her. I could tell he was about to say something just from his eyes, but before he could, I found myself in the lift and the doors closed in front of my eyes, and they were both gone.

I walked out of the apartment building and onto the street. Darkness had fallen whilst I'd been cleaning, and the sky was deep and coal-black. It's never really night-time in the city, though, because the street lights and the noise and the people won't allow it to take charge. It was a Thursday, but the weekend starts much earlier these days and a river of people passed by me as I stood there. You could tell they were on their way to a night out, because there was a fizz of excitement and the smell of fresh after-shave about them. Perhaps people find their weekdays so dreary, they need to find the edges of the weekend and pull them further and further across the week in order to cover up all the monotony.

Next to Rebecca's apartment block there was one of those twenty-four-hour convenience stores, which – considering how hungry I was – proved to be very convenient, and so I went inside and bought myself an egg and cress sandwich and a packet of salt and vinegar crisps. I sat on a bench across the road and ate them on my lap. Mother always looks down on people who eat in the street, but sometimes needs must and besides, what she didn't know wouldn't hurt her.

I watched them arrive. Rebecca's dinner guests. I could tell by the way they were dressed, but if it needed any confirmation, Rebecca was obviously so excited, she came down herself and let them in off the street. There were lots of loud voices and air kissing, but clearly these were business acquaintances because I didn't even see a hint of Ferrero Rocher from any of them. Suddenly, it all made sense. Obviously Rebecca didn't think I'd want to be there, because it was a work-related thing. She knew I'd be bored and so she saved me the dilemma of whether or not to turn down the invitation by not inviting me to it in the first place. She was so thoughtful. Such a good friend.

I looked down. I hadn't been concentrating properly on my eating, and pieces of egg and cress were scattered across the silky trouser suit. Usually, I'd be annoyed with myself for making such a mess, but I couldn't help but chuckle to myself. What a silly misunderstanding.

Rebecca and I would laugh about this one day.

26

'It was just routine,' Terry said.

Routine is something you do all the time. Routine crouches silently in your life, biding its time, mundane and ordinary. It is not mundane and ordinary to have the police call you on your landline and interview you for half an hour in a side room at the station. Being questioned about a murder isn't something you do all the time. I wanted to say that to him, but I thought better of it. We were in the van, trying to get to the supermarket. I'd put a towel down, but I still felt contaminated. It was the smell more than anything. Oil and dust and heaven knows what else. Terry stared straight ahead at the tail lights of the car in front, even though we were in a queue. Even though it didn't look like we were going to move any time soon.

'They spoke to everyone to do with the factory,' he said. 'I heard they even spoke to the managers.'

'Even the managers?'

'Well, you know. You wouldn't think they'd bother with men in suits.'

I wanted to say men in suits are often the most dangerous men of all, but when you're trying to coax information out of Terry, I've found you're better off sticking to the main road.

'What did they say?'

'Oh, you know. The usual.'

The queue moved a little and stopped again. In the distance, you could see a string of brake lights. Little red decorations against the tarmac. I looked at him.

'You know,' he said again. 'Where were you on this that and the other day. As if anyone remembers. I can't even remember what I was doing last week, let alone last month.'

'So what did you say, then?'

He turned to look at me for the first time. 'I told them I was with you,' he said.

We finally found a space in the car park. Everyone else did their big shop on a Friday night and so we did ours too. There is something comforting about following the herd, keeping in line, even if it makes that line very long and drawn out, because if everyone else is doing it then surely it must be the thing you should be doing as well. We drifted across the retail park, pulled towards the sharp white supermarket lights which hung against the black of an evening sky. A beacon of shopping and three for twos and things you didn't know you needed until they were put on a shelf right in front of your eyes.

'They didn't ask you about the van?' I said, as Terry tried to pull a trolley free from the stack outside the entrance.

He mumbled something that became lost in the clatter and rattle of one shopping cart bickering with another.

'Because that van's in a proper state,' I said. 'It needs a good sorting out before any policeman takes a look inside of it.'

He pulled a trolley free and wheeled it towards the door. 'Aye,' he said. 'You might be right.'

'I'll see to it,' I said. 'If you like.'

'You hate that van, Linda. You don't even like walking past it, let alone hoovering it out.'

'I don't,' I said and I put my handbag across my body, because all the magazines tell you to do this to avoid pickpockets. If you weren't careful, like me, anyone could take something, or even put something in there, without you even noticing. 'But I'd quite enjoy doing it. Getting it into the state I think it needs to be to make the right impression to a member of the police force.'

The automatic doors closed behind us and we were sealed into our shopping experience. Terry headed straight for the lager and crisps and I was forced to follow him along the aisles because it's much easier to let him sort himself out first and then I can take my time choosing the things I want to eat.

Life is so much brighter in there. The silver cans and the shiny boxes. All the rows of colours shouting at you to put them in your basket. Reassuring faces, staring down at you from packets and jars and containers. Each one making you think that's the only thing you've ever wanted to eat since the day you were born. Everything done for you. Washed lettuce. Grated cheese. Peeled. Diced. Chopped. Choose me! I am ready in ten minutes. Three minutes. Thirty seconds. Buy me! All you have to do is tear along the dotted line and I'm yours. Perhaps we'll eventually lose the ability to wash lettuce. Soon the little pathways in our brain will shrivel up and die, and there will be no one left any more who remembers how to do it.

Terry had already filled half the trolley by the time I'd caught up with him.

'On offer,' he said, walking back along the aisle, waving his hand over twenty-four cans of lager and three multipacks of salt and vinegar.

We stopped just short of hot beverages.

'I thought we might try something different for a change,' I said. 'Something nice.'

'Like what?' He wheeled along a few feet and reached for our usual jar of coffee.

'Like this,' I said.

I picked up another brand. It was made in a country I'd never heard of and it wasn't in a jar, it was in a packet. There was a picture of a woman on the front. She was wearing white pyjamas and staring out of a window and drinking her coffee made in a country I'd never heard of with a faraway smile on her face. I would have liked to smile like that, once in a while. It was the brand of coffee Rebecca drank. I knew, because I'd seen it in her kitchen when I was cleaning.

'It's an "Enjoy the difference" product.' I pointed to the little sticker on the front. 'Don't you want to enjoy the difference, Terry? Just for once?'

'It's twice the bloody price, Linda,' he said, and put it straight back on the shelf. 'I don't want to be that different.'

I would have paid more than twice the price to smile like that, I thought, and when his back was turned, I popped it into the trolley, hidden deep between the crisps and the lager.

When we got home, while the fish fingers were under the grill, I thought I'd grab my chance. It wasn't often you caught Terry when his eyes weren't tight shut or glued to a television screen, but at that moment he was idling about at the kitchen table. It was too good an opportunity.

'How was work this week?' I said.

I didn't turn around and he didn't answer straight away. He just shifted in his seat instead. It says a lot when people do that, I've found. As if shuffling about a bit and rearranging yourself might help you to come up with a better answer.

'Not bad,' he said in the end. 'Can't complain.'

'You haven't had any overtime recently.'

'No, no,' he said. 'Everyone's suffering at the moment, Linda. At least I've kept my hours.'

'I've not seen any wages go into the account, though.' I turned to face him. I'd still got the fish slice in my hand and I waved it about a bit to help me make my point. 'You know, those automatic payments they make.'

He stared at me with one of those expressions that could be filled in with anything.

'What payments?' he said.

'Your wages. The ones with your national insurance number as a reference.'

'Oh,' he said, '*those* payments. No, no, well you wouldn't. They've been having a bit of trouble.'

'I thought you said they were doing okay?'

'I mean with their banking system.' He shifted about a bit more. 'Had to pay me by cheque instead. Money's going into the account, Linda. Don't you worry about that.'

I turned back to the fish fingers. They were shaping up quite nicely. Getting browner and browner under the heat. 'I wonder when they'll have the Family Away Day this year. It's always in the summer, isn't it?'

'Oh, I don't think there'll be anything like that.'

'Maybe you can persuade them to pick Alton Towers this time. Or I could give Janet a ring in HR. She's always been very nice to me. Put in a good word.'

'Linda . . .'

'We should invite Janet around for a sherry. People do things like that with work colleagues, Terry. You see it in magazines all the time.'

'Linda!'

Terry's voice rose above the boiled potatoes jumping around in the saucepan, and the spit and crack of the grill. 'What?' I said.

'Linda, there's something I need to tell you.'

I turned off the gas. The fish fingers were done now. To perfection.

'What do you mean you lost your job?'

The food sat between us. Untouched.

'Six weeks ago,' he said. 'Made redundant.'

'Why in God's name didn't you tell me?'

He didn't move. He didn't even look up, he just stared at the cold fish fingers and the slices of bread sweating margarine onto a side plate.

'I was ashamed, Linda,' he said. 'I work. I bring money into a house, that's what I do. That's what I've always done, ever since I was sixteen.'

'You still bring money in, though, because it gets paid in. I've seen it, when I go to the bank.'

'Credit card,' he said. 'I signed up for a few and I syphoned money into the joint account so you didn't get suspicious.'

'But I see you drive off to work every day! You leave me little notes about things before you go!' I said, because when people tell you something you don't want to hear, you present all sorts of evidence back to them in the hope that they'll change their minds. 'I see you do it! I watch you pull out and disappear down the road!'

'You saw me drive off in the van. You just assumed I was going to work,' he said. 'If there are gaps in the truth, we fill those gaps with whatever it is we want to believe, don't we?'

'So where *did* you go?'

He sat forward, still talking to the tablecloth. 'I parked up on the moors usually, in a lay-by, until it went dark. I drove into the city a couple of times, but it was too risky. I might have seen someone I knew. Sometimes I parked the van a few streets away and walked back here. But you were always changing your work and messing around with your hours, and there were times I had to hide upstairs until you went to the shop or the post box.'

'All the creaking floorboards. I wasn't imagining it.'

He didn't answer. Instead, he pushed his untouched plate forward an inch, like he always did, and scraped his chair back across the tiles. He stood at the kitchen door and looked at me.

'Having a shower the minute you came in? Washing your own clothes?'

'I didn't want you to notice I wasn't covered in factory dust,' he said. 'I could fake going to work each day, but I couldn't fake the way I should look when I walked back in.'

'And the work friends you go fishing with on a Saturday morning?'

'I don't go fishing any more,' he said. 'Because I don't have those friends any more. Once you're made redundant, people give you a wide berth because if they spend too much time with you, they start thinking they might be the ones to go next.'

I heard the living-room door shut and the television spring to life.

27

'Have you been moving any of my things, Linda?'

Rebecca appeared in the hallway. I didn't turn around, but I was dusting that awful painting of her mother's and I could see Rebecca's reflection in the glass. It had become a routine now, me giving the flat a once-over each time I visited. I didn't mind, because that's what friends are for – helping out. Plus, it added a bit of extra interest to my week. Anything can be turned to your advantage if you think about it for long enough.

'Your things?' I said and I sprayed a bit of Pledge right on the spot where she was reflecting.

'Some of my make-up has disappeared and I can't find the earrings I keep by the side of the bed.'

'Nothing to do with me,' I said. 'The only thing I've done so far in the bedroom is a thorough hoovering – oh, and I gave your wigs a good brush as I went past because they looked a little bit . . . matted, if you don't mind me saying so.'

Rebecca scratched at the side of her head. 'Well, things have been switched around in the bathroom as well and I can't find my perfume.'

Jolyon peered around the living-room door. 'That won't be anything to do with Linda, that'll be you putting things down where they don't belong and forgetting what you did with them.'

I knew Jolyon would stick up for me. He's such a gentleman. We have a connection, Jolyon and I, you could tell by the way he sprang to my defence. He'd done a lot of that lately, because the more irritable and argumentative Rebecca became, the more helpful I'd tried to be. Helpfulness always starts off very quietly, but if you keep at it, it grows and grows, until one day people finally realise it's there and take some notice of it.

Rebecca scratched the other side of her head.

'Just don't . . . don't touch my things,' she said. 'Any more than you have to.'

Rebecca disappeared back into the bedroom, and for once she didn't slam the door behind her.

Jolyon didn't disappear. He stayed right where he was, leaning against the door frame, and he raised his eyebrows at me. I raised my eyebrows back. I was going to wink, but I decided at the last minute that it might be overkill.

'I'm very grateful for your support, Linda,' he said. 'You

always seem to be there when you're needed the most. Much appreciated. Especially when Rebecca's being so . . . difficult.'

I nodded and tried to make my eyes look sympathetic.

'You're more use around here than Rebecca is at the moment,' he said.

I was going to agree with him, but there was no need to throw any more coal on the fire, it was burning quite nicely all by itself.

'How's your husband, Linda,' he said. 'Terry, isn't it?'

I made one of Terry's whale noises.

'A pain in the backside, so no change there!' I laughed and it ended up being one of my loud laughs, but it didn't seem to bother Jolyon. 'Why do you ask?'

'Oh, nothing special – no reason,' he said. 'I've just heard . . . things through the grapevine. You know what this place is like. Rumours.'

'Rumours?'

'They're ramping up the hunt for this serial killer, aren't they? Interviewing all sorts of people. It doesn't mean anything, of course.'

'No, of course,' I said.

'It's just . . .' Jolyon glanced at the closed bedroom door and edged a little further into the hallway. 'The newspapers soon get a sniff of these things, you know. If it goes any further, they'll be after your side of the story and they'd pay handsomely for your . . . viewpoint.'

He made money signs with his hands. The way Mother does when she buys a lottery ticket.

'I just don't want you selling yourself short, Linda. That's all. You can always rely on me to guide you, you know. All you have to do is ask.'

When he'd gone back into the living room, I listened to see if I could hear them talking, but there was just silence. It was difficult to work those two out. They lived in the same flat, but you'd never think they were in any kind of romantic relationship, because there was never even a hint of affection between them. Although when I thought about it, if showing affection was a barometer of being in a relationship, you'd have to discount the relationships of most of the people I know. Including me and Terry. I squirted some more Pledge on the ugly painting. I shouldn't have been so liberal with that perfume, I suppose. I just couldn't resist having a little spray each time I walked past. The earrings I planned to put back, I just wanted to wear them to work tomorrow because the area manager was due a visit and I thought it might stand me in good stead if I made a bit of an effort. The clothes obviously hadn't been missed yet, but then Rebecca had so many, and half of them still had the price tags swinging from the labels. I only borrowed the oversize things – the baggy jumpers and big jackets – because Rebecca was so ridiculously tiny and I couldn't fit into anything else.

It was fun, though. Dressing up as someone else and walking around the shops. She never usually noticed when I'd borrowed something, and people were so much nicer to me when I was Rebecca. Plus, if I did it often enough, perhaps I'd start to forget where I ended and she began.

NOW

It took three days before I saw a doctor.

I kept trying to spot one, but it's easier said than done. I asked on several occasions, but each time I was told they were too busy or not available right now. You expect them to be on hand, lurking in corridors and answering important phone calls, like they do on the television, but in real life you only ever see them for a few seconds. They disappear into a room and then a little while later they disappear out of it again. I've arrived at the conclusion that television has a lot to answer for when it comes to public disappointment in medical personnel.

I managed to catch one the other day, quite by chance. He came to talk to the woman sitting next to me in the day room and she kept referring to him by name. 'Dr Richard,' she said, at the end of every sentence. 'Do you

305

think I'll be allowed to go home soon, Dr Richard?' and 'I wonder if you could ask them to give me some leave, Dr Richard?' I couldn't decide if Richard was his first name or his last, but he didn't look very much like a Richard, so I presumed it was his surname.

When the woman next to me had run out of questions, and Vahri had taken pity on Dr Richard and ushered her away, I decided to try my luck.

'Dr Richard?' I said.

He was just turning to leave, but he looked back and smiled.

'Yes?' He poked at the inside of his ear as he spoke, which I didn't think was a particularly hygienic way to carry on for someone in a healthcare role. 'It's Linda, isn't it?'

I supposed I'd have to get used to it. People knowing me before I knew them. Hearing the sound of my name before I had given it away. Strangers having right of entry to all the dark and quiet corners of my life.

'It is,' I said. 'I just wondered if I could have a quick word?'

He looked at his watch. I didn't think doctors were supposed to have anything below their elbows, but not only was he wearing a watch, he had on a long-sleeved shirt. No sign of a tie and he was walking around in a pair of jeans. If I was stood next to him in the queue in Sainsbury's, I wouldn't have given him a backward glance. I thought doctors were supposed to look like doctors, so everybody knows where they are. But perhaps it's different in here. Perhaps it's important that everyone looks the same.

'It won't take long,' I said.

He hesitated for a moment, but then he smiled and sat down in the armchair opposite. It was one of those leatherette ones. The kind that masquerades as leather, but you can sit there with peace of mind, because you can get most stains out of them with a damp cloth and a bit of determination. The only problem is, it makes the most unfortunate noise each time someone sits in it, because deception always comes at a price.

Dr Richard gestured with his hands for me to speak, which is fatal because that always frightens all the words out of my head.

'I just wondered . . .' I began, even though I couldn't remember what I was wondering. 'I mean, I was thinking . . .'

Dr Richard's smile stayed where it was. 'The thing is, Linda,' he said, because it isn't only policemen who take it for granted that everyone else is more foolish than they are. 'It's quite a complicated situation.'

'Oh, I know it is,' I said. 'I've been swimming around in it from the start.'

'Which is why it's important to hear what you have to say about it all. It's been very helpful.'

It wasn't often anyone described me as helpful and I made sure I waited in the moment for a little while to make the most of it.

'And it's helpful for you, too, I hope?' he said.

'So helpful!' I said very quickly, even though I wasn't sure if it was, because people very often ask you a question even though what they really want isn't an answer, but the sound of their own opinion gift-wrapped and given back to them.

'Good, good,' he said.

'I love it here,' I said. 'It's very calming.'

'Good, good.'

'I like the Pets as Therapy dog and the activities. I even like the guitar-playing on occasion, when it's not too boisterous.'

'That's great to hear, Linda.'

'It's just . . .' I leaned forward because it sometimes helped my voice to lean back. 'I wonder sometimes how it came to all this. One minute you're swimming along quite nicely, and the next minute . . .' I stared around at the blank walls and cushion-less sofas to try and find the end to my sentence.

'Stress is a very powerful thing. It can do so much damage to our minds and our bodies.'

'But do you think the medication is really necessary?'

Dr Richard stuck his finger in his ear again. 'I do, Linda. Especially at the moment. This has been an especially traumatic experience.'

'But so much of it?'

'Sometimes, we need a little help,' he said. 'Just to get back to a place where we can help ourselves.'

I decided I couldn't argue with him. Mother needed that kind of help after Dad died. She lay buried in darkness for weeks, paper-thin curtains doing their best to shroud the rest of the world from her eyes, and as regular as clock-work, she placed a small white tablet on her tongue to measure out the next four hours.

'I don't understand being sectioned either. It feels like a punishment but no one can be bothered to tell you what it is you're being punished for.'

'No one's being punished, Linda. This isn't a prison. You said yourself how much you like it here.'

'I do,' I said. 'It has the look of a small holiday and there's always someone to talk to.' It's always wise, when you tell an untruth, to weave in a truth alongside it, because then it means your face has an idea about what it should be doing.

'Well, there you are.'

'Then why do you need a piece of paper to make everyone stay put?'

Dr Richard didn't answer for a moment. When he did speak, his voice was a little lower. A little more careful.

'There are times when we might need other people to make our decisions for us.'

'Why?' I said.

'Because we might not see the world how it really is. We might be mistaken about things and we need someone to help us who can see it all more clearly.'

'But how do you know?'

'Know what, Linda?'

'Who are the people who are seeing the world how it really is and who are the people that are mistaken? How do you know which way around it is?'

He didn't reply at first, and even when he did speak, it wasn't really an answer. It was one of those imitation answers people use just to keep you quiet. Terry did it all the time, and Mother. A masquerade. Just like the chair he was sitting in.

'Let's just see how it all goes, shall we? Sometimes, these reactions to a stressful situation disappear as suddenly as they arrived.'

I was going to move on to my next question, but Dr Richard had already got up from the chair and was making his way across the room. Before he left, though, he turned back.

'There was just one thing I wanted to ask, if you wouldn't mind,' he said, because even doctors like to open doors into rooms in which they don't belong.

I told him I didn't mind. I told him to go right ahead.

'I just wondered . . . you must have suspected what was going on?' He shuffled about in the doorway, trying to find his question. 'When was the point where you put two and two together?'

'Oh, that's an easy question, I can give you an answer to that straight away,' I said. 'It was when they found the fourth body.'

28

They found her quite quickly. She hadn't been dead very long at all and she lay silent and still in the darkness, just inside the churchyard, by the far wall.

I've always wondered why they bother putting walls around graveyards. It isn't as though anyone would be very keen to get in, or particularly want to get out. Perhaps it's because we think putting a wall around something means it's less likely to bother us.

Mother rang and delivered the news to me as I was stacking the dishwasher. She'd been to the corner shop for emergency toilet rolls and overheard it in the queue.

'Thank heavens I ran out of double-ply,' she said, 'or I never would have known.'

Of course, she wanted to get down and have a gawp. There was quite a crowd going, she said, and Freda couldn't squeeze any more into the back of her Ford Fiesta because it would alarm the dog, so would Terry come and pick her up? She knew I'd never go, because I hate driving that van at the best of times, least of all in the dark.

'There's nothing worth watching on the telly,' Terry said. 'I suppose we could have a wander down.'

I'd rather have stayed in. I'd rather have sat in the kitchen by myself, wearing my nice dressing gown and listening to my music and looking through all the things I'd borrowed from Rebecca, but having Terry at home all day now meant that was out of the question. He could be quite insistent when he wanted to be, and Mother would only have made a song and dance about why I hadn't gone, so I put my coat on and walked down with Malcolm while Terry went to pick her up.

'You'll be safe with Malcolm,' Terry said before he drove off.

Malcolm stood on the pavement in his raincoat. His spindly arms stuck out from the too-short sleeves, and I could see the thin red capillaries threaded across his cheekbones. He did a small salute.

'Right you are then,' I said.

We walked a line of blackened roads through the estate, but every so often I caught a glimpse of Malcolm's face, jaundiced by the pool of light from a street lamp.

'Nasty business,' he said, as we turned the corner by the fire station.

'I don't know why we're even going down there,

Malcolm.' I pushed my chin further into the folds of my scarf. 'It won't achieve anything.'

'We have to show the police our support.' In the absence of a police officer he nodded back at the fire station instead, as if they were a vague relative. 'We need to demonstrate some kind of solidarity.'

'We could demonstrate solidarity by all staying indoors and watching *EastEnders*,' I said. 'Where it's warm and safe.'

'He won't strike again tonight, Linda. I can assure you of that.' Malcolm spoke with such certainty, it was difficult not to be taken in. 'I've been studying serial killers in recent days and it would be totally out of character.'

'Jack the Ripper?' I said.

Malcolm turned to me in the darkness. 'Pardon?'

'Jack the Ripper killed two women in one night. They found them within an hour of each other.'

'This isn't Victorian England, Linda. We're much more civilised these days.'

As soon as you turned on to Church Street you could see the crowd of people. They were gathered behind a ribbon of blue and white tape and a policeman stood in front of them all, waving his hands around. It looked like he was conducting a particularly unruly orchestra, where none of the musicians wanted to do what his hands were telling them to.

'There's nothing to see.' The policeman's voice drifted down the street. 'You're all wasting your time, you'd be better off at home.'

The group of people obviously disagreed with his assessment of the situation, because they shuffled and pushed, and if anything, they edged forward slowly, closer to the walls of the churchyard.

'Quite a turn-out,' said Malcolm. 'Considering it's a Thursday.'

Malcolm marched his way into the throes of it all, but I hung back a little. I've never liked crowds. Other people's breath and the smell of damp clothes. All those elbows and shoulders. There was too much noise as well, endless voices and opinions, and it felt as though everyone else's words filled up your throat and stopped you from being able to breathe. Anyway, it's always a better view from the edges. People don't realise just how much you can see.

There must have been close to two hundred people all in all. Most of them were from the estate, and I recognised their faces even if I didn't know their names. The Slaters were right at the front of the crowd and Single Simon was just behind them, his hands stuffed into the pockets of his bomber jacket. There was Freda and all the people she'd managed to fit in the back of a Ford Fiesta, and I spotted Tamsin as well, right at the centre, and she stared at me for a moment before she was swallowed up again by an ocean of faces. Even Andrea the vicar was there. She looked pale and weighed down, as though she was carrying something really heavy behind her eyes. Perhaps it was the location that bothered her, just as much as the murder. Perhaps where we die is just as important as how we die and to take your last breath within the shadow of a church made it feel like God had seen what was going on, but hadn't bothered to save you.

I walked around the periphery of the crowd, away from the shouting and opinions, and followed the twist of the churchyard wall up towards the little gate that led onto the back lane. The police had set up some kind of lighting and sheets of tarpaulin around the scene, but as you moved further away, the night took charge again and it became much darker. I could just make out the edges of the wall and the graves that peered over the top of it. The oldest bodies were buried here and the headstones were the most ornate, garlands of ivy carved into the stone and a wide variety of flora and fauna were chiselled alongside the names. Perhaps it felt reassuring to those left behind that the anchors and cherubs, the lions and the swallows, all carried the dead into the afterlife.

I had spent a lot of time in that churchyard over the years. It's strangely reassuring to sit amongst the dead and collect your thoughts, to think we will one day all end up in the same place, lying deep in the soil, forever listening to the church bells ring out the hours. There's a little seat behind a group of trees – you'd never know it existed unless you wandered from the path – and I'd sit with a sandwich and file away all my thinking. Some of the graves there were so old, the letters in the names had worn down until they were impossible to read any more. You didn't know if you were looking at a John or a James, an Ann or an Amy.

There was no chance of sitting on the little bench the night they found the body. For one thing, it was far too dark to be sure of where it was, and for another, you would almost certainly bump into a police officer on your way there. I could hear their voices in the distance. At first, you couldn't tell which voices were real and which voices drifted from their walkie-talkies, but the darker it became, the more easily you could distinguish between the two.

What the police were saying became clearer too. I took a few more steps in the wet grass. Normally, I would have stumbled or tripped, and drawn attention to myself, but I'd borrowed one of Rebecca's scarves and it felt like a talisman. It felt like wrapping it around my neck had lent me some of her grace. I could catch an odd word as I stood there, and further along, those odd words became whole sentences. They could tell the girl hadn't been dead long, even without the pathologist (who was on her way) because *you get a feel for this kind of stuff*. She'd been strangled, just like the others. With her own scarf. *You could just tell*, apparently, because even though these officers had only seen a handful of murders and were more used to dealing with shoplifters and stolen cars, there is something about being involved in a murder inquiry that alters the way you look at things. I knew what they meant.

No one knew her name until much later, and no one could search her body for any identification, because nothing could be touched yet. All they could do was stare at her under the fizz and glare of the incident lights, at the last expression that would remain forever on her face, and wonder what her story might be. Scientists used to think that the eye held an image of the last thing you saw before you died, like a camera taking a photograph. I watched it on a documentary at Mother's. They took the eyes from a beheaded murderer and made an image of the last thing he saw. Except no one could decide if the image was the blade of a guillotine or the steps he'd walked up in order to get to it, because no matter how unlikely the evidence and no matter how obvious the conclusion might be, people will always see what they want to see and then find a reason to argue with each other about it.

There was no evidence to argue about here. No witnesses. The girl was obviously on her way to visit a grave, but never managed to get there because *she still had the flowers in her hand*, one of the voices said. Funny time of day to visit a churchyard, if you ask me, but there's no accounting for people's behaviour. I have always thought dusk was much more worrying than night. In the dusk you can see things that aren't there and not see things that are. You know where you are when it's pitch black.

I was just turning to walk back down to the crowd before Malcolm noticed I was missing and organised a search party, when I heard more voices. They were still police officers, because they still spoke in the same, police-officer harmony with each other.

'Woman across the street came over to me and mentioned seeing a van earlier,' one of the voices said. 'Driving up and down past the church. Slow enough to make her notice.'

317

'White van?' said the other voice.

The owner of the first voice must have nodded, because the second voice said, 'Same here. Someone mentioned one parked down the lane at the side of the church a couple of hours ago.'

I looked down the lane. You couldn't see much in the faded light, but there were definitely no vehicles parked down there now.

Because the white van had long since gone.

I was hoping I could blend back in with the crowd outside the main gates, but as soon as Malcolm saw me he said, 'There she is, there she is, we've found her,' and he nodded very vigorously and pointed, so everyone turned around and stared.

'No need to panic,' Malcolm said, several times in different directions.

No one was panicking. Even before he'd finished speaking, everyone had turned back to continue their argument with a police officer who was trying to persuade them to leave.

'We thought we'd lost you, Linda,' he said. 'Wandering off like that.'

'I just needed a bit of fresh air,' I said. 'There's too much pushing and shoving down here.'

Malcolm tilted his head very slightly. 'Have you heard anything?' he said. 'Any information on what might have happened?'

'No, nothing. Have you seen Terry anywhere?'

Malcolm tilted his head very slightly the other way. 'I do believe he's over there.'

He nodded back towards the road, without letting go of his tilt.

'With your mother,' he added.

I looked beyond Malcolm's tilt where Terry stood with his hands in his pockets, staring across the tarmac. We were in the oldest part of the town, where Georgian houses spilled their steps onto the pavement and iron railings kept all the neighbours from interfering in your life. Mother was leaning against some of these railings, rubbing at her left hip.

'He's no idea what it's like to live with chronic pain,' she shouted across the street. 'I have crosses to bear no one even thinks about.'

I walked over to them because Mother's shouting always tended to outshout everyone else's, and people had started to look. She was leaning against old Dr Hollick's railings, which might have been a problem had I not walked past his grave only five minutes before. He used to spend all his spare time planting bulbs and there was no headstone for him in the cemetery because in spring he always lay deep under a carpet of daffodils. Rather than relying on stone-faced cherubs, perhaps putting on a decent floral display was the best way of persuading God to let you inside.

'I kept telling him my hip wasn't up to it,' Mother said, still rubbing, 'but he took not a blind bit of notice. Making me walk all that way.'

'All what way?' I said.

'Six streets away he parked. Six streets.'

I looked around, but the van was nowhere to be seen.

'I left it up by the hospital,' Terry said, snatches of air leaving his mouth in short white clouds. 'No point bringing it down here with all these crowds.'

We all looked over at the church gates. Most people were beginning to drift away in clusters of small talk, heading back to the warmth of their front rooms or a seat in the Red Lion.

'I thought it would be heaving,' he said. 'Much worse than this. Although I might as well go and have a gander, now that we're here.'

He crossed the road and headed towards Malcolm, who was always the best person to turn to if you wanted a lengthy summary of what might be going on.

I turned back to Mother, who had stopped rubbing her hip and was staring at me.

'He wouldn't even drop me off first,' she said, 'and then go and park.'

'Why ever not?'

'He said it would be too busy. Nowhere to pull up.' She frowned across the street. 'He said he didn't want people knowing his business.'

I frowned with her.

'Did he now?' I said.

29

They took Terry in for questioning. It meant nothing, of course.

I said as much to Mother, because she was on the phone and he'd not been gone five minutes. Someone must have seen them drive off and notified her. Malcolm, probably, who is ever vigilant. They came to the house and picked Terry up, which was a courtesy I didn't think the police were capable of. It was an ordinary car, but people aren't stupid. Police officers have a certain look about them you can recognise straight away, even when they're in their home clothes.

'I won't be long, Linda,' Terry said, as he was pulling his coat on. 'I'll be back in no time.'

I saw the detectives give each other a look, but I chose to ignore it.

'Good, because your tea will be on the table in less

than an hour,' I shouted, but the front door had already slammed shut.

Lots of people are questioned every day about all sorts of things. It doesn't mean the police think they've done anything wrong. It doesn't mean it will lead on to something else. I put my music on as loud as I dared and tried to walk off the adrenaline. I couldn't settle to a crossword, so I did a load of laundry. Wiped down some surfaces. Keeping busy is the best way to deal with anxiety, that's what they always say, and if you can manage to distract yourself enough, you'll eventually dig through all that worrying and find yourself a little bit of hope right at the bottom.

'It's because of the people who saw a white van near the churchyard,' I said to Mother on the phone. 'They'll be interviewing everybody who owns one.'

'Everybody?' she said.

I thought about it. 'Everybody who lives locally,' I added.

'They've got to your Terry quick smart, then. It can't be alphabetical, can it?' she said.

I didn't say anything back, and I could hear her sharp, excited breaths eating into the silence.

'He needs a solicitor,' she said. 'A defence attorney.' Because she watched so many American dramas, she'd lost the ability to remember where the Atlantic began and where it ended.

'There's nothing to defend him against,' I said. 'Not yet.'

*   *   *

In the end, he didn't get home until the early hours of the morning. I'd waited up, but I didn't want him to know, or the police, so I'd lain in bed in the darkness, watching the numbers change on the clock at the side of the bed. Little green lines, snaking one way and then the other, counting out the minutes and the hours. It was 2:08 when I heard the car pull up outside. I knew it was them, because you get to know the sound of everyone's car on a road like this, given long enough, and the car I heard was a stranger to me. There were a few low voices, the click of a passenger door being shut, and then I heard Terry's footsteps on the stairs.

A few minutes later and he was sat on the edge of the bed. His back was to me and I could see the shape of his shoulders in the glow of a street light through the curtains.

'Well?' I said.

'Well what?' he said, because Terry has always been very good at forcing someone else to find all the words for him.

'This is the second occasion the police have found you interesting enough to have a conversation with, and it's not like last time. They've singled you out especially. What did they want?'

'Oh, the usual,' he said. 'You know.'

'No, Terry, I don't know. Which is why I'm asking you.'

'I've answered enough questions in the past five hours without you coming up with some more,' he said. 'They just wanted to know more about the nights of the murders. That's all. What I was doing.'

'And what did you say?'

He lay back on the pillow, his back was still facing me. He pulled the duvet across.

'I said what I said last time. I told them I was with you,' he said.

Two days later, they came back for me. I knew they would. I was ready for them.

'We wondered if you'd come down to the station with us, Linda,' they said as they stood on the doorstep. 'Answer a few questions, that's all.'

I couldn't help myself. 'So, you want me down there now, do you?' I said. 'You won't be leaving me on the pavement this time?'

There were three of them – the tall one, the shorter one and DC Caroline. They all looked at each other.

The tall one said, 'It won't take long, Linda. Nothing to worry about.'

'I'll get my coat,' I said.

There are certain people who make you start to worry when they say there's nothing to worry about. Doctors, for example, and often accountants. But especially police officers. When a police officer tells you there's nothing to worry about, you know it's time to be concerned.

I slid into the back of their car. It smelled of chewing gum and upholstery, and there were even lines where a vacuum cleaner had moved over the seat covers, like a ploughed field. Clean as a whistle, it was. I even checked the little tray in the door panel and the pocket on the back of the seat in front, but you couldn't fault it. DC Caroline, sitting next to me, said, 'Are you all right, Linda?' and I told her I was perfectly fine, and no one said another word for the rest of the journey.

It was usually a fifteen-minute drive to the police station, but people were just finishing work and they spilled from offices and shops onto the pavements and the roads, and so it took twice the time to get there as it normally would. It had started raining as well, which didn't help. Giant splashes hit the windscreen and the tarmac, from the kind of storm that blows in from nowhere and just as quickly blows away again. People always behave badly in the rain, I've noticed. Pedestrians as well as drivers. Wet weather seems to make people more selfish.

We pulled into a small car park at the back of the building. I'd never seen the police station from this angle before and it was quite the novelty. You don't often get the chance to see things from a different view and so I made the most of it and had a good stare. The only other vehicle there was a panda car, parked in the far corner, and against the back wall there was an empty skip. Covered in graffiti it was, which made me raise an eyebrow because if the police couldn't control vandals in their own car park, what chance did it give anyone else? I was going to point this out as we walked across the concrete, but the shorter policeman said, 'This way, Linda,' and held open the back door of the station before I had a chance to comment.

I followed them down a series of corridors. I thought I

knew where I was, but I was seeing it from the opposite side, from a place I wasn't used to, and so everything looked familiar and strange all at the same time. It was only when they took me into one of the little interview rooms that I felt at home, because I'd sat in there on numerous occasions, reporting petty crime.

'Milk and two sugars,' I said, before they'd even asked.

'So you can't be certain whether Terry was with you that night or not?'

I stared at the new detective and shook my head. He was called DI Matthews and he had a moustache that was so skinny, I wondered why he'd bothered growing it in the first place. I hadn't asked him his first name yet, as it all seemed a bit more serious this time.

'Is that a "no", Linda?' he said.

'No. I mean yes, it's a no,' I said.

'So, bearing that in mind,' he said, 'it's fair to say he could have been out for a considerable time that night?'

'I suppose so,' I said. 'Although he could have been at work on a late.'

Detective Inspector Matthews looked at the other man, who was called Detective Sergeant Simsion and had no facial hair whatsoever.

'What was on the television?' I said.

'I'm sorry?' DI Matthews looked down at his notes as if the answer might be there.

'If I knew what was on television that night, it might jog

my memory. Although to be honest, with everything on catch-up now that's not really much help, is it?'

They seemed lost for words, so I took another sip of tea.

'What about one of the other dates?' said DS Graeme eventually. 'What about the twenty-ninth of December? Between Christmas and New Year?'

I leaned forward, over my milk and two sugars. 'The thing is, Detective Sergeant Simsion,' I said, and because it felt satisfying, I said it again. '*The thing is*, I can't remember what I was doing this time last week, let alone two months ago.'

Police officers clearly didn't like having *the thing* pointed out to them any more than I did, because DS Simsion gave me a glare and went all bristly.

'Let's change tack, shall we, Graeme?' DI Matthews gave a nod and leaned back in his plastic chair. 'I know this must bring back some bad memories, Linda. After what happened in Wales.'

'What happened in Wales has got nothing to do with it. What do you know about what happened in Wales?'

'To see what you saw and then have the police ask you about it. At that age, it must have been very traumatic.'

'I didn't see anything.' I knew my voice must have been getting louder, because they both sat a little straighter in their chairs. 'My dad was doing nothing wrong. The police put words in my mouth – their own words – because it suited them, and look what happened to my dad after that. It wasn't my fault.'

'Of course it wasn't.'

'And you're doing exactly the same again. He didn't do it, you know. He didn't hurt any of those girls!' I was definitely shouting now.

'Terry?' said DI Matthews.

'No.' I could feel everything get angry and heavy behind my eyes. 'My dad!'

'And Terry?' said DS Graeme.

'Oh, God knows where he is half the time! He could be in Timbuktu for all I know. Getting home at all hours of the day and night!'

The detectives looked at each other and I sat back in my seat. All the shouting seemed to have left me. It blew in and out again, just like the storm.

'Can you take me home now, please?' I said.

30

I didn't tell Terry about the police interview.

I didn't tell Mother either. There are some things in life which are just easier to keep to yourself because the problem with letting things drop like that is it only leads to more and more questions and before you know it there are questions spread out across your whole life, left, right and centre, like a tablecloth.

As it happened, I had other, much nicer, things going on and so I put the police away, parked them in a corner of my mind and decided to think about them later. Besides, I had far more interesting things to think about.

'Surprise!'

Rebecca had only opened the front door a little way, so I had to say it through the crack. I suppose I shouted it

really, more than said it, because Mother says that enthusiasm gets the better of me sometimes.

'Linda?' She frowned. It wasn't a temporary thing either,
it stayed put for ages.

'I knew you'd be thrilled!' I said. 'I wanted to surprise
you with it properly, so I've been standing on the pavement
for the last hour and a bit, waiting for someone to go into
the building so I could slip in behind them!'

'What's going on?' she said slowly.

I flipped my hair. '"Isn't it amazing?" I said to the hairdresser. "It's almost uncanny," I said, "how similar it is to
my best friend Rebecca's!"'

I'd booked the appointment. You have to at these kinds of
places. No popping in on the off-chance or ringing up the
day before. If you want to spend a ridiculous amount of money
on your own head, you have to plan it all well in advance.
The salon is on the top floor of the department store, past
the chained-up handbags and the hoity-toity sales assistants,
and down a little corridor. You'd never know it was there if
you weren't well informed, which I suppose makes it feel
more exclusive and stops undesirable people just wandering
in by accident and making a nuisance of themselves.

I found it by accident, the last time I was in the department
store. I only went in because I thought it was a cloakroom.
All that dark wood and windows you can't see through, and
I walked through the door fully expecting a row of cubicles
and a hat stand. Instead there was a young woman on a high
stool, smiling and asking if I'd made a booking.

'For the toilet?' I said.

The smile stayed on her face, but her eyes stopped joining in. When I didn't say anything else, she started pointing and waving her arms about, like cabin crew do on an aeroplane before you all take off. When I looked to what she was pointing and waving at, there were pictures of hair all over the walls. Not the huge technicolour posters you see in normal salons, but tiny black and white squares of people's fringes and a few inches of someone's parting. Images to inspire you to sit for a while in a squishy leather chair and a little while later, walk back down the little corridor a whole new person. At a cost, mind you, although there wasn't a price list anywhere to be seen.

'Oh, it's a *hairdressers*!' I said, and the young woman nodded very enthusiastically – so enthusiastically that her whole body decided to take part in it, but miraculously, she still managed to remain on her perch.

'Would you like to make an appointment?' She reached into a drawer and pulled out a large, leather-bound book.

I studied all the pictures on the walls. Small squares of people I couldn't be. Plucked eyebrows and button noses. Confident expressions and well-behaved hair that did as it was told instead of being argued with for fifteen minutes every morning. I tried to find myself in each one of those photographs, but I was nowhere to be seen.

'The earliest available window we have is two weeks on Tuesday,' she said.

I thought about Rebecca's hair. Not the wigs she wore,

but her real hair. The platinum bob with the sharp edges. I often looked at Rebecca in mid hair-flick. It wasn't difficult to catch her doing it, because Rebecca flicked her hair around a lot. It was shiny and straight, the kind of hair that was always up for flying around and enjoying itself but still remembered where it lived at the end of the day. If I tried to flick my hair, my fingers got trapped in thick, dark curls and even if I managed to find a way through, no matter how hard I tried, I could never get it all to return to the way it had been before.

'Can I choose who I want to be?' I said.

'Pardon?'

'I have a particular colour and a style in mind.'

She said yes, yes of course and wiggled around a bit more on her stool.

I scanned all the hair in the photographs on the wall until I found one that looked like Rebecca's. 'I want to be just like that,' I said.

She looked at the straight blonde bob. At the tiny nose and the perfect eyebrows on the model. And then she looked back at me.

'Perhaps we'd better book a double appointment,' she said.

It took three hours and four people.

It wasn't like the place I usually go, where one person turns their hand to everything. Where the same girl helps you out of your coat and washes your hair, and puts you under a drying machine and takes your money. At this hairdressers, you've no sooner got to know one of them, when someone else pops up and takes over. None of them speaks much, either. Although the man who did my colour kept lifting my dark brown curls into the air and staring at them, like he'd never seen hair before, and asking if I was sure about this.

'Is madame *certain* this is what she wants?' he said, because everyone in this building seemed to like speaking in the third person. Perhaps pretending someone else had walked into the room meant decision-making was a little easier.

I thought about Rebecca.

'Madame is *very* certain,' I said.

I was very pleased with the result, and I think everyone else was too, because they couldn't take their eyes off me when it was all done. Even the young lad sweeping the floor stopped what he was doing and leaned on his brush, and let his mouth fall open.

Everything was going splendidly until I got to the girl on the high stool and she smiled and told me how much it had all cost.

'Pardon?' I said, because I thought I'd misheard.

She said it again, only more slowly.

Thankfully, they took store cards, which was a blessing when I thought about it afterwards, because not only did I get my hair done, I also took several steps closer to another reward point and a free hot drink and small biscuit in the bistro on the fifth floor. So it was a win-win, as Mother likes to say. Besides, I thought seeing Rebecca's face would be priceless, and I was right.

333

She was so thrilled, she could hardly form a sentence and I had to stand outside the door for ages before she gathered herself and let me in. It was only when I stepped into the hallway that I could show it off properly, mind you, because it's surprising how much room it takes to flick your hair properly.

'Isn't it amazing?' I said.

'Amazing . . .' she said.

I ran my fingers through the straight, soft blonde of it, and it made the air in Rebecca's hallway smell of the department store and the hairdressing salon, and someone else's different life. They said it would take some 'keeping up', which made me laugh out loud quite a bit because it sounded like I'd have to chase after my new hairstyle through the streets, but it all worked out fine in the end because they sold me several bottles and jars I'd need in order to chase it properly, plus some electric hair straighteners to make sure it did as it was told when I finally caught up.

'I even bought some straighteners to go with it. They're just like the ones on your dressing table!' I said.

Rebecca took a few steps backwards, which wasn't really necessary because I'd finished flicking by then, but it was very thoughtful of her.

'We could be twins now, couldn't we?' I said.

If I thought mine and Terry's house took some keeping on top of, I hadn't seen anything until I started cleaning at Rebecca and Jolyon's. If I say I didn't take my Marigolds off from start to finish, I wouldn't be lying. It was the clutter, more than anything. Piles of books and magazines and little trinkets. Mementos, I suppose they were, but whatever they were supposed to remind people of, they had long since lost that ability, and so all the memories did now was gather dust at the back of the shelf or hang on a wall and never be looked at. Blind as a bat, those two. They walked past all these things every day and never took one jot of notice. I started rearranging them at first, trying to make the place look a bit more presentable. No one said anything, so in the end I started ridding out. Smaller things at first. Postcards and pebbles. Magazines from six months ago. Fragments of days long gone by, because I've found the most useful place to keep the past is in your own mind. It's much easier to explain everything to yourself if you spread all your memories out in your own head, instead of allowing them to live out their days in ornaments and letters.

No one said anything even then, so I moved on to throwing away bigger things. That awful wooden elephant next to the fireplace and a picture no one looked at any more. Chipped cups and drinking glasses in the kitchen cupboards that had long seen better days. I was quite proud of the progress I made, and I was doing them a favour because none of these things matched the apartment. You have to *curate your living space.* I know all about it because I read it in a magazine. I thought I'd save them the bother, because I was so clued up on it, and I even brought a few things from home that I thought might look nice. The orange and lemon glasses Terry's so fond of leaving everywhere, and the Liverpool FC mug because it matched the red tiles above Rebecca's sink. I've never liked it, myself. Greedy birds, cormorants. They're supposed to spy on people too. I know because I read it in a magazine. I knew Terry would wonder where it had gone, but I decided I'd just tell him it got broken, and I was so excited, I took the mug straight out of my bag and hung it at the back of the little stand on the draining board without even giving it a wash, which isn't like me at all.

'Perfect!' I said.

The place was beginning to look a whole lot better since I'd started taking care of it. That book I read was right. Tidying up really can be magic.

31

I didn't mind this new arrangement where I did a bit of cleaning every time I went to Rebecca's, because it made me feel useful and there's a strange sense of achievement when you manage to scrub and polish something so much, you return it back to being new again, and there's not a trace left behind of how it used to be. It was the same after my dad died. We cleaned the whole house. Top to bottom. Mother went to the hardware shop and bought every brush and cloth and big steel bucket they had, and by the end, it felt as though every trace of him had disappeared, because it's amazing how much of yourself you leave behind, even when you're dead. Notes left on scraps of paper, photographs of moments passed by, the cup you always liked to use, the shape of who you used to be in a well-worn cushion. Not just physical things, though; something remains of you in the air as well. Brush strokes of someone long since departed rest on door handles and windowsills. They walk the treads of a staircase and hide in the pull of a curtain. My mother scrubbed all of it away. There wasn't a whisper of him left.

Terry had already gone out on one of his little adventures, and he'd left a note on the kitchen worktop. It said DON'T FORGET TO LOCK THE DOOR and I folded it up and put it in my dressing gown pocket.

It took me ages to decide what to wear this time, because I'd built up quite the collection. I'd borrowed quite a lot of Rebecca's things now and they hung right at the end of the wardrobe, behind Terry's funeral suit. In the end, I went for a cream silk blouse and a pair of wide-legged trousers I'd found brand new at the charity shop, and which Mother would have had something to say about if she'd witnessed them. I put a pretty scarf on for a 'pop of colour', because that's what the magazines say you should do. It was the same one Rebecca had and when she opened the door to the flat she said, 'I've got a scarf just like that,' and I said, '*Have you?* What a coincidence,' and she scratched at her head again, which was becoming quite the habit with her just lately, and she let me in.

Rebecca didn't even say, 'Do you mind?' or 'Have you got time?', she just handed me a duster and a can of polish, because some words drift away and disappear as time goes on. I've noticed that with Terry. Words like *I love you* and *goodnight* and *how was your day?* It makes you realise which words are fragile and cling by a thread, because some of them break off so easily and are never heard of again.

After I'd dusted, I plugged the hoover in and dragged the chairs and the settee across the room, because I'd discovered Rebecca wasn't especially particular about what went on underneath her furniture. It was then I found it. The present I'd given her. It was still resting in the wrapping paper I'd chosen and the little card was hiding in a ball of fluff a bit further back. I was still holding it when Rebecca marched into the room, looking for her cigarettes.

'Have you moved them?' she said. 'I swear things keep disappearing in this flat. Either that or I'm losing my mind.' She said 'losing my mind' quite loudly and Jolyon looked through from the kitchen and shook his head.

I pointed to the little table underneath the window and she went over, opened the packet and lit one.

'What about this cup?' I said, as she walked back across the room. 'Where shall I put it?'

She stared at the cup and pulled a face. It had the beautiful gold foil *Rebecca* on the front, with little cherubs around the edges, and an extra – especially long-legged – cherub to make the handle. It looked even more beautiful in daylight.

'God knows where that came from.' She blew smoke towards the ceiling. 'Just chuck it away, Linda. There's enough junk in this flat as it is.'

She flopped down in one of the armchairs and frowned. 'You look quite nice today, Linda.'

'Thank you,' I said.

She looked at the back of the door, where I'd hung the jacket I'd worn.

'I have a jacket just like that,' she said.

But it was the kind of sentence that you say to yourself more than anyone else, and so I didn't answer back.

'Well, Linda, the time has finally arrived,' Jolyon said, as he came through from the kitchen. 'We're going to introduce you to our new business venture today. No time like the present!'

I'd been waiting for him to talk about it again. It had been on the tip of my tongue to ask each time I saw them, but I'd discovered long ago that the very best way to get someone to talk about something is not to mention it at all.

'I thought you'd forgotten about it,' I said. 'I thought you'd changed your mind.'

'I never forget my promises, Linda. We just needed to make sure you were the right calibre. Needed you to earn your stripes first.' Jolyon smiled one of his smiles. 'Come on, Bex. Run through what you're going to do.'

Rebecca was still looking at the jacket, but Jolyon's words seemed to snap her out of it.

'You're going to become one of Robin Hood's merry men!' She used her sing-song voice, because people think sing-song voices make harmful things sound less harmful.

'We need to set up a little page for you online. Make you all official. If you're going to help us with the business, you're going to have to have an online presence.'

'Why?'

'Because those are the kinds of things people check to make sure you're legit. No one trusts someone who isn't on the internet, Linda. You might as well not exist at all.'

'But I've never been on the world wide web,' I said. 'I don't see why I have to start now.'

Rebecca looked as though she was wrestling with something in her throat.

'Linda,' she said. 'Linda, if you're going to go out into the world and do our . . .'

'Charity work,' said Jolyon.

'Yes, charity work,' she said. 'You're going to need an online presence. No one will trust you otherwise. It's the first thing people do when they meet someone new. They look them up online.'

I couldn't argue with that.

'So you need a nice smiley picture and a little biography, and you'll be able to persuade anyone of anything. Just bring me a photo from home.'

'Oh, but I don't have any pictures of myself. Only my wedding photo.'

'No pictures? No photographs at all?' It was the first time I'd seen Rebecca look shocked about anything and she let go of my hands. '*Everyone* has photographs of themselves, don't they?'

'Not me,' I said. 'If you want a picture of me, you're going to have to take one yourself,' and I laughed a bit.

Rebecca nodded and blew more smoke around. 'That's what we'll do, then. We'll take some pictures. Especially now . . . with your new hair.'

'Wouldn't you want me to wear a wig, like you do in all your photos?'

'No need!' she said. 'Nobody knows you. You're . . . fresh as a daisy!'

'I really hate having my photograph taken, Rebecca,' I said. 'I'd really rather not.'

'Nonsense!' she said, getting up from her chair. 'It'll be a breeze, and anyway, we can just change what you don't like.'

'How do you mean?'

'We can make you thinner or taller. We can make your hair longer and your nose smaller. Anything you don't like about your face, we can just rub out.' She waved her phone at me. 'I've got an app.'

'Why not just take a photograph of someone thinner and taller, and with longer hair?'

'Linda!' She sighed. 'Look, if you really hate it that much, we can take them from a distance.'

'Like candid shots?'

'Yes, if you like,' she said. 'You don't even have to look at the camera. How about that? Plus, it'll take your mind off Terry.'

I could tell she wanted to pull the words back in as soon

as they'd left her mouth, because she looked all sheepish and not like Rebecca at all. There was no escaping him, though. He'd been in all the papers. The police said they'd taken a forty-five-year-old man in for questioning; they didn't say it was Terry but within twenty-four hours, his picture was all over the place. I don't know who tipped the papers off, but Malcolm had been unusually absent from the landscape for the past three days, so I knew who my money was on.

Rebecca said it was best not to take pictures in the flat and I agreed with her, so we walked to the little square with the statue and the park benches.

'Shall we take some outside the Co-op?' I said. 'I could pretend to use the cashpoint?'

Rebecca pulled a face. 'I suppose so,' she said.

I made her stand as far back as I could, but when I pretended to put my card into the machine, I could still hear the little click of the shutter on the phone's camera.

'Why don't we take some on the benches?' she said, and so we did. I sat and pretended to read a newspaper someone had left and then I leaned across and looked over the back of the seat and gazed at nothing in particular, like the models do in Mother's catalogues.

'Great, Linda.' Rebecca kept saying as she clicked away. 'You're a natural, Linda.'

My face ran out of expressions eventually, and I shouted over to her, 'Shall we go back – have we got enough now?'

'Probably, but let's get a few more just in case.' She pointed over to the little flower stall. 'Take off your jacket so it looks like it's a different day, and let's do some over there.'

The tarpaulin had been removed from the kiosk and there were steel buckets everywhere, all filled with flowers. Tulips and chrysanthemums, roses and daffodils. Because at this time of year, you can guarantee there will always be daffodils.

'I'd rather not,' I said.

'Linda, don't be so ridiculous.' Rebecca walked over and began taking off my jacket for me, as if I were a small child. 'It'll make a great shot.'

I stood by the stall, and the woman in the apron with a moneybag around her waist had an understandable assumption that if you were taking photographs of her flower stall, you were technically obliged to buy a bunch of flowers from her.

'How about some lovely daffs?' she said.

I looked down at the bucket. It was the beginning of the day and a crowd of them were packed in there together, fighting for space. Their stems sodden and pressed against each other, their sickly yellow petals shouting out for attention. I looked away again. 'I don't like daffodils.'

'Everyone likes daffodils!' she said. 'Some of my regulars love them so much, they say they wish they could have daffodils all year round!'

I narrowed my eyes and stared right into hers.

'Well, I don't,' I whispered.

She looked away and said, 'Right,' a few times and I allowed her to persuade me into a bunch of tulips. While she was wrapping them into their paper, I looked over at Rebecca and just at that moment, she took a photograph. I heard the little click on her phone.

'I'll delete that one,' she said later, scrolling through all the photos. 'We've got hundreds here.'

'No, no.' I leaned across and scrolled back. 'I think I like that one most of all.'

I was staring straight at the camera, and my eyes spilled with anger.

'You do?' she said.

'It looks more like me than any of the others,' I said. 'There's no point in pretending to be someone you're not, is there?'

32

Rebecca had taken to mumbling to herself as she walked around the house. It was barely noticeable at first. You could only hear it if you tuned your ears in properly at the beginning, although Jolyon must have tuned his ears in because I caught him looking over at her a few times.

Jolyon and I were getting along like a house on fire. He was so easy to talk to because he was interested in everything I said. Always asking me things. Especially about Terry.

'Have you had any press approaching you?' he said on more than one occasion. 'Because they will, you know, if Terry's a suspect.'

Jolyon was very familiar with the press, apparently. He'd had 'dealings with them', although he didn't elaborate on what those dealings were, which I thought was very discreet of him.

'They'll offer you money, you know,' he said. 'Quite substantial money, and you must promise me one thing, Linda.'

At this point he looked deep into my eyes and I held my breath to make the looking last a bit longer.

'What should I promise you?' I said and let all my breath out, although I would have promised him anything as long as it meant he kept staring at me.

'Promise me you'll speak to me first if they approach you. I wouldn't want anyone taking advantage of such a sweet person.'

I was a sweet person. No one had ever called me that before. No one had ever called me very much at all, if I'm honest. It kept me going all afternoon.

'Where have you put it?'

Rebecca's mumblings were particularly loud that day and she seemed to have collected them all up and she shouted at us from the doorway.

'Put what?' Jolyon said.

We were in the middle of a conversation about the benefits of tabloid journalism and he didn't seem to be very pleased at being interrupted.

'The *letter*. I had another anonymous letter this morning and I put it on the table in the hall and now it's gone.'

'Well, I haven't touched it,' he said.

'Nor me,' I said.

'It was right there.' She waved her hand back at the hall. 'On the table underneath that bloody painting.'

'Are you sure it was another one? Perhaps you just put the old letter on there by mistake.'

'Jolyon, I'm not stupid. This was different. It said DON'T THINK I'VE FORGOTTEN in big ugly capital letters. He's out there, you know. He's probably watching the flat right now.'

She marched over to the window.

'Darling, don't be so paranoid.'

'I'm not paranoid! I've had three silent phone calls now. Three. But they only ever happen when neither of you are here!'

'Why don't I run you a nice bath,' I said. 'Make you feel a bit better.'

'I don't need a *nice bath*.' She was still craning her neck to look down at the pavement. 'I'm fine as I am.'

'You've just been looking a bit . . . dishevelled lately.'

Rebecca spun around.

'Dishevelled?' She glared at me and then looked at Jolyon. 'Since when have I looked dishevelled? I never look dishevelled, do I?!'

'Linda's right. You do a bit, sweetheart. Just lately.'

'I beg your pardon? What do you mean, *Linda's right*?'

'You've just . . .' Jolyon sat back and studied her. '. . . let yourself go a little bit.'

Rebecca didn't say anything, she just glared at him.

'I mean, only a little bit,' he said. 'Easily rectified. Why don't you let Linda do something with your hair and make-up? She's very good at it, aren't you, Linda?'

I was going to agree with him because I'd been practising so hard over the past few weeks, but Rebecca marched out of the room before I had a chance.

It was just as well, because she might have wanted to put on one of her wigs and I'd taken a couple of them home on the bus, given them a wash and blow-dry, and they looked so good, I thought I might hang on to them for a little while. Just for fun.

NOW

I'd never set foot on a ward before this place.

Although ward is a loose term, because everyone wears their own clothes here and no one ever seems to bother taking a pulse or shoving a thermometer in anybody's ears. I suppose once your mind has lost its way, that trumps everything else and all your other problems have to wait their turn.

It's not for want of trying. People are always complaining of headaches and sore throats, and little bits and pieces they think might be wrong with them. It must help to pass the time, because Mother has a lot of that on her hands as well and she often specialises in the same thing. One woman in the day room said the government had placed a microchip in her ear canal and they were monitoring her every move from somewhere in Whitehall. No one took any notice.

Although I did spot one or two people briefly sticking their fingers down their own ears.

Everyone knew the microchip was a figment of her imagination, a symptom of the illness that crawled and crouched in her mind. That was an easy one to figure out. Even Terry would have spotted it, and he's never been very big on noticing details. Other things aren't so obvious, though. Other things take a bit more thinking about and sometimes we get it wrong, because we don't look at all the other clues in the puzzle. We just concentrate on what we'd like to see and use it as evidence to suit the answer we'd like to come up with.

They said my dad was depressed. They said he'd been depressed for some time and they didn't bother listening to me when I told them how happy we were. How we'd gone for a stroll that morning down the lane, and he'd walked with his hands in his pockets and kicked at the shingle on the footpath and laughed at my jokes. They didn't take any notice when I explained the conversation we'd had. How we'd talked about me wanting to go in for hairdressing when I left school, and he hadn't laughed at me like Mother did. How, instead, he'd told me I could be anything I wanted to be. All I had to do was pick the life I imagined I would lead and start walking towards it. They ignored all of that. Instead, they only took the words from me that they wanted. About what I saw when I walked into the room, about what they thought it meant. Not about what *I* thought it meant. They only took the parts that suited their own answers and they cut away all the rest. Leaving nice clean margins.

I had never seen a dead body before I saw my dad's.

He lay on the bank, a little further downstream from where I stood. He was muddy and pale, his lungs so full of water there was no room left in them for any air. I'd only gone down there to pick flowers. I'd seen some earlier, on our walk, and I wanted to put them in a vase on top of the piano. To make the room smile again.

He'd taken some of Mother's tablets, they said later. Because no matter what situation you might find yourself in, no matter how much you are tired of living, your body will always try to protect itself. To rescue you, just in case you change your mind. To be your saviour. The tablets would have stopped that, the inquest said. They would have made sure his mind slept whilst his body found its escape. They would have allowed my father, with weighted pockets, to walk into the shock of the deep, black water and to disappear forever.

They say 'stone cold dead' and they're right, because I touched his face. His eyes were wide open. You wouldn't think that, would you? On the television, everyone closes their eyes when they die, but it's not true because my dad stared back at me on that riverbank. I thought he might break into a smile and say, *'That got you, didn't it, Linda!'* or *'I'm only joking, Linda!'* but he didn't. He just stared. As though he'd had one last thing he wanted to say, but he'd run out of time in which to say it.

I don't remember getting back to the house. I know I didn't say anything. I just pushed past Mother, and I was covered in mud and reeds, so she followed the journey I'd taken to see what I'd just seen for herself. I could hear her screaming long after she'd stopped because some things get stuck in your mind and refuse to leave, even if you ask them to. I was sitting on the stairs when she got back, and she told me to get to my room and not come down until I was told. There was so much commotion. Shouting and vehicles and lights. I leaned right out of the bathroom window to see what was going on, because I knew no one would notice, and I watched the ambulance men crowd around my dad's body. His eyes were still open and he continued staring at me, as though he'd noticed I was there when no one else had. Because Dad was just like me. He always noticed everything. They'd got him wired up to all sorts of machinery, things I didn't understand, but I knew one of them was for his heart because the leads had been stuck onto his chest. All the leads went into a little screen, and I watched the little screen, waiting for the up and down pattern to appear. The pattern that tells you that someone is still here, that they still have some purpose left in the world. The same pattern that appeared in the glass on mine and Terry's front door.

But there was nothing.

Just a perfectly flat line.

33

'It's really simple, Linda. It couldn't be simpler.'

Rebecca was sitting on the carpet in front of me, her hands clasped together like she was saying a small prayer.

'I still don't understand what I'm supposed to do,' I said.

'Just keep the sales assistant busy.' Jolyon reached forward and ground his cigarette out. He had much more patience than Rebecca. Especially with me.

'How?' I said.

'Talk to them. Ask them questions,' Rebecca clasped her hands together a little more tightly. 'God, I don't know. Just make sure they're focused on you instead of on me.'

'And what will you be doing?' I said.

Rebecca looked over at Jolyon, who had already lit another cigarette and was wafting a matchstick about.

'She'll be shopping,' he said. 'But with a slight difference.'

Rebecca let out a tiny snort. She tried to wrap it up in a cough, but I spotted it. I spot everything. I wasn't born yesterday.

I looked at her. 'What does he mean?'

'He *means* . . .' she dragged the word out to give the other ones a chance to catch up, 'that I won't be paying for anything.'

'Shoplifting?' I said and I covered my mouth.

'It's not really shoplifting, Linda.' Jolyon sat back and stared up at the ceiling, where his smoke had formed a little yellow cloud on the paintwork. 'That's not a term I like to use.'

'Well what else would you call it?' I said.

'See!' Rebecca said. 'I knew this was a bad idea – she's not up to it. This is a big mistake!'

'Rebecca, calm down!' Jolyon pinched at the little bit of skin between his eyebrows. 'You've been so tetchy lately, just loosen up a bit. Linda's smart. She'll be just grand.' And he smiled a nice smile.

'The thing is, Linda, these big retailers factor in shop-lifting when they price things up. They assume these losses will happen, so really, *really*, we're just taking something we've already paid for.'

I smiled back at him. 'When you put it like that, it sounds almost acceptable.'

'Excellent!' Rebecca clapped and stood up. 'I have a list of things I need to get.'

She passed a piece of paper over to me. There was quite a mix on there. Make-up, household goods, clothing. All quite small things. Easily hidden.

'What do you want with a size fourteen silk nightdress?'
I said.

'They're not for me, silly.' She pulled her jacket from
the back of a chair. 'They're all things I've been asked to
get for other people.'

'And then you charge them a fraction of the real cost?'
I said.

'You've got it! The customer is happy, we're happy, and
the shop doesn't lose out because they're insured!' Jolyon
winked at me and I felt my cheeks warm up, because he
always had that effect on me.

'When shall we do it?' I said.

'No time like the present!' Rebecca picked her keys up
from the coffee table. 'The cleaning can wait until we get back.'

'What shall I wear?'

She glanced back at me. I'd got on a jumper I'd borrowed
from Rebecca's airing cupboard, although she was so blind
she hadn't even noticed, and a pair of trousers I'd bought
from work.

'You look perfect just as you are,' she said. 'No one would
ever suspect you were up to any mischief whatsoever.'

'When we get in there, just pretend you don't know me.'

We were walking through the shopping centre towards
the big department store, and I was forced to take two
steps to every one of Rebecca's.

'Why?' I whispered. I always whisper in shopping centres.
They bring it out in me.

'Because we don't want them realising we're together,' she said. 'Don't talk to me. Don't even make eye contact. We shouldn't even be talking now, there are cameras everywhere.'

'So how is it going to work?'

She stopped and looked up at the high glass ceilings.

'Remember what's on the list, Linda. Walk around the store. Linger in those departments and talk to some assistants – it's not difficult, the minute you slow down they pounce on you.'

'What will you be doing?'

'I'll follow you around. Discreetly. At a distance. While you're keeping them occupied, I'll acquire what we came for.' She put her hands on my shoulders. 'You can do this, Linda. I have every faith in you.'

Faith wasn't something people immediately thought of when they met me, and I didn't recall anyone ever finding it in me before. Even Mother, who booked a day off work for the resit before I'd even taken my first driving test.

We went into the store. Rebecca immediately disappeared off somewhere to my left, but the problem with telling someone to not do something is that it only makes them want to do it even more, and it was the same with not looking at Rebecca.

I couldn't help myself. Every time I turned my head I seemed to catch her eye, and the more I tried to stop it, the more it happened. At one point, she glared so hard at me over a tray of sunglasses, I was forced into an abrupt one-hundred-and-eighty-degree turn and I headed off towards the beauty hall. I felt safe in there because the smell felt like a lullaby and I knew there was make-up on the list, even if I couldn't remember exactly what it was. And then I thought of Natalie. I found her straight away. Right on the spot where she'd been before, wearing the exact same clothes.

'Hello!' I said.

I lifted my chin up to show Natalie my full face because I thought there was more of a chance of her recognising me if she saw me from a similar angle, but when she said hello back again I could tell there was a degree of puzzlement about it.

'It's Linda. Coppery eyeshadow Linda.' I smiled at her and closed my eyes.

'Right,' she said, but the right was very slow and not at all convincing.

'You said I was born to wear it. Although I haven't got it on now, obviously.'

I laughed, although it was probably a bit too loud because a couple of other people turned around and I could see Rebecca shake her head at the edge of my eyes.

'Right, yes. Linda. Of course. I remember,' Natalie said. 'What can I do for you today, Linda?'

I glanced over at Rebecca. It just slipped out.

'I just wondered,' I glanced again and I spoke very loud and slow, so Rebecca would know I was doing my job, 'if you could recommend me another eyeshadow. A different one. Although coppery is beautiful, I wondered if there was something a little less coppery. Just for a bit of a change.'

Natalie beamed at me. 'Yes, of course!'

I sat on the high stool again. I'd forgotten how slidey it was and my feet kept missing the little foot bar and stamping on the floor. A couple of other people turned around, and this time Rebecca definitely shook her head, because I looked back to check.

'Are you all right, Linda?' Natalie unscrewed the top from one of her little pots. 'You seem a bit jittery.'

I leaned round to see where Rebecca was and my foot hit the floor again.

'No, I'm fine. Completely fine,' I said.

Natalie looked across the shop floor towards Rebecca. 'Is that woman bothering you?'

'The woman who keeps staring at us? Continually?' I said. 'No, absolutely not. Not at all. Not in the least bit.'

'She's very rude. I can call security, if you like?'

'Really, it's not necessary.' I slid to my feet and whispered, 'I just feel a little . . . exposed.'

'Come on, let's take you around here.' Natalie picked up my stool and moved it to the back of one of the stands. 'We'll do your make-up on this side instead.'

I sat in my new position, and while Natalie sorted out all her little brushes around her waist, I stared through the stand at Rebecca and she stared back at me with furious eyes, between the lip glosses and the liquid bronzers.

'Well that was a complete waste of bloody time,' Rebecca said.

We were walking back through the shopping centre. I couldn't keep up this time, even with two steps to her one.

'I'm sorry. Let's try again – I'm sure I'll get the hang of it eventually.'

'You do realise we've completely blown our chances in that store. I won't be able to go back in there for weeks.'

'Then let's go somewhere else,' I said. 'There are lots of other shops.'

Conversation had slowed us to a stop, and we were standing right outside a women's clothes boutique. It was one of those where the mannequins were made to look as far removed from human beings as they possibly could, and they all had fourteen-inch waists and the same hairstyle.

Rebecca took the list out of her pocket. 'I suppose so,' she said.

I hadn't banked on it being so poorly lit in there. Rails of clothing crouched in semi-darkness, with the occasional spotlight emphasising a skirt or a pair of tracksuit bottoms. The music seemed to make it darker somehow as well. It wasn't like the songs I listened to, but wordless music that spilled from big speakers on the ceilings and sent its beat through the floor and the walls, and made all the little rails vibrate under your fingertips.

It was too hard to even see Rebecca, let alone avoid her. Each time I went round a corner she was there, and I had to turn and run away from her again. A few times I thought I'd managed it, only to look up and see her face right in front of mine. Potentially, I may have let out a few small squeaks, because one of the sales assistants came up to me and asked if I was all right. She had bright red hair in bunches and a big smile. Her name was Taylor. I knew this because it was written on a large piece of plastic that hung around her neck.

'I'm fine, Taylor, thank you,' I said. 'I'm just trying to avoid someone.'

Taylor and her pigtails swivelled towards Rebecca. 'Is that woman bothering you?' she said.

'Not at all,' I said. I gave her a glazed smile, the kind Mother is so fond of dishing out.

'Because there's CCTV, you know.' Taylor looked up at the ceiling. 'It's everywhere.'

'Is it?' I said. 'I hadn't noticed.'

Jolyon was quite nice about it all. I knew he would be. Even though Rebecca did lots of huffing and puffing when we got back, and tried to turn it into something far more dramatic than it was by parading different impressions of me up and down the living room.

'Honestly, Jolyon – she was literally this bad. Literally!' and she did a stupid walk, which was meant to be mine, I suppose.

'Really?' Jolyon said.

'Yes.' Rebecca was still doing the stupid walk up and down the carpet. 'Really.'

I didn't look at either of them. I decided to ignore the conversation and get on with my cleaning, because Mother always says if you can't be useful, at least don't get in people's way, but I did steal a small glance in Jolyon's direction, and he was staring right at me.

'I find that very hard to believe,' he said very quietly, and he winked at me without Rebecca even noticing.

In the end they both went to the pub and left me to get on with it, so I had the place to myself for once. I put my Marigolds on as usual. There's no point spending all that time cleaning somewhere if you're going to ruin it all by leaving smears and finger-smudges all over the clean surfaces, and I made quick work of it for once because neither of them was under my feet. Also, it did mean I had time to sort out my little surprise without anyone catching on. I knew Rebecca missed me when I wasn't there, so I'd taken the trouble of nipping into Boots and getting a photograph printed. It was the one Rebecca had taken of me by the flower stall, with me staring straight into the camera, and I'd put it in a little silver frame for her. I knew she wouldn't accept if I tried to give it as a present, because she's completely selfless, just like Tamsin, so instead I just slid it at the back of one of the shelves in the living room. I knew it was unlikely that she'd notice straight away, but perhaps she'd be sitting there one day feeling fed up and wishing I was there, and she'd look around and *hey presto!* There I'd be, staring back at her.

I was quite pleased with myself. So pleased, it must have gone straight to my head because I turned the handle of Jolyon's study instead of going into the bedroom. The doors were right next to each other and I was so full of my little surprise, I tried the wrong one by mistake. The one that's always locked.

Except this time, it was open.

Jolyon must have rushed off to the pub and forgotten.

He was bound to do it one day, because other people have minds like sieves. They can't help themselves. They get distracted by something shiny and new, and completely forget what's actually important. I knew the study was important the minute I walked in there, because it had that air about it. Different rooms have different personalities, just like houses, and this room knew it was the most interesting place in the flat.

It was quite gloomy because there were no windows, so I switched the light on. Luckily, there was no shade, just a bare bulb, which lit everything up nicely and meant I could have a good look around. You look with your eyes, that's what Mother says, so I made sure I didn't touch anything before I'd properly got my bearings. There was a large desk against the far wall. It reminded me of Terry's desk, piled with paper and full of clutter, except Jolyon's desk was twice the size and the computer on it was much smarter than Terry's. It was a laptop, even nicer than Mother's, and there was no sign of the Grand Canyon anywhere, just a swirly pattern on the screen that kept vanishing and reappearing, and trying its best to hypnotise you into guessing where it would turn up next. The other wall was filled with filing cabinets. The big metal ones like you get at the doctor's. I knew they'd be locked without even trying, because they had that look about them, so I went over to the desk instead.

There was a chair, of course. One of these modern spinning affairs with a giant spring stretched out in all its glory, because the things that used to be hidden people like to show off these days. Like open-plan offices and armpit hair. I had my apron and my Marigolds on, but I chose not to sit down. Instead, I decided to tackle the drawers. 'A tidy office is a tidy mind', that's what I'd say if they noticed. I wouldn't take any thanks for it, because gratitude wasn't necessary. I don't do these things to be thanked, I do them for the greater good.

The first two drawers were mainly old pens and creased receipts. Scatterings of paperclips and pencil sharpenings that hadn't managed to find their way to the nearest wastepaper bin. There was a ball of string and a few safety pins in the next drawer down. Lots of unused notebooks, because people buy these things thinking they have plenty to say, but as soon as they sit down in front of a sheet of paper, they realise none of it is really worth writing down. Behind the notebooks there was one of those padded Jiffy bags. I was going to dismiss it as being empty as well, but when I lifted it up a shower of bits of plastic fell out of it. It was only when I cursed and knelt down on the carpet to pick them all up again, I realised they were credit cards. Dozens of them. I thought, *Jolyon and Rebecca must have a lot of bank accounts between them*, but then I looked at the names on the cards and they were all different. People I'd never heard of. Except one of them. Linda Hammett. I'd heard of her.

I shuffled all the cards into a neat pile. I returned them to their Jiffy bag and pushed the bag to the back of the drawer when my hand hit a box file. I've never really held with box files because they seem like somewhere you just throw all your nonsense out of sight so you don't have to keep looking at it any more, but I pulled it out nevertheless and opened the lid and lifted up the big metal spring.

It was full of Rebecca.

Photographs. Not the neat and tidy ones that she had on the internet wearing all her different wigs, but messy and colourful photographs from her childhood. All different sizes, like photographs used to be. Pictures of teenage years, with posters on a wall of bands long since forgotten. Last day of school. Fairgrounds and fancy dress. There was even a photograph of her sitting next to her mum, which I was quite pleased about. A party, perhaps, or a holiday café. Her mum had aged terribly, I thought. Time hadn't treated her very kindly, although there was no mistaking her. You always get the face you deserve, Mother reckons. And she'd know.

Underneath all the photographs there was an old paper driving licence and a birth certificate, and even Rebecca's passport. At least, the passport had her photograph in it, but the name was different. It was the same name on the paper driving licence and the birth certificate too.

Karen Smith.

I gathered all the bits and pieces together and put them in a creased brown envelope I found in the second drawer down. A box file was no place to keep important documents like these. They needed to go somewhere safe. Somewhere not everyone could get their hands on them.

I smiled at Karen Smith before I sealed her away.

It felt like bumping into an old friend.

34

'We're just worried about you, Linda.'

Tamsin stood on the front step. She was wearing her pretty beaded jacket and one of those giant scarves that wraps itself around your neck a hundred times, yet still manages to almost trail on the floor.

Tamsin had never been to the house before. It's strange seeing someone you know with a different background and it always takes a moment to recognise them again, because the background and the foreground don't seem to match up any more.

I wanted to tell her that everything in my life was going exactly as I thought it would, but instead I said, 'I'm just a bit off colour, that's all.'

I saw her look me up and down in that subtle way people do when they think their eyes aren't moving very much, and I realised I was wearing one of Rebecca's dresses.

'You look really well, Linda. Considering everything that's been going on. Your hair looks . . . new. Not like your old style at all.'

'I haven't been myself,' I said. 'For quite a while now.'

'You haven't turned up for work in three weeks. You don't answer your phone. Head office wanted to call you in, but I said I'd try and have a word with you first.'

Tamsin tried to look over my shoulder, and I could tell she was after being invited in.

'I'll put the kettle on,' I said.

After she'd unwound herself out of her scarf and unbuttoned the little beads on her jacket, Tamsin sat down at the kitchen table. One of Rebecca's brochures was lying there. I'd just got it out to have a leaf through while I waited for the next load of laundry to finish, and Tamsin picked it up.

'This is nice,' she said. 'Is it yours?'

The kettle clicked and I felt a drift of steam wander into my face.

'No, it belongs to a friend.' I poured the water into the teapot. It spat and hissed, and I had to raise my voice over the noise of it. 'My best friend, actually. The one I told you about.'

'I see.' Tamsin turned a few more pages. 'She must be quite well off, Linda. Some of these things cost a small fortune.'

'She believes in quality, Tamsin.' I stirred the pot. 'As do I. Clothes are an investment and you only get one chance to make a first impression.'

'It depends on who you're trying to impress, I suppose.'

When I turned and took the teapot to the table, Tamsin had put the brochure down and she sat back in her chair, watching me.

'Have you been spending a lot of time with this friend you keep mentioning?' she said.

'Loads.' I poured milk into the mugs. I didn't bother using my best ones, because I knew Tamsin didn't bother with those types of things. Her mug at work had a big chip in it and half of the poppies had worn away. 'She's always inviting me over because I think she depends on me for company. It's getting quite embarrassing, really.'

I passed her tea but she didn't look at it. She carried on watching my face instead. I could see the question coming. It hovered around her lips for ages before it found a way out.

'How's it going, Linda? With Terry, I mean?'

I took a big sip of tea, because I needed to give my face something else to do for a minute.

'Oh, you know,' I said eventually. 'He's just helping the police. They're interviewing all sorts of people, not just him.'

'I haven't heard of anyone else being interviewed for this long.'

She said it kindly. Not like most people. Not like Mother's words with their serrated edges.

'They're just being thorough, Tamsin. It's a good thing, isn't it? We need the police to be thorough because there's no point being slapdash when it comes to a murder inquiry.'

369

She picked up her mug of tea and watched me over the rim.

'I hope your friend Rebecca is being supportive,' she said.

'Oh, very supportive,' I answered very quickly, just so there was no doubt in anybody's mind. 'She can't do enough for me.'

'And your mother?'

'Would you like a biscuit?' I said.

I thought it would just be a flying visit, but half an hour later, Tamsin was still at the kitchen table with questions wandering all around her face.

She talked about work quite a bit as well. New stock we'd had in, which was something that would usually interest me, but I just couldn't find anything exciting in it now. She also said the shop wasn't the same without me.

'People have been asking after you, Linda,' she said. 'Lots of customers wondering where you are.'

Which was strange because no one usually bothered with me from one day to the next. On the other hand, Tamsin was one of those folk everyone took to immediately. You see people like that from time to time and I can never work out what it is about them. I just know that whatever it is, I wasn't given any of it, because I never seem to have that effect on anyone.

'Not that it matters, but who's been asking after me?' I said.

Tamsin came out with a long list of regulars and passers-by. Even Nigel the butcher, who hadn't so much as given me the time of day in fifteen years.

'Everyone is very concerned,' she said.

The thought of all these people being concerned made a strange warmth unfold across my chest and travel down my arms.

'Tell me who was concerned again,' I said because I wanted to stretch the warmth out and make it last a bit longer.

She was halfway through repeating all the names when there was a knock at the door. It wasn't like Tamsin's knock had been, soft and a little bit hesitant; this knock was loud and impatient, and it made Tamsin and me stop talking and stare at each other across the kitchen table.

'I suppose I'd better get that,' I said.

I stood up and smoothed down my hair and my dress, and I was halfway across the kitchen when the knocking started again.

'All right, all right.'

I pulled at the door and argued with it, because it had started sticking in cold weather. I'd asked Terry to look at it but you might as well ask a brick wall.

'Where's the bloody fire?' I said, giving it one last pull.

When it swung open, there were half a dozen police officers standing on my front lawn.

35

The one on the doorstep was DS Graeme.

He was the only one I recognised, and he put some piece of paper or other under my nose and said, 'We've got a warrant to search the house, Linda — we'll probably have to take a few things away with us.'

Before I could even find something to say back again, the other ones were filing past me and into the hall. A great stream of them it felt like, all uniforms and stern faces.

'We'll be as quick as we can. Try not to worry,' DS Graeme said. 'Everything will be put back exactly how it was.'

Except it wouldn't, because no one is as particular as me, let alone police officers with their sodding great feet and clumsy ways. I could hear them upstairs, marching down the landing and opening all the doors. There was one in the front room, going through all the drawers in the sideboard. I could see him from where I was stood.

'I'll have to go over the whole house again!' I shouted. 'Bringing in all this muck from the outside! Whatever happened to good manners?'

'Sorry, Linda,' said DS Graeme.

It was the sorry that got to me more than the muck and the sodding great feet, because you don't realise you've become someone who needs to be pitied until you read about it in someone else's eyes.

When DS Graeme walked past me, I realised there was a female police officer standing right behind him. She was in a uniform like some of the others, but she had a kinder face and a little bit of mascara.

'Hello Linda,' she said. 'I'm Carol.'

She stepped inside as well, and I didn't give it a second thought because it doesn't take you long to get used to people just walking into your hallway without an invitation.

'Oh good, you've already got someone with you,' she said.

I turned around and Tamsin was standing in the doorway of the kitchen. She was still holding her mug of tea, but her face had changed. She didn't just look concerned any more, she looked frightened.

'There's no need to worry, Tamsin,' I said. 'It's all very routine and they're not going to make any mess.'

And then I burst into tears.

*   *   *

Carol and Tamsin sat either side of me on the settee in the front room.

They'd finished searching in there, DS Graeme said, and it was best to stay put and just let everyone get on with it. Quicker, he said, if I didn't follow people around asking questions and trying to help.

'Look at the state of this room.' I pointed at the mantelpiece. The tip of my finger was trembling and I tried to make it stop, but it felt like it belonged to someone else. 'Nothing's where it should be.'

Tamsin got up and straightened the wedding photograph.

'Those drawers aren't shut properly.' I nodded at the sideboard. 'Look at them!'

'We'll tidy up when they've gone, Linda.' Tamsin passed me the mug I'd left on the coffee table. 'It'll soon be back to the way it was.'

The tea was stone cold, and an orange film lay on its surface.

'Why are they doing this, anyway?' I said. 'What on earth are they searching for?'

DS Graeme walked into the room as I was speaking and I saw Carol give him a look.

'Terry's helping us with the inquiry,' she said, 'and we think it might be useful to have a look around to see if there's anything else we need to know.'

DS Graeme gave her a small nod. It was very subtle but I spotted it. I spot everything. I wasn't born yesterday.

'In the airing cupboard?' I said. 'And the pantry?'

'We're just being thorough, Linda.' DS Graeme stepped over the contents of a drawer one of the policemen had left on the floor. 'Best get it over with in one go, eh?'

I'd just about got used to their clodhopping all over the place, but then they started taking things away. Marching down the stairs with all sorts, I could see them from where I was sitting. Carol tried to distract me, talking about weekends away and city breaks, but I don't miss a trick.

They had two big vans parked up outside. I got up from the settee, even though Carol tried to stop me, and I watched them load up from the window. Bedding, Terry's clothes, all manner of things from the back bedroom. One of them was struggling down the driveway with Terry's computer.

'It's nothing to do with me, that thing isn't,' I said. 'I don't even know how to switch it on. Ask anybody.'

'Well, that's true enough,' Tamsin said, because people repeat everything you tell them about yourself, if you say it enough times.

DC Graeme took a notebook from his pocket and pushed through a few pages. 'There's just a couple of things we were curious about,' he said. 'If you could maybe help us out?'

For a second, I thought they might be talking about the laptop, but I'd taken it back to Mother's and of course there was no way they'd know anything about it. It's strange how a policeman standing in front of you makes your mind lose track of itself.

'Like what?' I said.

'Men's shoes.' He looked at his notes. 'Size nine. Wing walker boots – very hard to get hold of, it seems. Especially in the UK.' He passed me a photograph. 'Does Terry own a pair like these?'

I looked at the picture. 'Oh, he threw those out a few weeks ago. Ruined them at work, apparently.'

'Did you see him throw the boots out?'

I stared for a moment at another photograph. The one on the mantelpiece. The flowers in my hair. The uncertainty in my eyes.

'Well no,' I said. 'But I haven't seen them since. What was the other thing?'

Graeme checked his notes. 'A burgundy leather jacket. Man's. Size extra large.' He turned the page. 'Apparently, it's got a small pen mark near one of the pockets. Do you know why your husband tried to dispose of it in a charity shop?'

I looked at Tamsin. She had gone bright pink.

It was gone two o'clock by the time everyone left.

The vans pulled away, loaded with our things. DS Graeme thought they might have to call for another one, but in the end they managed to fit everything in. He gave me a list of what they'd taken. An inventory, he called it. As though giving it a posh name made it slightly more acceptable.

'It'll all be returned when we're done with it, Linda,' he said.

I looked at the list. There wasn't anything on there I particularly wanted back. All of Terry's clothes they could keep, as far as I was concerned, because it meant fewer things to wash, and the bedding needed replacing anyway. Even the computer wasn't much use any more. The keyboard was too annoying with all its missing letters, and besides, I could borrow Mother's laptop again if I needed to look anything up.

'Are you sure you don't want me to stay?' Tamsin said, after they'd all gone. 'Carol thought it would be best if someone sat with you. At least for a little while.'

'There's really no need.' I tried edging her towards the front door, but for every step I took in that direction, she took another one back into the room. 'I think I might just have a bath and call it a day.'

'If you're certain?' she said.

'I'm certain.' I went around her and opened the front door. 'Really.'

I watched her walk down the drive in her little beaded jacket and her twisty scarf, and then I went to the top of the stairs and followed the top of her head along the little alleyway at the side of the house, until I was absolutely sure that she'd left.

It was only then that I put my music on, as loud as I dared, and opened a new packet of Jaffa Cakes.

You can't beat a bit of ABBA of a Thursday evening.

NOW

Whenever you're brought into hospital, the first thing they always do is take a history.

It was the same with Terry's appendix and Mother, when she had one of her headaches. They put you in a little cubicle, curtained away from all the other stories, and then they ask you how you came to be there. It's no different in this place, except here it might take a little bit longer than it does to enquire about losing your appetite or a throbbing behind your left temple. Although even those problems can wander back in time a lot further than you might think.

Mother never used to get headaches in Wales. She was one of those 'pull your socks up and get on with it' type of people, and she expected everyone else to be the same. *'Don't give into it, Linda,'* she'd say, if I ever complained of anything. *'Don't let it get the better of you,'* she said when I tripped on the kerb outside Boots and sat and cried on the pavement. *'Mind over matter!'* Even when they X-rayed my ankle the next day and found out that I'd fractured it. Mother believed most problems in life could be solved with a soluble aspirin and a good dose of determination, even broken bones. Until she stumbled across one that couldn't. She hadn't had a day's illness in her life until all the trouble happened with my dad, then it was one day's illness after the next. Like bunting.

'Strong cheese!' she said in the little cubicle when they asked her about the history of her headaches. So they nodded and wrote it all down, and prescribed her something, because that's always far easier than pulling out the rest of the story and untangling what you might find hidden away inside it. It makes it much simpler to sweep everything away in a corner if you've only bothered to go back five minutes, instead of a whole lifetime.

They ask different questions with their histories here, of course. They don't ask how the pain started or how long the pain lasts, or do anything to make it feel easier. Although when you look at all the pain hiding away within these walls, it might be an idea to start. They ask about how you see the future, about whether you feel positive when you think about what lies ahead. *'Do you feel good about the way things are going?'* they say. *'Do you feel optimistic about the future?'* which is a bit of a daft question really, because if the first half of a film is rubbish, it's a pretty safe bet to

assume the second half of it will be as well. You can't say
that to them, though. You have to nod and smile, and go
along with it. When they ask you to rate your mood, you
have to play it down a bit. Tell them you sleep fine and
there's nothing wrong with your appetite, because if you
don't – if you tell them the whole history, right back to
where it started – you'll end up with someone following
you around all day long, watching what you do and waiting
for you outside the toilet. I know because I've seen it often
enough. One-to-one-ing, they call it. You have a whole
person to yourself to make sure you don't get into any
bother. Sometimes you even get two, if they think you
might be a bit of a handful. Not long ago, there was a big
strapping lad in here. Six foot four, very upset about something. They gave him three. Three people, following you
around all day, watching your every move. If he wasn't
paranoid when he arrived, he certainly was after that.

The doctor back in Wales was going to send Mother
somewhere like here, I think. There was talk of it behind
a closed door, because I sat on the stairs late at night and
tried to listen. Our GP was kind, and called everyone by
their first names.

'Eunice,' I heard her say from the stairs, *'it's hardly surprising
you feel this way'* and *'Eunice, I think it might be a good idea
for you to have some extra support for a while.'* I knew my
mother was sitting at the kitchen table in last week's clothes
and I knew the doctor meant she should go into hospital.

I stared at the daffodil painting as I eavesdropped. Its

yawning, garish, shouting yellows stared back at me, and I wondered who would support me if Mother was busy being supported by someone else. Then I realised it was only ever my dad who'd been there for me all along. Mother was like the daffodils, all show and no real use, and if she went somewhere else for a while, I probably wouldn't even notice the difference.

As it happened, there was no need, because the next day my mother got washed and dressed and started cleaning the house. Room by room. Surface by surface. Skirting boards and light fittings, and all the bits you normally turn a blind eye to. I don't know where she got her energy from because she hardly ate a thing. I'd try to make something for us, a sandwich or some cheese on toast, and she'd say, '*I haven't got the stomach for it, Linda — you have it all. Eat it up.*'

And so I did. Because grief does that to you. It makes you either eat far too much or far too little, it makes you not sleep at all or sleep far too much, and it makes you either turn into someone who needs to be supported, or someone who will never need the support of anyone else ever again.

36

'You really shouldn't be here, Linda.'

Each time DS Graeme reached for Rebecca's doorbell, PC Josh, the younger policeman with him said the same thing and interrupted. This was the second time and it was no more effective than the first.

'But I'm the complainant,' I said. 'I've got every right to be here.'

DS Graeme sighed. He obviously had a bit more common sense and was also a lot more eager to get home for his tea, because he said, 'Maybe having her here will help to sort it out more quickly,' and eventually the younger one agreed with him and the bell was pressed.

Rebecca opened the door in her dressing gown, which I knew was a distinct possibility because it was a pretty safe bet no matter what time of the day it was.

'Ms Finch?' said DS Graeme.

'What do you want?' Rebecca pulled her dressing gown tighter and made herself look quite small.

'We just wondered if we could have a few moments of your time? If you wouldn't mind?'

She let them in. Just like that. It's amazing what people will do when they're reduced to their undergarments. You see it in hospitals all the time and this is why doctors get away with blue murder.

Jolyon was leaning against the windowsill in the living room with a glass of whisky in his hand, and when we all marched in he turned the same colour as the far wall and quite a large amount of whisky spilled from his glass and onto a rug I'd cleaned not three days earlier.

'This is my . . .' Rebecca hesitated for a second because clearly, describing Jolyon wasn't an easy task. '. . . business partner,' she said eventually.

Everyone nodded at each other and Jolyon gestured at the tired settees and suggested that we all sat down.

The police officers introduced themselves and Jolyon said, 'It must be something worthwhile to send a DS,' and all his nerves escaped wrapped up in a small laugh.

'Linda,' said DS Graeme, 'Linda gets special treatment at the moment.'

Jolyon nodded very slowly and said, 'So what can we help you with today?' which made it sound like we'd accidentally walked into a men's outfitters.

PC Josh took out his notebook and scanned the page he'd written not twenty minutes earlier. As he did, he crossed his legs and knocked the cherub mug from where I'd left it, right at the edge of the coffee table, and the handle broke free and rolled under the settee.

'Oh, I am sorry!' Josh said. 'I do apologise . . .'

'Think nothing of it,' Rebecca said. 'Just a piece of tat. I can't even remember where it came from.'

I tilted my head to the side, in exactly the same way she liked to do. It was easy when you'd seen it so many times.

Josh returned to his notebook. 'We're here about an allegation of harassment by Mrs Hammett.'

'Harassment?' Rebecca looked at me and then Jolyon, and then back to the policeman again. 'She says *I've* been harassing *her*?'

'She does, Ms Finch. Yes.' DS Graeme leaned forward. 'Do you know Mrs Hammett? Have you met before?'

'Well of course, we've—' Rebecca was about to launch into one of her speeches, you can always tell by her eyebrows, but it was cut short by Jolyon, who coughed and stood up from the windowsill. 'Well, I know *of* her, I should say. Everyone knows of her what with . . . her husband.'

Jolyon sat back on his ledge.

'Mrs Hammett states that you've been following her around and taking pictures of her without her consent. Have you been taking photographs of her?'

'Well, only because—'

I could sense Jolyon on the move again.

Rebecca looked at her mobile phone, nestled next to a packet of cigarettes on the coffee table.

'I may have done,' she said. 'Possibly.'

'And you've been following her around the shopping centre?' PC Josh continued. 'We have the names of several shop assistants who can corroborate this and apparently there'll be some CCTV footage.'

I could hear the words stumbling around Rebecca's mouth, but none of them made it out. She looked at Jolyon.

'Bex. I think you need to be very careful about what you say.'

She turned back to the policeman. 'We may have been in a shop at the same time. At some point.'

PC Josh was writing everything down in his notebook. He was a very slow writer. I thought you had to pass tests in order to be a policeman these days but perhaps it's turned more informal.

'Why are you doing this to me, Linda?' Rebecca hissed her words, like a stage whisper, although I don't know why she bothered because everyone could hear.

'I don't mind you copying my clothes,' I said. 'I don't even mind you copying my hairstyle, but following me around all the time and taking my picture . . . It's just a bit too much.'

'Your hairstyle? I haven't copied your hairstyle, you've copied mine!' Rebecca flicked at her hair to back herself up.

DS Graeme looked at me.

'She's lying, detective sergeant. I'm afraid it's the other way around. I had a recent restyle and within days she was walking around with exactly the same hair. It's quite unnerving.'

'But I've had this style for years. I can show you photographs . . .' Her voice trailed off.

'The wigs!' she stood and started making her way towards the bedroom. 'I can show you my wigs!'

'You wear wigs?' DS Graeme said. 'Why do you wear wigs, Ms Finch?'

'Well, why not?' Rebecca called over her shoulder. 'I mean who doesn't?'

'I don't, do you?' I said to DS Graeme, but he didn't answer me.

When Rebecca returned to the room, she seemed a little more subdued and she sat down very quietly. 'They're gone,' she said.

'Gone?' PC Josh's pencil was still trying to keep up.

'He must have taken them. The murderer.' She looked at the policemen in turn, probably trying to choose the more sympathetic face because I've done it myself often enough. 'He's been here, you know!'

'Bex,' Jolyon was trying to whisper, but he didn't do a very good job of it 'you sound deranged.'

'I'm not deranged. You think I'm paranoid, but I'm not. He sends me letters and he rings up all the time!' Her voice sounded quite shrill.

'You're saying that you're acquainted with the man who's killed these young women?' said DS Graeme. 'That's a very serious statement, Ms Finch, I have to warn you.'

Rebecca sat back. She didn't say a word, and her face suddenly looked different. Not quite as perfect. Not quite as impossible.

'To be honest,' I turned to DS Graeme, 'I think it's my husband she was after next.'

'Terry?' Rebecca sprang to life again. 'What in the name of God would I want with your Terry?'

'I thought you said he visits you here and sends you letters?' DS Graeme said. 'Which is it to be – do you know Terry Hammett or not?'

'Well, of course I do.' Rebecca leaned forward, opened her cigarettes and lit one. I was amazed she'd held out for so long. 'The whole country knows Terry Hammett, he's on the front page of every newspaper you pick up.'

'Oh, she knew him well before that,' I said. 'They met when he enquired about buying the house she lived in before and I think she's been obsessed ever since. He's sent her letters since they met, I know that for a fact.' I thought about Terry's dirty great fingerprint on an envelope and all the little notes he'd left me, and I had to work really hard to stop myself from smiling.

'What?' Rebecca said, but no one took any notice. 'You live in my old house? That was Terry?'

'I'd often catch him on the phone to her – you can check his mobile because I'm sure there's a record – and I think he might have even sent her notes about the murders, because I caught him writing one once. You'd probably find a few of them if you looked around this flat.'

I glanced around, at the bookshelves and little wooden box on the mantelpiece.

'Has Mr Hammett ever been here?' PC Josh looked up from his notebook.

'Of course not!' Rebecca said.

'You just said he had.' DS Graeme sat back in his seat and sighed.

I could see the kitchen through the open door, where the orange and lemon glasses waited in a cupboard, and the mantelpiece, with all the little trinkets Rebecca took not one blind bit of notice of. A little stone cat curled into a basket that Terry was always moving when he couldn't find a space for his mug, and a pair of candlesticks that would never find themselves being introduced to any candles. 'I bet if you got one of your little paintbrushes out, the place would be riddled with him.'

'Have you ever been here, Linda?' said DS Graeme.

'You won't find any trace of me,' I said. 'I've never been here in my life. To be honest, it wouldn't surprise me if she knew more about all those dead girls than she's letting on.'

Rebecca made a small noise at the back of her throat.

PC Josh turned to me. 'How do you mean?'

'Well . . .' I said.

I waited. I waited until everybody's eyes were on me, and then I waited a little bit more, because it's not very often that happens, and I wanted to take it all in.

'I don't like telling the police how to do their job,' I said.

'No, no.' DS Graeme sat forward and smiled at me. 'Please go ahead, Linda. We're all ears.'

I smiled. 'It was the press conference, you see. The dead girl they found down near the canal. The picture of her with the Labrador.'

'The Labrador?' said PC Josh.

'Or the golden retriever. I never can tell the difference,' I said. 'Can you?'

'Don't worry about that, Linda. What was it about the photograph that bothered you?' said DS Graeme.

'Oh nothing *bothered* me,' I said. 'I was just amazed, really. Such a coincidence – such a stroke of luck.'

'What was?'

'People never notice, you see. They never look at the tiny details, the background of something, they only see whatever it is that's in front of them. What people want them to see. Not like me. I notice everything. Always have.'

'What did you notice in the background of the picture, Linda?' said DS Graeme. PC Josh had stopped writing altogether and was just holding his pen three inches above the page in his notebook.

'The front door!' I said. 'The front door the girl's standing next to – it's ours. You can tell. By the crack in the glass – just like a heartbeat, it is. Although I've only ever seen one on the television of course, because the ambulance men only managed to find a flat line.'

'Linda.' DS Graeme was still leaning forward. 'Just

slow down, love. Are you saying the murdered girl was at your house?'

'Well, not our house, because we weren't living there when it was taken, were we, silly? It was Rebecca's house then. They must have known each other. They must have been friends.'

'Are you out of your mind?' Rebecca leaped from the settee and began pacing around by the sideboard, although there was so much clutter and nonsense, pacing in that flat was definitely an interesting challenge.

I said I was very much in my mind, thank you, but no one heard because Rebecca started rambling over the top of me. Most of it was incoherent, but she did say *'working for us'* and *'don't try to pin this on me'* quite a few times.

Jolyon looked quite startled and tried to stop her mid-pace, but she managed to dodge him on each occasion and he gave up in the end.

'Take no notice,' he kept saying. 'She's been under a lot of pressure lately' and 'She's been paranoid for quite some time, officers. Talking nonsense. Accusing people of all sorts. She's not herself.'

'That would be right!' Rebecca's voice was so loud now, all the little ornaments on the mantelpiece began to shake. 'Rebecca isn't even my real name! My name is Karen Smith!'

'Rebecca, you're talking gibberish now!' Jolyon looked at the policemen and pointed to his own head and made whirly movements.

'I can tell you all about myself!' Rebecca was shouting now.

'I was born on the twenty-third of August. My father was born here but my mother was from Wales. I'm an only child—'

'Right!' DS Graeme stood very abruptly and made everyone jump, and Rebecca stopped shouting. 'This is turning out to be much more complicated than I could ever have envisaged. I think this all needs to go to the station. Can you get dressed, Ms Finch? We can wait a couple of minutes.'

I stood in the hall with DS Graeme whilst we waited. He didn't say much, he just shifted his weight about and coughed a few times, and kept asking if I was all right.

'We'll need to take another statement from you as well, Linda. In good time.'

'Of course, of course. Anything I can do to help the police force,' I said, 'and I'm there in a flash.'

'You're a good woman, Linda,' he said. 'Considering all you've been through.'

'Oh, my handbag – I've left it on the floor by my chair, can you just give me a minute while I fetch it?' I said.

After I'd collected the bag, I peered around the door of Rebecca's bedroom. She was pulling a jumper over her head. Quite tatty, it was. Not the kind of thing I'd wear at all.

'Your mother would have been proud, Karen,' I said. 'You remind me of her so much.'

'What?' Rebecca turned to me and I could see her eyes glittering in the semi-darkness. 'Why are you doing this?'

'You're like two peas in a pod. She was quite the expert at deception, as well.'

'You knew my mother?'

'Well, I wouldn't say *knew* exactly. She passed by me in the hallway a few times. It's a shame she's no longer with us; I would have liked to track her down, you know, like people do these days. On the internet. But failing that, I just had to make do with you instead.'

I could hear PC Josh breathing behind me even before he spoke, but he clearly hadn't heard a word because he just said, 'Come on then, Ms Finch, let's make a move, shall we?'

I walked back into the hall and stood next to DS Graeme. Without realising it, we'd both ended up facing the painting. The one on the wall just above the little table.

'What's that supposed to be of, then?' he said.

I half closed my eyes so the sight of it couldn't all get through at once. 'Daffodils. I think.'

It looked just the same as it always had, just the same as when Rebecca's mother had carried it out of our front garden in Wales. You wouldn't think anyone would want a memento of what had happened, but greed always gets the better of people in the end and besides, there are times we like to feed and water our misery like a small, exotic plant.

'Oh yes, of course.' He leaned his head a little to the left. 'You're right, it's daffodils. My wife always calls it a narcissus, though.'

I always knew I'd see those daffodils again. It was just a question of finding them.

'That's the proper name,' I said. 'From Greek mythology.'

'You know a lot about mythology, do you, Linda?'

'Oh yes,' I said. 'Narcissus loved himself. He loved himself so much, when he saw his own reflection in a stream, he was so besotted with the image, he couldn't look away.'

'So what happened?'

I stared at the daffodils. 'He drowned,' I said. 'That's what happens, I think, if you look at yourself too closely. You end up not liking what you see.'

'I didn't know you were so well read, Linda,' said DS Graeme. 'I'm very impressed.'

'I just remember a lot of details,' I said. 'You never know, do you, when it might come in useful.'

He pulled a little face at the painting. 'I can't decide if I like it or not.'

'I know what you mean,' I said. 'With some things, it's such a fine line, you can't always decide if you hate them or love them, can you?'

'No,' he said. 'No, you can't.'

'Although I've always hated this picture, ever since I was a child.'

The words were out before I could put a stop to them. The only mistake I'd made. Mother always said my mouth would be the death of me and it looked like she was probably right. But when I turned, DS Graeme wasn't there. He'd already gone to call the lift.

Jolyon had heard me, though.

He stood in the doorway of the sitting room with the whisky still in his hand.

'Linda,' he smiled. 'You're not quite the simple soul I first took you for, are you?'

'Probably not,' I said. 'But we see what we want to see, don't we?'

I could see him measuring it all out in his eyes. He was no different to Terry, really. A different accent, more expensive clothes, but they were peas in a pod. Both forever trying to decide which direction might work out best for them.

'You must be under so much pressure at the moment, Linda. The press must be desperate to talk to you.' He spoke slowly, as if I was still a simple soul, because once you've made your first impression, there isn't usually any room left for a second one.

'Oh, they are,' I said, equally as slowly, because people thinking you're simple can often work to your advantage. 'They all want to do interviews. I probably should have told you earlier, but there's a bidding war on at the moment between four of them and the amount of money they want to give me is unbelievable.'

'Really?' He stretched the word out so much, I didn't think it was ever going to end. 'When these policemen have gone, I think we ought to have a little chat about that. Maybe I can help take some of that pressure off you.'

I peered towards the front door, which was still open.

'Aren't you going to go with Rebecca?' I said. 'Make sure she's all right?'

'Oh, I think Rebecca's big enough to look after herself now,' he said. 'I'm much more concerned with making sure you're all right, Linda.'

And he smiled. The way only Jolyon could.

37

They charged Terry with the murders on the Saturday. Or it might have been the Sunday, I don't know. The days run away with you sometimes. I can usually work things out by remembering what I was watching on the telly, but it was all messed up with the football like it sometimes is, so I couldn't quite work it out. They held on to him, of course. I presume it was because they thought he might try and run off, which shows you how little research the police do these days, because there's no likelihood of Terry running anywhere. You've got more chance of knitting fog.

They turned up at the house again. Such a palaver. Loads of them there were, at the front door and at the back door, trampling all over the borders.

Whilst they were searching through the house, I asked

if they'd said all the words to Terry that they say on the television. The ones about remaining silent and using evidence against you. I've watched so many dramas, sat next to Mother, and so I know all the words off by heart, and I said them in my head as the officer was answering me. Although a few might have escaped from my mouth because a couple of the other police turned around and looked at me, and one of them asked if I'd like to wait outside whilst they finished checking the house.

'No, no,' I said. 'I want to witness all the evidence.' Because I've found that police officers respect you all the more if you speak to them in their own language.

After they'd gone I had a little hoover around, because you never know where people have been, and I opened a new packet of biscuits and put *Springwatch* on catch-up. It was all about magpies. They're very intelligent birds, are magpies. They plan ahead. Collect things that will be useful to them later. *'One for sorrow, two for joy,'* Mother always says, and she tips an imaginary hat and says good morning to them because she thinks it's bad luck if you don't. What Mother fails to realise is that you make your own luck in life. Good and bad.

Of course, I had Malcolm knocking at the back door, disturbing the peace, as they say.

'Are you all right in there, Linda?' he kept shouting. 'Is there anything you need?'

I wanted to shout back *There's nothing I need, thank you. I've got Chris Packham and a fresh box of Jaffa Cakes,'* but I didn't. I stayed quiet until he gave up and left, because if it's a choice between garden birds and Malcolm, the garden birds are always going to win.

Terry rang me from the station.

Less than an hour it took to charge him. I didn't think it would take long, but it was speedy even by my estimation. I suppose they had everything they needed by then.

'They're saying I did it, Lind,' he said down the receiver. 'They're saying I killed all those girls. Can you believe it?'

He sounded very small and frightened. Not like Terry at all. Not like someone who could fill a whole house just by sitting in it, but perhaps when you're charged with murder, you have to leave that version of yourself behind along with all the other ones.

I didn't know what to say. It's not the kind of conversation you expect to be having with your husband during your favourite television programme, so I just said 'Oh dear' a few times at everything he was rambling on about, and I tutted a bit, and then I told him I'd have to talk to him later because there was someone at the door.

There wasn't, of course.

Although it might have been a premonition, because thirty minutes later, Mother was on the doorstep.

'They're saying he did it, they're saying he killed all those girls. Can you believe it?' she said.

I knew she'd be there in record time. Bad news travels much, much faster than good news because people tend to leave good news to its own devices, but when it comes to bad news, they always make a special effort to help it on its way.

'Freda rang the minute she heard.' Mother pushed past me and walked around the bit of loose carpet. 'Straight away. Like the good friend she is.'

'How does Freda know?' I said.

'Her cousin's next-door neighbour's niece cleans at the station, Linda. You might as well have a hotline to the Chief of Police.'

I sat her down with a cup of tea in the front room, and let her babble on for a while. The problem with Mother is that she lives on her own, and people who live on their own tend to possess a backlog of things they need to say to everybody. I didn't really listen, if I'm honest, because Mother always sings the same song. I could hear the chorus of it, and it sounded very familiar, so I just let the verses pass me by. Although after a little while, I realised she'd gone quiet.

'Are you all right, Mother?' I said, as it was particularly out of character.

Mother's eyes were usually quite blank and empty, but there was a light in there now. Almost a spark. As if she'd finally found something in the world that was worth looking at again.

'Do you think he's guilty, Linda?' she said.

All sorts of answers swim around in your head when people ask you a question like that about your own husband.

There are so many different possibilities, and so many different variations, and it takes a while to sort through them all and pick which one is the best. I had to think for quite some time before I spoke.

'I think you know, don't you?' I said. 'You get a gut feeling, and it's very often the case that these gut feelings turn out to be right all along.'

'Like when we're watching an episode of *Midsomer Murders?*' she said.

'Exactly like that!'

I looked up at her and smiled, and the spark in her eyes had grown even brighter.

It didn't take long for the newspapers to find out, although they were obviously lagging a good hour or two behind Mother.

The first few times, I answered the door because I didn't know any better, but I soon got wise to it.

'No comment!' I kept shouting, because that's what they say on the television. 'I have the right to remain silent!'

Mother had been quite keen on staying and joining in with the shouting, but I sent her home as soon as she'd finished stretching out her opinion. The police station rang just after she'd left, and said I might be better off staying somewhere else for a few days, but I told them I had my music and a pair of earphones, and I wasn't going to be driven out of my own home by a small misunderstanding. I asked if Terry would be granted bail, because I've heard them ask this on the television as well, and the line must have gone a bit funny because the policeman at the other end went silent for a minute, but then he said no, no, Terry would remain in custody and I had to hold back a small laugh because he made it sound like 'custardy'. It was good to keep your sense of humour, I told him, even in times of crisis, and I put the receiver down just in time for *Coronation Street* starting.

Terry hated *Coronation Street*.

NOW

They bang a little gong when it's time for dinner, just like they do in old-fashioned seafront hotels. The gong has a tiny drumstick with a woolly end, but they have to hide the drumstick away somewhere when it's not being used, because otherwise the gong goes off morning noon and night and everyone gets confused about whether they should be eating or not.

'That's my cue!' I said, when I heard its chime.

The only other person in the day room was Vahri. She was hoovering the rugs before she finished her shift and she smiled at me.

'You're a good soul, Linda,' she said, above the sound of the hoover.

'Not really,' I said. Even though her words made my face warm and I really wanted to ask her to say them all again. 'I only do what anyone else would.'

'But they wouldn't, though. Not for all these weeks.'

'I just wish it helped, Vahri. I don't mind at all visiting every day, if it helps.'

'Oh, but it does. The doctor said it means a lot that you're here, even if she won't see you. He said it will help with closure.'

I hated that word. It made every situation sound like it had a door you could just shut to and all the trauma you'd gone through would conveniently disappear behind it, never to be seen again.

'I just struggle to understand how she ended up here,' I said. 'She just isn't the type.'

'Who is? No one expects to wake up on a mental health ward, do they?'

I shook my head.

'She just seemed to unravel.' I made my voice into a whisper. 'One of the officers told me she completely lost the plot at the police station. Screaming and shouting, and saying all sorts of nonsense. Her business partner told them she'd been unwell for quite some time. Very paranoid, he said. Not even sure who she was half the time.'

'They had to bring her here, Linda. I don't think they had much choice. She needed to be assessed.'

'How is she doing?' I said, and I did the special listening head tilt.

'Not so good.' Vahri sighed and stared at the rug, as if the answer to my question lay in the little knotted tassels at its edges. 'She seems so different from when she first arrived.'

'How do you mean?' I said.

'She's more withdrawn, less chatty. When she first arrived, she was full of talk about why she shouldn't be here, but now . . . she more or less keeps herself to herself.'

'Does she now?'

I wanted to say keeping yourself to yourself isn't always a decision you make on your own, but I didn't, of course. Instead, I said, 'It just goes to show any one of us can break, Vahri. Rebecca was fine one minute, and the next she ends up in here, looking down when everyone else is facing straight ahead. Keeping herself to herself.'

Vahri nodded as she vacuumed around my feet.

'Nothing is ever as it seems, is it? Look at my Terry, for a start.'

The hoover paused for a little too long at the edge of the rug and it started eating into the tassels and making a strange noise. I should have known better than to mention Terry. I forget people haven't got the stomach for it.

'Oh dear,' said Vahri.

It was only a formality. The guilty verdict. That's what the police said.

'Something's got stuck,' she said.

I wasn't sure what convinced them the most. All the searches on his laptop, searches for girls who'd eventually end up murdered, or the notes he'd written to Rebecca and his fingerprints all over that typed envelope. They said the envelope and all those anonymous letters people received were printed in our back bedroom. '*Distinctive*', they said the printer was, because it smudged all the words. Most probably, though, it was when they found his DNA all over the victims, and the victims' DNA all over his van. You can't argue with science, that's what Mother says.

I smiled at Vahri, to make her feel more comfortable. 'It's amazing what you find in a hoover bag sometimes, isn't it?' I said. 'When you clean properly like you and I do.'

She looked up at me and nodded.

'Why don't you leave this until tomorrow?' I said. 'We can walk out together.'

Vahri swiped us both off the ward with her little card and we walked across the car park side by side. The sun was just going down. It felt yellow and peaceful. Silent, almost. I thought about what I'd do when I got home. I could watch whatever I wanted on the telly and I could even leave the washing-up until tomorrow if I felt like it. I was supposed to be meeting Jolyon for supper, to talk about our next move with the press, but I decided I was going to cancel. I could only take Jolyon in small doses, especially if it involved a meal. He's such a loud swallower. I've told him about it on several occasions, but he takes not one blind bit of notice.

'This is me!' I said, when we reached my car. I'd got rid of the van, of course. Bought myself a nice little hatchback. Clean as a whistle. Not a mark on it. 'Which way are you going, Vahri?'

'Oh, I get the bus,' she said. 'Out of town, up towards Clayton.'

'I'm going that way,' I said. 'Why don't I give you a lift?'

She hesitated. 'I'm not sure. I'm not sure if I'm allowed.'

'I'm only a visitor,' I said, 'I'm not a patient, and besides, it'll get you home a lot quicker than the bus will.'

I opened the passenger door. She hesitated, just for a moment, and then she smiled back. 'If you insist,' she said.

I made sure she was safely inside before I closed the door. 'I even know a shortcut,' I said. 'I'll get you there a whole lot sooner, don't you worry.'

But of course, she couldn't hear.

I switched on the ignition and all the little lights appeared, and the pinging noise started to tell you to put your seat-belt on, and the child locks activated automatically, because that's one of the best things about modern vehicles. They're so safety conscious.

We'd only been going for a little while when she said it. Perhaps it was because we'd left the hospital and she could cross more lines, or perhaps it was because people just can't help themselves. Even Vahri.

'Do you mind if I ask you something?' she said.

'Of course not, Vahri. Ask away!' I said, because it didn't really matter any more.

'Didn't you ever have an inkling? You know. About your husband?'

I moved my hands slightly on the steering wheel. I didn't want to make any marks on such a pristine car, although of course I had my gloves on.

'You never really know anyone that well, do you?' I said.

'No one shows all their true colours, only the colours they want other people to see. Plus, once you've started killing, it's very difficult to stop. Even though you know you should. Even though you've come to the end of the story.'

I could hear the hesitation in her breathing.

'I guess so,' she said. 'But I wonder why he chose those particular girls. I mean, they weren't connected to each other, there was no motive, so why them?'

'Vahri,' I said. 'Do you ever hear a piece of music and it makes you remember something? Or you smell a certain smell or taste a certain food, and it makes you think of something else?'

'Yes, of course. Everything holds a memory, doesn't it?'

'Exactly. It does. But what holds a memory for me might not hold the same memory for you. Ice cream might make me think of happy holidays, but it might make you think of miserable tonsillitis.'

'Okay, I suppose that's true.'

'And winged eyeliner or soft blonde hair or skin that still holds on to a summer tan might make someone so angry, so very angry, they could find themselves committing murder.'

She didn't ask any more questions, but I could hear her breathing. Hesitant, unsure, just on the edge of anxiety.

We drove along the little road until we got to a 'give way' sign just at the edge of the woods. I looked across, meaning to check the traffic, but instead I found myself staring straight at Vahri in the silence. Just the slow tick of an indicator, and a hundred trees hiding any light that remained in a dusky evening.

'I like your scarf,' I said.

ACKNOWLEDGEMENTS

Writing a novel is always an isolating experience, but the last eighteen months have provided an increased amount of isolation for all of us. On this strange journey we have travelled together, I would like to thank my amazing agent Susan Armstrong and the wonderful team at C&W for their continued support, kindness and friendship. A huge thank you also to Suzie Dooré, Ann Bissell and everyone at HarperCollins for taking such good care of my words (and me). Your belief in my stories means so much.

In this peculiar landscape, the connection between readers and writers has become even more valuable, and I owe a huge debt of gratitude, not only to the fellow authors whose words have kept me company, but also to my own readers. Your tweets, messages, letters and emails bring so much joy and I don't think you will ever realise the difference they make.

The characters in this novel are, of course, purely fiction, but two of their names were very kindly given in exchange for very generous donations to CLIC Sargent, a charity supporting young people with cancer. Thank you to Vahri (and mum Elaine) and to Graeme Simsion for your kindness and generosity. I hope you like your alter egos! Lastly, thank you (as always) to the patients I met on my many travels through the NHS. I do miss you.